For Alex: this, and everything else

JUBILEE

JUBILEE

SHELLEY HARRIS

ISIS
LARGE PRINT
Oxford

First published in Great Britain 2011
by
Weidenfeld & Nicolson
An imprint of the Orion Publishing Group Ltd.

Published in Large Print 2012 by ISIS Publishing Ltd.,
7 Centremead, Osney Mead, Oxford OX2 0ES
by arrangement with
Orion Publishing Group Ltd.
An Hachette UK Company

British Library Cataloguing in Publication Data
Harris, Shelley.
  Jubilee.
  1. Large type books.
  I. Title
  823.9'2–dc23

ISBN 978–0–7531–9052–4 (hb)
ISBN 978–0–7531–9053–1 (pb)

Printed and bound in Great Britain by
T. J. International Ltd., Padstow, Cornwall

"I will provide you with the available words and the available grammar. But will that help you to interpret between privacies? I have no idea."

Brian Friel, *Translations*

Prologue

One two-hundred-and-fiftieth of a second

The photograph in front of you was taken in one two-hundred-and-fiftieth of a second. Your first thoughts, when you look at it, are of the decades that place themselves between you and it — what a museum piece it is! How retro, what a laugh — the haircuts and flares and the archaic Union Jacks. Quite right, too — we all have Crimplene lurking in our past and sometimes it's fun to be reminded of it.

But this photograph was taken in one two-hundred-and-fiftieth of a second, and thus is not just about the Seventies, or 1977, or June 1977, or even the seventh of June 1977 (a Tuesday, as it happens). There's a greater precision here. This is about 13.03 and twenty-nine seconds (give or take a few hundredths of a second) on Tuesday the seventh of June 1977, in this particular place, with the photographer crouching three yards, one foot, four and a quarter inches in front of Number 4, Cherry Gardens, Bourne Heath, Bucks.

So, tempting as it is to look at this picture for generalities, take a closer look: the single strand of hair flying up and away from this girl's glossy fringe; the corner of a lapel bent back on that boy's shirt; three crumbs on the table next to the plate of cakes. Take your time. You could perform an inventory of every curve and angle, every glance and gesture, their precise juxtaposition unique to this moment.

And when you do look, this photograph — like all photographs — will tease you a little. Because you can examine it all you want, you can enumerate every detail, but after a while the things you really want to know are exactly those things that are unavailable to you. There is nothing internal here; it's all surface. You want to know what, *precisely*, they were thinking in that moment, what happened before the shutter opened, and after it closed. This photograph was a point on a trajectory for these people, and what it's hiding from you is the most interesting thing of all: what happened before, what happened next.

CHAPTER
ONE

Spring 2007: What Happened Next

Satish has been awake for nineteen hours when he gets his first rest. Lying neatly on the single bed, he breathes slowly, and begins the wind-down to sleep. Without the diazepam he has to do this alone, but he has strategies. In the street outside an ambulance has just arrived; there's the dying fall of the siren, the *thunk* of the doors being opened. He suspends himself between attentiveness to his sleepless condition and a carelessness of it; a small shift either way and he'll be lost.

He starts with the breathing: in for four, hold for four, out for four, hold for four. He continues like this for a minute or two, feels his pulse rate drop, relaxes his shoulders, rolls on to his side. Here, he reminds himself, it's crucial to keep counting the breaths. It's when you think you're falling asleep that you become sloppy; then you might as well open your post, read the paper, or take a shower; you won't be sleeping any time soon.

He breathes and counts, breathes and counts. The room around him is alien. Let's go to a different place, thinks Satish. At home, Maya will be enjoying the run of their double bed (something she will not admit, but he knows it's true). She might be lying at a slant, one foot poking out of the covers on her own side, her head on his pillow. She will have been asleep for a long time already. His on-calls are her excuse for an early night; once, he rang home at nine o'clock and woke her.

Asha will be out cold too, he's sure, her cheek imprinted red by the corner of a book, or striped with the tiny hairlines from the edge of the pages. Awake, she's balanced between a young girl and a teenager, can't wait to get on to the next thing, but sleep draws her back into childhood. Maya would rescue the book from under her, but only Satish would fold the pages the right way and bookmark it. The children are quite used to these services being performed while they sleep; Asha has never once commented. Mehul will be damply unconscious, his room filled with the loamy scent that marks the territory of boy.

Satish's parents' room is more of a mystery. In the delicate business of communal living, he has drawn lines to ensure everyone's privacy and his own sanity. He trespasses now though, slipping through their door unseen. His father is asleep but his mother, liberated from the demands of the family and her own sense of obligation, sits up in bed, cardigan around her shoulders against the chill, turning the pages of a book or magazine slowly so as not to crackle them and wake her husband. One night, when Satish had returned home late, she came quickly to the bedroom door, to warn him that Mehul had been ill. Satish noticed a book lying face down on the duvet, his mother's reading glasses on the bedside table, his father sleeping, oblivious. When his mother caught him peering at the book, she smiled. "*Mansfield Park*," she said, and he felt the warmth of complicity.

It's comforting to move through the rest of the house, to hear that particular night-silence that is a sort of settling. Satish drifts down the stairs, through the hall, into the kitchen. He opens the fridge so he can see the light and hear the drip and click of it, then quietly moves across the dining room's bare boards, and into the lounge. He lies on the broad sofa, drawing Maya's blanket round him, cocooning himself.

Just breathing now, not counting, forgetting his earlier admonition to himself. Just breathing because snatches of nonsense are running through his brain, which is surely a good sign, fragments of sentences that mean nothing, or seem important, but when he rises up to take hold of them they skitter away. He is reaching out to Maya, pulling the blanket around himself, closing the door . . . he's nearly . . . almost . . .

And then his phone is ringing. He locates it on the bedside table, eyes closed, and puts it to his ear.

"Yes?"

"Dr Patel. It's the reg. She's struggling to put in a line. Can you come?"

Satish can feel the adrenaline kick-starting him, shaking him out of his fragile doze. His hands twitch. "The *registrar* can't get a line in?"

"No. She's struggling."

"She needs a consultant for that?"

"Yes. Sorry. They're in room 5."

He wants to argue with this woman — he was so close to sleep! — but there's no point; he's properly awake now. He swings his legs on to the floor and reaches for his sweater. This had better be good.

An hour later, Satish returns to the bedroom, pauses, then turns round and leaves immediately. His bladder, full from the cups of water he has drunk through the day, is swollen and prickling. But soon he is back on the narrow bed, hands folded on his chest. He thinks of the little brown bottle in his briefcase. A second dose would take the edge off, make sleep come more easily. Should he? No. No: he has rules about these things.

He starts to think about his home again, but this time it shrugs him off; it's 3 a.m. now and there is no chance of the house shifting a little in its sleep to let him burrow in. Frustration bobs to the surface but Satish pushes it under; frustration will keep him awake.

Satish breathes and counts. He strategises. Let's play All The Beds I've Ever Slept In, he thinks. All the beds.

Bed One, Kampala, although he cannot remember it. His parents' bed, he thinks.

Bed two, Kampala. He can remember dark wood and a mosquito net, its colour intensifying as it rose above him. Did he spend much time each night, staring at that gathering of white on the ceiling? It's an image that comes back to him effortlessly every time he plays this game. He thinks of himself, scaled down, five, four, three, lying there just as he's lying here, staring up but breathing a different air. It was a richer air, he thinks — can this be true? — a bit of sweat, a bit of spice, the scent released from sun-warmed earth. It's something like a kitchen-smell. But how would he know? He's never been back; it's an émigré's fantasy.

Bed three, Ranjeet's place, Bassetsbury. The weight of blankets on him, the cold a new discovery. Satish remembers the chill of the air as it entered his nostrils, his body warming it on its way down to his lungs. In Ranjeet's house, he perfected a new way of lying in bed, falling asleep on his tummy, hands balled in fists at his neck to pin the blankets around him, a seal against the autumn night. In the morning, invariably, he would awake on his back, his shoulders and the tip of his nose cold.

Bed four, Cherry Gardens. The best nights were the rainy ones, and there were plenty of those. His dormer window was a drum, his room a sound box, and the noise kept telling him he was safe and dry, safe and warm and dry. Satish's room was special.

Somehow he can rest here, and he does so now. He's ten, or eleven, or twelve. His duvet quilt cover is dark blue and he lies under it, listening to the rain, not able to hear the telly downstairs because of the wet thrumming above him. He knows Mummy and Papa are in the sitting room, doing the mysterious things grown-ups do when you're not with them.

All the kids in Cherry Gardens are asleep. Satish thinks of them, each in their own bed, sleeping tidy or sprawled, surrounded by the objects that recall them. Down the street there's Sarah, with her make-up, her magazines and Snoopy paraphernalia. Her mother, Mrs Miller, would be downstairs making notes on a clipboard. Her dad might be fixing something.

Over the road, Mandy is sleeping. Where to start with Mandy? The contents of her secret box, he supposes, the prepubescent treasures spilling out of it: the leather pendant, the lipgloss, the chocolate mouse. There's a smell to Mandy's house, too. It's the smell of baking. That's what Mrs Hobbes would be doing, of course, in the kitchen. Her dad would be somewhere else. Just that: somewhere else.

Then Cai, Satish's next-door neighbour, and his younger sister Colette. Colette . . . he thinks of scooters, hair bobbles, cuddly animals, generic kids' things.

Cai, of course, had his cultural contraband, the stuff that would *really* piss off his dad. Satish imagines it now, sitting in the drawer waiting to be discovered. Cai's dad — Mr Brecon — doesn't know about it yet. He's downstairs in the sitting room with Mrs Brecon. They're watching *It Ain't Half Hot, Mum*, and Mr Brecon is laughing and laughing . . .

Satish rolls over. His pillow smells nice; it smells of himself, his hair. Finally he sleeps.

Satish sleeps for four hours. He's finally summoned to consciousness by his travel alarm, its dutiful beeps telling him: shower, handover, home.

But he can't go home, not yet anyway, because once he's over at the hospital his replacement rings, claiming a traffic hold-up. No one seems to need him for a bit, so Satish retreats to his office and sits, bleary, at his computer, clearing messages while he waits. He scans the subject lines: a second opinion, a paediatrics

8

conference, the legalities of a recent firing. Towards the end, there's something else.

It's from Colette. The subject line says *Happy and Glorious*, and his fist clenches. Then he opens the email and reads what she has to say, and he can't believe she's saying it. It's *Colette* — his friend — and *she's* telling him there's going to be a reunion, a new photograph. They want Satish to be in it. He knew it would come eventually, but he couldn't imagine it would come from her. She's sent him a copy of the picture. He double-clicks on the attachment.

He's been ambushed. Four hours of sleep have not prepared him for this. And with a kick of anger he remembers how this photograph, this bloody photograph, has always ambushed him.

When he was twelve, when it all happened, he felt stalked by the thing. It first turned up in his local paper, as they had expected it to, one image in a round-up of Jubilee street parties. But it was special, you could tell even then, and the nationals got hold of it, and it started reproducing promiscuously: in broadsheets, tabloids, and a Sunday supplement souvenir edition. It lay in wait for him at school; it followed him home. His Cherry Gardens neighbours couldn't get enough of it. They bought everything it appeared in and the newsagents kept selling out. For a few weeks it was everywhere he looked, and each time he saw it — whack! — it gave him a good thumping. People called it "the Jubilee photo" or "that street party picture". Its photographer, Andrew Ford, called it "Happy and Glorious".

Over the years it has ambushed Satish many times because of its endlessly flexible applications. For a while it seemed central to his country's view of itself, a snapshot of a nation in harmony. It was used — the irony! — to illustrate Britishness, or the Jubilee, or in arguments about the monarchy or multiculturalism. He remembers how politically versatile it was. It allowed racists to deny that Britain was racist (*of course we aren't: didn't you see that lovely picture in the paper?*) yet provided a neat reference to Empire, and a gentle hint that assimilation might prove a better model than multiculturalism. Here he was after all, an Asian boy happy in his white-majority Buckinghamshire village, accepted by its good-hearted people, and posing only a minimal threat to house prices.

It was used, too, by those who constructed a different story for the picture. For them, "Happy and Glorious" helped to redefine what "English" might mean, to posit a new normality in which your mate might be Asian, a Britain in which black immigrants were British too, and as patriotic as their white countrymen. But even these ideological tussles didn't earn the picture its status as a National Treasure. That came later.

There's a noise at the door, a token knock. When Satish looks up he sees Niamh, the team secretary, already halfway across the office.

"I've sorted through these for you," she says.

"Not now."

"I'm sorry." She stops.

"You should knock and wait."

"Oh. OK."

"Knock and wait next time, please."

"I'll remember."

She retreats, stepping back before turning away from him. Satish stares for a few moments at the desk, at an arbitrary patch comprising the corner of his keyboard and the lid of a pen. It's time to look at the photograph. He's going to make himself do it. He'll pretend he isn't Satish at all. He's someone else, someone detached from this entirely. This isn't history — national, personal, familial — it's *art*. He's going to make an *aesthetic* judgement. Think about the composition. It's part of the reason for the photograph's endurance, the pleasing balance of the thing . . .

The photograph is taken from the head of a very long table, but with a shallow depth of field, so that only those seated nearest to the camera are in focus. Behind them, the table narrows as it stretches away, a blurred runway of paper cups and plates and cakes and crisps and Coke.

Only six people can be seen with clarity. When Satish looks at them again he feels a rise of nausea. He finds he's pushing his chair back, just in case he needs to leave. There's Colette and her dad, Peter Brecon. There's Mandy and Sarah. More to the point, here is Cai, and here he is himself, plump of cheek, his limbs already showing signs of the disproportion that will take hold of them in puberty. As the acid gathers in his stomach Satish tells himself that this is just an icon and its subjects are ciphers; they are significant only as tokens of something else. It doesn't even look like the real world, he reminds himself, but is black and white, as all newspaper photographs were back then; he remembers newsprint coming off on his hands. And it's thirty years old now. Look at us, he thinks. We look dated. We look funny. Don't take this so seriously. Look at the clothes, the hair. It was long, long ago. Look at those people.

He starts with Peter Brecon. He's nearest to the camera on the right-hand side of the table, head turned slightly away so that his face, framed by the dark curve of his comedy sideburns, is in profile. Both his arms encircle Colette. She's grinning, kiddish, maybe six years old, and she perches on her dad's lap, facing the camera squarely. Where was Mrs Brecon that day? She didn't sit with the rest of the family, Satish remembers that (he remembers, too, hiding in her house, hearing her cry in her bedroom). He peers along the table and spots her — an arm, a shoulder, no more. Here, at the front of the shot, Colette is sitting stiffly upright for her moment in the spotlight. In her right hand she clutches a plastic Union Jack, a cameo of the Queen at its centre. With her left, she is pulling at the bottom of the flag, its plastic is straining at the wooden strut.

Next to them, a bit further down the table, is Sarah. She too is in profile, staring across the table at Mandy, unsmiling. Sarah's shoulders are bare, and she's wearing the kind of skimpy top usually seen on women whose curves would inhabit it properly. On her rangy, eleven-year-old frame it hangs loosely, its descent down her chest interrupted by the merest suggestion of

12

breasts. Mandy, dark-eyed, shiny-lipped, meets her gaze. Neither acknowledges the camera.

Between them, and all along the table, Union Jack plates and cups are set out at neat intervals on Union Jack table-cloths. Here and there, dishes of food have been placed; he can see a pyramid of fairy cakes and remembers their meticulous red, white and blue icing. There's a platter of small spirals — his mum's chakli — and, further up, an amorphous pile he knows is the coronation chicken. There, at the point where sharpness is lost and the blurring begins, arms are reaching across to distribute food. Forks are already moving towards mouths, cups are being lifted.

Outside that charmed circle at the front of the picture, expressions can only be made out with difficulty. Satish sees a woman turning, smiling radiantly towards the camera: Colette's teacher friend, Miss Walsh. Mrs Miller, Sarah's mum, is next to her. Those two blobs are Stephen and Paul Chandler, Satish knows for sure. He cannot find his own parents and sister, but he remembers exactly where they were: halfway along the trestle table near the Tomineys, Sima staring longingly down at his end, itching to move.

The sounds outside Satish's office have changed again. There are steps, and a gentle knocking, and then silence: Niamh again.

"Come in."

She eyes him warily. "I'm off now. I really do need to get these to you today."

"Yes. I'm sorry about earlier. I had to concentrate. On some . . ."

"Of course." She's holding the sheaf of papers to her chest and coming over to the desk. Satish sees it in split-screen: Niamh getting closer, the photograph waiting on his monitor. He stands and leans over the desk towards her, reaching out for the papers. She stops far enough away and hands them over.

"Thanks," he tells her. "See you next week." She leaves.

I'll get this over with, he thinks. I'll just look at Cai and me, then I can go. His eye locates the photograph again, moves down past Mandy, towards the front of the table once more. There's Cai, and then there's Satish. He's right at the front of the picture, the key compositional element.

Cai sits sideways on his chair, his back to Mandy, his face towards the camera, one arm around Satish's shoulder, the other hand resting a quarter inch from Satish's cheek in a kind of Morecambe and Wise happy-slap. Satish's Union Jack hat is about to fall off. It obscures his expression, so that all anybody sees is a comical half-grimace. Out of sight and across the road in Cai's back garden, the barbecue glows hot, the hamburgers are charring.

He wonders what it felt like for Andrew Ford, the invisible framer of this scene, resplendent in denim and cowboy boots. Satish remembers the photographer squatting down, feet planted wide apart on the tarmac, holding the camera at roughly the height of his subjects' faces. He'd grasped the long lens underneath, adjusting it deftly in a motion so suffused with adulthood and competence that Satish was winded by envy. In the end the photograph was the product of chance, Ford reeling off a string of clicks, and Satish doesn't know which moment this was: the first, the second, the ninth? Ford didn't ask them to look his way; that was why there was this rag-tag feel, this diffuse attention.

Chance served Andrew Ford well. After those first, hyperbolic weeks, people stopped caring so much about the Jubilee. The news went back to normal. Elvis Presley died, Satish started at his new school. The photograph found other places to be — in lofts, in scrapbooks, in bins; Satish didn't care. He wasn't visiting his neighbours' houses much any more, but when he did, he'd sometimes catch sight of it. As the months went by, even that lost its impact. Skewered with a drawing pin or propped on a mantelpiece, it curled until all he could see were the things behind the photograph — other pictures, stuff he didn't care about, writing that had nothing to do with him.

Then, one day — it was the next summer, a whole year had gone by — a boy in his class brought in a copy of the *NME*. On the front cover: Riot Act, a new band. They slouched against a wall, avoiding the camera's gaze, all tight trousers and discontent. Inside was an interview, and a picture of their LP. Satish just looked at it. Then someone said: "Shit. It's Patel."

For a minute he couldn't understand what he was seeing. Their record cover was a version of "Happy and

15

Glorious". They'd made the picture look different, but it was the Jubilee photograph all the same. He was in it. The band was in it, too; ragged cut-outs of them squeezed in between the real people. One lolled, smoking a cigarette. Another had his head on the table. Satish could see other changes, too: instead of the Coke, there was a bottle of whisky; Sarah wore a ring of black round each eye; Colette's flag was burning and they'd put smudges of colour all over the photograph — red on Peter's lips, red and blue on Satish's hat. The album was called *The Only Language They Understand*.

Satish took the magazine and walked straight out of his prefab classroom, out to the end of the field where there was a gap in the hedge, and on to the pavement. He found a bin a few yards on and stuffed the copy of *NME* in there, down under other rubbish even though it made his hand dirty, down where it couldn't be seen.

Lucky Andrew Ford. With the hindsight that Satish now possesses, he can see Ford's success as inevitable; a smooth upward curve. After the album cover came profitable outrage: just what did that graffitied photograph, that ambiguous album title, imply? And to use *children* . . . Riot Act became huge, and a thousand disenchanted schoolboys leaned against walls, hoping they looked like their heroes. The *Bucks Gazette* was suddenly a tight fit for Andrew Ford, who was taken up by post-punk London. As "Happy and Glorious" spun away from him (the endless pastiches, the cultural referencing), he became the chronicler of a new England, its underground and — not long after — of Thatcher's Britain.

16

By March 2007, as Satish sits at his desk, ambushed again, Ford can credit to that picture his international reputation, both his wives, and all of his homes He's planning a major retrospective, Colette says. He wants to take a "Thirty Years On" reunion photograph in Cherry Gardens, a re-staging of the famous image. The *Sunday Times Magazine* wants to do a feature on the project. He'll need them, those important six people, but most of all he'll need Satish. How about it?

Satish is jabbed by a fierce spike of anger. He can't believe what she's asking him to do. He can't understand how Colette fits in, why she's mixed up in this at all. He resents having to make any decision, any pronouncement about it. He wishes Ford had never taken up the idea, but Ford knows no more about what happened that day than any other outsider — why should he? Ford looks at his masterpiece and sees, besides the money, the leapfrogging career, only smiling faces, party clothes, the bloody Union Jacks. How could he see anything else? Colette is a different matter. What was she thinking? Maybe it's this: that what's past is so long past it doesn't matter any more. Satish considers the years it has taken to knit these memories into a manageable form and thinks it would be wise for her to fear, for all of them to fear, just as he does, the pulling of the thread that might set them unravelling.

CHAPTER
TWO

It's Saturday afternoon and Maya's in her tracksuit bottoms and vest, bouncing from foot to foot in the hall and breathing out loudly, rhythmically, each time she lands to her right. Her hands are clad in lilac boxing gloves and as she dances and huffs she slams them against each other.

"Come on! Get on with it!" she tells Satish. "Come and have a go if you think you're hard enough."

The second pad is always hardest to get on, his hand immobilised by the first; in the end he traps it under his armpit and slides his fingers in that way. He's never told Maya how much he hates this ritual, how bemused he is that his wife, this gentle soul, would want to spend her spare time knocking seven bells out of . . . anything. When she fixes the pad with that focused gaze and lands one on it, he wonders what it's standing in for. The whole process is unsettling, but it's dull too, standing there for thirty minutes with his hands in the air. Plus, she looks a bit funny in her lilac boxing gloves and sometimes he has to force himself not to laugh.

"You look weird, Papa," Asha tells him. She's lounging on the bottom stair, book in hand.

"Thank you, Asha," he says. "Do you have homework to do?"

"At the end of this chapter."

"Homework?"

"Just let me finish this." Her skinny legs are encased in black, thin tops layered over her skinny torso. She slaps the book face down on the stair and reaches up to tighten her ponytail.

"Right," says Maya. "You done? You ready? You want a piece of me? You want a piece of me?"

"One chapter," says Satish.

"Sati! Any more of that and you'll distract me," says Maya. "I might just hit the wrong thing." She's exaggerating her bounces, bobbing from side to side. She dances up to Satish and bops him gently on the chest, on the nose. Then she puts her guard up and he can't see her breasts any more. He realises he's been watching them, the way they sit differently in a vest.

"I'm going to start with jab, jab, cross. OK?" She points to his right pad.

"OK."

She starts slowly, pulling back into guard position between punches, naming them as she lands them: jab, jab, cross. He concentrates on what he has to do, the pads at her shoulder height, meeting the blows with a little resistance, a little pushback each time. Sometimes she doesn't land square, and then his hand is knocked askew, but not too often. It's flowing nicely now, the crosses coming right across her body, from the back foot to the leading hand, and packing a proper wallop. Under her bare feet, as she twists, the hall rug skews.

"Papa?"

"Ye-es?"

"Did you hear about Daksha's dad? He's famous."

Eleven years as a parent have taught Satish the art of half-listening. He can catch the cry of authentic fear, the yell of actual pain, and filter out anything less consequential. He'll never be able to multi-task, but this comes close.

"You know *Be My Guest*?"

"Umm . . . no."

"Papa! God!"

"Asha! Language, please!" Maya puffs. "Right, Sati. Change." She frowns at the pad and swaps foot positions. Leading from the other side she starts again: jab, jab, cross. He'd like a cup of tea, he thinks. He'd like a sit-down with the paper. Mehul's out with his grandparents buying his school uniform and he'd even rather be doing that. Jab, jab, cross. His shoulders are aching.

"Satish? Just watch the angle there. You're a bit out." Maya reaches across to adjust the pad.

"*Be My Guest*. It's this TV programme. You know, TV, the thing in the corner? Big screen?"

Maya snorts. "Asha . . . has . . . a . . . point," she says.

"Daksha's dad was on it. There're four people. They do, like, dinner parties for each other."

"Oh yes?"

"It was on last week. Daksha's dad won. He got a thousand pounds."

"Very nice."

20

"He was in the paper. Daksha brought it in yesterday: *Asian Lite*. There was a picture of him in their kitchen."

"Good for him."

The pounding against his hands has stopped. Maya lifts her gloves to her head, pushing them over her ears. She frowns.

"What are you doing?"

"I'm trying to tuck my hair behind my ears. Don't laugh. I can't do it with these things on."

"Here, let me help."

"Anyway," he hears Asha say. "Daksha's, like, this celebrity now."

"No," says Maya. "You're just taking the mick . . ." but she lets him reach out to her. Giggling, she dips her head forward and he brackets it with the curve of the pads. There's her face, her hair, the flush and warmth of her, and he strokes across her cheeks towards her ears. There's nothing to feel, an inch of leather and stuffing between them, and so he has to remember what it feels like, his fingers against her skin, the architecture of her bones.

"Hmm. Not sure how to manage this." He pushes at her ears ineffectually. They're both laughing. There's a Velcro rip and her glove comes off. He leans down to her, but she turns away and searches the hall table for something.

There's a gentle thumping behind them: Asha making her way lugubriously upstairs. She'll hunker down on the beanbag they keep on the landing — there's the shingle sound of her sinking into it. She'll read her book, keeping an ear open for her parents, and send down waspish comments when she feels like it.

"Bingo!" Maya's found two of Asha's hairclips and puts them on: sparkling plastic butterflies, one on each side.

"Good choice," Satish says. "Didn't Prince Naseem wear something like that?"

"Enough! Let's go!" But now she's having problems with the glove; the Velcro strap won't do up properly.

"Bugger!"

"I can hear you, Mum!"

"It's different for adults!" Maya calls up. Then she mutters: "I'm sick of this. I'll just be a sec."

She goes to the door that links the house to the garage. Satish sees the light flickering.

"What are you doing?"

"I'm looking for duct tape. I just want to . . . hold on." He sees her through the half-open door, peering into the toolbox. He goes to the bottom of the stairs.

"Asha?"

"Yeah?"

"*Yes.* I was serious about that homework."

"I've done my Maths. My War project's due in . . ." But as she's talking, his attention leaves her again. He hears the lid of the toolbox shut, Maya sighing. He turns to see what she's up to; she has his briefcase in her hand.

"Wait! What are you doing?" He rushes into the garage and snatches it from her.

"Ow! What are *you* doing? I told you, I need duct tape —"

22

"Well, it's not in there."

"I was just clearing this shelf."

"I don't like my stuff being moved."

"There's all sorts of crap in here. I thought someone might have . . . hey!" She reaches across him and emerges, duct tape in hand. She holds it up in front of his face. "On your briefcase shelf," she says. "Behind your briefcase."

"Well, it shouldn't be."

"Well, if you don't like it, may I suggest you're overdue a tidy-up?"

Upstairs, Asha shifts. "Chill!" she advises them. Satish and Maya look at each other. There's a brief moment of standoff, then she smiles.

"Yeah, chill," she says. "Dude."

"I just —"

"Chill," she repeats. "Or your ass is grass."

Jab, jab, cross, hook, hook: her hands are coming across at right angles, a side-on impact, and he has to angle the pads down after the first three punches. This takes more concentration, the change in position; it's easy to miss a beat and mess things up.

"I talked to Sima about your dad's birthday." She slams into the pads on the stresses. "She's got no idea about his present."

"OK. Don't talk. Concentrate."

"I can do both — whoops! It's good for me. Keeps both sides of my brain working."

"I'll think of something for Papa."

He sees the angle of her arm, her fierce face behind it, as she hooks across and connects. Upstairs, he can hear Asha shifting in the bean bag. Maya's finding it harder to talk now; she leaves her words unfinished. Then she stops on a half-hearted cross and leans forward, hands on knees, mouth breathing, reaches out for the water bottle stationed on the windowsill.

"Hold on . . . Just a minute." She swigs and bends over again. Satish stretches his hands behind him, crunching his shoulder blades together. He rolls his head and closes his eyes. No one requires him; it's a moment of peace. He hears Maya's breathing slow down and then, just when he thinks they're about to start again, she says: "Colette rang earlier. She told me about the photo."

He keeps his eyes closed. What does Maya know? Find out. Carefully.

"What did she say?"

"She said Andrew Ford wants to get all of you together again. She said she'd sent you an email. Didn't you get it?"

Instinctively, his hand has moved to the top of his right arm. He finds he's standing there hugging himself, only he can't feel anything because of the stupid pad. He opens his eyes. Maya is looking at him quizzically.

"Yes. I got it. What else did she say?" He uncurls and holds the pads up at shoulder height.

"Put some uppercuts in," she instructs. "Two, after the hooks. Pads facing down. OK?"

Jab, jab, cross, hook, hook, uppercut, uppercut, the last two coming towards his chin, blocked by the pads. Once she's in the rhythm he tries again.

24

"What did Colette tell you?"

"Ford wants to take another picture. The papers want to do articles. Publicity and fame! She's *very* keen."

Ford *wants*? Satish knows what he wants. He wants to give Colette what for. He wants to shout at Maya. He wants them all to be quiet and leave him alone.

"Think I'll duck out."

"Why?"

"I'm too busy. The rotas . . . it won't work out."

She's hit her stride and she pounds away, hammering her words into the pads. "Everyone's busy. They'll be flexible about it."

He has to concentrate on placing his hands: three punches upright, two lateral, two facing down. She's moving faster and he doesn't want to make a mistake.

"It won't work out, Maya."

"It might."

"I'm not going to do it!"

"OK." Jab, jab, cross. "How about you tell me . . ." Hook, hook. ". . . what's really going on?"

His arms jerk sideways and the uppercut slams into him. There's a blow, his head judders back, and he's bitten the side of his tongue. Maya's trying to touch him, but he's pushing her away.

"Oh God, Sati. I'm sorry. Are you OK?"

He nods. His mouth fills with the metallic taste of blood. She's pulling her gloves off. "Let me see. Open up . . ."

He pushes past her into the kitchen, slips off the pads and opens his mouth under the tap. He spits out red, then pink. He wants to bellow. It escapes him as a low hum while the water shifts on his tongue.

"Sati?"

He turns to her. "I'm all right. My fault."

"Let's pack it in."

"No." He looks at the pads on the floor. "My turn."

He's not done this before. Maya's padded up and he's refused her sweaty, lilac gloves.

"It's stupid to do it without gloves. You can break your hand like *that*." Maya clicks her fingers.

"Hold them up, Maya."

"Stop being so proud. Lead with the top of the metacarpals. Never tuck your thumb in. Keep it outside, to protect it. Start gently."

"Pads up."

She sighs and holds up her hands. He copies what he's seen her do, slowly at first. He feels the shock of the blow travel up his arm. Maya's OK, though. She shudders very slightly each time he lands a punch, but she's fine, and soon he can concentrate on just hitting. He can land them harder, and faster, and there's a mantra in his head — jab, jab, cross — which helps him keep time. There's only the pads, the centre of them, and it's OK to hit them, to really hammer them, because Maya won't be hurt and each blow makes him feel better.

This is him, jab, jab, cross, hook, hook, very strong, very powerful. He can look after himself; don't mess with him. He sees them, sees them in front of him. Cai and Sarah. He sees the Chandler boys, Stephen and

Paul. He sees Mrs Miller and Mr Brecon and Mrs Hobbes, the whole lot of them, and he is absolutely, absolutely not afraid of them, so much so that he can . . .

Cross, cross, cross, cross, cross . . . Just lay into them. Bam! Bam! Bam! They cannot stop him, and he will not stop. He will hit and hit and hit. He is completely unafraid. He is . . .

"Satish? Satish! Stop!"

He is completely unafraid.

"Satish! Please stop it!" Maya is shouting at him. She's stepping back, away from him. He can see Asha behind her, halfway down the stairs, her mouth open.

Satish crouches down and rests his head on his fists. He breathes. He can hear Maya's voice. "Satish?"

It's OK.

"Sati, tell me what's wrong."

Everything's OK.

CHAPTER
THREE

Since the email, Satish's night-time strategies don't seem to be working. He can't do his breathing, or play All The Beds, or roam his house unseen. There's only one place he can go, and one time, too, that lets him in as easily as you like. Because in those restless nights, 1977 welcomes him. Cherry Gardens invites him in — every door is open, he can just stroll inside.

There's the dormer window of his childhood house, jutting out at the front, the bay beneath it. He can see his bedroom and the sitting room dimly behind the glass — no nets for his mum. There's the front porch with its light that looks like an old-fashioned lantern, the brass number 4, the nameplate — *Dawlish* — which was there when they arrived. There's the green front door. He walks through it, moves up the stairs, up and round, following their backwards twist. He arrives at the door of his room. He's looking for something, as he always is on these night rambles. He's searching for an explanation, a chain of cause and effect, something with a beginning, middle and end. In particular, he's looking for a beginning. He wants to find out where it started.

28

Maybe it started here: in his own bedroom, on Jubilee morning. He pushes open the door. There he is, twelve years old, standing near the window. And here's Mandy. She's come to see him.

Mandy had brought something to show him. She was holding a long cardboard box. She lifted the lid, reverently, and he heard the *sh-ish* of tissue paper. Mandy spread her fingers to move aside the wrapping. Three oval soaps lay underneath, creamy-white and snug against their cardboard partitions.

"It's special soap, for the Jubilee," she told him. "My mum bought it at Murray's."

He looked at her quizzically for a moment. "Your mum bought them?"

"Yes! Look at them, will you?"

He turned his attention to the soaps. Each one had a sepia photograph of the queen set into it on a transparent plastic disc; Satish could see the dots that made up each picture. He scratched at the surface with his fingernail.

"Careful!"

"I *am* being careful. I just want to see how hard it is. Will it wear down like the rest of the soap?"

"I don't know. That's not the point. Do you like them?"

"They're OK. They're just soaps." He leaned down and sniffed. "They don't smell of much."

Satish had bought his mum Aqua Manda bath foam for her birthday; he knew the importance of powerful fragrancing where women's toiletries were concerned.

But now, looking at Mandy, he had the sense that he hadn't given her the right answers.

"They're really nice, though. Special, like you said. I haven't seen any like these before."

Mandy smiled at him, placated. They were in Satish's room, its familiar landscape glamorised by the flickering, dappled shadows of the bunting. Since early morning Satish's dad and Mr Brecon had been on ladders, stringing triangular pennants across the street under the eaves of the houses. Every few yards there was also a line of Union Jacks with the queen pictured in the middle of them, wearing her cloak and crown.

There were no cars parked in the street; it was empty and waiting, a sweep of uncluttered tarmac between two rows of identical semis: the same wavy roof tiles, the same dormers, the same patches of green at the front, the same brick pillars marking the entrance to the same concrete driveways. At either end, Cherry Gardens was anchored by homes of eclectic design: corner houses, owing allegiance neither to Satish's road, nor to the streets adjoining them. Aside from these mavericks, there were only subtle variations: the colour of a door, a rockery instead of a flowerbed out front, a ceramic house number in place of a metal one.

The men were nearly finished. The ladders stood at the entrance to Cherry Gardens, where you could turn in from the village's main road. Resting his elbows on the windowsill, Satish peered down to where the men were working, flattening his cheek against the glass. They were putting up a banner, their finishing touch, and he read it backwards: "Reign She May Long".

30

Looking up, it was hard to see past the lines of red, white and blue; they cut off the sky. When the wind lifted, as it did now, the bunting swayed and bounced like the roof of a tent.

He heard Mandy come and stand beside him. Her elbow was on the sill, touching his. He wanted to move away and he wanted to stay there. Satish kept looking forwards; her house was opposite his. She had the dormer room, too. He concentrated on his arm, not letting it push any nearer, not letting it pull away. He thought about food.

In her kitchen, he knew, Mandy's mum was decorating fairy cakes in red, white and blue. He visualised glass bowls of bright colour on the marbled Formica of their counter, vibrant dribbles of sweetness that hardened as they trickled down the sides of the cakes. Satish was a connoisseur of Mandy's mum's fairy cakes; he liked the icing best when it had just lost its gloss and a thin matte crust had formed over the stickiness underneath. This held true for only a very short moment but if you pushed against it with your tongue, you could taste the sweetness and feel the give of it without breaking through.

Beside him, Mandy was standing quietly, looking out over the road. He thought he should say something funny, or clever, but wasn't sure which words he could enlist to do that. Her elbow was a constant pressure against his. If either of them moved, something would be switched off. He thought of electricity experiments at school: light bulbs and circuits. He remembered the muffled snarl of the buzzers.

31

Mandy was his secret. When they all played together, him and Cai, her and Sarah, she was like most of the other girls he saw at school: she went on about pop stars and laughed about things that didn't make sense to him. He'd liked her, and he'd watched her, just as he watched the others, trying to understand how it worked between them, but they hadn't been friends. Then one day he'd met her in Jennings' Field, the bit of waste ground near the school that he'd cycle around on bored afternoons. She was alone too, which had surprised him, but he'd eased his bike down beside her, and they'd talked.

Without Sarah she was more fun, more up for a laugh. She did impressions of some of the teachers in school, and told him about seeing Mr Tominey in the nude through his bedroom window one night. Satish imitated Mr McLennan, their headmaster, as he called the school to order before assembly — "and . . . *sit!*" — which made Mandy giggle. Satish repeated his performance, hoping to hear her giggle again.

They talked about their families. Her mum and dad were going out to a party that night, she said. Her mum had bought a new dress and was spending the afternoon at the hairdresser's. He could see it: Mrs Hobbes, elegant in her long gown, her hair piled up high. He couldn't picture Mr Hobbes in a jacket and bow tie though; in fact, he struggled to imagine him at a party at all. Satish had only ever heard Mr Hobbes say two things: "I'm warming her up," shouted into the house as he headed to the car in the morning, and "I was hoping for red, actually," after Satish's dad complimented him on his new Granada. Unless the partygoers were keen to discuss motoring issues Mr Hobbes would be at a loss. Certainly, Mandy didn't have much faith in him.

"It's not like he ever enjoys it," she said. "Mum says all he does is sit in a corner and eat cheese. Then he spends the next day complaining about the other guests. Do your parents go to parties?"

He thought about it. "Not like that. We go to my Uncle Ranjeet's place a lot, though. He lives in Bassetsbury."

"What do you do there?"

He knew what she was asking now. She wanted to know what Asian people did, about how it might be different.

"We talk and eat." There were things he couldn't tell her about, things English people didn't understand. He thought about Ranjeet's family shrine, which took up the whole dining room. Auntie Manju washed and dressed the image of Vishnu every Sunday. Mandy wouldn't understand that. He offered her something else, "sometimes they make me and my cousin play music", and shot her a sideways glance as he said it, waiting for her derision.

"They once made me do a ballet dance at my uncle's house," Mandy told him. "They brought a butterfly costume and made me wear it."

Satish received this in silence. He picked up a stick and spun the back wheel of his bike. A few moments later they both got up and made their way through the field, onto the main road. Neither of them said anything, but when Mandy turned the corner into Cherry Gardens, Satish slowed down. He waited for a bit, leaning on his bike, to give her enough time to get home. When he heard the sound of a door slamming, he started moving again.

After that they'd get together when no one else was around, each instinctively knowing that each was a liability for the other: she a girl, and a younger one at that, he the acknowledged outsider. She grew used to greeting his mum quickly at the door before slipping upstairs to his room, and he became used — gloriously, deliciously — to the treasure house of baked goods that was Mandy's mum's kitchen.

Looking out of the window on that Jubilee morning, Satish followed Mandy's slow gaze, taking in his neighbours' homes, performing imaginary cross-sections to reveal the industry going on in each one.

Fairy cakes at number one; Jubilee celebration cake at number three (Miss Bissett standing on a ladder, the better to reach the summit of her creation); no food at number five (Miss Walsh was providing the drinks); coronation chicken at number seven (huge platefuls of creamy-pale lumps. Satish wasn't familiar with the dish, but it had met with warm approval from many of the adults). On his own side, there were the Chandlers at number eight (the Chandler boys, large and intimidating, sliced tomatoes and lettuce with flashing cleavers), whilst next door to him, Cai Brecon — lucky beggar — stoked a fire in his garden as his dad had volunteered to do the barbecue. On the other side, the Tomineys at number two were providing jelly and ice cream. In their

34

kitchen, he felt sure, elaborate, wobbling creations only previously seen in comics or on children's TV sat waiting to be revealed to the astonished revellers.

In his own house, Satish had been barred from the kitchen since breakfast. Between his mother's anxious perfectionism and his sister Sima's sulks — press-ganged into cooking she would adopt, at nine, a sullenness that prefigured her adolescence alarmingly — the atmosphere was unbearable anyway. They were making great bowlfuls of crispy chakli and would later steam dhokla, cut it into squares and put it out on the long tables at the last minute, warm and sprinkled with mustard seeds still popping from the heat of the pan. Thinking about the snacks made Satish's stomach feel tight. When his mum cooked, he would usually hang around the kitchen, trying to grab what he could when her attention was elsewhere. He liked to sneak a curl of chakli before she'd let him, when it was still too hot to eat safely, passing it from hand to hand, judging the moment when it would not-quite burn his tongue.

Mandy leaned towards him, nudging his shoulder with her own, then left it there so that he could feel her warmth along his upper arm. She'd seen something.

"Hey, look! It's Colette. What's she *doing*?"

Below them, Cai's little sister was standing in the street, right in the centre of the road, bending her body backwards, face to the sky, her eyes clenched shut. She was grinning, her cheeks forced into squirrel pouches, and she held her hands out on either side of her, presumably to balance herself, though as they watched she staggered backwards. Mandy made an explosive sound in the back of her throat. Satish covered his mouth and laughed through his nose.

"What on *earth* is she —"

"Look at her! She looks such a —"

"She's just — quick, hang on, you can't —"

Colette had dropped her strange pose, but not moved from her position, as her dad advanced towards her from the end of the street. She waited for him, still grinning. He held one end of a ladder and walked in long strides, his free hand sweeping back and forth, feigning a military march. Satish's dad brought up the rear.

"Stop it, she'll hear you." Satish grabbed Mandy's arm and shook it gently, trying to silence her. They stood next to his bed, where the box of soaps had been placed, and he was aware, all of a sudden, of himself touching her. He liked Mandy, and he liked being with her, and as they both slowed their laughter, he allowed himself to wonder what other things might be possible. The sun went in again and the room darkened slightly. This quick moment felt like privacy. He glanced at Mandy's face, saw nothing warning him off and, filled with the spirit of adventure, he stepped towards her.

CHAPTER
FOUR

Satish is finally home after a tough run of nights. He decompressed on the drive back from London: twenty-odd miles down the M40 to his town, which, in its well-heeled Georgian charm, is a lifetime away from the modest semis of Bourne Heath. Not so far by road, though; just a little further down the motorway, along the valley, up the hill, and he'd be right back where he started.

He's discharged his paternal duties and put the kids to bed. As ever, they've felt his absence, Asha more cuddly, Mehul more wired than he would be in a normal week. Satish's mum, displaying an Austenian delicacy, has gone up to her room early, and even his dad has now caught on and joined her. Satish and Maya are alone in the kitchen.

There's a rhythm to this end of the day. It goes on in his absence, but rejoining it affords him a deep pleasure. Maya will prepare the children's packed lunches for the next morning, tutting over their nutritional foibles, but indulging them nonetheless. An apple, always, for Asha, but no tomatoes, ever. Mehul's craving for cheese is met with one of those little red-waxed balls Maya hates. She mutters as she slips it into his lunch bag. Satish leans against the hob, watching her work. He likes the back of her neck, the space between her hair and the neckline of her blouse. It's an unguarded, vulnerable place; he remembers how she'd nuzzle that same spot on her babies, and he can watch it unnoticed. His fingers drum the countertop beside him. Their gallop keeps pace with the thing in him that is not at peace. As Maya drops her head forward, her thick hair rides up, exposing a little more skin.

"Tired, Sati?"

"Not yet. Still running on adrenaline. Work was interesting, though. A couple of good catches."

"Yeah?" She pours juice into Asha's sports bottle. He knows she misses it, the bustle of the ward, the drama of it, being at the centre of things. She even misses the more pedestrian satisfactions of her stint as a school nurse. He knows she's waiting for the moment — maybe three or four years hence — when the kids are old enough not to trouble her conscience, when she can go back to work and not feel guilty. They're crying out for good people. She'll walk into a job.

"Three-day-old baby girl, blue. Transposition of the great arteries."

"Oh, God. Heroics."

The baby had come in from a hospital thirty miles away. Lights and sirens, the registrar crouched in the back of the ambulance with the patient. "It's a close one," the reg had said. "Hurry." What you had to do, in these circumstances, was not catch the fear around you.

You had to breathe, loosen your shoulders, be methodical.

Satish had performed the procedure in the Cath Lab, a room so quiet he could hear his own exhalations as he fed the catheter through the child's blood vessels. All the clamorous things outside the lab — the ambulance, the registrar, the parents prowling the waiting room — those things were behind him now. The mercy dash was in its final few centimetres: the steady advance towards the heart, into it, and down to the septum, the wall dividing the chambers. There it was on the screen: the tiny hole which had kept her alive so far. Satish breathed slowly in and out, focused on keeping a steady hand. Narrowing his eyes, he inserted the catheter into the hole. Then — carefully does it — he inflated the balloon at its tip, and the hole stretched larger. When he'd finished, the balloon withdrawn, he'd watched the screen to see oxygenated blood rushing across the septum through the space he'd widened. It happened again, and then again as the heart pumped. The baby had sighed and twitched in sedated sleep, raised her fist off the table and then settled it down again. The nurse turned to Satish and smiled: "Nice one."

Now Maya stops what she's doing for a moment and turns to him, smiling also. "That is a good catch. Very satisfying."

Satish stills his fingers — just a few minutes, be patient — and reaches out to Maya. He touches his thumb to C4, her fourth cervical vertebrae, just below the jut of her skull, buried beneath the warm skin and hair. When she doesn't shake him off, he traces the length of her spine, letting his hand tilt as the bones undulate beneath it.

"Satish . . ."

"I know, I know. Just let me . . ."

She lets him. She remains pointedly motionless, her work arrested. When he reaches L4, the penultimate lumbar vertebra, the tips of his fingers come to rest inside the beltline of her jeans. He loves the parts she hates, the extra fat she laid down here to have their kids, the little swells of flesh she never used to have, which she will sometimes besiege in brief, doomed bursts of dieting. He wants to stroke her there, but she won't let him, not now, standing in the halogen light of their kitchen.

"Maya, shall we —"

"Don't you want to know about my day?"

"Yes, of course." He can listen and clear up, it'll go that much quicker. He scrapes the food waste into the green bin.

"Asha's been picked for a dance show. There are only three other girls doing it. She's very proud."

He switches the lights out in the lounge, in the dining room. He calls through: "That's good."

"She was full of it when I picked her up. She's going to be a mermaid."

"She's done well."

"Mehul's not firing on all cylinders," Maya says, when he's back in the kitchen. "Trouble in paradise."

"What do you mean?" He picks up the expensive knife, the one they can't put in the dishwasher, and takes it to the sink. He turns on the hot tap and water sluices down the blade.

"He's fallen out with Tom. Playground stuff. I had to do the talk: you know, sticks and stones."

"What happened?"

"Tom's been saying things about Mehul. So Mehul came out of school today and he was a bit down in the dumps. That's all."

Satish turns the tap on more. He holds the blade in the gush, tilting it up and down, sending spray over the edge of the sink.

"What's Tom been saying?"

"Satish," says Maya. "Let it be. They're just kids. It'll be sweetness and light next week."

"Hmm."

Maya gives him her head-on-one-side look. Her expression is hard to read at this angle, but it looks alarmingly like compassion. Satish turns off the tap and reaches for the dishcloth.

She points to her nose and smiles. "He said something about Mehul's nose. He has the Bhatt nose, poor boy, and Tom teased him about it. You know eight-year-old boys, always the witty ones."

"Just his nose? Nothing else?"

"Yes!"

He looks at Maya, proudly sporting the Bhatt nose. "I like that nose," he tells her. "It's a good nose."

"Thanks. Hey, can you go through the kids' bags? I need their reading records for tomorrow."

The bags lie under the hall table, dumped there when the children came in from school. Maya's vision for this table owes much to country-house dramas. She imagines an expanse of polished mahogany, a neat pile of letters, a vase of carelessly arranged blooms. Instead, in this inconvenient, servantless world, there is a saucer of unclaimed trinkets, a mound of football cards, and a sagging bag of ballet clothes. Satish drags the kids' rucksacks out from underneath. Mehul's reading record ("The green one!" Maya calls through) is dog-eared and stained with orange juice. Asha's can't be found.

"It's not in here," he tells Maya.

"It must be. It always is."

"It isn't!"

Satish looks in the pockets: snapped pencils, an apple core, a crumpled newsletter. He empties out all the junk and makes a pile on the floor. There's a sticker promoting road safety, someone else's tie, a tattered notebook, a cigarette.

A cigarette.

Asha has a cigarette in her bag.

It's a bit squashed, and shedding flakes of tobacco. It was stuffed into a side-pocket, the last place she'd think her parents would go.

He holds it away from him as he enters the kitchen. "Look."

"Oh shit," says Maya.

Satish is up the stairs and into Asha's bedroom before he can think clearly. He shakes her awake.

"Wha —?"

"Sit up."

"What's wrong? Papa?" she says, her eyes wide.

He turns on the light and Asha hides her face under the duvet.

"Look!" he tells her. He holds the cigarette up in front of him.

Asha emerges from the covers and sees what he is holding.

"Oh, God!" she says.

"Stop that language. Do you know where I found this?"

"It's not what it looks like. It's not mine," she wails.

"Then why was it in your bag?"

Maya has arrived and is leaning against the doorframe. "None of that, young lady," she says.

"It's not mine. Honestly." Asha spreads her fingers in a counterfeit of nothing-to-hide. "It belongs to someone else. Someone's brother!"

"Who?"

Asha looks from Satish to Maya. She shakes her head.

"I think it *is* yours," says Maya.

"It isn't!"

"Then —"

"I can't! If I tell you, you'll tell their parents, won't you?"

"Absolutely," Satish says. "You can be sure I will. Do you smoke?" He waves the cigarette in front of her. "I can see you didn't smoke this one, but do you smoke?"

"No! I never would!"

They look at her, waiting for more.

"I never would!" she says again.

"I sincerely hope you're telling the truth," says Maya. "How many times have we told you how dangerous it is? And Charlie's granddad, when he died? You remember why he died?"

"Yes, yes!"

"Do you remember how Charlie *felt*? Did that have any impact on you at all?"

"Yes! But I don't smoke."

For a second they are all quiet. Satish can hear movement in his parents' room.

"This," he says, making little stabbing motions at the cigarette. "This would suggest the opposite."

"You have a cigarette in your bag," Maya tells her. "That makes us think you have smoked, or are *thinking* of smoking. It makes us think that *you* think it's OK."

"It's not OK!" Asha shakes her head vigorously.

"Right," says Satish. "As of now, you are grounded. For two weeks. No going out, no visits from friends . . ." Asha starts to cry, ". . . no swimming on Saturday. You can stay at home and help your mum."

"And we will be talking about your choice of friends," puts in Maya. "And who gave you that cigarette."

Asha slides down into the bed and pulls the covers under her chin. She turns to face the wall and sobs loudly, a sort of showy *boo-hoo*. Maya snaps off the light and they leave.

From the kitchen, they can hear her continuing to cry. Maya grimaces. "We needed to do that, didn't we? The shock —?"

"Yes," Satish says. "She won't do that again in a hurry."

"Do you think she's actually tried it? I've never smelt anything on her."

He considers. "No. I think she was just being silly."

"Peer pressure? She's only eleven . . . she's normally so sensible."

"I know."

"Her friends, though . . ."

"Who do you think?"

They look at each other, then simultaneously: "Daksha."

"Daksha's brother?" says Maya.

"Probably." They stand in the quiet of the kitchen. As Satish winds down from the adrenaline rush — the discovery, the confrontation — the craving asserts itself again. Time for bed.

"Let's go up," he says. "Do you want me to do the honours?"

She hesitates. "OK."

He always does the honours, it's part of their night-time routine. She'll make the packed lunches and he'll store them overnight in the second fridge, their embarrassing, climate-changing monster. They hide it in the garage. Maya doesn't like the dusty concrete of the floor there, or the chill of the place, so she always lets him do it. Tonight she sighs and drifts upstairs as he opens the door from the hall and slips inside.

In the garage, the fluorescent lights take a while to trigger. They make tinny, effortful *pings* in the flickering darkness. Satish leans against the door while he waits for them to come on: there. He wedges the lunch bags onto the bottom shelf of the fridge, then double-checks the door behind him. It's closed, and will stay that way. No one is left downstairs and Maya is already padding around in their room above him.

His briefcase sits on a shelf by the door. He always dumps it there when he gets in. He tells the family he likes it that way, the separation of work and home. He asks them not to touch it because its contents could be important: hospital paperwork, cases to review.

Maya gave him the briefcase when he first started at Central Children's. He remembers the smell of leather, Maya running her fingers down its brown flank: "Butter-soft", she'd said. It's not what they have now, the younger doctors with their messenger bags slung over their shoulders; this is a proper briefcase. Satish feels the seam of the handle pressing against his fingers when he carries it. There's room inside for all his papers, leather loops for his pens, a buckled front pouch for his wallet. The briefcase also has an inner pocket, discreet enough for his needs. He unzips it.

There's the current bottle, in a plastic bag sealed with a clip in case of spillages. There's a spoon in another bag next to it. He pulls them both out, aware now of the time, of the need to get upstairs before Maya remarks on his absence.

Satish pours the liquid into the spoon: a precisely calibrated dose. He watches the white solution roll out of the bottle and waits until the spoon is full, over-full, the dome of the meniscus held in tension, then he takes it. There's a second measure, then he flips the spoon upside down and licks it clean, child-like. The medicine leaves a membrane of sweetness, designed for younger palates, clinging to his mouth. He sweeps his tongue around his gums to rid them of it. In a minute, he'll wash it down with some water. He fears the smell of it giving him away.

Maya will be getting into bed now. The memory of her skin is on his fingers. He slips out of the garage, and goes upstairs.

CHAPTER
FIVE

Somewhere in the nebulous hours of the night, Satish is still looking for a convincing origin story. Surely that was the start of it, he tells himself: me and Mandy in the bedroom; that was how it began. It's a comforting formulation, but he's not such a fool as to believe it. He knows that by the time Jubilee morning came, things had already been set in motion. The signs were there in the way Sarah's mum treated him, in Satish's solitary playtimes at school. They were there in the way people talked to his parents.

Satish can look back now to those endless meetings about the party: the Entertainment Meeting, the Decoration Meeting, the Food Meeting. He could have seen the signs, if he'd known where to look: there was trouble on the way.

The Food Meeting was an all-female affair held one Sunday afternoon in the Millers' sitting room. Satish, at twelve, the weight of impending manhood upon him, felt discomfited by his presence among the women. But, he reasoned, Cai would come too, and Mandy might be round to see Sarah, and they could all go up to her room, so it was OK, really.

In the event it had not been OK at all, and he had wished himself scrubbed out of the place entirely, because his mother's contribution to the Food Meeting had been mortifying. In the beginning the discussion had been organised and focused. Mrs Miller had a clipboard. She took notes as the women talked, and was soon able to present them with a provisional menu. Satish, banished with Sima to a corner of the room, spent his time depleting the supply of chocolate digestives and eyeing the door. Where was Cai? The only moment of controversy so far had been Mrs Brecon's suggestion that, with coronation chicken on offer for the adults, the children should have hamburgers, grilled on a barbecue in her garden. Miss Bissett demurred:

"That seems somewhat American, doesn't it? Shouldn't we be celebrating our own food on that day, of all days?" She frowned at her skirt, picking some unwanted detritus — fluff or cat hair — from her knee while the group took this in. When Mrs Chandler intervened, it was with the same effortless batting-away of obstructions that Satish had witnessed in her dealings with her sons.

"We're having coronation chicken, aren't we? Think about it: spices from India. Everybody loved that, first time round."

"That was a tribute from the Empire — quite different," retorted Miss Bissett. "We have enough American influences in this country already, don't we?"

Mrs Brecon pressed her lips together and looked away. Little Colette, squashed up against her on an armchair, glanced quickly at her mother's face. From the settee Mrs Tominey, Satish's ally because she let him hop over her fence to retrieve lost balls without asking each time, addressed Miss Bissett.

"Of course I see your point, Verity," she said. "Quite right. This American nonsense is all over the place. Hard to work out what's British sometimes. But how many of the children are really going to eat spicy chicken?"

Mrs Miller glanced at her notes. "You know, it is rather a grown-up menu at the moment. What about using good old British beef for the burgers, Verity? Would that be a happy compromise?"

Miss Bissett's smile was a grudging admission of defeat, and the conversation moved on to dessert. With the inclusion of beef in the menu, the children's food had been put definitively beyond Satish's grasp, and he wondered again about coronation chicken and the pleasures it might offer. Then the sitting room door opened and Cai appeared, beckoning. He'd come into the house quietly, sneaking through the back. Satish went over to him.

"Cai! Nice entry. Are you undercover?"

"What?" His friend frowned. "No, we're not playing spies. I was just getting some stuff sorted out. Listen, come upstairs. Be really quiet."

Satish looked at Sima, and then back at Cai. His hesitation was for form only, and she knew it; cutting her eyes away from him dismissively, she reached for another biscuit. Too young or too old for the other kids in the street, and indentured to her mother, she was used to being the odd one out. Sima usually played in other houses in other streets, with girls she'd met at school. She didn't expect much from Cherry Gardens, Satish told himself.

Sarah's door was shut, a plastic Do Not Disturb sign depicting Snoopy asleep on his doghouse. Satish reached for the handle.

"No," whispered Cai. "Listen."

Behind the door, the girls were playing a record. Satish could hear a bouncy piano accompaniment, a loping drumbeat. He looked at Cai, quizzical.

"What is it?"

"David Soul," said Cai. "It's completely spastic. Listen."

They moved quietly up to the door and pressed their ears to it. The blond fluff of Cai's hair tickled Satish's lips and chin. David Soul was duetting with a high-voiced woman.

"It's a *soup recipe*," Cai told him. "A musical soup recipe."

Satish tried to make out the words amidst the sound of his own hair rubbing against the door and the occasional thumps and creaks from within. Cai was right. The song was a list of ingredients; he caught a reference to tomatoes and onions. There was mention of garlic. He and Cai looked at each other, world-weary. David Soul exhorted the woman to mash some black beans. Then suddenly the track finished, the needle scraping across the grooves. In the silence that followed, they could hear the girls talking.

"You said he was a seven," said Sarah. "Most *men* couldn't do that. Believe me, I know."

"What? How?"

"I can tell you —"

But Sarah's revelation was cut off by a swell of violins. The boys groaned.

"Not this crap again!" muttered Cai. "It makes me want to *puke*." Satish nodded agreement. They'd heard the track incessantly the previous winter. Now here it was again: *Don't Give Up On Us, Baby.*

"That stupid film," whispered Satish. "When he sings behind that fence thing."

"That spazzy horse," said Cai. Satish agreed. A car was cool, a horse was spazzy. He knew that.

Whatever the girls had been talking about, they'd stopped now and were giving themselves freely to the music, singing along with varying degrees of tunefulness. After a while the boys could hear more movement in the room — were they dancing? Satish could make out soft thuds, and muffled commands from Sarah ("*Now do the thing with your shoulders . . . No! Like this!*"). Satish tried to imagine what was going on in there. They could be acting the song out in dance, like Pan's People.

Cai put his fingers down his throat and mock-puked. Quickly, Satish did the same. Then, as David Soul turned his attention to rain and stars, Cai put his hands together: index fingers forward — a pretend gun — and levelled it at Satish. "I'm Starsky," he said.

"What?"

52

"I'm Starsky. You're Hutch. OK?" Cai started doing the tune from the programme. He pointed at the door with his gun. "In there."

And then Satish realised what he was supposed to do. He didn't watch the programme much. He hoped he'd remember enough.

They crept up like the cops did on TV: one each side of the door, guns pointing up. Mandy hit a particularly tricky high note. Cai nodded towards the door handle. Satish pushed it gently down, hoping the girls' attention was elsewhere. He gave Cai the thumbs up, and Cai jumped round, aiming a kick at the centre of the door. It burst open and they rushed in, more or less as Starsky and Hutch might, accompanied by the gratifying sound of Sarah screaming. She lowered her arms from the beseeching position they'd been in. The door rebounded and knocked Cai into Satish, but he quickly righted himself and held up his improvised gun again, pointing it at the girls, then into the corners of the room.

"What the hell are you doing?" shouted Sarah.

Satish crouched under the window ledge and then sprang up, aiming a few shots into the street. Cai threw open the wardrobe and hauled out a jumper, pointing his gun at it.

"Wankers!" Sarah said, checking the door.

Satish got the record player in his sights and squeezed off a couple of rounds. Cai leapt onto the bed and then sat down hard on it. Satish remembered that: Hutch jumping on the car in the intro sequence.

"Just get out! Get *out!*" Sarah howled at them then, quieter, to Satish, "You just bloody get out!"

Behind her, Mandy was corpsing, looking at Satish, and then looking away. The boys retreated a safe distance, then both lifted their guns once more — simultaneous, Satish felt warm with it, and fired one last time. They clattered downstairs, turning to each other as they reached the sitting room, landing there for want of a better place. As he entered, Satish could hear his mother talking.

"Of course the children will eat them! Satish loves them. Satish, don't you love your chakli?"

Satish's mood flattened. He wished he'd stayed to fight with the girls. Most of all, he wished that Cai had. Instead, his friend was beside him, and Satish wondered whether there'd be a price to pay for this later on. He answered his mother with careful neutrality: "Yeah, I suppose so."

"He does not *suppose so.* He loves them! Takes them from the kitchen all the time when I am making them. They are a lovely snack."

Miss Bissett gave an exasperated sigh. "I'm sure they *are* lovely," she said, "but they're not British food, are they? Do let's remember this is a particularly *British* celebration."

"I live here. I am British now. She's my Queen too." There was a shifting in the room. Sima looked at the floor. Above them, Satish could hear movement as Mandy and Sarah's performance resumed. Even as his abdominal muscles crunched, he sensed that the conversation had moved beyond food and even felt,

54

though this may have been a retro-fitted response, an untrustworthy memory, that his mother had been quite clever. With those final four words, she had occupied the territory of patriotism. Mrs Miller, hostess and mediator of disputes, stepped in.

"Of course she is, Neeta. You say they're crispy snacks for the kids? Looking at this list, there's lots for everyone already, so if the children really don't like them, there's plenty more to eat. It's another reference to the Empire, really, isn't it?" This to Mrs Tominey, who smiled noncommittally. In the chair by the window, Satish's mum looked down at her lap.

"Are you happy with that, Verity? Lots of English food, like your lovely fruit cake, and some more . . . cosmopolitan contributions, too?"

Miss Bissett pursed her lips and raised her eyebrows. "I don't want to cause trouble. I'm sure that sort of thing is very appreciated in your household, Neeta, but it seems an odd dish to have at a Silver Jubilee party. I suppose it doesn't matter, really. Add it to the list."

The ensuing silence was deftly handled by Mrs Miller, who set about filling teacups and recirculating the biscuits. Satish, feeling hot and weak, turned to Cai. "This is boring, let's go back upstairs."

Later, in the sanctuary of her own kitchen, Satish's mum was to rail against the lot of them.

"I've taught History, remember!" she harangued Satish, when his dad had heard enough and retired to the lounge. "'Tribute from the Empire' indeed. I know what was going on in that Empire! You need to know, too. Do they even bother to . . .? Bloody coronation chicken! I will not touch it! Not one *mouthful*! And you —" catching Satish as he was shuffling towards the kitchen door, and pointing a wooden spoon at him for emphasis — "You shouldn't either!"

CHAPTER
SIX

Satish sleeps late, and when he wakes the house is quiet. He tries to guess the time from that silence, from the quality of light on his eyelids, and the messages his hungry body is sending him. When he opens his eyes, the clock confirms it: ten past eleven.

Hanging up on the wardrobe is the T-shirt Asha gave him for Diwali. It's another of her attempts to modernise him. He likes it well enough, but he needed it explained. It's khaki, with a row of medals printed on the chest. On the back, it says "Chief".

"Chief?"

"Yeah. The Kaiser Chiefs. You know . . ."

"Oh, yes." He didn't know.

"Go on. Put it on."

He'd come downstairs in it and she'd howled, hiding her head in a sofa cushion.

"No, Papa! God!"

"Asha . . ."

"I can't believe . . ." She went over to him. "Not with cords. You wear it with jeans! And not like that, tucked in! Pull it out."

Satish did as bidden. The T-shirt hung sloppy over his hips, but she seemed happier. He wonders now whether Maya left it out for him, or Asha herself. She might be contrite after last night's discovery of the cigarette: contrite, or sulky. He puts it on.

After breakfast he sets off. The town slips around him, and he passes through it at one remove. The pavements are busy with buggies, and his progress is slow. He stands aside, smiles politely, and tries not to make eye contact because he needs to think. He's working up a script.

Between the wine shop and the hair salon there's a cut-through, a covered passageway used for fag breaks by shop assistants and hairdressers. There's no one there now though, and it's dark and private. Satish faces away from the street. He leans against a wall and mutters to himself.

"I'm surprised you thought it appropriate," he says. "I was surprised you thought . . . I was taken aback when you . . ."

On the ground there's a scattering of cigarette butts. They're soft underfoot.

"No, that would be out of the question . . . To be honest, I was disappointed that you found it necessary to call my home . . . Well, I'm sure I don't need to remind you that . . ."

Ridiculous. This is language from a business letter. Why can't he get this right?

"Given what you know of the events of that day . . . Do I really have to remind you that . . ." His voice echoes back to him in the confined space. He checks the street behind him; shoppers move across the passageway entrance, framed for a moment in forward motion, eyes forward too. They're oblivious to him. Then: "You and I are friends. What the hell were you thinking?"

When he enters the wine shop, Colette is at the back, squatting down to refill a low shelf. He takes in her tight top, the way her too-short skirt rides up her thighs, and tests himself for a sexual response, as he has to with Colette from time to time. No: she's never quite stopped being his mate's kid sister. She's looking like a child today as well, pigtails wonkily erect at the sides of her head; only when he is closer can he see the lines around her eyes. She rises, her polite customer-service face already forming its greeting, then she recognises him.

"Satish!" He's gripped in a bear hug, her cheek squashed to his chest. He lets her do it, doesn't respond. After a moment she loosens her hold and looks up at him. "You're really pissed off, aren't you?"

"I'm a little surprised, I have to admit."

"It was a surprise for me, too. Andrew Ford! After all these years!"

"How did he find you?"

She flinches and pulls away. "Don't be cross."

"Why did you do it? You, of all people, know better than that."

"Oh, don't be cross. Please, Satish."

He can't let her get to him. He looks down at the floor: rough wooden boards, a filament of straw. Billy Bragg is playing softly on the shop's stereo system. The phone call: she told Maya about the photo.

"You called Maya."

"We often talk. What's the problem?" She looks up at him. Big eyes.

"Don't be disingenuous. You know what the problem is."

Footsteps interrupt them. It's Oscar, Colette's boss, coming from the storage rooms. He inserts his head through the doorway, leaning forward into the shop with his hands anchored either side of the frame, his long hair falling over his face. He rocks there, back and forward.

"'Right, mate?"

"Yes thanks, Oscar. You?"

"Yeah, fine. You want a cuppa, Colette?"

She looks him slowly up and down. Satish knows that look, and he pities Oscar. "Cheers," she says, dismissing him, and he rocks back out of view.

"Total pash," she murmurs. "I've started smelling his coat."

"Don't change the subject!" Satish's voice sounds strident in the quiet of the shop. "You shouldn't have called Maya about it. You've placed me in a difficult position."

"I didn't mean to." Then, quieter: "Does she not know?"

"You *know* she doesn't."

"Then I'm sorry. I've made things hard for you."

"Yes, you have." Billy Bragg's guitar fades, and in the silence between songs Colette reaches up to touch Satish on the right arm, just below his shoulder, and he schools himself not to smack her hand away.

60

"I'm sorry. Really sorry," she says. Then the shop door bangs open, rammed by a buggy, and a customer struggles in.

The toddler is parked equidistant between two displays of bottles, its mother's instinctive geometry planting it so both are just beyond fingertip reach. Satish watches Colette as she works. She is asked for recommendations, and as he listens he smiles, despite himself. She's doing it by the book: two suggestions only, she told him once, an old retailers' trick.

"One choice and they feel bullied, more than three and they're confused. So you go easy on them — two choices, and they'll buy the one you're most enthusiastic about, even if it goes over their budget." He can hear her patter now.

"Actually, how about this one? It's a couple of quid more than you wanted to pay, but it's gorgeous. Really passionate producer, cracking wines. You get more for your money from Chile, and it's a perfect match for the food."

She holds the bottle flat, label upwards. There's a flourish to her movements that Satish rather likes; she puts each bottle on display, presents it like a temptation. You don't have to take this from me, she is saying, but look how delightful it is.

He thinks of the lines he hasn't used: *what were you thinking?* It's a decent question. What *was* she thinking? She's mercurial but not insensitive. He's trying to work this out when the question slips away from him, just like that, and he's staring at a line of bottles, overcome by his lassitude. Diazepam's great for that, he thinks, it keeps you in the moment.

He can hear the sound of Colette's transaction finishing, the door opening and closing. He is held by the luxury of inertia. He doesn't move until he hears her voice.

"Satish?" she's saying. "Satish? Are you OK?"

"Yes, of course." He sniffs and shakes his head.

She's looking at him, holding his gaze a fraction longer than he's comfortable with. He rouses himself.

"Why did you call Maya? What were you thinking?"

"It'd be all right, you know. We've all grown up. Everyone's different now."

"It will never be all right. We may have grown up. Whether we're any different is another matter." Then he realises what she's said, and he can hear his voice go higher as he asks: "What do you mean, 'everyone'? Who else have you told?"

"Well, I thought I'd just put out some feelers. See if people were up for it."

"*Feelers!* Who?"

She starts to turn away but he stops her, grabbing her by the shoulders. "Who have you told about this, Colette?"

"Don't, Satish!" The fabric of her top snaps out of his grip and she retreats behind the counter. She doesn't say anything for a moment. "Well," she says. "I know Dad can do it, and Cai might. They don't count, do they, Dad and Cai?"

"They do. Who else?"

She rubs at her arms. "I haven't found Mandy yet."

"No Mandy?" And there's an unpoliced little fall of disappointment.

"No. But I've found Sarah. I don't know if she could even do it. Satish, she's got this tiny baby and he's ill, and she's desperate about him, you can tell."

"Don't even try it!"

But she does try it, palms up, all trust-me, leaning over the counter towards him to make her point. "But that's what I'm saying. She's different. Everyone's different now."

"People don't change."

"*You* have. Think about that."

"I'm going. Don't mention this to me again, please."

As he turns for the door, Oscar enters carrying a steaming mug, its faded design proclaiming: 1994: First Free Election In South Africa.

"Tea, Colette," he says.

Colette ignores him and shouts after Satish. "*You* have changed!"

The old-fashioned bell at the top of the door tings as Satish leaves. He hears Colette shout out: "Living well is the best revenge!"

And he hears something else too, as the door bangs behind him and the next song begins. It's the opening glissando of *Dancing Queen*.

CHAPTER
SEVEN

The generations had tussled about the music for the street party. In the end, the adults had made a small concession. During the meal, music from the Fifties, the only *appropriate* music, insisted Miss Bissett, would be playing on the PA system. This seemed to galvanise the parents; Cai complained to Satish about an interminable Saturday afternoon spent listening to the 78s his dad had hauled down from the loft. But after the meal, when the tables were cleared away, the kids would be allowed to play their own tape. They were invited to make a suitable compilation for the occasion. Thrilled with the responsibility, they held their own Music Meeting the Friday before the Jubilee in Mandy's sitting room.

David Soul had been an early, controversial choice; Cai had argued the case against by grabbing Mandy's single, placing it in front of his face and whining, in falsetto: "Tomatoes and onions! Ooh, baby!"

"What's your problem? He's Hutch! You *love* Starsky and Hutch!" Sarah was fierce in her defence.

"He's not Hutch," offered Satish. "He *plays* Hutch."

"Yeah," agreed Cai. "And he's not going to be on the tape."

While Mandy recovered her record from Cai, Sarah loyally jotted the contentious name down, reading it aloud as she did so, a sideways shot Cai chose to ignore. Satish's sister put in a word for the Dead End Kids ("Thank you for that suggestion, Sima," said Sarah, her pen immobile). Mandy added Abba, and Cai countered with Roxy Music, while the Stranglers were put up against Bony M. When Sarah listed David Essex and IOCC without any reference to her companions, the fragile civility of horse-trading broke down once more.

"Get it!"

Cai lunged across to Sarah, grabbed the notebook and flung it to Satish. As the girls headed for him, Satish ripped out the offending page and stuffed it in his mouth. His tongue worked against it as Sarah whacked him on the chest, overbalancing him onto the settee, but it was less soluble than he'd expected. Mandy grasped the protruding ends and started to tug.

"What on earth?" Mandy's mum had come into the room. "What are you doing?"

The others straightened up. Satish pulled the paper out of his mouth. It peeled off his tongue dryly. Cai murmured, "Sorry, Mrs Hobbes," and she tutted at them.

"I've done some flapjacks," she told them. "Ten minutes. In the kitchen."

When she left, Sarah reached out to rescue her notebook. "Splat-eesh," she hissed.

"Spaz," he returned.

"Splatish" wasn't making so much of an appearance any more, and when the name did surface Satish found himself almost inured to its impact. Sticks and stones, he told himself. It was a nickname thought up by one of the Chandler brothers during his early months in Cherry Gardens. At first, Paul had called him "Diarrhoea" — a little skid mark on the whiteness of Bourne Heath. Then Stephen, the younger and brighter of the two, came up with "Splatish", and the pun had stuck for a long while, lingering until it was finally neutralised. In that sense it was like "Paki", a term used so frequently in the daily hustle of the playground that Satish had been mystified when his casual mention of the term had seen his dad barrelling in to the Head's office to complain. This tactless intervention, which threatened so much of the painstaking work Satish had done to shore himself up socially, would not be allowed to happen again. His job was to party the blows, or absorb them. He didn't need a protector.

Later they sat at Mandy's kitchen counter, flapjacks in hand, glasses of milk lined up in front of them. Mandy's mum's flapjacks came soused in sweetness. Satish had once asked her what she put into them to make them so nice. "Golden syrup," she'd said. What else? he'd asked. "More golden syrup," she'd told him.

The can was still out on the side. Satish loved the picture of the lion and the bees, the old-fashioned look of the tin. He reached for it, dug his little finger into the notch around the lid and pulled it along, collecting a build-up of syrup. He popped the finger into his mouth and sucked. Cai was talking.

"So I've got two more to get, Battleships and Rally Cars," he was telling Mandy. "And then I'll have four gift cards, and then Satish will get one more, and he'll give me his gift card. So that's five, and I can get a free pack. I'm going to get World Record Holders."

Sima dropped down from her bar stool.

"I'm going home," she announced.

"Top Trumps is brilliant," Sarah put in. "I've seen Cai's Cars pack. It's great."

But Cai wasn't looking at her. He was facing the other way, towards Mandy. "It's fun," he told her. "You can play it with me, if you want."

"Yeah. Great. Maybe," and she winked at Satish as she turned away from Cai. "Which ones will you get, Satish?" she asked. Under the counter, her knee nudged against his.

Out in the hall, he could hear his sister thanking Mrs Hobbes, preparing to leave. "Bombers," he said.

"Fighters and Bombers," Cai corrected.

"Same thing," said Mandy, but Satish made a mental note. There were so many things to remember, so many little details to keep hold of. You had to know which music to like, which sport to play, which words you could use to sound cool, and which ones made you sound like a spaz. But he'd bent his mind to it; he'd been doing that ever since he arrived in Cherry Gardens.

From the outset, displaced from Uganda, plunged into the cold shock of an English autumn, Satish had deployed his resources as quickly and as effectively as he could. He had an eye for detail, and a readiness to be flexible about things. He willed his body to get used to the latitudinal facts of life in Europe; gone was the reassuring rhythm of the equatorial day where the hours of daylight and darkness were measured with an even hand. Here, waking up in the dark, walking home from school at dusk, he could feel the night jostling him. Dampened by the drizzle — what mediocrity! — he thought sometimes of the rainstorms visited on them back home, passionate downpours that hammered the land, then were dried in an hour by the tropical sun. Later, in the aftermath, a cloud of grasshoppers would descend, the slowest of them grabbed by Satish and his friends and offered to the Africans as food. He'd watched, entranced, as they pulled off the wings and ate them straight away. Once, when she was old enough to feed herself but too young to tell their mum, he gave one to Sima.

These losses were to be borne, but there were good things about England, too. The afternoons might be gloomy, but at least he was allowed to play outside in the growing dark, not ushered in when his mum started getting worried for him; these streets were safe. And then there was the first time he saw milk money being left out: Mrs Brecon put a pound note under an empty bottle, and he watched her front porch, peeping through the hall window every few minutes until bedtime, waiting for it to be swiped.

"It'll be there in the morning, Sati," his dad had said. "We're not in Kampala any more."

In Kampala Miss Slater was a graceful oddity at Satish's school, with her white skin and impeccable deportment. Courtesy had informed all her dealings with the class. Whatever she taught them — although

Satish could not, once he had left, recall any specific academic gain — was shot through with politeness and respect.

The adult Satish looks back on this now with a jaundiced eye; he is intelligent enough to realise how chaotic, how uncivilised was the world in which Miss Slater believed herself to be, therefore how necessary the redress of her invincible *politesse*. But as a child, Satish just thought she was courteous, and she was one hundred per cent of all the white people he knew. When he was told his family was going to live in Britain, he envisaged a nation of such adults, cordial and refined in all their dealings. And on that particular evening Satish remembered Miss Slater, and then he knew: of course they could leave the milk money out at night.

Miss Slater's legacy was short-lived. After he moved to Cherry Gardens, Satish wasn't thrown by his peers' behaviour; every kid is used to the casual cruelty of other children. However, sitting alone in Sarah's kitchen one day, perhaps six weeks after his arrival in Cherry Gardens, Satish heard a whispered argument in the dining room, just the other side of the closed serving hatch.

"What are you doing, Sarah? Why's he here?" That was her mum.

"He came home with me after school. Can he . . ." That was Sarah, speaking at normal volume. Mrs Miller shushed her. "Can he play?"

"Absolutely *not*. Listen Sarah, Daddy and I think . . . I'm sure he's a nice boy, but he'd really be better off with his own people."

Satish thought: does she know Uncle Ranjeet? Does she mean my cousin? Mrs Miller continued.

"So I'm going to say *no*." There was a brief silence, and a sigh. "He can't stay. Are you going to ask him to leave, or shall I?"

Satish, listening, spilt an experimental bead of milk onto the work surface. He placed his glass on top of it and started moving it around.

"He just came back with me after school," Sarah repeated. "I thought he could . . ."

"Well, he can't. And I'm not going to say it again. Now, you or me?"

Sarah, sullen: "You."

Satish drew a milky "S" across the counter with the base of the glass. A moment later Mrs Miller came into the kitchen, and he slid off the bar stool to greet her.

"I'm so sorry, Satish, but Sarah has to have an early tea today. She didn't realise. So you'll have to go home, I'm afraid!"

Miss Slater had not prepared him for this, though she had prepared him admirably for the courteous exit he managed to make — "Thank you very much for having me, Mrs Miller" — and, he sensed, she might even have been impressed by the unruffled way in which his hostess managed to dispatch Satish from the house. It was a shock, this loss of innocence. Adults could be wicked, even white ones: cruel and rude while appearing to be polite and welcoming.

His family stayed in Cherry Gardens, became a fixture, and Satish thought Mrs Miller had become more used to having him around. He didn't go to their house much, but when he did he was allowed to stay. On Jubilee Day, in the rushed final moments before the street party, Sarah's mum positively welcomed him into the kitchen, letting him take dishes out to the waiting table. When Sarah called him Splatish, he was reminded that she was not an adult yet; she said it to his face.

Back in Mandy's sitting room, negotiations about the music continued. Sarah listed the tracks, and Cai volunteered to tape them over the weekend. It was a hotchpotch in the end, because David Soul got in, and so did the Stranglers. Boney M and the Ramones were both included, because nobody would back down.

When the two boys crossed to their side of the road afterwards, Cai told Satish, "I've got something to show you. Come over for a bit."

Up in his room Cai pulled open a drawer, shoved stuff out of the way, and retrieved something from underneath. It was a paper bag, printed with the red scorpion logo of the local record shop. From it he pulled a square of royal blue cardboard with the familiar cameo of the Queen in its centre, the same oval which now decorated houses and car windows, petrol stations, mugs, soaps. But in this picture the eyes were blindfolded, and the mouth gagged with strips of words seemingly cut from a newspaper, ransom-note-style. "God Save The Queen" it said. "Sex Pistols".

"Paul Chandler bought it for me on Saturday," Cai told him. "Mum and Dad would kill me."

"Yeah, they would. How are you going to listen to it then?"

"I've already heard it, at Paul's house. It's brilliant. Don't tell anyone."

They looked at the single together. It was dangerous; you couldn't hear it on the radio. But now Cai had it stashed in his sock drawer.

"Better than bloody Boney M, eh?"

Satish nodded. "Yeah, but you couldn't put this on with Abba and IOCC. They'd kill you."

"I've thought of something, though. My dad —"

There were feet on the stairs: Colette. Cai ran back to the drawer with the record. Satish went towards the door in case she came in. She didn't.

"Cai?" They heard the sound of her fingernails scratching the door. "Mum says it's teatime. She says you should say goodbye to Satish now."

Then they heard her pad back to the top of the stairs: a grunt, a thump, a faint squeaking, and Satish realised what she was doing: straddling the banister, getting resistance with her damp palm so she could control her descent. Little Colette, sliding all the way down to the hall, hoping her mum wouldn't catch her in the act.

CHAPTER
EIGHT

And now he's convinced he's going to be caught.

There's nothing concrete he can identify. All his procedures continue as usual. In the three months since he started taking diazepam, Satish has perfected these procedures: the visits to the garage at the end of the day, the swift dose, the evidence tucked away in his briefcase. At work he's extremely careful, ingenious, even. He visits the drugs cupboards on a strict rotation, and always when no one else is around. He could write his own prescriptions, but that would need careful management: a different pharmacy each time, and scrupulous record keeping. So he's explored other sources, going to his GP for a consultation. Satish sat in her office and they had talked shop for a bit, while he wondered what to tell her. The truth had seemed too complex, she'd misunderstand. Instead, he cited an upcoming conference and his own prespeech nerves. They'd laughed about it together. She had prescribed quite happily: blue pills in a blister pack, an adult formulation. He keeps a bottle of water in the garage to wash down the tablets. He has everything covered.

Satish watches for signs of cognisance in those around him: a searching look from a colleague, a quizzical one from Maya. He checks himself in the mirror frequently, but there's only him, the way he's always been. He audits his face, his hands, but there's nothing to see. He knows it's coming, though. Someone's going to find him out.

The medicine's not always doing what it should, either, but he won't increase his dose — he's strict about that. So here he is, at 2 a.m, downstairs in his lounge and not asleep or even sleepy, trying to keep himself occupied. He's organising the CD collection (alphabetical, by artist). On the coffee table are piles of cases, decanted from their shelves, and a smaller pile of discs beside them. They've become untethered during incidents that will, he knows, be denied by everyone he lives with. He may as well do this himself.

He's trying to track down a Robbie Williams case when his mobile phone, filed on the mantelpiece with his keys and wallet, pings at him. It's a text from Colette: sorry sory sorry there r reasons

He replies:

Go to sleep.

The thing to do is to make sure all the CDs are rehomed, then redistribute the ones which shouldn't be downstairs anyway. Some of Asha's have found their way here, and —

r u awake!?

Go to sleep. Not an approp

He struggles with the word, all fingers and thumbs, before giving up.

Not now.

The reverse will also be true; there is a growing pile of CDs in Maya's car. Not all of them have cases, either, so that means he'll have to match them up —

hang on

Satish looks at the phone, waiting for more, but nothing comes. He wonders whether he's sleepy enough yet: nothing. An itching in the veins tells him he needs to be moving, doing something. He goes back to the pile.

The CDs are like a chronicle of his life. Of *their* lives, his and Maya's. A chaotic one, which won't be ordered in the ordering of it, Abba next to the Bombay Vikings, Oasis a forerunner to the Pogues. Satish considers a different arrangement, by person, or by chronology. He could trace their years together in this way, from his time as a Senior House Officer back in the early Nineties. He'd noticed Maya at work and had gone to pick her up one night before some group event. Arriving at her room he had heard music coming from behind her door: a foul-mouthed, stomping song he had later learned was called "Bottle of Smoke". The lyrics contained words he'd barely ever said, and yet there she was, listening to it, singing, and thudding: was she pogo-ing? He knocked on the door and the thudding stopped. The music was turned off and Maya appeared: puffed out, flushed.

"Right, soldier," she said. "Let's go." His scrotum tingled.

Maya made everything new. Satish was a dynamic young doctor, and his provenance, to a girl born and raised in Portsmouth, seemed glamorous. After three weeks she saw him naked, the scar on his arm dismissed as a botched vaccination. A year later, he asked his parents to arrange the marriage. They still have the song from their wedding. Satish is looking at it now, "Bindya Chamkegi". Maya insists that the mix is "edgy".

Then there's the Sheryl Crow album that reminds him of Asha's birth, and the Best of Madness CD Maya bought around the time his parents moved in. She'd play "Our House" loudly, and he never knew whether she was being cheerful or ironic, and, it being a tricky subject, he never asked. There's "Brimful of Asha" which they'd play to their daughter, aged two or three. He remembers Maya dancing with her in the lounge, her face burrowed into Asha's neck. Mehul had just been born then, a tiny two handfuls. Satish's lad.

Satish could order his music like that, in a way strangers would find baffling, a private chronology, starting with the Pogues. Before that, before Maya, there's not much to speak of. Nearly nothing. Maya has sneaked something in under the wire, though. A couple of years ago she went to a Seventies fancy dress party (flares, platforms, afro wig). Her outfit won her a prize, and here it is: fluorescent yellow, a pink strip of ransom-note letters across the bottom: *Never Mind the Bollocks*.

The headphones are the old-fashioned, bulky kind. Asha would crack up, but she's not here to witness it. Satish puts the CD in, clicks through the tracks to the one he wants. He thinks of Cai going on at him about the Sex Pistols, trying to get through to him:

"I want to play it at maximum volume, yeah? I want it to smash the windows."

He'd found Satish in Jennings Field and started this unsolicited proselytising. It was a week before Cai was due to leave for South Africa, and Satish didn't want to talk to him at all. He got up and walked away, but Cai followed him.

"Listen! When I put it on I can feel my hair standing up and my skin tingling. It makes me . . . I feel sort of strong, unbeatable. It's like I've got this power and I don't know what to do with it. I want to *destroy* things. Do you get it?" Satish kept walking.

Now his head fills with the noise of it: "God Save the Queen". At first it's almost like some kind of Fifties rock "n" roll, then after those early bars, it takes on a raw, anarchic edge. Satish closes his eyes, blanking out the sofa, the coffee table, the flatscreen TV. He tries to see it as Cai did: a grey street, the movement of brown and orange curtains, the sameness of it all, the things he wanted to leave behind. Satish moves to the music: a dipping bob, his fists clenched. He shuffles and twists. What did Cai do? He bounces on his toes, the coiled wire of the headphones slapping against his shoulder. He jumps: knees together, his body an exclamation mark. He is Cai. He jumps higher, raises his hands. He punches the air. He mouths the words, most of them wrong, but he *is* Cai. This is what he felt.

The song ends in a messy drum roll, a final percussive flourish. Satish leans against the wall, panting. When he opens his eyes, Colette is standing beside him.

He yells before he can stop himself, the noise banging inside his head.

"Sorry," she mouths. He pulls the headphones off and drops them. They clatter to the floor.

"What are you doing?"

"Sorry! I didn't want to wake anyone up. I thought you knew I was coming. I —"

"Oh God!" Anger and fright and embarrassment are tussling inside him. He presses his hand to his chest. Colette steps towards him but he moves away. "What are you doing here?"

"I said I'd come. 'Hang on', I said. I texted."

"But it's . . ." he glances around him ". . . it's two thirty."

"More like three. But you were awake. What are *you* doing?"

"I'm organising my CDs."

A laugh escapes her and she claps her hand to her mouth to control it.

"And listening to music. Why are you here? How did you get in?"

"I came in through the garage. Maya lets me, if she's out."

"We're not out, though —" The garage. He pushes past Colette and through the hall, opens the garage door. It's all there: his briefcase undisturbed, everything as it should be. She's followed him.

"That was a bloody stupid thing to do, Colette," he says, returning to the lounge. "And presumptuous."

"Don't! We need to talk."

"About what? We've talked. Go home."

"Satish . . ." She looks up at him. "You have never, ever turned me away. Don't send me home."

He falters. It's the most presumptuous thing of all, to remind him of that. The bare-faced cheek. He starts sorting through the discs again.

"We've got through worse than this, haven't we, Satish? Way worse."

He's not so sure. Back then, she was the only one suffering. It was the mid-Nineties, and she'd come to him out of the blue, nearly twenty years after the Brecons had left Cherry Gardens. Skinny with addiction, a cautionary tale, she had turned up on his doorstep. He and Maya had only been married a short while and Maya hadn't even heard her name mentioned before. "You were the only one I could think of," Colette had told Satish. Maya had reached past him and pulled her inside.

"You took me in," she reminds him now. "You helped me get clean. And that's the thing. That's why I need to talk to you."

This, then. Suddenly, he has to sit down. He lowers himself onto the sofa, takes one breath, two, then squares his shoulders and looks at her. "Go on. Say it."

"OK." She sits next to him. "To understand all is to forgive all, yeah?"

"Go on."

"OK. It's about my dad."

"What?"

"The Andrew Ford thing. It's about my dad. You need to know."

He has to break apart what she's saying, quickly, and put it back into this new order, an order in which he isn't about to be found out, to be disgraced. He wants to grin at her, but remembers he's angry.

"What about your dad?" he asks.

"Well . . ." Colette twitches her head sideways. "It's awful. Things are crap for him right now."

So things are *crap* for Peter. Satish finds he's not uncomfortable with this notion.

"Do you know where he's living?" Colette adds.

"I know he's in London. Catford, is it? What does that have to do with the photo?"

"He's living in this shitty hostel. I saw him two weeks ago and he wouldn't even let me come in and see it. Shitty. You could tell. And he hates his job. Do you know how I know everything's crap?"

"No."

"Because the whole time I was with him, the whole time, all he could talk about was how *great* it was. You know, it's a positive *advantage* that he and Mum are living so far apart, because it means he can put in a few more night shifts." Her fingers stab the air, placing ironic quotation marks around the words. "It's great that he's working long hours because he says he can just *pay off the debt quicker*."

"Well, maybe he's right. Maybe he just needs to do that for a while, put up with it."

Her glance is a rebuke. "He's rubbish without Mum. He's lonely, I think. I know he took that money. He was a bloody fool. She makes him say it, makes him call it

... fraud ... embezzlement. It's like part of his punishment."

"Colette, it *was* fraud. He did those things. He was lucky, too. The bank could have prosecuted him."

"Well, I wish they had!" Her voice disrupts the air between them. "I absolutely and bloody wish they had, because then he would still be in South Africa, with Mum, and he'd probably have had this *tiny* prison sentence which would be much, much more bearable than all these months of pain. Do you know how much he took?"

"Roughly . . ."

"Two hundred and fifty thousand rand. Do you know how much that is? It's barely sixteen grand. Bloody fool! I wish they *had* prosecuted. They only reason they didn't was because of the publicity. And she — Mum — makes him come over here because she says it's easier to get work, but it's hard, you know . . ."

"Colette . . ."

"We had lunch. I paid the bill and he was crushed." The last word is stretched as her mouth distorts. Suddenly, she's crying.

"Oh, no. Don't do that." He imagines Maya waking, his mother coming downstairs. "Don't cry, Colette, come on."

But she does for a while, moaning softly, and he lets her. He notices his hands are shaking and gets up to close the lounge door. She tails off, sniffs and looks round the room. "Shit. I need a tissue."

He won't pretend to care about Peter's predicament, but he has to stop this crying.

"At least he has you here in England," Satish says, bright side. "And Cai." This triggers a fresh bout of sobbing.

"It's awful with Cai. He's still furious about the whole thing. They're hardly talking. Nothing's going to be right until Dad goes home again. Nothing. That's the problem, Satish. I should have told you about it. I'm sorry. That stupid email —"

"He'll work off the debt and then he'll go home. It'll happen sooner than you think."

"I just don't know how long he can hold out, or how long him and Mum can be apart and still stay together. I can't give him any money, I don't have any, so I thought . . . that was the only reason I asked you to do the photograph, honestly."

"I don't understand."

She looks up at him. Her nose is pink and rivulets of mascara run down her cheeks. "The money, Satish. Andrew Ford will pay us to be in the photograph."

"Listen, Colette, I doubt he'd even consider paying. That's wishful thinking. He won't do it."

"Yes he bloody will. I told him: we aren't scenery. We're people, and we're the only ones who can do this for him. It wasn't like that for the first photo, but it is now. He needs us."

"Well, good for you. He approached you with this?"

"I told him we'd have to give up time to do this, and he'd made enough money out of us already. We made him rich. So I said that if he did pay us I'd —"

"You'd what? What did you say you'd do?"

"I said I'd make sure everyone turned up. Fifteen hundred pounds each. I promised him. I said you'd do it for me."

He can't think what to say. He has nothing, no queue of words waiting in his mouth, nothing that might do as a response. He lets out an empty breath.

"Satish, I know you're angry, but I had to think about Dad. My money and his, that's three thousand pounds and there might be more down the line. Newspapers, magazines. I can't just leave him like this. I can't shut the door on him. You couldn't, either, I know it."

But Satish *can* shut the door on Peter: let the wolves get him. He can see Peter doing it to *him*, can see it with clarity even now: the older man breaking his gaze and turning away from the glass, as if the window made what was happening not real, as if he were absolved of responsibility by the fragile division between them.

"No," he says.

"Think about it," she tries again. "Think about your dad, when things went wrong for him."

"Colette," he warns her.

"A few money problems and he's in the shit. You were able to help him out. But what if you hadn't been able to? Wouldn't you have tried *anything* for him?"

"It's not the same. Your dad is . . ." Finally he says: "Your father's a resourceful man, Colette. I'm not doing the photograph. End of discussion."

Colette bites down on her bottom lip. He can see her fighting the inclination to beg, to persuade or manipulate.

"Well, that's it," she says finally. "End of story."

"I'm tired. You should leave."

And it's nearly a perfect exit; he's silent, and pissed off, and in full possession of the moral high ground and he's at the door, and holding it open for her when he remembers, this is *Colette*. He wants to part in high dudgeon and he wants to give her some comfort, but he doesn't know how to do both. He grimaces, then moves towards her. She bends her head obediently while he drops a small kiss on her forehead and hopes it feels perfunctory.

"Go home," he tells her. "Get some sleep."

CHAPTER
NINE

The night before the Jubilee party, Colette had trouble sleeping. She woke early, excited, and lay in bed until she heard her dad get up. She'd promised to help him with the decorations.

"Just you, me and Ram," he'd told her. "God knows how that's going to work out! So I could do with a bit of company, some cups of tea. I'll wake you up when I'm ready to go."

"I bet I'm up before you!" she'd said. "Dressed and ready!"

He'd smiled at her, reached out to stroke the back of his finger down her nose. "You're on."

In the event it was boring, this grown-up work going on high above her, the occasional talk passing over her head. She did bring them tea, ordered from her mum in the kitchen and transported sloppily, one mug at a time, down the pavement to her dad and Mr Patel. Dad had her hold the base of his ladder for a bit, then she experimented with what happened when she let go: nothing. She needed a wee so she left, and he didn't stop her. The morning dragged. The sun came out, went in again. Colette examined the barbecue in the back garden, poking around in the ashes underneath the rack, putting the tip of her tongue to her black fingers then wiping her hands down her jeans.

"I AM THE ALL-POWERFUL ONE!" a voice behind her shouted, and she screamed.

Her brother loomed over her in his pyjamas and dressing gown, arching his arms and wiggling his fingers. "Power!" he shouted again, his eyes wide. "You are in my power!" Then he did a sort of hopping dance on the patio.

"Cai! You gave me a real fright!"

"Were you scared of the all-powerful one?"

"No. You were just really loud."

He looked at her hands. "Burgers later! Magic, yeah? Where's Dad?" She told him. "Right," he said. "Fancy doing something a bit more interesting, then?"

He took her into the shed, and made her swear ten different ways that she wouldn't tell. Then he found a box of matches and a squeezy bottle hidden high up on a shelf. When they came out again, he made Colette go first and told her to check for grown-ups.

"Right," he said, when the coast was clear. "We'll do it behind the shed."

Behind the shed was a space no one cared about. It was useful because you couldn't be seen from the house, and exciting because there was no fence so you could get into other people's gardens — people who lived behind their road, in Chapman Lane. Cai did this a lot. He'd been caught once and a policeman came to tell their parents about it. Her mum had said she was *livid*.

"We're going to start a grass fire," Cai explained. "They have them all the time in Australia. They cause devastation. They kill kangaroos."

"But I don't want to kill kangaroos."

"We don't have any here, do we? It'll be fine."

"What if they find out who did it?"

Cai gave her a gentle push. "They never will. These grass fires just start on their own. No one will guess. We're going to squirt some of this stuff over there," he indicated a tuft of grass and an adjacent dandelion, "then we light it and — boom, whoosh!" His hands sketched a pillar of fire followed by a flattening of the land. "OK?"

She nodded.

"Great! You do the bottle, I'll do the match."

"I don't want to do the bottle. What if it burns me?"

"It won't. Only once it's lit. You'll be fine."

"I don't want to."

"All right. Don't. I'll find someone older to do this with. Someone who's not so scared."

She thought about it. "Do you promise I won't get hurt?"

"Yeah. And if it goes well, I'll tell you the C-word."

Cai showed her how to tip the bottle and aim it at the grass. At first it squirted too far, but she worked out how to adjust it, and then kept going until the grass and the dandelion were soaked.

"Right," Cai said. "Let's light it. Stand back."

He took the bottle from her and put it round the side of the shed. He struck a match but it went out. While he was trying the next one, she noticed a movement near the dandelion. A beetle was making its way towards her, tilting from side to side as it ambled, its black back slick with fluid. When Cai threw the match, it would be burned. Colette reached out for it.

A moment later there was a jumble of sounds, the *ch-ick* of the match, and Cai shouting her name, and a sort of whoomph.

She felt him grab her round the waist and they both tumbled backwards. In front of them was an explosion of fire, just as Cai had said there would be. They sat where they'd landed and watched it blaze, then burn lower. The dandelion was gone, and so was the beetle. There was a rough circle of black, but the fire didn't spread the way Cai had said it would. They waited until it had all gone, till they could smell the charred stuff.

"That was brill!" said Cai. "Did you see it? It just went up — wham!"

He reached a finger into the blackened grass and touched it lightly, pulling his hand away as he made contact. "We did it wrong though. We'll do it better next time."

"OK."

"Next time, we'll make sure the grass is really dry."

Later, Colette went out into the street again. It was magic. No cars — they'd all been moved — and up there, as high as the roofs of the houses, stretched line after line of pennants and Union Jacks, running almost to the end of the road, where her dad and Mr Patel were finishing up. She stood right in the middle, on the white lines, without worrying about traffic, and tilted her head back until all she could see was the sky and the bunting. Above the flickering pennants were skidding clouds, and clearings of blue. Another clearing was coming along soon.

Colette closed her eyes in anticipation, bending her knees slightly to stop herself falling backwards, and listened to the noises of the street. She could make pictures from those noises, like a guessing game. Behind her, there was an open window with music coming from it, loud and jangly. The Chandlers, probably, Stephen's room, the front one. Mr Chandler would be banging on his door soon; she heard him through the wall sometimes. You could collect even better swear words from Mr Chandler than from Cai. *I'll break your fucking neck!* he'd shout. *You insolent little bastard!* Cai had promised he'd tell her the C-word, but she knew it anyway: *I'm not taking this crap from you!*

Colette could hear her dad and Mr Patel ahead of her, at the entrance to the road, scraping a ladder along the ground and talking quietly. She smiled. It felt good, having Dad just there, being able to hear him. Somewhere nearby a front door opened and closed. There were slow, grown-up steps. Mrs Miller, coming to see what was going on? Then the steps got quieter, moving in the other direction, until she couldn't hear them any more.

When the sun finally came out, it was a wall of red against her closed eyes. She squeezed them even tighter. Her face felt warm. She stayed like that for a while, tipping her head back, until her neck hurt and finally the world shifted under her feet. She steadied herself, then heard the clang and rattle that was the adults packing up a ladder: job done. Colette prepared a smile for them as they marched towards her, her dad at the front saluting to her jokily and Mr Patel behind him, bringing the back of the ladder into line. As they headed for the garage, her dad brought down his hand and jerked his thumb backwards. "Ladder-wallah!" he whispered, then snorted a laugh. Colette stared over his head and up to Satish's window, which was rendered semi-opaque by the sun. Inside the room, she could see two figures.

"You all right, Collie?" The ladder offloaded, her dad was coming over to her. "What you doing, then?"

"I don't know." She shrugged. "Just looking at the street."

He crouched down next to her, holding her gaze for a second, then swept his arm theatrically across her field of vision. "What do you think of all this, then? Not a bad job?"

"Brilliant. I can't wait."

"Yeah. We'll give you kids a good time. In a few minutes I'll be finished up here, then we'll look for Cai, see if we can't get a bit of help out of him."

As her father straightened again the street darkened, its brief moment of sunshine gone. They both looked up and saw it at the same time: Satish's window was a little more transparent and the figures in his room could be seen moving behind the glass. They were moving towards each other. Colette felt goose pimples on her arms in the cooling air. She wanted to turn for

90

home, but she stayed where she was. Above her, there was Satish, tentatively reaching out. Colette squinted, trying to identify the person with him, still just a shape, a silhouette really. A girl. Then, in her height, in the blunt line of the bobbed hair, she was suddenly recognisable: Mandy, of course. Satish's hand touched her arm.

Years later, watching two cars collide ahead of her on a motorway, Colette had cause to recall this moment. There was the same sense of inevitability, of the implacable geometry of the thing, the trajectories converging here, now, unstoppably. There was the same fear too, adrenaline jumping in her blood as she stared up at the window, though it was by no means clear to her, looking back, how she knew to be frightened. Soundlessly, Satish ducked his head as he came closer to Mandy, then veered quickly round to place a kiss on her cheek. Colette gawped.

Tall beside her now, her dad grabbed her hand, jerking her back slightly as he sometimes did when they were about to cross the road together. She heard him breathe in sharply as Mandy, bold, came forward again. The two watchers froze, mouths open, eyes raised, waiting for the next instalment. Satish had let go of Mandy and stepped back, but now she leaned towards him — was she holding his hand? — and brought her mouth up to his and kissed him on the lips. She took her time about it, Colette thought, and wouldn't Sarah be proud of that? It made her feel little, all of a sudden.

Her dad was gripping her hand hard. He'd gone very still, and she craned upwards to see his face.

"Little bastard," he said quietly, more a statement than an expletive. "Little Paki bastard." Then he looked down at her.

"Go on in," he said tightly. He paused for a moment, then: "Get Cai out here. Now." The lovely morning felt spoiled. Colette wanted to make it right again but she didn't know how, and she hurried away to do as he said.

CHAPTER
TEN

The journey to Sima's place takes half an hour. Satish's parents are following in their own car.

"How are you doing?" Maya asks, as they ease out of the driveway.

"Fine."

"Really? I thought you didn't sleep so well last night."

"Dad!" yells Mehul from the back. "Can you stop? I've forgotten my DS." Satish hesitates, pressing on the brake.

"No," Maya tells the boy, shuffling round so she can see him. "I don't like you taking that thing anyway. You can play with your cousins." She turns to Satish again. "I woke up last night and you weren't there."

They swing round the war memorial at the top of the high street and head out on the road to Bassetsbury. "I'll be *bored*," complains Mehul from the back. Satish hears Asha telling him, "Shut *up*," but applies selective deafness. No such luck with Maya.

"So you can't sleep," she says. "What's the matter?"

"Can't you sleep, Papa? Are you OK?"

"I'm fine, Asha." He glances at Maya, who's slipping off her shoes. "I'm fine," he repeats. "Busy time at work."

"Hmm." She props her feet up on the dashboard and looks out of the window. For a while she's quiet, watching the hedge running next to them, a rider on a horse the other side of it, glimpsed in flashes where the hedge is sparse. Ahead there are cars waiting to turn right. He slows down.

"Is it trouble getting to sleep or are you waking up, then?"

"Forget it," he says, casually. "I'm fine."

"Mum! Look!" Asha leans forward, taps Maya on the shoulder. She points to a sign, an A-frame set on the pavement next to them:

Retriever Pups. Cast Iron Cookware.

"Can we?"

"We've got enough cookware at home," says Maya. Satish knows she is delighted with herself, biting down on her smile.

"No, *really!*" says Asha. She bangs the back of Satish's seat for emphasis.

"What are you looking for? Casserole? Frying pan?"

"Mummy, you know that is actually annoying," puts in Mehul.

"We are buying neither pots nor puppies," says Maya.

There's a brief silence. Asha mutters something. Then Mehul pipes up: "Asha said bloody hell."

"You said *what?*" asks Maya, twisting round in her seat.

"God!" says Asha.

94

"And we don't want any of that either, young lady," Maya tells her.

"Why is Mehul allowed to tell on me and no one tells him off?" asks Asha.

"Mehul, don't tell on people. Asha, don't swear."

In the back of the car, Mehul yelps.

Maya turns to Satish. "So what's up? Spit it out."

Satish wonders how quickly he could unclip his belt and exit the car. He imagines himself rolling to safety like they do in films, landing in the hedge and watching the car travel on without him. But I'm driving, he thinks. They'd crash.

"Look, kids!" he says. "Look at the dog in the back of that car! Look at his ears!"

"Aww!" they say, in unison, and Asha starts up again. "Mum please! I'll do all the walks and make sure he's, like, fed and everything."

"No," says Maya.

Asha heaves a theatrical sigh. "Can we not do just one interesting thing?" she asks.

"Nearly there," says Satish. For a short while there's silence, Maya watching the road, Asha and Mehul quiet. Satish relaxes his shoulders and realises he can drop them a good inch. Two inches.

"I heard you and Mum talking about that photograph," Asha pipes up. "She said publicity and fame. Is it true? Are you going to do it?"

His shoulders rise again. "No."

"Oh, go on, Papa. It would be *fun*. You'd be, like, a celebrity!"

He says nothing. They've nearly reached the motorway. Maya looks steadily at Satish. He can see her out of the corner of his eye, unflinching.

They arrive at Sima's place in a tumble of noise, Satish getting the kids out of the car, Mehul reticent, Asha scrambling to be first. Maya stops in the driveway and frowns, reciting her list of things forgotten, things to be remembered. "Got the dish, Sima's book, kids' pyjamas. Satish, did you bring the toothbrushes? No, hang on, they're here . . ." He knows she's not addressing him, not really, and he walks to the front door.

Asha rings the bell and they're still waiting for an answer when the second vehicle in their little convoy draws up behind them. Satish's mum and dad get out, bickering gently.

"Ask about their mechanic, Ram. Get the number. I'm fed up with this constant squeaking. You've left it long enough . . ."

"Do you know how much he charges? I can do it myself. Waste of money . . ."

Then the door opens and Gita is there, his little sister's littlest girl, already a lofty twelve to Asha's eleven and carrying the weight of her advanced age with dignity. Her greeting is schooled and formal: "Hello, Satish Mama! Welcome! Come in!" Satish wants to laugh at her but suppresses it, bending to kiss the top of her head instead. He's not fooled for a moment; Gita, the spit of her mother as a kid, will be upstairs in no time, continuing his daughter's social education with the blend of authority and inaccuracy that marks all such discussions between children. It was ever thus, he thinks. And, indeed, as his sister emerges to greet them, Asha is hauled upstairs by her cousin, and he can already see the doors closing on their private world.

"Come on in! It's chaos of course!" Sima hugs him, her skin sheened with sweat from the kitchen. Around him, there's the noise of reunion. They are ushered into the lounge, taking their fragmented conversations with them. Mehul is encouraged to play upstairs, and he does so grudgingly, still muttering about the absent DS; younger than all three of his cousins, he's a misfit boy in a house of girls. Satish's mother has brought a gift, two jars of the chutney she made this week, and the women disappear into the kitchen.

As their voices fade, Satish's father makes for the chair he always sits in. He's lowering himself into it when Sima's husband Manik enters; Satish feels his hand squeezed in a hearty, brother-in-law grip.

"The drinks are coming. Sit!" Manik tells them.

"So, my latest find. Listen to this!" Satish's father leans forward in his chair. "Electric mower, Qualcast, ex-display. Guess how much?"

"Forty?" offers Manik.

Ram frowns in disapproval.

"As new! Higher than that."

"Fifty?"

"Lower. A little." He gestures with thumb and forefinger, a pinch less.

Manik leans back. "Forty-seven?"

"Forty-six. And based in Bassetsbury, so buyer to collect. Thank you." This to Maya, who's come in with his drink. "A bargain. Just in time for spring. Bidding ended at midnight. Got in with thirty seconds to spare!" He takes a satisfied draw on his nimbu pani, the sweet lime and water concoction which really belongs to the heat of Uganda or Gujarat, but which he has never quite lost his taste for, even in the chill of England. Is this eccentricity, wonders Satish. Is this old age? He looks across at his father, his sweater fraying, his trousers and shirt mismatched, the shoes he's had since 1982, and he wonders whether Manik might just be humouring him. Silly old man, wise old man. For a second Satish balances between the two, and the thought of the former pulls up a great wall of defence in him. Manik shakes his head and Satish gives him the benefit of the doubt; you're a bit fuzzy today, he tells himself. You're not thinking straight, so just go with it for the moment. We're next, anyway.

"You have more patience than I do," says Manik. "Going through those lists of stuff, checking the bidding . . . The girls love it, though. On it all the time."

Satish looks across at the mantelpiece, where his nieces smile out from silver frames: they are toddlers, they are at a party, they are forced into brief, uniformed solidarity for the school photographer.

"Didn't Gita get something on eBay?" asks his father.

"Yes, she did. Her iPod. Now, of course, she's plugged into it night and day. I'm not sure it was such a bargain any more."

"Oh! Kids will always do that. You should have heard the rubbish Sima played when she was a teenager. And no headphones, unfortunately . . ."

Satish, hearing them commiserate together, feels himself rocked to a familiar rhythm. He's caught up in the old patterns of behaviour he watched as a child, only now he's the dad, inhabiting the bass rumble of men's talk that reaches up through the floor to his kids, round the corner to his wife in the kitchen. She's there now, politely asking for Sima's chai recipe, while his sister refuses with equal courtesy. He hears his mother reprise her complaints about the malfunctioning car. A couple of seconds later, Maya is in the lounge again, bringing him his chai, remonstrating with him about the barfi sweets he's been snacking on. He lets the words patter about him, welcomes the hazy distance bestowed by last night's dose. He feels middle age settle upon him comfortably and takes another bite. The milky sweetness of the barfi is reassuring. He licks the floury residue off his bottom lip and smiles. His sister has turned out to be a decent cook.

It didn't always look that way. During the painful early years of her apprenticeship in the kitchen he'd wondered who would crack first: Sima, whose resistance seemed a denial of her very gender, or his mother, in denial herself, her cuisine a refusal to admit they'd ever left Uganda.

His mum had evinced a constant dissatisfaction with the ingredients she could find in England, and in Cherry Gardens her demeanour was that of an army field-cook, working under intolerable conditions, forced to make the best of what was available. Notwithstanding her complaints, she displayed an admirable inventiveness. Satish could still remember their home in Kampala, the strings of green chillis hanging from the kitchen ceiling. His mum would buy them at the market, hang them for a few days in the dry equatorial heat, then pound them to a powder. Installed in the dampness of Bourne Heath she continued to disdain shop-bought spices, and instead commandeered the airing cupboard for her precious chillis. She'd take a bus ride into Bassetsbury to buy them fresh, then hang them from the water pipes amidst towels and sheets. Even so it wasn't uncommon, as the family tucked into a meal, to hear her softly tutting at what she'd been reduced to.

In those early days in Cherry Gardens, when he was still young enough to want to stick around, Satish would spend time with his mum in the kitchen. As she prepared the meal, she'd murmur her mantra over the food. "We thank the food, and we ask forgiveness for killing it, even the plants," she told him. As she chopped herbs or sliced chicken, she taught him about the hierarchy of living things, with the cow at the top, the one animal they could never, ever eat.

"Cows are like our mothers, because they give us their milk," she'd say. "You wouldn't kill your mummy, would you, Sati?" Some things changed, as they adapted to their new lives in Bourne Heath, but this never did. Later, when Sima was old enough to learn, he'd heard his mum instructing her in the order of things, in the hierarchy of nature and the maternal benevolence of the cow.

But Sima had proved to be less than biddable. Wilful even at five when she was just rinsing rice and rolling chapatis, she was a sullen malcontent at the age of nine, by which time she was chief vegetable chopper and washer-up. She'd pull a kitchen stool over to the counter, raising herself to roughly their mum's height, and the two would snipe at each other over the spinach and lentils. By then Satish was just an occasional visitor, passing through. He'd grab any stray bits of food he could, then leave, heading outside to a game with Cai or upstairs to his room. Sima would watch him soulfully as he went. Careless of her suffering, he nevertheless tuned his senses to what was happening in the kitchen, keen not to miss any treats, and on a special day he'd not go far. That smell when the barfi was being made, sweet-sweet as the ghee started boiling, a promise of what was to come. Then when his mum added flour to the pan it changed: the smell you get at the start of rain. He'd time his entry into the kitchen, letting the fragrance of just-cooked barfi guide him, and then make off with a portion while it was still warm, the top sprinkled with almonds. Sometimes there would be a pan for them both to pick clean, the strings of melted sugar welded to the stainless steel, yielding to their nails and teeth.

Now, Sima's calling the children for their tea, and Maya is busy retrieving them from their various nooks around the house. Satish knows what's happening in there right now; his sister in perpetual motion,

101

kitchen-to-table-to-kitchen, ferrying hot bowls of rice, dhal and chana nu shaak for the kids. They will clatter down the stairs soon enough, hungry and restive, elbowing for room, chorusing their thanks to his sister. It was just the same when he was a child, in Auntie Manju's time; unlike Satish's parents, Ranjeet's family were strict vegetarians, and Manju's virtuoso cooking was more than just hospitality. It was a counter-argument.

But even Auntie Manju didn't make puri, the showy flat-bread Sima always lays on for Satish's visits. It will keep her working over a crackling pot for a good while yet, but they all adore her for it. Come to think of it, maybe now would be a good time to pop into the kitchen. Just a brief visit, cast an eye over the family . . . In the lounge, his father and Manik have entered into a vigorous debate about car servicing, and he'll not be missed for a while. A little tower of puri is building on the plate next to Sima's stove, but it won't be there long. If he's quick, he'll get in before she transfers it to the table.

Easing up from the sofa, Satish reflects that his search for gastronomic pleasure has been a life's work of sorts, a proudly international enterprise which, even in childhood, reached beyond the boundaries of his mother's kitchen and into other, more alien territories. In Cherry Gardens, "going round for tea" was common practice, and if he wasn't doing it himself, he was on hand to catch the preparations for other people's. Mandy's mum made a great macaroni cheese: creamy sauce loaded with cheddar, then even more piled on

102

top and browned under the grill. He loved the elastic crispness of the topping against the squish of the sauce. Mandy's mum would pop a tiny portion on a side plate for him if he were around when she was cooking it.

At a Boxing Day drinks party in Sarah's house, he had grazed the tray of nibbles, one of everything, just to see what it was like: little sausages impaled on wooden sticks, a totem pole of cheese and pineapple, the fruit still dripping with the syrup it had been canned in. He couldn't stand the cavernous pork pies — the jelly made him retch — but the vol-au-vents made up for that, and he ate as many as he could, until Mrs Miller discovered what he was doing and, sibilant with vexation, confiscated the tray.

As time went by Satish added to his repertoire of exotic foods: the bizarre, the scrumptious, the nauseating. He drew up lists in his head, a catalogue of his discoveries. Toad-in-the-hole, the name of which made him shiver in delight; mushy peas; scampi; egg-and-bacon sandwiches; chips and mash and roasties — every iteration of the glorious potato; faggots; fry-ups; fish and chips; jelly and rice pudding; apple pie and Arctic Roll. Everything, bar beef, had to be tried. He wondered what might happen to him if these were the only things he ate. Would it build up a Britishness in him, all this English food? Might it drain his colour, sharpen his football skills, send him rushing into church? The thought was a wicked one; he was playing with fire. Safer by far, and more familiar, were the meals at home, or the dinners they had with Auntie Manju and Uncle Ranjeet.

Ranjeet's place was great, their first refuge after they'd left Uganda. There was tension in those early days; the rest of the family had quit Kampala some time before, but Satish's dad had refused. In the end he'd had no choice. Idi Amin scoured the country of Asians and the four of them had fled. They arrived on Ranjeet's doorstep with nothing, then filled up his Bassetsbury semi, waiting to move on again. And when they did — a worse crime this, far worse than their inconvenient destitution — Ram chose Bourne Heath and placed an unacceptable four miles between himself and the rest of the family. Satish can't remember any of the rows which later became legend, but fragments of them lived on, in throwaway comments designed to remind Ram of his role as the errant younger brother.

All the more comforting, then, that throughout Satish's childhood Ranjeet had offered a welcome, no questions asked. At Ranjeet's, Satish and Sima could lose themselves in the hurly-burly of the extended family, and there wasn't all this endless explaining of things. Cousin Dinesh was there, Ranjeet's son, four years older than Satish and ripe with wisdom. They'd smirk at each other knowingly as their parents traded news about the prodigious achievements of their boys.

"Dinesh has been getting excellent marks in science," Uncle Ranjeet would confide, grabbing a handful of dhal biji, the crunchy spiced lentils he adored. "Biology, chemistry . . . he's taking after his old man!"

"Very good, very good," Satish's dad would agree. "Satish's teacher, too, is very pleased with him. He's a

104

real all-rounder, she says. You know, good at all sorts of things. You listen to him now, on the tabla. Are these children going to play for us?"

The kids would be rounded up and made to play songs for the adults, and Satish would try to look casual for Dinesh's sake whilst trying really hard for his dad's and be exhausted and relieved when they were finally allowed to escape outside.

While they threw a ball in Ranjeet's garden, or lounged around on the grass, his cousin would tell tales of life at the boys' grammar school. There wasn't much Satish could do to compete with this; all the things he might say would be old hat, so mostly he just listened. Dinesh was going to be a doctor, he told Satish. A really good one, better than his dad. He'd work in London, not some rubbish local hospital. And he'd be a surgeon, too, or an anaesthetist. He lingered over the word, though whether from pleasure or the struggle to pronounce it correctly, Satish couldn't tell.

Satish's family went to Ranjeet's for the fun stuff, too, the things that didn't fit properly in Cherry Gardens. Best of all was the spring festival, Holi. They left Bourne Heath, dressed in their oldest clothes, the ones they could ruin with impunity, waving politely to their neighbours as they climbed in the car and headed for Bassetsbury.

When they arrived, they were made to eat lunch first and they did it in a hurry for once, distracted from their food, peeking out into the garden. There were buckets by the side of the shed, filled right to the top with coloured liquids — pink and green, orange and blue. A pile of water pistols waited next to them. Sima caught Satish's eye, sniggering, and pointed at Uncle Ranjeet. From where they sat they could see boxes of bright powder on the patio and the domes of balloons, multi-coloured, jostling in a washing-up bowl outside the back door.

When Auntie Manju said the children could get down — release! They tried coaxing their uncle onto the lawn, and when he feigned resistance they grabbed him instead, hauling him by the arms, Dinesh pushing him from behind. In the garden, the world was turned upside down: kids against adults, the grown-ups losing. They scrambled to attack Ranjeet — a water balloon full in the face, an exploding splash of red. He held up his arms in useless defence, giggling, while the children did their worst. Splashes of yellow across Ranjeet's clothes, purple soaking his hair, orange squirting at him from hastily filled water pistols.

Then the kids collided during the chase, or maybe it was Ranjeet dodging them too effectively, and suddenly nobody was safe. Dinesh rushed up to Satish, hands full of green powder, and smacked it onto his cheeks, then smeared it down his neck and T-shirt. Satish made a grab for one of the balloons but Sima got there first, raising it unsteadily and launching herself at her cousin.

Auntie Manju joined in, and Satish's mum. When people were wet enough they were attacked with more coloured powder, which clumped on eyebrows and the tops of heads, silting into the folds of Manju's sari. Satish's dad stood, fastidious, at the edge of it all until they spotted him, Satish leading the charge, and went on the attack.

"In the name of Lord Krishna!" yelled Sima as they pelted him with pink and green and yellow. Satish's mum took handfuls of purple and shook it over her husband's head until he stood, caked in colour, coughing and laughing.

For high days and holidays and sociable weekends, Uncle Ranjeet played host. Satish got used to falling asleep on Dinesh's floor, his quilt wrapped round him, lulled by the sound of adult talk from below. But one Saturday, a couple of months before the Jubilee, his cousin had news.

"We're coming to you next week. There's going to be a National Front march down our street!"

Satish took this in. "A march?"

"Yeah. Right down our street. Mum and Papa want us to come to you for the day."

"A proper march? And we can't stay for it?" The National Front was in the papers a lot. They wore braces and boots and shaved their heads. They waved Union Jacks. Nothing this exciting ever happened in Bourne Heath.

As Satish had feared, the excitement of the day — Ranjeet's downstairs window was smashed with a brick, his neighbour's young daughter had stood at her gate, screaming at the marchers until her dad dragged her in — was experienced second-hand, and after the event. In Cherry Gardens, Satish's mum laid on a feast for the family, showing off all the culinary skills she usually did not get a chance to demonstrate. Sima, playing in the garden, threw a ball awry and knocked the fan out of the kitchen window. She turned to her brother in horror, lower lip already wobbling, eyes wide. When their dad came out to yell at her, Satish stopped him.

"Sorry, Papa, It was me. I just . . . I threw too hard." His dad hesitated, looked closely at Sima, and at Satish, then stretched out and cuffed his son. Satish closed his eyes against the blow, but when it came, it was more like a stroke. He opened his eyes to find his father still looking at him.

All the things he was to do later, the medical degree, the marriage, inviting his parents to live with him when things got tough, all that made him a good son, a dutiful one. This, though, was something different. The look his father had given Satish was the sort of look any son would want to see on his father's face, a kind of deep and private pride. Once he'd seen that look, a boy might spend a lifetime trying to earn it once more.

Now Satish plays the good father himself, kissing his kids goodnight, fetching their sleeping bags from the car. When the children are in bed the adults eat, and afterwards they play Teen Pathi, shoring themselves up with enough chai to see them through the early hands. Sima plays cards like a demon, needs watching all the time. His father, equally competitive, is apt to distract his opponents with desultory talk of one sort or another before going in for the kill. Satish resigns himself to his losses, and hopes Maya will play sharp tonight. She smiles across at him from the other side of the table.

"Into the pot!" They've all brought supplies of bitty little five pence pieces; the coins chink into the bowl.

"Dealer . . ." Manik nods towards Maya who shuffles cleanly. She loves this bit. Satish hears the slide and click of the cards as they're dealt out. Manik and Sima pick up theirs, have a quick look, and Sima glances at her husband.

"So," says Ram. "Those roadworks at the Bassetsbury roundabout. Another four months, they think. How are you managing your journey each day, Manik?"

"Oh, it's stressful, of course, very time-consuming," Manik tells him. "And all the other routes, they're just as bad now, with the overspill."

"Terrible," Ram agrees. "Neeta, are you betting?"

"Blind," she replies, slinging another coin into the pot. "Manik?"

Manik looks round the table. Everyone does their best to be unreadable, apart from Sima, who grins and dips him a heavy wink. "I fold," he announces, pushing his hand away.

Then it's Satish's turn, blind too, another five pence in, and his dad's commiserating with Sima about her own commuting problems.

"The thing with teaching is, there can be no lateness, eh, Sima? I suppose you have to start everything so much earlier in the mornings?" He lobs in his stake. He hasn't looked at his cards yet.

"Inevitably," she agrees. "It just takes — oh, hang on." She aims two coins at the bowl. "It just takes a bit more organisation. I haven't been late yet."

"I fold," says Maya, after a peep at hers. Next to her, Satish's mum looks unimpressed with her own hand.

"Fold," she declares. "Ram, concentrate on the game!"

"How are those reports coming on, Sima?" says Ram.

"Oh, the reports. Well, they're coming on slowly, Papa. They always do. We're using this computerised system now, this, um . . . comment bank, it's called. It's meant to make the process quicker, but you know these things — they never live up to the hype. Satish?"

Satish is looking at his cards. He has a pair, and a low one at that: two fives. "Folding," he says.

With just his father and sister left in the game, Satish knows things will turn a little more entertaining. Each has a talent for bluff and double-bluff, and both are hungry to win. He sits back to enjoy it. Sima looks at her cards once more. She purses her lips together, taps the table with her nail, lets out a sigh. This one's a bluff, he reckons; she's not really studying her cards in the way you do when you're willing them to say something else, so she must be quite happy with them as they are.

His father hesitates, then slings in two coins; gulled, he's upped the stakes. Sima tips four into the pot.

"OK," she says. "Over to you, Papa."

His dad smiles broadly, scoots his hand over to the pile next to him and counts out two five-pences. "Sima," he tells her. "Show me what you have."

They turn their cards together. Sima's lips remain pursed as she assesses their hands; hers is an eight, seven and six, different suits. Not bad, but definitely beatable — there's been a little daring in her play, as

110

usual. Her father pushes his into the centre of the table: a three, a ten and a king, all of clubs. She's won the pot. Sima raises her eyebrows, crumples her face into pathos.

"Oh, Papa! I was so distracted by that talk of reports and paperwork!" she hams at him. "I nearly lost my concentration! How will I ever manage to count all this lovely money?"

They laugh, father and daughter eye to eye across the table. Manik wanders into the lounge to retrieve the remaining barfi and Maya slips into the kitchen. Satish watches his dad and sister laughing at each other, and is aware of his mother watching him watching them. It's compelling, this family life. It can be onerous and fractious and sometimes plain dull, but here they are anyway, against all expectations. When Amin threw them out they escaped in the night, just them and what they could carry: a suitcase and £55. No one thought they would flourish, but they have done. They have flourished in open defiance of Idi Amin and the summer of '77.

Neeta starts to gather in the cards, ready for her deal. As she's tapping them down, Maya comes back, glass of water in hand.

"Hey, I meant to ask," she says to Satish. "Did you ever talk to Colette about that photograph?"

Satish looks straight at her and shakes his head minimally, but she looks away and doesn't catch it. His fingertips press into his thighs.

His dad asks: "What's this? What's going on?"

"It's nothing, just . . ." He shakes it off with a shrug. ". . . domestic things. Boring. Stakes into the pot. Let's play." Behind him, Satish hears a noise, and jumps: but it is just Manik.

"It didn't sound boring to me," says his dad. His mum says, more loudly than she needs to, "Right, come on Ram. Into the pot!"

Satish keeps his eyes down. His nails scratch at the fabric of his trousers. He hears the coins going in, sees his pile of cards grow — one, two, three — as his mum moves her quick hand around the table. When she's finished he can hear the others appraising them, or guessing at them, the little sighs and tuts, the bluffs.

"What did I miss?" asks Manik.

"Let's start play," says Satish.

They are seated round the table, volatile, but settling now. Manik peeks at his cards, picks up two coins and rubs them against each other. If he puts them in the pot then Satish can bet, and Sima will, and they'll be thrown into the game themselves; momentum will save him. Satish waits. Manik turns to Sima.

"No really," he says. "What did I miss?"

"Shush, now. You betting?" But the coins stay in Manik's hand.

"Something about a photograph," says Ram. And now he's looking at Satish, quizzical. Neeta sighs and her body jerks slightly with the kick she's administering to his shin. Sima leans back in her chair, folds her arms and watches him, too.

"It's nothing," Satish tells them.

112

Maya glances between the family members. She looks at Satish and frowns. "Yes, it is. It's that Jubilee photograph. Andrew Ford is doing another one."

Satish could slap her, actually hit and hurt her; he has no idea why she can't read the signs, why she won't shut up. They are ranged against him, his father worst of all, craning forward now, ker-ching! in his widened eyes.

"Andrew Ford is doing another photograph?"

"Yes, Papa. But . . ."

His mother places her fingers on her cards. She pushes at them, rubbing them minutely to and fro in front of her.

"It's a thirty-years-on photograph," Maya tells him. "The *Sunday Times* wants to do a piece. Colette says Satish is important for it, and Andrew Ford's very keen to have him there. He —"

"*Sunday Times!*" repeats his dad. This is starting to tip just a little out of control, with the emergence of his terrible, coercive paternal pride, so now is the time to make it very clear, totally clear that —

"It won't happen. I just can't do it."

"Satish?" says Maya.

"But why?" asks Ram.

"I'm too busy. It's just a PR exercise anyway." There's a sound in the hall, and Maya's up and out.

"So it's PR," his dad continues. "Who cares? For people to see you again, and to know what you've done since. A doctor — Central Children's! — your lovely family. Do the photograph."

113

Satish needs to flatten the curve of his rising anger. He presses his cards under his palm. In the hall, Maya is remonstrating with Asha ("Get back to bed!" "But Mehul's keeping me awake. He's being a pain.")

"You know," his father continues. "We came to this country with so little. Look at all you have now. That's what I'd like to see, in the *Sunday Times*. That's what I'd like other people to see. Back then, who knew what you would do?"

"I can't do it. I'm too busy."

But his father isn't interested. *Busy* is a trifling thing. He's remembering their journey, his own tenacity, Satish's rise.

"We've always been proud of you, Satish. But look at this! All you have." He gestures towards his son as if his achievements are lying on the table between them. "It's important, you know. What are immigrants? All we hear: they live in detention centres, they clean our houses. You need to show them something different."

No he doesn't. If nothing else, he has earned the right to that. "Papa, this isn't about politics. It's a publicity stunt."

Maya returns to the table; in the dip of her head, in her pursed lips, he thinks he reads contrition. He thinks she knows now, when it's too late, when contrition is irrelevant, that she has somehow steered this the wrong way.

His father will not let go. "Why do you not want to do this?" he asks, and he's abandoned casual interest or jovial enthusiasm. His tone is gentle and probing and thus takes a step closer to the truth of the thing. Satish

114

sees himself surrounded. He clamps his mouth closed, scared he'll supply an answer. He searches for the clever thing, the killer argument, the way out. Then it comes to him.

"No," he tells them. "And that's that. I'm not going to do it." They all need to hear it: his family, Colette, the lot of them. He'll say it as many times as he needs to: no.

In the quiet, two coins fall from Manik's hand into the bowl. Three cards lie in front of Satish. They can start playing again.

CHAPTER
ELEVEN

Sometimes, being six was about wanting to be eleven. For Colette, it was about Mandy and Sarah. Being around that relationship of theirs, that axis of power and desire, was a heady thing. You could lose your bearings completely. You'd veer towards the two of them, heedless of the dangers of running aground or breaking apart. If you were six, Mandy and Sarah put out a siren call, and here was the pull of it: if you were six, they were just about everything you wanted to be.

They were unattainably eleven, unreachably sophisticated. At school assembly they sat, subversive, in the back rows near the really big kids — the fifth years like Cai and Satish.

Colette would see Mandy and Sarah at lunchtimes, playing Elastic with their friends. Somehow, when she caught sight of them, they were never the ones on anchor duty, standing bored with the loop stretched round them. Instead, they were always the jumpers, flicking their feet in and out of the white twists. Her memories are of their insouciant anklesies, their focused kneesies, their occasional, contortionist waistsies which would bring the game to a triumphant end.

At home, Colette was sometimes allowed to break into their lair and watch their mysteries up close. "It's just little Colette," Sarah would say, as she opened the bedroom door on one of Jan Brecon's visits. Once inside, Colette watched the girls putting on the make-up that was forbidden in public. They used blue and green eye shadow, a legacy of Sarah's sister Diane, liberated from her bedroom after she went off to be a nurse. They ran snail trails of roll-on gloss over their lips. Its artificial flavours — peppermint, bubblegum, strawberry — became an olfactory token of those private times. Once, Mandy bit the ball out of the top of the vial and just poured the gloss on. It looked like plastic on her mouth and, where her lips met, it went white.

Their bodies fascinated her. Sarah already had breasts — just small ones, but they counted. She had bought a halterneck top and was trying it on for Mandy.

"Can you tie a good bow? You can help me if you want," she told Colette. Sarah held the top snugly at the front, then fed the straps through to her. Colette tied carefully, balancing the lengths of the loops and ends so that it looked pretty hanging down. Sarah had freckles on her back, and her shoulder blades were like wing stumps. Colette reached out to touch her, a tremor in her hand. She wondered what it would feel like: the warmth she would meet, the hard and soft of it. Her fingers looked grubby beside Sarah's clean skin. She let them make just the lightest touchdown, four fingertips across the rise of bone.

"Ouch!"

"Oops. Sorry. I —"

Sarah twitched her shoulders in distaste. "Your hands are freezing! What are you doing? Get off!" She frowned at Colette for a moment. "Did you tie the bow?"

"Yes. It looks nice."

Sarah turned away from her towards Mandy, from whom she demanded a more informed assessment.

Once Colette had turned six, the older girls had taken upon themselves the responsibility of tutoring her in matters cultural, biological and sexual. No one knew how to kiss except Mandy and Sarah; the girls made sure she knew how to snog on a first date, why no one liked David Cassidy any more, and which boys at school were worth fancying.

"John Andrews, yes," Sarah said. "He's good looking. I like Richard Greenwood. Well, everyone likes Richard Greenwood because he's gorgeous. But really gorgeous boys only like the best-looking girls, so it depends if you're one of them." Sarah ran a hand across the flicks at her temples, sweeps of hair lacquered to solidity with repeated spraying. Mandy, lying on the bed, rolled over and shared her own wisdom.

"Yeah — good looking's good, of course. But being a laugh is good, too. I like it when —"

Sarah cut across her. "And don't go for anyone shorter than you, even if they're good looking. So no one like Robert Meade, OK?"

Colette tried to nod sagely. Robert Meade?

118

"He'd be good as a friend, though," advised Mandy. "For boyfriends, try to go for boys in the year above. Dominic Irving's nice, I think."

Sarah's judgement was swift and damning. "Eeughh! His hair! His shoes! Mandy! Dominic *Irving*! His stupid hair!"

"It's not that stupid. Anyway, I didn't say I really liked him. He's quite nice, that's all."

Sarah sighed heavily. "He's all wrong. I have to tell you *everything*."

"Yeah? Well he's better than some." Mandy widened her eyes and pouted. Her voice went up an octave. "Ooh, Stephen, can I watch you play football?"

Sarah frowned. "Shut up."

"Go on, Stevie-boy. Can I listen to you shout at your brother? Can I?"

"I said shut up!"

"Stephen, I think I LOVE you. Ow!"

"Well, not everyone agrees about boys," Sarah said, with a final tug at Mandy's hair. "Just don't go for someone short, or younger, or really ugly." She leaned down towards Colette, dropping her voice to a mock whisper. "Like Dominic stupid-hair Irving."

When one problem page correspondent in *Jackie* wrote in fear of an early death — "I'm bleeding, and I don't know why. I can't tell my mum because I'm too embarrassed" — Mandy and Sarah enlightened Colette with girlish enthusiasm. She left that day a little shaken, and somewhat unclear as to the details of the process. She was fairly sure that her winkie was involved, and

119

absolutely certain, after a vigorous debate between the two bigger girls, that Ruth from 5A had Started.

Even when they didn't notice her, she noticed them. She watched them, "going down the shops", "going up the rec" and, on one thrilling occasion, "going up the off". They came home with two cans of Cream Soda.

Sometimes she'd catch them playing separately. Not Sarah so much, but Mandy. Colette at the end of Cherry Gardens, counting all the red cars, and Mandy coming round the corner from the main road with her bike, getting a fright when she saw Colette there.

"Gordon Bennett!" she said. "You scared me!"

"Can I come to your house?"

"No. Sorry. I'm having my tea." She walked away. There were two more red cars, and an orange one that probably didn't count, and then Satish appeared from the same direction. "Hello, Colette," he said, and ruffled her hair. She ducked out from under his hand and watched him turning into his drive the way Mandy had turned into hers a couple of minutes before: a mirror image, the two houses opposite each other. In her head there was already a triangle: Sarah's house, Mandy's house, her own. Now there was a line, a short one, between Mandy and Satish. After that, she watched the line between their doors and saw them on it sometimes, running, looking both ways, slipping quickly into each other's homes. On Jubilee morning they must have managed it without her seeing.

That day Colette had woken up early to help her dad, and seen her new clothes draped playfully over her chair. There was the red pinafore which had caused so many quiet curses during its production. The blue blouse with leg o' mutton sleeves had been a womanly touch and far too old for her, but she had begged for it and loved its graceful lines, the sleeves bagging gently at the long cuffs. They were propped up on the chair back, the pinafore hem reaching the edge of the seat, new white socks hanging down from it to red patent shoes on the floor. It was as if Colette had put them on, then dissolved inside them. She would show the outfit to Mandy and Sarah. They would tell her how smart she looked.

"They're to stay clean, all right Colette?" her mum had lectured. "Keep your sticky fingers off them until it's nearly lunchtime. Jeans and T-shirt for the morning."

It was a long morning, waiting for the party to start. Her dad put up the bunting, and they saw Satish and Mandy kissing. Then it rained and that took ages, all of them waiting indoors for it to stop. Only after that, when the tables had been set out along the street, did it really start to look ready for the party. Miss Walsh brought out the paper cups and plates. Colette was sent to find stones to weigh down the Union Jack tablecloth after one gust whipped it up and sent cups, bowls and plastic cutlery tumbling onto the tarmac.

It was time to get excited. Colette stood at the head of the table and gazed up its length. It was perfect and untouched. Colette pictured it just an hour into the future, when the festivities were due to start. Soon, she thought, really soon, they could pour Coke into the paper cups, and put hamburgers and cakes on those plates. She could make a mess — nobody would tell her off — and would not have to finish her main course before she had pudding. She might sit next to Mandy, or Sarah. She heard a scraping two tables down; Mrs Miller was pushing a chair back into place, before turning and wandering back into her house to cook, or rest, or get changed. The thought occurred to Colette that now, with everything ready, her mum might let her put on the new clothes. She ran towards her own front door.

Her parents were in the kitchen. When Colette came in, they both turned towards her.

"Can I get ready now?"

Her mum glanced up at the kitchen clock. "We've got about an hour. I suppose so. You can keep your outfit clean for an hour, can't you?" She sounded tired. There was a puffed-out feeling about her. As Colette turned to go upstairs she felt a silence weighing between her parents, and though she dawdled on the way to her room, hoping to hear what happened next, they remained quiet.

When she came down again, hungry for approbation, her dad had gone. She had dressed with great care, putting the socks and shoes on first because they were her favourite things, then polishing the red patent on a bathroom towel, just in case. After she had dressed, she had pulled the pinafore skirt up and tugged the blouse sharply down, wiggling a bit so that it sat properly on her shoulders. Her mum would do her hair in the kitchen.

122

"Look at me!" She entered with a grin.

"Oh, Collie. That's lovely. Go on then, give us a twirl." As she spun, her mother's eyes narrowed.

"I really struggled with that piping. Is it a bit wobbly? Hang on, stop a minute." She looked at the pinafore closely. "No, I think we can just about get away with that. What do you think?"

"It's great," and then, a beat later: "Thanks, Mum. Will you do my hair?"

"Yes. Brush and bobble." Colette nipped into the hall to pick them up, then stood obediently as her hair was brushed in great scrapes against her scalp.

"Up or down pony?"

Colette considered. She thought of Mandy and Sarah. "Down pony. Please."

Her mum started stroking the hair downwards in long movements, pausing sometimes for quick little catches underneath to bring it all into line. The soft hairs at the nape of Colette's neck twanged in pain. She tried not to make a fuss. When the ponytail was done, her mum knelt in front of her, pulling strands out to curl around her ears.

"Lovely. If you hang on, I'll let you have some hairspray. Special occasion." She came down with her big gold can of Elnett, redolent of grown-up elegance and babysitters coming.

"Close your eyes." Colette braced herself while her mum sprayed round and round in the air above her. Opening her eyes a little too early, she could see the particles float down on her arms and hands. She could feel them settling on her face.

"Oh, no. I don't like it, Mum. It smells funny."

"Don't complain. Please." The syllables fell sharply between them. "It's meant to be a nice treat. If you really don't like it, go upstairs, wash your face, pull out your ponytail, wash your hair, start again." The room went quiet. Colette couldn't work out where this had come from, what she'd done wrong.

"I'm doing my best," her mum said. "It's just a bit of hairspray, for Christ's sake."

Holding still at the shock of the swearing, the bitterness of it, Colette searched for the magic words. "I didn't mean anything bad. I'm . . . I didn't mean anything . . ."

Colette had seen her mum like this before. She didn't want to be cross, but once she'd started she found it hard to stop. Colette knew it was up to her to fix it, to help her make friends again.

"I'm sorry, Mum. I'm just not used to it. I'll go and look in the mirror. I bet it's nice." When she came back from the bathroom, trailing words of comfort: "It looks ace. Really brilliant," she could see this had done the trick, though whether it was her words or her absence that had achieved this, she did not know.

"It does look good, Collie. I'm sorry. I'm just tired. Tired and grumpy. Give us a hug." Her mum pulled Colette against her belly and held her there. When they separated, she pursed her lips in a squashed smile.

"Hey, I know. How about one final treat? You want?"

"Yeah. Yes, please."

As her mum disappeared upstairs, Colette looked down at herself, a sweep of red polyester, white socks, the gloss of her Mary Janes. She leaned over experimentally, letting her skirt fall forward to obliterate her knees, then her buckles, then everything except the shiny curves of red at the very tips of her shoes. When her mum came back down, she was holding something behind her back.

"Now, how about . . ." — she pulled her hand round with a flourish — ". . . this?"

It was her clay sun pendant, Colette's favourite. She'd never been allowed to wear it before. It wasn't red, white or blue, like they were meant to wear that day, but Colette decided not to let that matter.

"Wow! That's great! Thanks, Mum. Can I wear it out?"

"Yes you can. Special treat. Let's pop it on."

Colette dipped her head, reached towards the smiling sun as it bumped against her tummy, then watched as it rose higher. When it got to the V of her collar, it stopped.

"I'll just tie a little knot here; make it a bit shorter for you. There! Perfect!" Her mum tucked the extra length of cord into the back of Colette's blouse and the two stood silent for a moment.

"You look lovely. Why don't you pop over to Sarah's? See how she's getting on. Ask her mum if she needs any help, OK?"

"OK."

At Sarah's, Colette was greeted by Mrs Miller, her apron clotted with patches of orange mush.

"Come in, Colette. Quick!" She held one arm away from her, sticky with the mess, and grasped the door latch delicately between the finger and thumb of her other hand. "The apricots came through the top of the blender. Now I've got to do it with tinned. Come inside."

In the kitchen, a corner of tiling and the underside of a wall cupboard bore fruity witness to the accident. Mrs Miller busied herself with a cloth.

"How's your mum getting on? Not much for her to do now, I shouldn't think?"

"She's fine. She said, could she help?"

"That's kind, but I'm OK. We'd just trip over each other. Tell her to enjoy the rest. Hey!" She looked at Colette, surprised. "You're really smart! Are those your special party clothes?"

"Yes. Mum made them."

"She did a great job. Lovely red, white and blue. Wouldn't the Queen be pleased? Do you want to look in on Sarah?" Colette nodded. "Go on then! Tell her not to dawdle."

Upstairs, Snoopy barred entry to Sarah's room. Colette knocked with her fingertips.

"Who is it?"

"Colette. Your Mum said I could come up. I've got my new outfit on."

There was a short pause, then Sarah opened the door, peering round from behind it.

"Come in. I'm in the nuddie."

Colette looked at her quickly, a narrow paleness, the beesting breasts, then looked away.

"What are you wearing, then? Do you like my blouse?"

126

Sarah, pulling something from her wardrobe, glanced back. "Yeah, it's nice. I thought I'd wear my jeans — blue — and this."

It was her halter-neck top, the one she'd tried on before, when Colette had tied the bow.

"It's really nice. White and blue. I could tie it for you, if you like."

"OK."

Sarah pulled on her pants, then her jeans. She turned her back to Colette, wriggled into the top and settled it across her chest. Patient as a horse being shod, she waited while Colette tied the bow.

"How does it look?" She turned for approval.

"Great. No red, though."

"I've got red. Look at these. They're new." She held up a pair of red wedgie sandals, with long straps that wrapped around her ankles. When she stood up in them, she wobbled slightly. Colette glowed with the luxury of it; Sarah was hers for a while. Had Mandy even seen these new shoes?

"That looks great. Really good and . . . sexy." She stumbled on the words she'd heard them use. She looked into Sarah's face for confirmation that it was the right one.

"Thanks. And look: this is new. It's from Mandy. Her mum gave it to her, but she didn't want it. She said I could keep it."

Sarah held up a necklace: an enamelled heart on a silver chain, its lobes fat and pillowy. More red.

"That's kind of her." Colette was quiet as Sarah turned towards the mirror to put it on. After a couple of slips she secured it, then started on her hair, brushing it into Farrah flicks, then soaking them with hairspray. She studied herself from the front, from one side, from the other. When she stepped back, she almost trod on Colette.

"Oh! You're still here. Thanks for helping, Colette. Doesn't your mum need you?"

The moment was nearly gone. Soon, Sarah would be walking up the road to show Mandy her outfit, and sitting next to Mandy at the party, and — Colette could see her doing it right now — reaching up to touch her new necklace and thinking how generous Mandy was. Colette needed something special to stop those things happening, to stretch this moment a little longer, and in searching for this special thing she thought about her brother, Top Trumps and the Citroën GS.

Cai was completely mad about Top Trumps. He'd never sit still to do his homework, was always fiddling and wriggling and wandering away from the dining room table, but he'd spend hours in his room with his cards.

"You know my secret weapon?" he told her one morning. "It's the Citroën GS. Everyone always thinks it's a really bad card. It almost never wins. But when you look at the whole pack, it has the highest revs! Of any car!" That was what she needed. A Citroën GS. Then, suddenly, she had it.

"I saw something funny this morning, when me and Dad were putting up the decorations."

"Hmm?"

"It's something about Mandy."

Sarah paused, lipgloss in hand, and looked at Colette, who continued slowly. "It's something she did . . . with Satish."

"What did she do?"

Colette paused, enjoying it. She had Sarah to herself, for a little time. "She kissed him. On the lips."

Sarah angled one hip out, jutted her jaw. "I don't believe you! She fancies your brother."

This was news. Colette faltered. Had she really seen it? Yes, definitely. And her dad . . . She tried again.

"I was with Dad. We both saw it. Dad was cross. They kissed in Satish's room. He kissed her first, on the cheek. But she kissed him too, on the lips, for a long time." There was something about the grown-up way Mandy had done it — all of it, not just the kissing. The grown-upness made Colette feel funny, sort of left out.

"I don't believe you," Sarah was saying. "How do you know, if it was in Satish's room?"

"We saw through the window. Honest."

"She fancies Cai," Sarah repeated. "And Satish is a Paki, anyway. She can't fancy Satish." She gazed out of the window for a moment. "Anyway, your mum will be wanting you. We'll go out together."

"Where are you going?"

"To Mandy's. Come on. You're not to tell anyone about this, Colette. I'll be really cross if you do."

"Am I coming to Mandy's too?"

Sarah laughed. "No. You're going home. This is for us big girls." Forestalling argument, Sarah held the door open and gestured for Colette to leave.

CHAPTER
TWELVE

Maya has spent the afternoon making lists, and now Satish is getting the fall-out. It's the end of the day, but she's not winding down. She's putting the children's packed lunches together and running through the things he needs to get done. He won't remember half of it.

"It's really time to redecorate our bedroom and your study. I'll get a couple of quotes but I need you to sit down with me and talk about colours."

"Colours?"

"Yes. Don't complain. I'll do everything else. The water softener needs more salt, and your car is due for a service. Asha's dance thing is after school next week and I know you can't come, but have a word with her about it so she knows you wanted to."

"Salt, car, dance," he says, but he's thinking about the sweet viscosity of his dose, about the curve of the upside-down spoon against his tongue.

"She's a mermaid."

"A mermaid?"

"Don't worry. I'll jot it all down for you." She zips up the lunch bags and dispatches the countertop mess with centrifugal speed: knives and chopping board to the sink, cheese and red pepper to the fridge, crusts to the green bin. She pushes the lunches across to Satish: "Will you?"

"Of course."

Satish has a minute or so in the garage, and then it will start to look suspicious. He stacks the kids' lunch bags on the bottom shelf of the fridge, fumbling in his hurry. Maya doesn't go upstairs immediately; he can hear her bustling about in the hall and it makes him twitchy. They are separated by the width of the door, no more. He hears her muttering: "Shoes, shoes, shoes." If he gets out the diazepam and she comes in and catches him . . . If he delays and she starts to wonder what's keeping him . . .

Doing without is not an option; he'll have to get it over with. He gets his briefcase down, snaps it open, and is about to pull the zip on the inner pocket when he stops. There's an envelope in the back compartment. He didn't put it there. Satish draws his hand out and yanks the case open further, tilting it so he can get a better look. There's a word on the envelope, mismatched letters cut out from a newspaper. It says, *read this.*

He stares for a moment, not touching it, getting used to the fact of it. This could still be innocent, he tells himself. It could be — he searches for innocuous things this could be. There are none. He knows what this is: it's the heavy hand on his shoulder, the one he knew was coming, right here, in the same place where he keeps his . . . medicine! In a sudden panic, he jerks

131

open the zip and feels inside: a bottle, a plastic bag. It's still there.

"Satish?" Maya's right outside. The handle starts to turn.

"No! I mean, don't! I'm . . . lifting something . . . heavy." (But he wants to shout at her, dreadful things. He can feel them waiting in his throat.)

"What? Do you need a hand?"

"No! I'm just . . ." He puffs loudly, bangs his fist against the door. ". . . I'm right behind the door. A couple of suitcases slipped."

"Oh." She's quiet for a beat, then: "I said you should have a tidy-up."

"Mm."

"I'm going to bed, OK?"

"Yes. I'll be there soon. I'll just sort this out." He hears her go up, the familiar creaks and a muffled padding as she takes each stair. In her wake he has time to feel disgust at what he's becoming, a latent emotion that dissipates quickly, like heat from the skin when you walk into cold air. He lies, he stumbles over his words; he is losing his dignity.

He reaches towards the bottle again, but then he diverts — a sleight of hand, tricking himself into it — and picks up the envelope instead. He tells himself: it's not what you think, it'll be fine, but even as he does so he feels the distance narrowing between himself and something terrible. He unseals the envelope, a forensic exactitude preventing him from ripping it indiscriminately. Inside, there's a folded piece of A4 paper, the words in type.

Do the photograph or I'll tell your secret

He feels his lower intestine liquefy. He needs to sit down, or lie down. He leans against the fridge and slides to the floor, puts his head between his knees. He finds he can't think in any way that's useful. It's the betrayal, after everything, all these years and his own loyalty: Colette.

And then he goes over it again, the envelope, his name, the threat inside, re-reading it all in case it was quite different, and his panic had blinded him to what it was really saying. It's such an extreme response, such a baffling thing to do. And if she was capable of writing this note, this terrible and unbalanced thing, then she might do everything else, too. She might tell them. He needs his dose.

There's a quiet knock at the door and he springs up, shoving the letter into his back pocket. A dark head appears.

"Papa?"

It's Mehul.

"What are you doing? Why are you still up?"

"Not *still*. I woke up," he slurs. "I'm thirsty. Mummy said you'd give me some water."

"Oh, well . . ." Satish lifts the briefcase onto its shelf and has a quick look round. "Well . . . all right. Come to the kitchen."

Mehul walks beside him, slumped forward in tiredness. His hair lies every which way, his pyjama top skewed to one side. Satish hugs his son to him, a hand round his thin shoulder, then half-fills his Spiderman bottle with water.

"Go to bed," he says and Mehul turns away, somnambulating, and retraces his steps.

Satish watches him go, impossibly fragile, right foot treading down the cuff of his pyjama trousers, left hand clutching the water. In his sleepiness, Mehul bumps up against the banister. He takes the stairs slowly, both feet on a step before he'll rise to the next one. Satish waits it out, this slow ascent, and it's like the countdown to his decision: what to do about the letter, the sleepy tread — bump-bump, bump-bump — a heartbeat, a ticking clock. When Mehul reaches the landing, Satish's time is up.

He switches off the kitchen light and goes back to the garage for his dose.

CHAPTER
THIRTEEN

Satish isn't ready to deal with the note yet. He can't find a way to think about what Colette has done. He approaches it from the margins, imagining the new photograph as a reality, imagining what the others would look like thirty years on. He tries to envisage them ageing, speeding them through the years like time-lapse photography. He knows a bit about Cai already. Colette has told him some things about her brother: he went bald early, she said. Other than that, he doesn't look much different: a bit more solid round the waist. He has a long-term partner. They can't have children. He's a lion keeper in a zoo. Satish roared when he first heard this; it's a child's fantasy of a job, or else the first line of a joke. But no, Cai really is a lion keeper. Not too far away, either, just a journey round the M25. You should go, she'd told him mischievously. Take the kids. Satish doesn't know what future he had envisaged for Cai. International spy, for a while. Rock star, politician, criminal. Cartographer, he might have said, remembering their early years of friendship.

It was Cai who'd mapped out the territory for him when he first arrived in the street, who had helped him achieve a kind of belonging. They didn't play together at school; there, Satish was a lone explorer, and Cai was with his own tribe. Satish had had to learn for himself the subtleties that marked you out as a native: which bits of the school were no-go; you avoided the far end of the field because that was where the Years Fives always went, and you wouldn't be caught dead on your own in the adventure playground, not at eight, it was for the littlest kids. But groups were different. He watched gangs of bigger boys storm the climbing net, hollering their way to the top, reminding the Infants who was boss. If you ever needed to hide at lunchtimes you could try the first aid room, a prefab near the swimming pool, which was left unlocked and unmonitored. It wasn't meant to be empty, but the volunteer fifth-years who manned it nearly always deserted their post. You could usually stay for as long as you needed, breathing the comforting scent of TCP, smirking at the Kiss Of Life poster while you went undetected by your enemies.

Home was a different matter. Cai transformed the landscape of Cherry Gardens for Satish, making it familiar, knowable. He can't remember when they first met. There was no special moment, just a few nods on the way to school, a grunt of recognition when they found they were in the same class. Their parents met each other more formally, at Neeta's insistence. He recalls the preparation of the sitting room, and the hours his mum spent making food for their visitors. In the event, Mr and Mrs Brecon had hardly touched the delicacies, a cause of great rejoicing for Satish: all the more for him. The adults had chatted with restrained politeness, but the boys had the best of it, slipping upstairs to play early on without too much of a preamble.

In Cai's company, Satish learned who was OK and who to avoid. He met Mandy and Sarah, from the year below. Like him, they got to play with Cai after school hours. The Brecons' next-door neighbours, the Chandler boys, were older, and objects of veneration for Cai. The Chandlers were "brilliant", he told Satish, and he watched them for clues about his coming maturity, much as Satish watched his new friend for ways of navigating his environment.

The Chandlers were an anomaly in Cherry Gardens: loose cannons, lads who edged just the wrong side of all the indulgent terms which make bearable the behaviour of children. They were not *mischievous*, or *quite a handful*, they even surpassed that merry catch-all, *boys will be boys*. These boys showed clearly what they would be; one school legend had them chasing a younger kid up the climbing frame until he reached the top and, with nowhere else to go, dropped from it onto the tarmac below. Their quarry broke his leg, and when Satish had tried to discover what this boy had done to prompt the attack, no one could tell him. He wondered if it had mattered. Of Satish himself, they were contemptuous, not because of the things he *did* — there was nothing he could learn here, nothing he could modify which would change their attitude — but because of what he *was*. He tried not to be around much when they were present. Yet Cai adored the Chandlers, braving their quixotic moods, thrilled just to be in their presence. He didn't seem overly concerned about their attitude to Satish, either. "They're just having a laugh," Cai would tell him. "Don't take it so seriously."

When he first came to Cherry Gardens Satish would see Paul and Stephen ahead of him most mornings, bigger boys making erratic progress towards school. Stephen wore his uniform carelessly, his body a skinny presence inside, his slender neck ring-fenced by his shirt collar. In the winter, however cold it was, his coat slouched off one shoulder. Big brother Paul inhabited his clothing more conventionally, neater tie, buttoned-up shirt, and there was more of him to do so anyway: he was not muscled, not fat exactly either, but dense somehow. Despite this, Stephen was often the one who took charge, and when they'd left primary school for Bassetsbury Boys' it was him, though younger and scrawnier, who was said to get the High School girls, impressing them at the bus stop and on the brief twenty-minute journey before they were segregated again.

In those later years Satish was near the top of the primary school himself. The Chandlers would now go the other way in the mornings, slouching grim-faced past his house, or jostling up against each other, Paul lazily aggressive, Stephen twitchy, like a ferret. That was the thing about Stephen, the thing that made him instantly recognisable, even at a distance, those quick movements of his. Sometimes Satish would hear them, the occasional shout or laugh in the quiet street, and he would go to the window to catch sight of them. Theirs

138

was a different way of being from the one he knew with Sima, or saw between Cai and Colette. They seemed incapable of leaving each other alone, nor could they ever be quite comfortable close. It was a relationship of attraction and repulsion, as if their fraternity could be found in the tension itself. Satish had opportunities to observe this himself sometimes, at weekends or after school, when the brothers deigned to hang around with Cai, and Satish didn't know how to get out of it.

When the weather was decent the Cherry Gardens kids would gather outside, not in their street which, though quiet, was still a through-road, but in the next one along. A dead end, this street butted heads with the close their school was on. There was a tree and some fencing, with a sizeable gap between them that you could squeeze through as a shortcut to school. It was a good place to meet and talk. Someone usually brought a football, so there were kick-arounds in between the chat. With Cai, Satish would play self-consciously; learning footie had been crucial to his first months in England, and his skills were still rudimentary. But once the Chandlers arrived, things became more serious, and he'd play on the fringes. The talk shortened, till there was just the bump and scuff of the ball on tarmac and the boys shouting each other's names in accents they'd learned from *The Sweeney*.

"Cai! Caiseeyy . . ."

"Paul! Over 'ere!"

"To me, Steve-ay!"

The Chandler boys were bigger, faster, more skilled. If they wanted to, they could tackle the younger boys

139

and take the ball off them, moving the game down the street. Then they would come at each other, half-laughing, grimacing, tackling hard, the ball between them just an excuse. When they were finished they'd chip it over a hedge and leave, or boot it as far as they could, sometimes out of the road and into Chapman Lane, where it would languish until one of the younger ones rescued it.

Occasionally Mandy or Sarah joined in, kicking straight-on with the front of their feet so that the ball pinged off at uncontrollable angles, or rode up onto the toes of their shoes. The lads would look at each other knowingly, or take over and keep the rest of the game to themselves, or sometimes just retire from play. Sarah was always swift to notice, moving to the sidelines and offering inexpert support ("Brilliant kick, Stephen!"). Mandy was usually the last to stop, her final pass uncollected, before she'd realise she was suddenly playing alone.

Often, the kids would just talk. "I've got toad-in-the-hole tonight," Cai might offer, an opening gambit. "We've had sausages three times this week. It's been rubbish."

"We're having chops," Sarah would tell them. "I hate chops."

"I like lamb chops. Not pork. I think it's chips tonight though," from Mandy.

A murmur of approval. Satish thought about chips, and the advert that was on telly now for a cooking oil which "locked in" flavour. On the advert, the woman had a little key to unlock each piece of food. It made

140

you think about the specialness of each mouthful, how crunchy and clean it might taste.

"Chops are shit." Paul and Stephen had finished their kick-around and Paul's swearword felt like a slap. Satish saw Mandy look round: no adults to hear. "And toad-in-the-hole's shit, too," Paul went on. "What you having tonight, Splatish?" The brothers headed for the kerb where he was perched, and stood over him.

"I don't know. I think my mum's making some paneer — some cheese. Maybe that." The moment he'd said it, he cursed himself.

Stephen laughed, and stepped a bit closer so that the toes of his shoes were almost on top of Satish's. "She's *making* cheese? Has she got a cow? A sacred cow? Does she milk it?" He mimed it in that jerky way of his, wiggling his shoulders up and down, opening and closing his fists.

Sarah was giggling. "A sacred cow!" she echoed.

Satish pulled his feet out of the way, scrunched his legs up under him. He looked at Stephen's plimsolls and tried to imagine Stephen being whacked with them. His dad did it, Colette had said. She'd heard him do it and told Satish. He tried to think about that, while Stephen hopped up and down and the others laughed. Satish hoped it made a mark on Stephen's bum and that he cried. He hoped that he, Satish, would be granted the pleasure of hearing this himself one day.

When Satish looked up again he saw Mandy: jaw set, eyes fierce, staring at Stephen. She wasn't laughing.

It was hard to know what to do. Sincerity could be fatal. But he couldn't say anything. Next to Stephen, Paul was looking down at him, his face expressionless.

"She just boils milk. I don't know — she does it with my sister."

"Vith your sister?" echoed Paul, wobbling his head from side to side.

"Do you just eat cheese, then?" enquired Stephen. "On its own?"

"Ve do!" Paul wobbled at his brother.

"No." Satish risked an upwards glance at him, then looked away. Mandy was standing up, taking a step towards the Chandlers.

"We have spinach with it," he said quickly. "We love spinach." He stood up, his legs shaking, and found himself looking at Stephen's chest. "We really love spinach," he said again.

"Eeergh!" Stephen exploded. "Spinach! God, yuk!" He stuck out his tongue and made gagging noises. Paul put two fingers into his mouth. Out of the corner of his eye, Satish could see Mandy, frozen. Sarah laughed with the brothers, screwing up her face, and Cai guffawed.

"God! That's disgusting! Spinach!" Stephen hawked a couple of times, leaning in close to Satish. Saliva boiled at the back of his throat. Then he spat, twisting his head and sending a stringy gob onto Satish's trousers. Satish made his throat go hard so he wouldn't gag and waited for the next thing — the punch. But suddenly Stephen turned, and Paul turned with him, both understanding that they'd spent enough time with the kids now. They moved away, still giggling and grimacing, then Stephen nipped back, slapping his hands onto Satish's cheeks: the old joke. He chafed at them, making Satish's lips slap against his gums with a wet noise, then withdrew his hands and stared at them, exaggerated puzzlement on his face.

"Nope," he said, shaking his head. "Still not coming off." He wiped his hands down his jeans.

Paul sniggered and the two of them headed off towards Cherry Gardens. Cai called after them — "See ya!" — but his shout was not returned and the pair disappeared, leaving the dregs of the joke behind.

Without the Chandlers, Satish could breathe easier. The four of them would often meet at their tree, or in a garden, or in Mandy's sitting room, Cai lying on the floor with Mandy's cat Hendrix on his chest, its front paws squeezed between his fingers. As Cai talked — about the Damned, about their teachers, about what Sarah's sister Diane might have done in her Mini in the Sports Centre car park — Hendrix would gesticulate for him, expressing shock, or disappointment, or fury on Cai's behalf. After Diane returned from a holiday to Lloret de Mar, her travel stories occupied the group for days.

"She drank sangria all the time," Sarah told them. "It's this punch stuff. She drank tons of it, and one night she threw up and she passed out and when she woke up there was sick all over her bed."

There was a mutter of disgust. Mandy, stretched across the settee, added, "My uncle went to Ibiza and he ate donkey. Or was it dog? Anyway, that made him sick, too."

"Donkey!"

"People are always sick in Spain," Cai said. "Sick or the squits. It's well known. You can't drink the water, and if you swim in the sea there are bugs that get inside you." Hendrix covered his eyes with his paws.

"Yeah," said Sarah. "Diane said that. She said there were all these bugs."

"There's this one that's really disgusting," Cai went on. "Do you want to know?" They did. "You swim in the sea, and if you're a boy there's this worm that swims up into your donger."

"Eurrghh!"

"Yes. It swims up into your donger, and your donger swells up and goes purple and if they can't get you the right medicine in time, they have to cut it off."

Satish's hands moved to his crotch. "No!"

"Yes!" Sarah put in. "It is true, because I've heard it from other people. You lose your willy completely."

Cai nodded. "You're just left with a hole to pee out of. And every time you pee, it hurts so much you have to bite on something." Hendrix clasped his paws to his ears and shook his head from side to side. Behind Cai, Mandy grinned at Satish and circled her finger at her temple.

"I'll tell you what," said Sarah. "It wasn't just drinking. Loads and loads of people were Doing It all the time. Basically, if you didn't want to Do It you locked your door at night, but if you did, you'd just leave it unlocked, and people would come in, and you'd just Do It with them."

Mandy narrowed her eyes. "No!"

"Oh, yes, I promise you."

"Just went in?"

"Yeah."

"And Did It?"

"Honestly." The room was briefly quiet. Cai must have relaxed his hold on the cat for a moment, because suddenly Hendrix scrabbled with his back paws and was out of the room. Mandy began chiding Cai — "Were you being gentle with him?" — and Sarah frowned, her moment gone.

"Well —" she tried, sitting forward in her chair. Then, "Well!" a little louder. "I'll tell you what, I know it's true, because one night Diane left her door open, to see what would happen."

Cai looked up. "Oh yeah?"

"Yeah. And what happened was, *she Did It, too.* It was one of the Spanish waiters who came."

As one, Satish and Mandy turned towards Cai. A revelation like this required his stamp of authority.

Cai waited for a moment, then beamed. "Oh, José!" he shouted, scraping the word against the back of his throat, bending it to his atrocious Spanish accent. "I hope you are wearing a Rubberrr Chonny!"

Cai made Cherry Gardens familiar, but never predictable. Where was the fun in that? He was the purveyor of the new and the risky, a genius at creating danger and then tempting you with it. One afternoon at his place, there was something waiting on the kitchen counter. It had been left to cool, its glaze dulling as the heat evaporated from it. Satish eyed the dish with interest: wormy strands of pasta, stained red where the edges of a dark sauce had oozed. Satish could make out carrots and onions, maybe bits of celery. Cai came in trailing Sarah.

"Spag Bol!" he enlightened his friend. "Brilliant!"

"What's that?"

Cai assumed a cod Italian accent, like something from an ice-cream advert. "E-Spaghetti Bolognese-ee! Haw-he-haw-he-haw! You not have thees?"

"No. Is it good?"

"Ees great! Ees — ow you say — complete skeel! You try?" He pulled open a drawer, looked for a spoon. Out of the corner of Satish's eye, there was movement: Sarah shaking her head.

"What's in it?"

"Ees-a the meence. You know?" He'd found a teaspoon and passed it to Satish.

"Beef mince? I can't have that. I'm not allowed."

"You not allowed? But why?" Cai widened his eyes and spread his hands, a cartoon of Mediterranean idiocy. Satish hesitated before attempting the accent too.

"I get big trouble, you know? Much trouble. Me not allowed-a beef!"

"Really?" Suddenly Cai was all Bucks again. "What would happen? Would your gods punish you? Would you go to hell?"

"I don't know about that. My mum and dad would be angry, though." He saw the glint in Cai's eye. "I don't want to anyway," he added pre-emptively. "I've never eaten it. Cows are sacred." His friend snorted his derision. "I can't eat beef. Ever."

146

There was a moment's silence, and Satish thought he could see Cai running through some options. He was preparing himself for them when Cai suddenly changed tack. "Hard luck," he said. "Spag Bol's brilliant." Then the three of them went upstairs to play.

And sometimes there was just Mandy. She'd come into his room quietly and that was the first he'd hear of her, or they'd meet in the scrubby grass of Jennings Field, or at her place. Often they'd see each other across the way, she at her bedroom window, head tucked under the nets, he at his. He'd lift his hand to wave and let it rest on the windowpane. When he pulled away there would be the residue of his touch on the glass, a smudge of palm and fingers. On Jubilee morning, as the party was drawing closer, she'd written a note on a big bit of paper and held it up so he could read it — TROUBLE! — with a smiley face as the dot on the exclamation mark. He'd gone over straight away.

Mandy was trouble: that was for sure. She was a safe kind of trouble for him though, her peccadilloes a sort of circus act he could ooh and aah at from the safety of the benches. There was a certain thrill to it. She was unpredictable, like Cai, but the secrecy of their friendship protected him from her misdeeds. She was also a little subversive. There was something about her that picked at the edge of life in Cherry Gardens, not least her secret friendship with Satish. He couldn't explain why, but he knew it: Mandy was a foreigner, too.

With her, Satish could say pretty much anything; there were no rules here. He got used to her way of

147

thinking: a little off-beam. She'd tell him, "When I get older I'm going to live in the Swiss Alps with my husband and loads of children, and I'm going to dress them all in curtains like in *The Sound of Music*." She wanted them to select one pair of curtains from each house that might be up to the job. Some of the things they talked about were a bit girly, but Satish played along; Mandy was a mate.

They maintained an impeccable subterfuge. If Satish was having a laugh with Cai and Mandy and Sarah passed by, he'd let his gaze roll over her with the same casual attitude he used towards her friend. Once or twice he'd found her and Cai chatting, and he'd flick her a quick, "Hiya," before turning his attentions fully to Cai. Only when things were safe, when the others were concentrating on something else, would they risk a glance, a quick bit of contact. She'd widen her eyes, or cross them comically, and he'd grin, then look away. Sometimes they'd go two weeks without meeting; other times they'd see each other for days in a row.

Mandy was fascinated by the family shrine tucked away in his parents' bedroom, the artefacts crammed onto a shelf next to the dressing table. She loved the image of Lord Krishna, blue in limb and face, red-lipped, gold bracelets and anklets and crown. Mandy picked up the bell to ring it and Satish grabbed it back in a panic. Then she dipped her finger in the red kumkum powder, smearing it over the back of her hand, and blew on the incense cone, dislodging the ash that clung to it. In the wake of her visits, Satish would have to perform a hasty clean-up job, so they wouldn't be found out.

In return, Mandy showed him her parents' exotically separate bedrooms, her father's devoid of pictures or ornaments, the bed unmade, the curtains closed even during the day. Her mother had a bedspread decorated with elephants ("she brought it back from India!') and a red scarf over her lamp. Mandy made Satish plan his own grown-up bedroom, and designed one down the corridor for herself. One time, when the Chandler boys had been blowing off steam with him, she came round to his place and they didn't say much at all, just sat in his room and listened to his mum and Sima arguing downstairs.

It took a while, but the hard-won territory of field, playground and street began to seem like home to Satish. It was always good to go over to Bassetsbury to see his cousins, but when his dad told him to get ready for Temple, he found he wanted to play football with Cai instead. After a while, he started asking if he could, and just once or twice his father actually let him.

And now, thirty years on, Satish wonders what he might possibly have to say to Cai, what they'd ever talk about if they met. They would have to find a way of being with each other: two middle-aged men, two strangers. House prices, he thinks. Work. Or maybe — he gets a sudden image of Jubilee Day, the downpour in the morning — maybe the weather.

In the days following the Jubilee, people had talked a lot about the weather: how it had drizzled on and off, how lucky Andrew Ford had been to snatch the few bright moments in which to get his photograph. Satish remembers that drizzle, and the oppressive greyness of it, but more than that, he remembers what happened when it rained.

The rain came when the men and boys were busy setting out the tables. In the kitchens of Cherry Gardens, tempers were short. When Mr Brecon knocked on doors — "any strong men in there? The tables need moving!" — fathers and sons left their homes with gratitude. At Satish's house, as he and his dad prepared to leave, Sima bolted out of the kitchen. She'd managed to pull on one of her shoes when her mum called her back: "Ladki kahinki! This dhal won't stay hot forever!"

Satish and his father walked out into a street lined with gaping front doors. They headed for the Chandlers' garage, where the Austin Princess had been evicted the night before to make room for the trestles.

Mr Chandler was directing operations. "Watch it, you divvie!" he said, as someone scraped the corner of a table against a wall, or misjudged the arc of a turn.

Out in the street, fathers barked commands and their taciturn sons shammed as old hands: the less you talk, the more you know what you're doing. Colette was there too, scampering by her dad's side, yelping suggestions that everyone ignored. Once a few of the trestles were in place, Miss Bissett came out of her house.

"Should we start setting the tables now, Peter? I think Susan's got the things in her — oh, bother. That's entirely typical."

150

The drizzle had thickened into proper rain, rather than the fine mist they'd been able to ignore until now. Satish, manoeuvring a table into position with Cai, felt wetness seeping through his T-shirt.

"Get inside, lads!" That was Mr Brecon, already on his way into Miss Bissett's with Satish's dad. Miss Walsh, head out of her door to gauge the rain, called to Colette:

"Want to come in here, lovely?"

"Can I, Dad?"

He looked over from Miss Bissett's door. "Go on, then — but be *good*."

Satish turned for home. Across the road, Mandy's dad was knocking on his own front door.

"Pam?" he was saying, then: "Mandy? It's Daddy." He bent down to the letter slot and called through it. "Can you let me in, love? I'm soaking out here."

It was only when Satish reached his door, a fresh assault of rain soaking his shoulders and the back of his neck, that he realised it was also closed. Cai's wasn't, though. Cai's stood wide open. He jogged across the two driveways and thought of Mrs Brecon. She was inside, probably. Would she mind him sheltering there for a minute?"

Inside, it was quiet. Satish could see there was no one in the kitchen. He stood for a few seconds, feeling chilled for the first time. With the front door open he was still in a relatively public space, but he didn't know where to go from here. Outside the street was empty, a screen of rain between him and the houses opposite.

He wiped a hand down his nose and remembered the banned record lurking in Cai's drawer. He wanted to see it again. Turning, he trod softly up the stairs and went into his friend's bedroom. In the drawer, beneath the socks, was the bag containing the single. Satish reached under the clothing and felt something hard and cold brush against the back of his fingers. He snagged it with his fingernail — a thin metal bar — then tugged. As it emerged from the drawer, straining at the black fabric it was attached to, Satish saw that it was a safety pin.

When he'd pulled the whole thing out, he could see what Cai had done. The safety pin held together a long slash down the front of a T-shirt. A shorter cut, nearer the neck, was adorned with a second pin. On the back, in ragged white paint — Liquid Paper? — were the words: "No Future". Satish ran his finger over the lettering. It felt bumpy. His nails made tiny clicking sounds as he ran them across the soft cloth, then onto the letters, then off again.

Like the single that rested in its hiding place at the bottom of the drawer, this was a talisman; it resonated with danger and the possibilities of a different world. Had Cai used his parents' scissors to make the cuts? Where had he got the safety pins from? How had he managed the slow job of writing on the T-shirt, the material rucking up under the brush, without his mum walking in on him? Satish knew he would not have been brave enough for any of this: not even brave enough to keep such a thing in his bedroom. He did not allow

152

himself to imagine a time and place when Cai might wear this terrible, admirable, perilous garment.

It was as he was putting the T-shirt back in the drawer that Satish realised he was not alone in the house. He had forgotten to wonder about Mrs Brecon's whereabouts but now he could hear a noise coming from Cai's parents' bedroom. He eased the drawer shut, then stood very still. It was a most unexpected noise, and hearing it filled him with apprehension — a series of low, monotonous keenings, each ending in an exhale. It took Satish a long while to identify the noise, partly because of his surprise, but partly because its perfect balance of misery and anger acted as a sort of camouflage. Mrs Brecon was crying.

Satish couldn't sneak back down the stairs. If she spotted him now, she would know how badly he had trespassed. Stuck in Cai's room, Satish listened. Mrs Brecon — her name was Jan, he knew — continued like this for a while longer. After a bit, he heard her breathing hard, and then: "Bastard — no! Bastard! God!" He controlled his own breathing carefully, feeling exposed in the middle of the room, the first thing she'd see if she came in. Satish looked around. Anywhere he could shelter, under the bed, behind the door, in the wardrobe, was too long a journey, too fraught with the dangers of discovery. Floorboards could creak, hinges squeak and give him away, so Satish stayed where he was. Outside the rain had stopped, but he couldn't tell what was going on in the street; Cai's window overlooked the garden. He could see Colette's scooter abandoned near the shed, a stack of plastic patio chairs, the barbecue.

Next, he heard movement. He froze as Mrs Brecon, sniffing, came out of her room and went into the bathroom. When she started to run the taps Satish slid around Cai's door, not touching it, and tiptoed down the stairs. Coming outside again was a relief. Everyone was back in the street, exchanging rueful comments about the weather. When Satish saw his dad pulling a table into place, he rushed to help him.

CHAPTER
FOURTEEN

The mother in front of Satish is trying not to cry. She turns away from her daughter and looks pointedly out of the window. On the bed the girl fiddles with a cardboard sick bowl. Satish is doing rounds with Kawther, the registrar. Clare Munroe is with them.

"This is Dr Patel," Clare tells the girl. "You met Kawther earlier, didn't you?"

"Yeah." The girl runs her fingers round the rim of the bowl, bending the edges up.

"Jess and I discovered a mutual loathing for Coldplay," says Kawther. Jess says nothing. Her mum comes away from the window to sit in the chair beside her, and Kawther addresses Satish: "Jess Roberts, post-viral myocarditis, recovering well but not tolerating food."

"She threw up," says her mother. "Last night and this morning." She smiles apologetically and looks down at her clothing. She's wearing green scrubs provided, he assumes, by some sympathetic nurse. She looks exhausted, washedout, like a junior doctor at the wrong end of a long shift. "I'm Alice," she says, and reaches out to shake Satish's hand.

"You've been vomiting, Jess?" he asks.

"Yeah."

"And how are you feeling now? Still feeling sick?"

She shrugs. "Yeah. It comes and goes."

"All right. We'll see what we can do about that." He turns to Kawther. "We'll need to check bloods."

"Done. Electrolytes fine."

"Good. A single line ECG?"

"Yes, we did that this morning. All fine. Normal sinus rhythm."

"All right. Good."

"What does it mean?" asks Mrs Roberts — *Alice*, he reminds himself; they like this first-name stuff at Central Children's. "Is it to do with her heart? Is it the medications?" Two weeks ago, her twelve-year-old was completely healthy. Since then she's travelled from ambulance to theatre to ICU to high-dependency unit to ward. Mrs Roberts is punch-drunk.

Jess is the victim of events both nasty and arbitrary; the Coxsackie virus that nearly killed her might, instead, have caused a sore throat, or a temperature. She might have had a couple of days off school. She might have had no symptoms at all. The catching of it was arbitrary, too: the sneezed droplet which she could have evaded, the wayward microbes which might have lain untouched. But she had caught it, and after those first few innocent days (sore throat, fever) the virus made for her heart, inflaming its fibres, disabling it: sending her here.

And now she's throwing up and it might be nothing, the luck might run her way this time, or it might be cardiac failure. *What does it mean?* her mother asks, and Satish reminds himself that the question is a medical one.

156

"It's relatively common in recovering patients," he tells her. "Jess's bloods and ECG look fine." He looks at Jess, folding the sick bowl in half, making it into a mouth she then opens and closes. No breathlessness. "I'm just going to examine you now," he tells her. "Is that all right, Jess? I'm going to listen to your chest and feel your tummy." She nods her assent and Clare helps her sit forward. Beyond the closed curtains, someone laughs.

Jess has the remains of a temporary tattoo on her back. He can't make out what it once was — it's all black spikes and fragmented edges.

"Breathe in and out for me, Jess. Nice and deep, if you can."

He imagines Jess at a sleepover with her friends, like the ones Asha has. It's always been a mystery to him, what they do once the bedroom door is shut, but surely it's things like this, putting tattoos on each other, giggling together. No creps; her lungs are clear.

"That's all fine, Jess. Just your tummy now. I'm going to need to press on it." He nods at Clare.

"I feel a bit sick," says Jess. Her mother whips away the bent bowl and puts a new one in her hand. Clare strokes her back. They wait. Kawther runs her fingers along a fold of her hijab. Satish notices the repeated print on the material: lines of red-scarfed teddy bears.

"It's OK," says Jess after a while. "It's gone."

Clare lies her flat and pulls up her gown, resettling the sheet over her hips. Satish rubs his hands together, warming them. "I'll try not to push too hard," he says.

His fingers press Jess's abdomen, up towards the lower edge of her ribs: nothing. "Take a deep breath," he tells her, and then he can feel the edge of her liver, only just: thin and firm.

"That all feels quite normal," he tells Jess.

"So, what does that mean?" her mother asks.

"It means there's no sinister cause for Jess's sickness. It's not very pleasant for you, I know," he tells the girl. "But we can do something about it. I'm going to give you some medicine to stop you feeling sick. See if we can get you eating again. Clare?"

"Yes?"

"IV Metoclopramide, 50 milligrams."

"So can she go home?" says Jess's mother.

"I'm going to suggest we keep her in for a little while longer. I know it's a disappointment, but I just want to be cautious. We'll leave her a couple of days, reassess on . . . umm . . . Friday."

On hearing this last word Jess's mother slumps at the shoulders but she nods. "Of course, absolutely — whatever you think, really." She drops her voice. "Just, it's hard. You know, I'm not complaining. My other kid's at home, pillar to post. Got to find another few days' care for her."

Satish looks at the clock: he has a meeting in fifteen minutes and needs a pee before that.

"Are you worried about this? Will it stop her getting better? You just said you were happy with her heart. I don't understand . . ." Her fears come in a rush, as if they've been racing to reach her and have just caught up.

158

"It's not optimal," he says carefully. "But it is very common. I *am* happy with her, cardiovascularly. I just need to make sure that when she goes home, she continues to make a good recovery. I'm sorry. We really do have to wait a little longer on this one."

Alice Roberts looks out of the window again. He sees her hand go up to her face.

"You could go home for a night or two," Clare says, moving closer to her. "We have some fairly expert babysitters at Central Children's. Medical degrees and everything."

"No," Alice says to the window. "But thanks anyway. I couldn't leave her on her own. We'll be fine."

Satish leaves, nodding his thanks to Kawther. A few steps away, and Clare is beside him.

"That Metoclopramide," she says. "Just wanted to check. You did say 50mg?"

"Yes. IV."

"Fifty?"

He thinks. Fifty?

"No! Fifty? No. I didn't say that. Five. I said five."

"OK."

"I said five."

"I'll give her five."

"I said fifty just then because you did. But before, I said five. Definitely." Fifty would cause overdose and loss of muscle control, the patient twitching and jerking, her face contorting. He'd never have said fifty.

"OK. Five."

"And get Jane Oshodi to see Mrs Roberts. She needs patient liaison. She's under a lot of stress."

159

At university, Satish had a housemate called Lawrence Potten, an English student for whom Satish's chosen profession seemed an ideological and pharmacological goldmine. Pharmacologically, he had it all worked out: wait until you're filling in for a houseman, doing ward rounds with one of the more distractable nurses. (Lawrence was, he assured Satish, an expert in distractable nurses.) Swipe some Co-Proxamol from the drugs trolley, sell it on and receive a nice little supplement to your student grant. Satish had refused, of course, but Lawrence's plan was so accurate, and so very precise, that he knew it came from insider knowledge. Who were these *other* medics, he'd wonder, these swipers of drugs, these corrupters of youth? What sort of doctors would they turn out to be?

Lawrence had more luck with the ideological aspect of Satish's job. In particular, he was obsessed by the cultural significance of the white coat. He considered its semiotics, its effect on interpersonal dynamics. One day, Satish noticed that his coat and stethoscope had gone from their peg on the back of his door. Two hours later, Lawrence returned with them.

"Bloody unbelievable!" he told Satish. "Incredible!" Satish caught a waft of Lawrence's aftershave as he bounced closer. His spiked hair juddered with enthusiasm.

"Lawrence, what did you do?"

"I went to the hospital! I walked through the corridors wearing it. Even a couple of wards."

Satish winced. "That's completely irresponsible."

"It was *fine*. It was a revelation! It's like being Superman, isn't it? You walk past a group of people and they turn to you, they lift their faces to you. They're hopeful. They think you're going to solve their problems."

For some reason this threw a switch in Satish. "I do solve their problems!" he remonstrated. "That's the point! What do you think med students *do*, Lawrence?"

"I just said —"

"You did a stupid, irresponsible thing. Stay out of my room. Don't take my stuff without asking. Don't do that again."

Lawrence retreated. "I just wanted to see. I thought it was amazing," he said. "Amazing, walking round like that all day."

And of course, he was right. It *was* amazing. Even in those first sweaty weeks on the wards, when he didn't know his otoscope from his elbow, the white coat was transformative. It was magic, a cloak of visibility, and it didn't just make people notice you, it made people *need* you.

A couple of years after he'd started at the hospital the board had looked at ways of making the place less formal. Plenty of paediatric centres had abandoned white coats by then, and there was an enthusiastic lobby for Central to follow suit. Satish remembers his own arguments for retaining them. He'd cited studies and anecdotal evidence, suggesting that they were a comfort to anxious parents. He'd pointed out the practicalities. He lost.

When Satish walks the corridors of his hospital — as he does now, leaving Butterfly ward and heading for the lift — he operates without the benefit of his white coat. He wears a stethoscope and an ID card around his neck and carries a file in his hand, all of them vestigial, all of them what is left after the removal of that comforting, archaic costume. Around him patients, and the parents of patients, look up momentarily as he passes by, scanning him for evidence. He can see them checking his face, his ID, lingering on the folder he carries as if it might pertain to them in some way: contain news that's been longed-for, or dreaded. He avoids eye contact, always aware of the proximity of the next thing he has to do.

When the lift doors open, Mike Halloran gets out. "Satish! Departmental meeting Thursday!"

"Yes. I got the memo." Behind Mike, the lift is emptying. Soon the doors will close again, and Satish will have to wait.

"It's a lateish one." Mike's a fly-boy, like all cardiac surgeons: crack one chest and you think you're God. Talented though. All the women have crushes on him.

"Don't worry. I'll be there." He really needs to get upstairs, but Mike's still in front of him, hands in pockets. The lift doors slide shut. Satish wonders if he's meant to make small talk at this point, a sort of how's-the-wife-and-kids, like he hears the other doctors doing.

Mike says: "Heard about Bill Mezrich up at St Agnes?" So: small talk, then.

"No."

"Fired." Mike raises his eyebrows knowingly. Satish is meant to ask why.

"Why?"

Mike grips an imaginary glass and shakes it in front of his face. "Booze. On the sauce. Went into theatre pissed."

"That's . . . that's terrible."

"Anaesthetist halted the op."

"Oh, God. Poor Bill."

Mike frowns. "Poor Bill? Satish, he went in there *pissed*."

"I know, but still . . ."

"Sat next to him at a conference once. Like being in a bloody brewery. All the stories will come out, now that he's gone."

"Mike, can I . . .?" Satish needs — very badly — to get away. He gestures at the lift.

"No problem. On my way." But he hesitates. "Some of us will probably be going to the Duke for a drink afterwards. If you wanted to come . . ."

All the stories will come out. Satish, stripped of his medical props and sitting at a pub table. Satish with all his protection missing, the job, the urgency, exposed amongst them and looking for safe things to say.

"I don't know. It depends what time . . ."

"Yeah, I know. Well, if you want to. Push the boat out." He grins and walks backwards, away from Satish, who reaches out for the lift call button and presses it.

"All right. I'll see you at the meeting."

Mike swivels on his heel and walks away, lifting a hand in valediction.

Satish waits for the empty lift, the private space. Sometimes, simply staying upright feels exhausting. There is a need, now, to comb over the details of that last conversation, to check for the subliminal nod and wink. What does Mike know? What has he guessed? But Satish is denied even these few moments of privacy, because when the doors finally open there's a woman waiting beside him to get in. She struggles with a buggy, her baby balanced in the crook of her elbow. Satish recognises the awkward stance: this child has had recent heart surgery, and can't be picked up under the arms. He moves to help her, pulling the buggy into the lift behind them.

"Thank you so much." He presses the button for his floor, asks her for hers. She's tall and bony, well — groomed, a contrast to the frazzled mothers who have to make do with hospital bathrooms for their morning ablutions. For some reason he isn't predisposed to like her, he finds, and he's trying to work out why when she frowns at him and glances down at his ID.

"Satish?" She says it quietly. And suddenly he's looking at Sarah again.

The doors haven't quite shut yet. There's still time. He takes a single stride across the floor but as he does they close. There's a view of the corridor, a shrinking vertical slot, then just metal, and they're shut in together.

"I didn't know you worked here," she says.

He doesn't answer her. His hand moves up to stroke his scalp through his hair and then he stops himself doing it.

164

"You're a doctor here?" she says, hesitant.

He can hear his breathing coming faster and he wonders whether she can hear it too. He can't find a comfortable place for his hands: folded across his chest, in his trouser pockets, resting by his side, they migrate away from wherever he puts them. He looks briefly at her and knows from the concern on her face, from her own indrawn breath, that she's about to say something far more perilous than small-talk.

"Yes," he puts in quickly. "I'm a cardiologist."

"Oh!"

He's silenced her. Five floors of this, he tells himself. Just five more floors. He watches the red on the buttons flick upwards as they climb.

"This is Louis," she says. "He was born with Fallot's."

He looks at the child. At maybe seven months, the boy's a little too old to be happy on his back and he flails for an upright position.

"He was fine. Well, we thought he was fine. Then our GP heard a murmur."

She'd have had an apparently perfect baby. The paediatrician would have done an echo to look inside that perfect chest, not yet assaulted by a sternal saw, no ridge of scarring down its centre, and seen an imperfect heart twitching in the darkness, the misdirected blood flashing Doppler blue amongst the red.

On the third floor, the lift bounces to a stop and the doors open. Satish retreats to the opposite corner, waiting for incomers. There's silence from outside. After a moment Sarah leans out: "False alarm," she tells him, and just as Satish realises he could nip out himself, the doors close again.

"Nancy Driscoll operated last month," she says. "This is our four-week check. Is she good, Nancy Driscoll? We googled her. She seems to be good."

"Yes. Nancy's very good."

"They gave us Suraya Ahmed as a cardiologist. We hadn't even thought about that, about a cardiologist, or about the care he'd need afterwards — honestly, you just hope there will be an *afterwards* — so we hadn't looked her up or anything. What's she like?"

"Suraya's excellent." He hesitates. "Everyone here is excellent."

The lift has bumped gently to a halt. Finally, it's her floor. As she rolls out the buggy she asks him, "Are you going to do this photograph?" but he steps back into the lift without answering her. She gives him a tight smile as the doors close, and then she's gone.

CHAPTER
FIFTEEN

Her Saturday mornings were usually spent with Mandy. They'd call round for each other about ten: enough time for a lie-in, for Mum to nag her to *get up, you're wasting the day!* She'd have a long soak, nick some of her mum's bubble bath and lie there in the suds reading *Jackie* or *Pink*, shouting at her dad when he wanted to come in. Then she'd spend half an hour getting dressed, trying on different things in front of the dressing-table mirror; she liked to wear nice things on Saturdays, even if she and Mandy ended up doing nothing special, just hanging around in each other's bedrooms.

One Saturday they decided to go down the shops. The Jubilee was a few weeks away and they'd just been told they should wear red, white and blue to the party.

"My mum's given me money for something new," Mandy told her. "D'you fancy a look in Valerie's?" Valerie's was Bourne Heath's only clothes shop, a boutique next door to Mac Fisheries in the little parade at the centre of the village. Valerie was a real person, the mother of one of the kids in their class.

"Yeah. Let's go. I'll see if Mum will let me have some money, too." She did, four pounds; Sarah stuffed it into her purse.

On the way there they played "My House, Your House", a travel game that Sarah's parents had taught her, adapted by the girls for the short walk into the village. Mandy and Sarah would take it in turns to claim ownership of each house they passed, giving free rein to their disgust or envy at the way the lots fell. After Sarah staked possession of Ragstones, a picturesque Victorian semi, Mandy performed an impromptu impersonation of Gerry Carter, its ancient inhabitant, shambling her way past its dirty windows. Their headmaster Mr McLennan lived a few doors along from Ragstones, and when his house fell to Mandy, Sarah knew her lines: "Ooh, you could live with him there! Lenny McLenny, I love you, ooh!"

They stopped off at the Wavy Line before they went to Valerie's and bought a supply of sweet cigarettes. Sarah had watched her sister Diane smoking for real, her hand stiff, her wrist slightly bent; she replicated this, and Mandy copied her, as they made their way to the boutique, the powdery-sweet taste in their mouths.

Valerie — Mrs Weston — was undressing a window dummy when they came in. As she turned to greet them the figure wobbled and tipped.

"Whoops!" She righted it. "Hello girls. You doing a bit of shopping? Your mums with you?"

Sarah nodded a yes, Mandy shook her head, no. The dummy stretched a frozen hand towards them. The fingertips had bits chipped off.

"Lovely! D'you need me for a minute? Or are you happy to browse?" No, yes. The girls smiled and retreated into the shop.

168

"I've already got blue," Sarah said. "Jeans. So I want a top, red or white. What are you looking for?"

Mandy considered. "Dunno. Maybe a skirt. I like those tiered ones."

"I've got one of those," Sarah said. "My orange one."

Mandy fiddled with a hanger. "Yeah, I know."

Mrs Weston let them try on lots of things, even things they couldn't afford to buy. The window kept her busy for a while, and then she came over and asked them, "What sort of thing are you looking for?" Sarah remembered the way her mother talked in shops, and tried to talk like that.

She bought a halter-top in the end, a white one, and you could really see her boobs in it. So now she had blue and white. At the counter there was a little stand with pendants on it. She liked the leather ones, tooled with suns or rainbows or birds, but they weren't the right colour. There were some hearts on silver chains though, a brilliant, deep red and really pretty. Mrs Weston was wrapping the top.

"How much are these necklaces?"

Mrs Weston squinted at the tag. "One pound twenty," she told her. "How much have you got?"

"Three pounds ninety-eight."

"Sorry, love. The top's three ninety. The necklace will still be here on Monday. Go home and ask your mum if you can have it as a treat."

"OK." Sarah looked longingly at the pendant, imagined it dropping down towards the V of her new top, the perfect finishing touch. She paid and left the counter while Mandy bought the skirt she'd chosen.

Next to a display of belts and hats were some bras: Triumph. She knew these from the TV advert — *Triumph has the bra for the way you are*. It showed all the different kinds of girls who might wear Triumph bras and when she watched it, Sarah tried to pick out the type she was: sophisticated, cheery, romantic. As she and Mandy left the shop they sang the jingle:

"Whether you're *ooh-ee*
Or whether you're *doo-wop-wop-wop*
Triumph has the bra for the way you are!"

They didn't see Lee Davis coming towards them until it was too late; he must have heard them singing that stupid song. But it was only Lee after all. Sarah had seen him at playtimes, hanging around the infants' area with his little brother: a real no-no. Cai never played with him and he was generally considered a bit of a spaz. He smiled at them and, as she kept walking, Sarah realised that Mandy wasn't with her any more. She'd stopped to talk to Lee. Sarah turned back immediately.

". . . some clothes for our Jubilee party," she caught her friend saying.

Sarah intervened quickly. "You coming, Mandy?"

Mandy looked at her for just a second, then dropped the smile from her face. "Yeah, of course," she said, and swung away from Lee.

As they waited to cross the road Sarah pushed out her lower lip with her tongue and asked: "Were you habing a mice time with Lee ben, Manby?" — and

Mandy laughed and said, "God, he's such a spaz," and then it was clear and they crossed.

As they turned into Cherry Gardens Mandy stuck her hand into the back pocket of her jeans. "I'm glad you didn't buy that necklace at Valerie's. I've been meaning to give you this."

On her palm, tangled up in a lump, was a red heart on a chain. Sarah looked at it.

"It's the same as Mrs Weston's."

"Yeah, I know. My mum bought it for me, but it doesn't suit me. It'll look better on you. Go on, have it," and she pushed her hand towards her friend.

Sarah reached out for it. She undid the knotted chain, easing it apart gently. "It's just the same," she said again, when she'd finished and was holding it up between them.

"Yeah. She probably got it from there. Don't tell her I gave it you. She'll be upset."

"OK. Thanks."

"You've got the whole thing now — red, white and blue."

"I have. Maybe I'll get my mum to buy me red shoes, too."

It was lunchtime. Both girls would be wanted back at home. Sarah walked to her house alone, thinking about the Jubilee party and how great she'd look in her red, white and blue.

On Jubilee Day she did look good, she knew it. As predicted, her mum had bought her some red sandals, grown-up wedgies she'd had to practise walking in before the day. They were the same colour as the

171

pendant Mandy had given her; she looked like a fashion picture in one of her own magazines. Colette, yapping beside her as she got ready, had said as much, and then she'd said, cutting straight across the warm feel-good of the morning, that she had something else to tell her, "something about Mandy".

Sarah knew it couldn't be true. Mandy had told her, swearing her to secrecy, that she fancied Cai, and that he fancied her back. The two girls had planned the first kiss together; Sarah made Mandy practise on the back of her hand. She'd taught her about Frenchies: he should do it first, then you know it's OK for you to do it. Not too much tongue. Even if he's a sloppy kisser, never, ever wipe your mouth afterwards — it makes you look like a kid. Close your eyes. When it had happened (Jennings Field after school one day) Mandy had come straight to Sarah afterwards, and they'd gone over it together. Scale of one to ten? (Seven, said Mandy.) Length? (Dunno. It felt like a long time.) What did he do with his hands? (He put one on my shoulder. He held his bike with the other.)

So Sarah knew it wasn't true, what Colette was saying. But she was saying it anyway, and that could ruin things for Mandy — for both of them. Mandy needed to be warned.

Sarah found her sitting on her bed in a pair of *Love Is* pants. Across the floor tops, skirts and trousers were scattered.

"Hi," Mandy greeted her. "It doesn't look right. I don't know what to wear now. Oh! You look nice. The necklace is great."

172

"Yeah. Thanks." Sarah closed the bedroom door. "Listen, Mandy. I've just been with Colette. She told me something — well, it's really silly, but you could still get into trouble over it."

Mandy frowned. "What?"

"She says — well, you know what she's like, she'll say anything — she says she saw you *kissing* Satish! *Kissing!* In his *bedroom!*"

Mandy's hands went up to her face, covered her mouth and nose. Over her fingertips, her eyes were wide.

"Oh, no!" she was saying, and her voice echoed a little in the hollow of her hands.

"I know. What if she says that to someone else? And what if they believe her? Satish!"

"Oh no!" Mandy said again, and when she took her hands away from her face Sarah could see she was laughing.

"It's not funny, Mandy. Your parents will kill you!"

Mandy stopped her giggling. "I know. I know they will. It's not funny." Then she smiled again, sheepish.

"She said her dad had seen you, too. What was she talking about? Do you know?"

Mandy wasn't smiling now. "Her dad saw?"

"She says. What did she mean? Were you at his house or something?" Sarah had perched next to her friend and was looking solemnly at Mandy: crisis mode.

Mandy had found something interesting on the quilt cover and was tracing the swirly pattern with her finger. Then she looked up at Sarah again. "Oops," she said.

"What?"

"I was in his room." Mandy stretched across the bed to where a denim skirt lay crumpled, and started to pull it on.

"*Why* were you in his room?"

Mandy was still not looking at her, Sarah noticed. She faced away and tugged at the zipper in little jerks. "We were just chatting," she offered. "Just — you know — looking at the street. The decorations."

Sarah stood up, listing sideways on her new heels. She went round to plant herself in front of Mandy, stared down into her face.

"With Satish? Just looking at the decorations? *With Satish?*" She searched her friend's expression, tried to find some sense in what she was saying. "Why?"

"Just . . . did." Mandy turned away, fumbled in the wardrobe and came out with a white T-shirt. There was something else, thought Sarah.

"Was Colette right? Did you kiss him, then?"

Mandy dived into the T-shirt. Through the top of it, Sarah could see a circle of dark hair. Her friend stayed inside, pulling the fabric back against her face so that you could make out her nose, her lips, the sockets of her eyes. She nodded.

"Bloody hell!" Sarah shouted. "Satish! Bloody hell! Mandy!"

Mandy emerged. "Keep your hair on. So Colette and Mr Brecon saw me. Why should he care? And if Colette tells anyone, no one will believe her, she's just a kid."

"She might tell Cai. He might believe her."

At this, Mandy sobered slightly. "Yeah. I know."

"Bloody and bugger, Mandy! And yuk anyway. Yuk! Splatish? I bet he smelled horrible."

Mandy paused. "No, he didn't, actually."

"Then I bet he *tasted* horrible."

"Not really."

Sarah heard movement downstairs, then Mandy's mum shouting up. "Are you girls all right up there?"

Mandy moved to the bedroom door. "Fine, Mum. Just trying on stuff." They heard her go back into the kitchen.

"Can't you see how this could really get you into trouble?" Sarah asked. "Can't you see how wrong Satish is?"

"He goes round with us."

"Cai lets him hang around," Sarah corrected. "But he never, ever plays with him at school. Haven't you noticed that? At home — well, he lives next door. Cai sort of has to let him come too." Then she hesitated. Did he? Why did he? "Anyway," she rallied. "Kissing him! It's so *wrong*. Can't you see that?"

"No."

That was absolutely typical.

"Mandy, you're useless! I have to tell you everything, don't I? Look at all this!" Her spread hand took in the posters on Mandy's walls, the contents of Mandy's dressing table, the clothes on Mandy's floor. "Your clothes are nice now, and you go round with fun people at school, and you're friends with Cai, the Chandlers, that lot. It's been really hard work, helping you do that."

"Hard work?"

"Yeah. But it's OK. You go round with us now. What's going to happen if they find out about this? And what about me? If they think I'm your friend, and they know you've done this . . ."

She'd hit home, she thought. Mandy walked over to the dressing table and looked down at it, at the bangles and necklaces and the little can of hairspray she'd bought for the party. Sarah moved closer to her, lifted her arm to put it round her friend's shoulder, but Mandy stepped away.

"So what?" she said. "So what if they know? Why should I care? I *like* Satish. Satish is fun. He's a laugh. I like talking to him."

Her voice was getting louder and Sarah felt her mouth slacken. This wasn't the Mandy she knew. She couldn't believe what she was hearing. Then she realised — oh my God! — and she moved to the door before delivering her *coup de grace*, the blow Mandy wouldn't recover from.

"You fancy him!" she told her friend. "You *fancy* him!"

At last, this seemed to stop Mandy. She opened her mouth, frowning. She gazed across at Satish's house. Then her face closed off and she got that hard look which meant she wouldn't see sense.

"Yeah, you're right," she said finally. "I do fancy him. I fancy him a lot. I think Satish is brilliant and I don't care what you think. I don't care about Cai or Cai's dad. I don't care about the Chandlers or any of that lot. And mostly, I don't care about you."

"Mandy!"

"Take it and stick it up your bum!"

* * *

When Sarah left Mandy's house, her first thought was to closet herself in her bedroom for a while and work on some damage limitation. Then she glanced over to the other side of the street, across the long table with its Union Jack covering, the cups and plates in place, ready for the party. It's pretty, she thought. Opposite her, Satish's house was unreadable: door shut, windows unoccupied. Then she looked across at Cai's place, and the Chandlers'. Her eye snagged on something incongruous, a thatch of blond hair poking up from the pavement on the other side of the table. It was Cai, squatting down in front of his garden wall.

CHAPTER
SIXTEEN

It's the early hours, and Satish is still awake. Maya lies beside him, her breathing shallow, her feet finally warm, resting against his. He's pushed them away but they keep moving back towards him, and although it's a complete invasion of his space, if he keeps disturbing her she'll wake up and require conversation. He's been staring at the dark shapes of their bedroom: the irregular skyline of Maya's perfume bottles on the dresser, the lattice at the foot of their iron bed, the wardrobe door slightly ajar, a deeper darkness inside.

He thinks about the garage, the briefcase, the bottle.

There is light in here, too; he has had time to take stock of it. Yellow streetlight slides under their blind, and the phone in its cradle emits a blue glow. There's even — he's spent several minutes trying to find the source — a circle of white on the ceiling. It must be a reflection of something, only he can't work out what. And amongst the darkness and the shapes and the light there are his thoughts; they are elliptical, curving away from him then slicing back towards him until he is desperate to sleep, if only to stop them coming.

It's about the diazepam, and his thoughts go something like this: he calls it medicine, a dose, and then he tells himself, come clean — it's a *drug*, it's *your* drug. He lets himself think in terms of his usage, he risks the word reliance; am I becoming reliant on it, he asks. And then he taunts himself: admit it, it's an *addiction*, and then he sends that thought away from him because it's ridiculous, and when it comes back it has changed, and this time it's about Colette, and what action to take, and why she's doing this to him.

His first thought was to go straight to her and have it out. But that doesn't make sense yet; he can't work out why she wants this particular thing so much, why the photograph matters to her enough that she'd blackmail him. It can't be the money, for this is as precarious and indirect a route to money as he can think of, and troublesome too. It is hard work. The note is cruel (Colette's not cruel) and underhand (she's not that, either).

Maya shifts beside him and he lies still, waiting for her to settle again. Her feet move away. They move back. There's a thought tapping at him, but he's batting it away. *What if Colette is using again?* When you're using, irrationality is normal, cruelty easy. The blackmail doesn't make sense if she's straight. But what if she's hooked?

We both are then, he thinks, and this is an utterly unacceptable thought, because he is not like her at all.

This is unbearable. He needs something else to do.

Satish has new mail: a message from Colette. It's short: Cai would love to see Satish — their own reunion, regardless of the photograph. She's taken the liberty of giving Cai Satish's number.

Bloody Colette! All she does is take liberties. Satish can't think what to do about this new message so he dumps it in his Action folder. It's all closing in on him. He remembers Sarah, materialising at the hospital.

Time to take some control. Knowledge is power. There's nothing you can't find out on the net, he reminds himself, as he puts her name into a search engine. He types carefully, pressing on the keys, trying to keep the noise down. He knows only her maiden name and there must be a thousand Sarah Millers. He knows nothing about her now, that's the problem. Or, almost nothing. What was the name of her son? Leo? Leon? God, his memory. Louis. He inputs *Sarah Miller Louis* and scrolls down, sifting the references. There it is.

"Miller Stevens Productions", they've called their family website. It's slick, no rough edges, more like a company site than a family one. There's an extensive gallery devoted to Louis — his birth, his early weeks, various family members cooing over him (is that woman, chic and greying, pearl earrings and a black polo-neck, Sarah's mum? Is that the formidable Mrs Miller?). There's a restlessness in Satish's fingers. He shakes them out, jazz hands over the keyboard. On screen there's a jump-cut, a sudden leap forward in time, and Louis is six months, seven months. He's being held by a smiling Sarah outside Satish's hospital, he's being fed in a bouncy chair.

180

They wouldn't have operated straight away. And until they did . . . well, in this gallery there's no record of what happened. There's nothing, no pictures of the time in between, when Sarah didn't know how it was going to turn out. That void is full of bad things, he thinks; parents too scared to take a photograph in case it's the last one, in case their child dies and his picture waits in the camera, waiting to take them unawares. Satish feels a creep of compassion but pulls back from it. On the homepage there's a link to "our other great collaboration". He clicks on it.

Sarah is in PR, it seems, and here's all the guff you'd expect: she "navigates a rapidly changing society". She "engages in two-way conversations with clients". Had Satish thought about it, this is exactly the future he'd have mapped for her.

The study feels close around him. There's no elbow-room. Satish finds himself rolling his shoulders, stretching his arms, trying to get a bit of space. Good, long strides, that's what he needs, not this cramped little box. Maybe he should go for a walk.

He thinks of looking up Cai or Peter Brecon, and doesn't think he can, just yet. Who then? Someone safer. This one's easy. Satish Patel. UK only. *Dr Satish Patel. Dr Satish Patel cardiology.* There he is.

There are so many hits: a conference on paediatric cardiology (Dr Satish Patel presenting on "The Physiology of Congenital Heart Defects"), his listing on the Central Children's website, a cardiac intensive care course (Dr Satish Patel presents on "The Blue Baby in A & E"), his listing on the advisory panel of a medical charity (Dr Satish Patel: Cardiac Disorders). This is serious stuff. The references go on to a second page. No need for personal websites or blogs or any of those other vanity projects.

Some fresh air might help. He leaves his desk, rolls up the blind — quiet, slow — and hefts the sash to shoulder height. There's a soft thump as it settles.

This is all he needs: a spring night, the cool of it, and the dark. The road outside is empty and he can lean right out into the dark and breathe, and breathe. Behind him there is comfort, the accumulated evidence of his success: framed qualifications, family photographs, the books and journals he's contributed to. He can control anything that might threaten these things. He's done so in the past. Stephen Chandler's letters, for example. He controlled them.

They started three years after the Jubilee, long after the Chandlers had gone to live up north. A Manchester postmark landed on his parents' doormat, giving Satish the terrors. Andrew Ford had made it big by then. It was after the Riot Act cover, after Ford had left the local paper and you could see his photos in the Sunday magazines. That first letter was full of adolescent outrage. How dare he, asked Stephen, how dare Ford make his money off the back of them all? How come they got nothing for it? They should get together, challenge him. They should . . .

Satish had torn the letter up, sweating. A year or so after that, he got the second letter, and a few years later, the third. They continued like this, on and off, making their way to Satish from a different town each time. One even came from Australia. Satish was also moving around in these years, of course: to university, to hospital, to a new one, but somehow the letters always found him. He thought they were probably going to other places, as well: to Colette, to Mandy.

He couldn't always tell what had prompted them, why they should come *now*, rather than at any other moment. Sometimes, he could guess. There was an arts programme featuring an interview with Ford at his New York loft. Two weeks later the next letter came. When Ford's autobiography was published, Satish received another one. As time went by, Stephen's nebulous fury coalesced into a plan, then reformed into another. His prose veered from vitriol to project management: they would all hire a lawyer; they would launch a class action suit; they would picket an exhibition of Ford's work.

Satish had talked himself down: these were just bits of paper. They weren't Stephen, and Stephen wasn't about to come for him. He tore them up, every one. Satish controlled them.

He breathes, and breathes. There were good things about the past, he tells himself. There was Mandy.

The thought lifts him and he returns to his desk, enters "Mandy Hobbes" in the search engine, and there's a Mandy Hobbes straightaway, top of the list. It's something French, a language school: "école supérieure de langues étrangères appliquées" it says, all very trendy, lowercase. The site offers him the choice of French or English text. When he selects *English* the words fragment into one of those irritating slow intros. He slides the mouse around the screen, searching for a "skip" button, but can't find one. He wonders whether this really has anything to do with Mandy, *his* Mandy, and if it does, what turns her life has taken to bring her here. The company offers translation, management training, events and facilitation services. "Where do you want to be tomorrow?" it asks.

Her name's there in the "people" list — "staff" being presumably too stodgy — but there's no photograph. He still doesn't know if it's her. *This* Mandy Hobbes founded the company in 1998. She could be his Mandy Hobbes; she could be a stranger.

He searches again: "Mandy Hobbes", "Amanda Hobbes", looking in social networking sites, scrolling through the photographs of American teenagers and hoping he might find her among them. It's useless. He tries "Paris Hobbes blog" and "Mandy Paris blog", but she's not there. He searches pictures of people who share her name, closing the pages before the images have fully downloaded. He can see already: they're all wrong — too young, or too old, their hair the wrong colour. He remembers that hair.

He looks at the clock on the computer; it's nearly 3 a.m.

May as well do Cai. Do it quickly. He finds him straight away, on the Animal World website. Satish clicks on the reference.

Cai's mentioned on the Big Cats page. The only pictures here are of animals: a tiger, a jaguar, a pair of lions. *Come and meet our playful lion cubs, Harry,*

Hermione and Ron, the copy urges. *Or look in on Tequila, our jaguar. Section head Cai Brecon welcomes you to the world of the big cats, where the wilderness comes to you.*

Wild Cai, prowling Cherry Gardens. You could never guess what he was going to do next. Satish wonders what it's like for Cai now, handling those fierce creatures. Does he ever feel nervous?

Satish pages back. There was something else, another complete "Cai Brecon" reference. It's something unexpected: The Red Bean Boys, they're called, a Cajun band, operating out of Watford. Cai's the guitarist, apparently. There's a bit of video, the band playing Gloucester Cajun Festival. Cai on film.

Satish starts the clip and rests his face in his hands. The reproduction's terrible, as if the band were playing in a biscuit tin. An insistent four-four beat, and it's a song he knows, "Bad Moon Rising", but with plenty of squeezebox and fiddle. Is the voice Cai's? He can barely make out the guitar. His fingertips drum against his skull in time to the music. He looks at a curve of brown the shape of a guitar, the light coming off it. The figure behind it could be anyone.

Cai is a zookeeper, and he might or might not be a Red Bean Boy, but this film leaves Satish none the wiser.

He doesn't want to finish the job at all, but there's a sort of completist urge in him now. Do it fast, he tells himself. Get it over with.

There's nothing on any UK-based search, so he looks at South African sites instead. Peter's name turns up one reference, a golf club newsletter dated about a year ago. It's too long to read so Satish skips between phrases: *Say goodbye to Social Secretary Peter Brecon . . . return to the UK . . . wish him luck in his new project . . . farewell braai.*

Right, that's Peter. Swift exit, face-saving "new project". Tell us about that project, Peter, Satish thinks. Tell us! You're going to work for minimum wage in London to stop your house being repossessed. You're going to separate from your wife. You're going to be ostracised by your son. Satish iterates every last humiliation, feeling around inside him for any pity, the tiniest scrap of it. There's none. What a glorious thing that would be, to pity Peter. What a glorious, powerful thing.

It's cold in here. He goes over to the window and pulls down the sash. A couple of inches should do it, he thinks: the Goldilocks solution — not too cold, not too warm. But the frame is heavy and he pulls too hard. It travels right down to the sill and lands with a crash. Before he can think straight, he's followed it with the fist to the glass, a sideways punch that makes the window rattle. Satish prepares for another blow, for catharsis, but in the time it takes to draw back his hand he's already remembered his sleeping family, how upset they'd be to wake and find him like this, the questions they'd ask.

Quick. He deletes his search history. Two clicks and it's gone, untraceable. Soon Peter will be wiped from public memory. Whoever updates the golf club website will see that long-ago newsletter and think, it's time this went. And that'll be him, gone: just like that.

Satish looks at the clock for justification: Three forty-two. You can't say he hasn't tried. Three hours till he's up, five till he's working. He could do it, he knows. He could stop any time he wants to, but tonight's been . . . tricky.

As soon as he's decided, Satish leaves the study. He knows the places to step so that the floorboards won't creak and as he's making his way downstairs, he suddenly remembers that advert from his childhood. I'm a secret lemonade drinker, he thinks. I'm trying to give it up but it's one of those nights. He almost laughs.

He opens the garage door, taking account of his own pounding heart, the clench in his belly. He hates this part now: the first sight of his briefcase. He unfastens it and checks the interior, but tonight there's no note waiting for him: situation normal.

Satish unzips the internal pocket. Part of him is not here at all; he's scanning the house for noises, for anything that might reveal him. He reaches into the pocket, and his fingers hit an edge of paper.

No no no, he thinks. He peers in, hoping for the bottle, the bag, the spoon. They're here, but this other thing is too, right in here with them, a second envelope: *read this*.

He rips open the envelope.

I mean it. I will tell about the medicine, do the photograph

He kneels on the concrete floor and tries to produce a clear thought amid the cacophony inside his head. He stays there until he pulls out something coherent: this is enough, he tells himself. It's time to face her with it. It's time she stopped.

He pours his dose, hands shaking, the medicine spilling over and dripping sticky onto his pyjama bottoms. Then he picks himself off the floor and leaves the garage.

He doesn't know how far Colette will go, or if he will be able to stop her. And if she exposes him? He'd lose everything, starting with his job. That would hit him hard: the loss of it, and the shame of that loss. But right now it's not the job that takes up his thoughts, that forces him to stop at the bottom of the staircase and sit down. On the third stair is one of Mehul's socks — just the one, balled up, inside out. He'll have shucked it off and abandoned it, forgetting its existence in his pursuit of the next bit of fun. Satish's life is full of detritus like this: single socks, half-read books, school bags, spilled milk on the table where they've been eating breakfast, mud down the back of his car seat, tell-tale sweet wrappers on the floors of their rooms, a toothbrush left on the side of the bath.

If Satish is exposed, Maya may leave him, and take the children with her. Colette threatens him with a tidy life. The thought leaches the blood from his face. He needs to see his kids.

In Asha's room, he picks his way across the littered floor to her bed. He perches on the mattress and leans over her. In the half-dark, her face is a quick sketch, a handful of features intersected by the rise of her cheek. He puts his face into her hair and breathes in.

The book she was reading has fallen off the bed. Satish places it on her bedside table. He adjusts the duvet, covers an exposed foot. Her room is filled with evidence that she, even now, at eleven, is starting to grow up and away from him. He's thought this before, thought how fast it's all moving, but now he thinks he'd just like the chance to be here while she does it. There's clothing on the floor of questionable appropriateness. There's a photo collage of her friends above the bed: they stick their tongues out at the camera, they cuddle cats, they gurn. On another wall there's a picture of her latest crush, a popstar who was doing GCSEs this time last year. He was discovered — she has explained this to Satish with great patience — when a camera crew visited his school to do a fly-on-the-wall documentary. Satish, equipped with his dad-response, felt that the boy would have been better off staying in class. But he'd just nodded and smiled.

On her desk is a pile of CDs, and he reaches out to tidy them, lining up the edges. The top one has a black and white photograph on the cover: a man smoking, his eyes half-closed as he inhales. This isn't appropriate for a girl of eleven. He remembers the cigarette in Asha's bag. It's just this sort of image that . . . He sifts through the others. A line of young men looking sullen and unshaven; a girl on a bike, the CD case adorned with a "Parental Advisory" sticker. The next one . . . the next one is *The Only Language They Understand*.

Here's the picture again, lit with smears of colour, doctored so that Riot Act are sitting round the table with them. Here's Satish, Cai's arms around him, hat askew. As the adrenaline subsides, Satish thinks it's like being phobic about spiders, or birds, or other commonplace things; half your terror is about when you might see them next. On the album cover, the lead singer has just taken a drag on his cigarette. Smoke eases out of his mouth. Neil Listick: that's what he called himself. Inserted between Sarah and Peter, Neil Listick slumps, but his gaze is directed straight at the camera.

Satish has never heard Asha listening to Riot Act, or talking about them. Has she even listened to the album? Does she care about them, beyond her dad's picture being on the cover? And if she's interested in that, why has she never mentioned it to him?

When he leaves, he stands for a moment in the doorway and fixes the image in his mind. There may be a time when he needs this: Asha in the midden of her room, fast asleep and innocent.

In Mehul's bedroom, Satish touches a panel on the lamp, calling up a rising tide of light that illuminates his son, head curled forwards on the pillow. He kneels next to Mehul's bed and tucks him in. He looks at his profile: the Bhatt nose which his friend Tom has taken exception to. He hopes Maya's right, that it's just sticks and stones, playground politics. But he doesn't think Maya's ever encountered playground politics in quite the way he did, and he's not sure he trusts her judgement on this. Tomorrow he'll ask Mehul about it

— subtly — to check if it's still going on. He'll watch for the signs.

Perhaps it's the dose kicking in at last, but Satish feels calmer here. The blackmail is a problem to be solved, that's all. He's going to fix it. He lies down next to Mehul, who rolls onto his back and flops an arm out sideways. Satish lets it rest against his chest then reaches out and touches the lamp again, pulling darkness down into the room. He closes his eyes. There's a margin of warmth around his son and he wants to stay within it. Just him and Mehul. It'll be OK. He's going to make sure of that.

CHAPTER
SEVENTEEN

Peter woke early on Jubilee morning, roused by noises from his daughter's bedroom. He lay there listening to her bed squeak, to the curtain rings clatter. Jan slept on. He waited two minutes, three, then he went to fetch Colette.

"I've been awake for ages!" she told him.

"I'd never have guessed."

They slipped out of the house without disturbing the others, and he wondered how long it would take her to get bored, how long before Ram Patel started to grate on him. Looking up to gauge the weather, that British reflex, he could see it would be grim. Bits of blue, slabs of grey. The day felt chilly. As he stepped across his driveway the front door opposite swung open. Ram, dressed in a sweater and jacket, greeted him.

"Good morning, Peter. I see you are ready for work."

"Yep, bang on time."

"Of course. Neeta's been up for an hour already. I'm finding it best to stay out of the kitchen."

Peter acknowledged this with an upthrust of his chin, making his usual internal adjustment to Ram's speech, the regular peaks and troughs that put lilts in all the wrong places. "Right," he said, heaving up his garage door. "Ladders in here."

They started at the other end of the street, working slowly towards their own homes. It went pretty smoothly, Peter directing things, Ram quietly efficient. As the morning went on, more front doors opened, and there was a stirring in Cherry Gardens. People commented on the bunting, offered help, bustled off to do their own jobs. Colette's early enthusiasm did wane quickly, and she became restless. When the Hobbes' door opened a few houses down, she darted forward — "Mandy!" — then stopped and frowned.

"Oh, it's just her mum."

"A good thing, too," Peter told her. "She's bringing us a cuppa. Cheers, Pam."

"No trouble," she said, handing up Ram's. "You've got a Mandy Special there, Pete." He looked at the mug she'd given him. A rainbow arched its way around it, painted with a quavering hand, slivers of white showing between the strips of colour. Pam was smiling up at him.

"Good girl," he said. "Tell her well done."

Colette wandered off. The two men drew level with the Chandler house, then Peter's own, then the Patels'. Up on the ladder, fixing a line of flags under the eaves, Peter came face to face with Ram's son, Satish. On the other side of the glass he was just a few inches away, staring out at the street and the houses opposite. Satish acknowledged him with a little smile and a dip of the head, but he didn't move as Peter worked on, and didn't say a word to him either. It felt like insolence.

193

Strange boy, he thought, and tried to quell his annoyance. Always quiet. Always had been.

He wondered what bound Satish and Cai together, and what future their friendship might reasonably have. The question was irrelevant really — in two months' time Cai would be gone from Bourne Heath to their new life in South Africa; still, it gave Peter pause for thought. There could be no real future for a friendship like that. The boys inhabited different worlds, and the older they got the clearer that would become. Better for Cai to make a clean break now. Take today, for instance: there was Ram across the way, putting up bunting for an event that was not his celebration at all, really. A significant day for the English, but surely not for the . . . What were they, exactly? Indian? Ugandan? He had never been clear. But this was neither their country nor their culture, and no matter how many Union Jacks they raised, they would always be waving someone else's flag.

Peter made the line secure and gave Ram a thumbs-up. He got down from the ladder, leaving Satish alone above him, gazing out of his window. In the end, like goes to like; a natural balance is in place. You could whine about it, and plenty of people did these days, but you couldn't fight it.

When they'd finished their work, Peter found Colette idling in the road, itchy to get the party started. Must keep her occupied, he was thinking, and make sure that brother of hers is just as busy, keep him out of trouble. And where was Jan, for God's sake? These were his preoccupations in the slow seconds it took for him to

194

turn away from his daughter and glance down the street at his handiwork.

Timing is everything. In the perfect choreography of the moment he raised his head as the sky darkened, dimming the reflection off the line of windows above them, and a movement suddenly caught his eye, just . . . there. There, in Satish's room.

Despite the distance, the pane of glass between them, Peter recognised her immediately and from the gut. Then Satish reached out to touch her, held on to her arm, came towards her, ducking his head in an echo of that nod with which he had acknowledged Peter's presence earlier that morning. That cunning semblance of shyness. Girls always like that, and Mandy clearly did, because all of a sudden he kissed her, and she let him. It took Peter a couple of seconds to process what he was seeing, and then he understood, and he wanted to shout, to grab a brick and fling it at the window.

Instead he drew breath and yanked Colette back as if, failing all else, he could at least pull her out of the way of this thing. Then the two of them waited, passive spectators, to see what Mandy would do next. She'd been released by Satish so she could have walked out, could have done it easily. Instead, and without hesitation, she stepped back towards him and kissed him — so confident, so grown-up — on the mouth. The wrongness of it disabled Peter. He felt out of control, not an adult any more. The little bastard, he thought. He said it out loud, not loud enough, though. "Little bastard. Little Paki bastard." Somewhere below him, he heard an "oh!" of surprise: Colette. Calm down, he told himself. You can deal with this. Think of the best way. Give yourself some time.

"Go on in," he said to Colette. "Get inside." He thought for a moment. He had to get her out of the way — but what next? Then he knew. "I want Cai out here. Now."

By mid-morning on Jubilee Day, Peter reckoned he'd done his bit. The decorations were up, trestles out, the rain-washed street ready for the party. He could see women bearing down on the empty tables with cloths and cups so he left them to it. Colette would stay to help or hinder. He could pop inside for a while, just until it was time to light the barbecue.

The house was silent. Peter stood for a moment and listened, then slipped into the kitchen. He was peckish, wanted something, not quite sure what, and rummaged around for a handful of custard creams. He had a tune in his head, the music from that bread advert; "Doo-doo-doo-dee-doo, doo-dee-doo-dee-doo". He walked into the sitting room, narrating — "It were rough in t' Bourne 'eath . . ." smiling at his own wit.

In the sitting room, Jan was waiting for him, and in that moment he knew, even as he was concealing his mild shock at seeing her there, he knew she'd found him out.

"Hello, darling." He smiled narrowly. "Thought I'd grab a few minutes' peace."

Jan looked up at him from her armchair, head tilted, body still.

"Good timing, Peter. I wanted to talk to you. Why don't you sit down?" He felt himself instantly rising to

196

annoyance and he worked to slow his ascent, a diver trying to avoid the bends. He sat as bidden, and she peered at him curiously. Her eyes were pink, a little closed-up.

"I found the oddest thing this morning in our building society book. I can't make head nor tail of it. Wondered if you could help me." She reached over to the coffee table, where their savings book lay, its front cover bent up with repeated opening. She offered it to him.

I can't take it, he thought, or I'll look like I'm buying into this, like I'm a kid and she's the teacher. He realised he was still clutching the custard creams and relocated them to the settee in one brisk movement.

"Jan, I think I know what you're —"

"No," she dead-ended him. "No, do look at it. Go on — it's really odd."

"There's no need. I know what —"

"*Look* at it."

She was unrelenting. Peter reached out for the book and turned to the most recent page. He scanned the deposits and withdrawals, which were just as he knew they would be. This was always going to happen, he reminded himself. Concentrate, get your story right; there's nothing she can do about it. Jan was speaking again.

"What's strange, if you look on that page there, what's really odd is that the money we saved for South Africa — you see there, the £700 left after we'd bought the boat tickets? — that money's gone down.

Someone's taken £300 out, a couple of weeks ago. Looks like your signature, right there."

She pointed to the incriminating knot of ink, her hand shaking. He wondered if he could derail this right now with some tenderness, take her fingers in his and hold them, stroke her and pacify her. It didn't seem likely; she was all hard lines, her mouth, her cheekbones, the V of her lapels levelled at him, the glossy helmet of her hair armour against his advances.

"The thing is, Peter, we must have saved up for — what? — two years to get this money? Now half of it is gone. Any ideas?"

He sighed and ran a hand through his hair. "I know. I know about this. I mean, I did this. I should have told you earlier."

"And you didn't because?" Mock puzzlement.

"I knew you'd be angry, Jan. I knew you'd be like this."

"Well, good decision. Great decision, because finding out like this, just coming upon it, that's a great decision. Where is it, Peter?"

"What?"

"Where's the money? Can we have it back, please?"

Outside in the street there was a sudden escalation of female voices, a communal whoop cut off at its crest by laughter. Through the nets he could see Pam Hobbes giggling with Susan Walsh. At their feet squatted Colette, frog-legged, peering at something in the road. He watched her for a moment, for as long as he could, enjoying her absorption. He couldn't see her face, but the intensity of her engagement with the snail or stone, or insect, whatever had caught her eye, was there in the dip of her head, in the stillness of her crouch. But here was Jan. She wanted the money back.

"We'll get it back. But not for a while. I invested it."

Jan pushed a half-laugh, a plug of air, out of her mouth. "In what? What did you invest it in?" She closed her eyes against the answer.

"A new business. Howard at work recommended this bloke, this businessman, he's very enterprising. He's going to build these houses in Spain, sell them to English people. Great return. We could get £200, £300 back on top of what we've given him."

"When?"

"Well, in a couple of years' time. Maybe three. He's got to build them then sell them. We could double our money, Jan."

"What if it fails?"

"It won't fail. Everyone's going over there now. It can't fail."

"But what if it does? What do we get back then?"

"Well, nothing. But" — as she drew breath again — "it won't fail, Jan. It can't."

"It can, you stupid man. I can't believe you work in a bank and you don't know this. It *can* fail. It probably *will* fail. And even if it doesn't, two years, three years? How does that help us? We need the money now! We're going over there with nothing else, Peter. And we — oh, God — we saved so hard!"

She faltered and started to cry, but when he reached out to her, it seemed to galvanise her into further rage. She stood up and pushed him away.

"Don't touch me! Don't even touch me, Peter! We saved so hard! The bloody fifty-fifty sales, the hand-me-downs for the kids, eking everything out. No holiday at all last year, just to save a bit more money. What were you *thinking?*" She yelled the last word, wrenched it from her vocal cords: he could almost feel it. He stood up quickly, tried to quieten her.

"Jan, I'm sorry you're angry, but I think this was a good decision. I think we'll be pleased I did this. In two or three years —"

"And what will we do in the meantime? There's no leeway now, you know. You'll have to find a job, and bloody quick. As soon as we get there. And the kids. I could . . . You . . . I . . ." Then she left the room.

Alone in the ticking silence, Peter looked around him. Three custard creams sat on the arm of the settee, a fourth lay on the floor just in front of it, victim of his hasty scramble to silence his wife. The savings book had wedged itself down the side of the chair. As he leant down to rescue it, he looked at the street outside. The party was ready. He performed a quick assessment of his situation. Jan was angry and upset, but he recognised this phase of the argument, and was glad they'd got there: she had shouted, cursed him, become frustrated and weepy. She'd exhaust herself on that, freeze him out for a bit before returning to chide him in those softer ways that gestured towards a kind of acceptance. It would be OK; it was just a matter of getting from here to there, and for that she'd need to see a little submission . . . just a touch, nothing heavy-handed. He moved to the kitchen, where she was leaning against the sink, looking out into the garden.

"Don't be like this, darling," he told her. "Please. Just trust me. Everything will be all right." She bit her lip and looked straight at him.

The silence held, and who knew what might have dropped into it, had not a noise from the front door arrested their discussion: Colette. "Hi!" they both greeted her, and as she unbuckled her shoes in the hall Jan stepped a little closer to Peter. Confidingly, she told him, "You're a shit."

Next job: the barbecue. This was comforting, physical work devoid of emotional nuance, a chance to get his hands dirty. Peter hauled the sack of charcoal from the shed, slammed it down next to the little brick tower on the patio. He'd built the barbecue two springs ago with Jan's brother and it had been a laugh, a sort of grown-up scout camp, wielding the trowel as if they'd known what they were doing, scraping the mortar from between the bricks, slapping it on to the next layer. His brother-in-law had taken it all a bit more seriously, he remembered; you could tell the different parts they'd worked on even now, Trevor's side priggishly neat, his own constructed with a cheerful, you've-missed-a-bit sloppiness.

The barbecue had ushered in two great summers — "who needs Spain?" he'd joked to Jan — and they'd felt expansive, continental, as they spent weekend lunchtimes on the patio eating black-crusted sausages, chops or chicken drumsticks. Sometimes the Chandlers or the

Millers stopped round for a beer or a glass of Mateus, extending the day until it became teatime, and he'd pile some more charcoal on the embers and they'd start all over again. It was a good way to live, he thought, the adults sociable, the kids in and out, all welcome.

Peter fetched his matches and the squeezy bottle from the shed and nipped back to the patio, taking care to shield them with his body; Jan hated him lighting the barbecue like this, and he didn't want to antagonise her any more today. Standing with his back to the house he squirted the lighter fluid over the black lumps, waiting for the shine to dull, for it to sink in a little, or evaporate. Then he lit the match and threw it in quickly, grinning as the charcoal ignited with a *whump*.

"You starting the barbecue, then?" Peter jumped and bent down hastily, tucking the bottle out of sight, but it was only Cai, his pre-pubescent voice a simulacrum of his mother's.

"Yeah, all started. What have you been doing with yourself?"

"Stuff. Seeing people."

He was far too young for this attitude, thought Peter: twelve going on seventeen, with his evasion and his mono-syllabic replies. He wanted to get his voice broken before he started in with any of that.

"You can help me now, Cai. There's burgers in the fridge, top shelf. Bring them out, will you? I need to get this going. And bring us a plate too, to put them on."

Cai turned away from him and headed for the back door, scuffing his shoes on the concrete as he went, a

202

rhythmic scrape, scrape from the plastic toes of his plimsolls. Peter caught himself starting forward in a rebuke, then quashed it before he'd said anything.

They worked together to open the boxes, slipping the burgers out of their wrappings and piling them up on the plate. They could wait there until the party was due to start. He thought of Jan and her hygiene issues.

"Get the net thing from the kitchen," he told Cai. "That thing your mum puts over cakes."

Cai went in and started banging around, opening and closing cupboards. "On the counter!" Peter shouted as Cai came out holding it. A lacy dome, it opened and shut like a parasol. Cai was pulling on a toggle to make it go up and down.

"Can I leave after this?" he asked. "I said I'd help Mrs Miller with something." It was embroidered with flowers. He'd look a right ponce.

"Put it over the burgers," Peter told him. "You seen Satish?"

"Yeah. He was doing the tables with us, wasn't he? With his dad."

Cai picked up one of the boxes they'd just emptied and pressed down on the corners to flatten it, sending the flimsy cellophane inners floating down onto the patio.

"Pick those up, will you, Cai? Don't just bloody leave them there."

Slowly, his son bent to retrieve them, one by one. His movements wobbled the table, so that even as he piled them up, they started to slip towards the edge again. Peter's fingers itched.

"I'm surprised he's showing his face, after that performance this morning. I suppose he thinks he can get away with it. Probably no idea anyone saw him."

"Mmm?" Cai was focused on the burger box again, rolling it into a slim cylinder. "What did you see, then? What did he do?"

"You know. I told you. He was kissing Mandy in his bedroom."

"Yeah. I know. But what was he doing exactly? Was he kissing her? Or was she kissing him?"

Peter thought for a moment. "He kissed her. He went towards her and kissed her. I don't know if she wanted him to."

Cai looked at him through his makeshift telescope. "You saw it? You're sure?"

"Sure. So did your sister. Cheeky bugger. And he gets away with it, scot-free." There was a silence between them. Peter tried again. "Someone needs to teach that kid a lesson," he said.

A breeze moved through the garden. Peter heard the soft crackle of the burger wrappings as they drifted onto the patio.

Cai's exposed eye screwed up tight. "Can I go now, Dad?"

Peter sighed. "If you must. Make sure you're back in time to change."

"Yeah." And he said this last as he headed for the gate, scuff, scuff, scuffing his way through the fallen packets and out of the garden.

★ ★ ★

204

Peter saw Cai once more before the party, briefly. He'd changed (white shirt, red jumper, blue slacks), then nipped downstairs to check on the barbecue from the French windows. The garden was full of kids. Satish was there (Peter's hands clenching up, his arms getting ready to swing at him). But as he peered through the glass, he realised there was no need. Cai was doing it for him. On the patio, Cai and Satish faced each other, watched by Paul and Stephen Chandler. Satish was half-crouching up against the fence, one hand reaching behind to steady himself, the other held up in front of him, palm forward. Peter thought of Hammer Horror films, the priest proffering the crucifix to ward off evil — "Back! Back!" — and he smiled involuntarily.

Cai was shouting something at Satish, reaching out to grab him. On the barbecue the initial blaze had subsided to a steady glow, a banked-down heat that would be perfect for the burgers. Peter saw this in a moment, and in that same moment Satish looked through the glass and saw him. Cai, a hand's-reach away from the boy, stopped what he was doing, and for a few seconds the fight was suspended, Peter looking at them looking at him. But it was too late to stop anything happening — Cai was nearly upon him, and why would you, anyway? Kids meted out a rough justice, to be sure, but it was a natural justice, and probably long overdue.

In the stillness of the garden, Satish began to move. He slipped away from the fence, skirting Cai. One more step and he was behind him, both boys staring into the dining room. Cai won't do it with me watching, Peter thought. Time to go.

He turned away from the window; there was Jan to find, and a bit of peace to be made before the party started. He'd better get on.

CHAPTER
EIGHTEEN

Satish has been asleep for two hours when he gets the call. The sleep was hard-won, fragile. He's lying on his back somewhere dark and when his bleeper goes off he can feel himself being jerked towards consciousness. It takes a half-second to register: bed, table, empty walls, door with its institutional handle. He's on call. Even as he's coming to, he's already reaching out to grab the bleep. It's a crash.

Pyjama bottoms off, trousers on (wobbling backwards onto the bed, one foot caught in the leg), sweater on, grab ID and keys, down the stairs in a slithering scramble, out of the door, and across the narrow street to the hospital where the entrance is a funnel of light that sucks you in and you dodge and weave around the people dallying in reception, jog down the corridor, rub the grit from the corners of your eyes, find the lift and fall on the call button, leaning against it to get your breath back as you watch it rise. And in the lift there's a hiatus. You rest against the wall and steady your breathing, your body slightly bent. Then there's a little bounce as you reach the right floor and then you're off again, through the double doors and running, sidestep the gurney, nudging the porter as you do so. Round the corner, a banging in your throat, sweat in your armpits. Past the empty reception desk, past the clock which tells you it's just after three in the morning, past a shout which may or may not have been for you, but this isn't the time, and there's the registrar, Kawther, waiting for you outside the Cath Lab, her arms full of files and paper and X-ray images.

"Kawther."

"Seven-months-old boy; five-weeks post-Fallots' repair. Mum noticed racing heartbeat and distress. Brought him in herself. ECG confirms it — he's very sick. He's in there." She gestures to the lab behind her.

Kawther's good, and she's usually right, but Satish holds his hand out for the test results anyway. She pushes a printout towards him.

There's an aesthetic balance to a normal ECG, the gentle foothills of the P- and T-waves between the peaks of ventricular beats, curves and angles in a dignified advance. But this — this is nothing like that. It's textbook SVT, a staccato run of spikes across the page. This heart's running so fast you can't even see the P-waves. Kawther is spot-on.

"Get parental consent, now," he tells her. "Have you paged an anaesthetist?"

"Just arrived."

He makes for the Cath Lab door. As Kawther turns away he hears her say, "Good luck," and then, when he does not answer, he hears a "Sorry" under her breath. He wants to ask her what she means, but she's halfway down the corridor and there's a sick child waiting. He pushes open the lab door.

208

The baby lies on the bed in his nappy, waxy-pale and panting. His body's already gone into deep shock. The anaesthetist is setting up. Charles, Satish remembers: Charles Bennett. Clare Munroe is assisting. Charles acknowledges him with a nod.

"I'm going to shock him," says Satish. "I'll get some adrenaline out in case he arrests."

"Great. We're almost there," Charles tells him as he tips back the child's head, pulls his mouth open, and bears down on him with the tube.

Satish goes to the drugs cupboard. All at once the serendipity of it strikes him, and he pushes away the thought that this is inappropriate, that this is a terrible time to be stocking up, because he knows he can do it swiftly, and that the child won't suffer because of it, and that no one will be any the wiser. He glances up: Charles is leaning over the baby now, focused on the task. Clare has one eye on the monitor. Satish slips his hand into the cabinet, palms a bottle from the back of the middle shelf and slides it into his pocket. Then he takes a second bottle, from the top shelf this time, and places it on the instruments table.

"How are you doing?"

"Fine."

Satish washes his hands. The clock ticks. 3.10 a.m. He reaches for the defibrillator.

"He's out?" he asks.

"Out." Clare steps away from the bed, turns her full attention to the monitor. Charles is bagging the child now, pushing oxygen into his lungs. They're ready.

"Charge."

As the defibrillator charges, Satish watches the child's chest, its speedy rise and fall. In that brief moment he thinks of Mike Halloran, the fly-boy, and of all those cardiac surgeons with their God-complexes. Maybe they need it, those golden boys, because it's not like that for him. This is a moment of calm. He's going to do his job. He leans forward.

They all jump when the knock comes on the door.

"No!" shouts Satish, low and clear. He extends the paddles towards the baby. Outside there's a scuffling sound, voices. The door bursts open; he sees Kawther looking stricken, but he's focused on the woman in front of her. It's Sarah, and as she lunges into the room, he realises: this is Louis.

"Wait!" she tells him. "Hang on! What are you doing to him?" She comes so close he has to swivel to prevent her from touching the paddles.

"He's very sick, Sarah. I need to shock his heart, try to get it back into a normal rhythm." Satish reaches over, replaces the paddles, dumps the charge. He can see the baby — her baby, he corrects himself. Sarah sees him, too, intubated, bagged, unmoving under the weight of the anaesthetic. Her expression falters.

"I know he's sick. I want to know what *you're* doing to him."

Charles and Clare have heard her emphasis. They twitch towards Satish, like watchful meerkats.

"I'm the duty consultant tonight, Sarah, and I need to act quickly. Please step outside with Kawther. She'll explain."

"You're pressuring me."

"He needs help right now."

"You're —" Then she puts herself between Satish and the bed, her hands held up defensively. She's wearing the scarecrow outfit of a mother pulled from sleep by a medical emergency: the baggy sweatshirt, pyjama trousers, shoes without socks. "This is happening too fast. You're pressuring me. I know he needs treatment; I just don't think *you* should do it."

Kawther breaks the pause that follows. "Mrs Stevens, it's the middle of the night. Dr Patel's the duty doctor, and Louis needs help right now."

Sarah's still holding a hand out to keep Satish away from Louis, her other hand pulling at the hem of her sweatshirt. When she speaks next, he's taken aback by the force of her words.

"I know he needs help. I'm not stupid. I just don't want *you* to give it. I want another doctor. You won't — he won't . . ." She turns to Kawther. "I have good reason to believe that Satish — Dr Patel — won't do the best for my son. He's emotionally involved. He's not the right person for this. Call someone else."

Kawther's a professional, but this is solid gold, Satish can tell. He can imagine how this will play out in the staff canteen: *emotionally involved*, she'll tell them. *Satish!* Charles shifts at the head of the bed. Clare looks up from the monitor. Satish wants to throw them all out, to get rid of the witnesses. Instead, in the quiet following Sarah's statement, he knows that something is required of him.

"Sarah and I knew each other as children," he tells them. "That's what she's referring to, I think. We didn't get on well back then, and until last week I hadn't seen her for over twenty years. Sarah, you're understandably anxious about Louis, and I think that's making you feel . . . unreasonable things. I am not emotionally involved with you or with him." Every word a clue, every word a window to see into.

"His blood pressure's dropped," says Clare. "Systolic of 70."

"Listen, Sarah." Kawther's voice has taken on an edge. "Louis is in a critical condition. Dr Patel is straight down the line, I promise you. Nothing would interfere with his treatment of your son."

"I demand someone else!"

"There is no one else. No one. And there's no time."

Sarah sets her jaw. "I don't trust you," she tells him, her voice unsteady. "This is unethical."

"Satish . . ."

"Clare?"

"Systolic's down to 60."

"Charles?"

Charles is bent over Louis. "He's getting harder to oxygenate."

"I've got a bloody good lawyer!" Sarah's saying. Both her hands are fisted, her arms rigid at her sides. "He'll go over everything you do here, every decision. He'll *have* you. If anything happens to my boy, he'll have you."

"Sarah, I'm going to ask you to leave." Satish reaches over to charge the defibrillator. "And I'm going to tell you why. Louis's BPs have dropped to a dangerous level. He's about to arrest."

212

"Oh God, oh God . . ."

"I'm in a room with two other people, and I couldn't get anything past them, even if I wanted to." He feels the bottle in his pocket, bumping against his hip. "You need to trust me. You need to leave."

"Do you want an apology? For something that happened thirty years ago? For a mistake made by a kid? Frankly, if that's what it takes, I'll do it: I'm sorry. Take care of my boy. Don't hurt him."

Her raised voice has brought a nurse: Satish can see her barrelling down the corridor towards them. Then Kawther pulls Sarah from the room. As she disappears from view she looks towards the bed, to Louis, small and exposed, then across at Satish.

"Tell me I can trust you," she says.

Satish meets her gaze, the paddles raised and ready.

"Of course," he replies, and then the door shuts.

Most paediatricians will tell you that their job changes once they have their own children. For Satish, the change happened like this: once Asha was born, he realised he was treating two sets of patients every time he did a consultation. The child had always been there, the kid with a hole in the heart, or narrowed arteries, or the more complex issues: transpositions, tetralogy of Fallot, cardiomyopathy. There were always kids with symptoms to treat, and he'd prided himself on his effectiveness as a practitioner. He'd mitigate the breathlessness, the recurrent chest infections, all the things his patients had to live with. He'd time their interventions just so, seizing the optimum moment.

With his own fatherhood, however, came the shock of discovering what the parents had to endure; not theoretically, every decent medical school taught you that, but viscerally. Asha was a few weeks old, with a fever and a rash which Satish, during the sleepless night of his daughter's first illness, had become convinced was meningitis. He'd argued with Maya, fiercely and uncharacteristically, that they should rush the baby to the nearest A & E, until Satish's own mother had woken, and come in, and imposed her good sense on them. The next morning it had felt like a kind of insanity. He'd let himself wonder: what if Asha had really been ill? What if they'd had some other doctor give them bad news about their child, the kind of bad news you cannot negotiate with? All the things you'd fear if they happened to you — breathlessness, chest infections, open heart surgery — they would be nothing compared with watching it happen to your kid.

In the months following this unsettling discovery, Satish's professionalism was able to reassert itself. His detachment returned as it does to all good doctors, but his perspective changed in the process; all his cases were multiple now, the patient and the patient's parents, their happiness up for ransom.

So, as the door closes behind Sarah, he knows exactly why she is trying to stop him treating her son, why she rails at him and threatens him and abases herself. She wronged him once, and now her entire happiness, her ability to laugh, to make love with her husband, to sleep, to think of the future with any kind of pleasure, lies with him.

214

★   ★   ★

The clock shows 3.18. With Sarah gone, the room is quiet again. Karma, he thinks. Karma is not retribution. It's the natural outcome of the choices we make. How strange that their lives should have come round to this: this meeting in a hospital in the dead hours of the morning, her son struggling on the bed in front of him. Exactly how wicked would you have to be, at eleven, to bring this upon yourself at forty-one? She was not wicked enough for that; nobody deserved that.

The paddles are ready, their red lights glowing. "Clear!" He leans forward and places them on Louis's chest, spanning the heart. There's a *click* as they discharge their ten joules, and Satish turns to the monitor: nothing. The heart's still in SVT.

But maybe Sarah has a second chance coming to her. He charges the machine again: "Clear!" Again, the click. Only this time, he sees immediately: he's done it. The heart's in sinus rhythm once more, the waves and spikes rising in stately predictability. They all wait, unwilling to rely on it, then Clare says: "OK, systolic rising: 80," and Satish breathes out. Charles says, "Good job," and Satish puts the paddles back.

Satish has rules about the stuff he takes. He always gets it straight from the drugs cupboard — a risky process but, he thinks, a more ethical one. Otherwise it's a case of prescribing it for a patient and then taking it yourself, and you wouldn't want to do that, not when it's for anxiety and the kid's preop and terrified, and won't get any calmer because the diazepam's safely tucked away in your case. Satish knows this because he did it once — only once — and it was so terrible that it became his first protocol. There are other rules: never increase the dose. Take it once a day, before bed.

By the time he's reached his room again he already knows he'll break this last commandment. He left the lab by a circuitous route, along intricate back corridors, rather than pass through the room in which Sarah was waiting. The benevolent influence of his earlier dose has long receded. He's shaking, avoiding eye contact with the few people who are up and about, trying to control himself because his breath is juddering out of him. When he gets into his room he leans against the door to close it, then squats down, resting his forehead on his hands.

"Oooh!" he's saying. "Oooh!"

He sounds like Maya did in early labour, like someone surprised by pain but breathing through it anyway. Sarah, and Louis, and that appalling, public melodrama. Her shouted apology, his privacy breached. He reaches into his pocket. By now, he can estimate his dose just fine, no need for a spoon, even. He takes a gulp, and then another. The taste of it is a promise: you'll be OK soon. Wait it out. Her voice comes back to him, sorry. I'm sorry, and then he thinks of that other sorry: the quiet one, from Kawther just after she'd wished him luck.

What did she mean by that? Why should she think he needs *luck?* Does she doubt his abilities? Do others?

The thought fills him with panic, and then a sudden sadness comes. He wants to go somewhere safe, where he doesn't need to protect himself all the time. But when did that last happen? When he was a kid, he thinks. In Cherry Gardens, before it all fell apart. With Cai. And Mandy — always with Mandy.

He thinks about Mandy, and he sleeps.

CHAPTER
NINETEEN

A few weeks before the Jubilee, Satish was round at Mandy's house. They were playing Truth or Dare in her bedroom, Satish maintaining a courtly restraint (Dare: stand on your head. Truth: where would you most like to go on holiday?), Mandy being less scrupulous. He chose Truth twice and regretted it. (Which girl from school do you fancy? Have you ever heard your parents Doing It?) When it was his turn again, he risked a dare instead.

"OK," she said. "Steal one of my mum's cakes."

"What?"

"Steal a cake for me. Go on."

"I can't. It involves other people. Your mum. You can't involve other people. It's a rule."

She stepped close to him. She smelled of Pears shampoo, the same stuff he and Sima used, but it was sweeter on her somehow, and stronger. When she spoke, quietly, next to his ear, he could feel her breath warm. "It isn't a rule. You asked for a dare. Do it."

Mandy's mum was polishing the dining room table. They could see her from the kitchen, through the serving hatch. When she spotted Satish, she waved a can of furniture spray at him.

"Hi, Satish. You all right?"

"Yes, Mrs Hobbes. I'm getting a glass of water." He reached up to the cupboard, pushing the hatch door closed as he did so. Mandy, crouching below counter level, shot up a hand and re-opened it, wider than before.

The cakes were in front of the serving hatch. She'd made scones, their sides softly concertinaed, pasty-pale and studded with raisins, arranged in serried rows on the cooling rack.

"I'm just pouring the water now," he shouted through, sloshing it into the glass. He waited until Mrs Hobbes had started on the bookcase, her back to him, and made it fast. It was a smooth operation: grabbing the scone, still warm, the flour gritty against his hand, dropping it to Mandy, who chomped into it straight away.

"Mmm," he said. "Nice water. Thanks."

They left the kitchen, Mandy rising once she was out of her mum's sight.

"Great dare," she whispered, still processing the last of her mouthful. Then she swallowed and whipped her arm behind her back; Mrs Hobbes was coming.

"You down here too, Mands? What are you up to, then?"

Through the kitchen door Satish could see what he'd missed before. There had been twelve cakes: three rows of four. But now he'd nicked one, there was a gap; she'd see it immediately. He thought fast.

219

"My glass!" he said, holding it up, and went to put it noisily on the kitchen counter. He heard them talking in the hall.

"We're just mucking around," said Mandy. "Satish needed a drink."

He tried rearranging the scones, leapfrogging replacements into the gap, shifting them around. Nothing worked.

"Well, I'm done with the dusting," said Mrs Hobbes. "Done and dusted! Garden next."

She'd have to go through the kitchen to get to the garden. She'd see the cooling rack, and then — he looked at Mandy, the remains of her scone behind her back — Mandy'd be for it. He put the scones back where they were, with the gap at the front, then he spread his fingers to widen it. When Mrs Hobbes came into the room, he puffed out his cheeks.

"I'b horry," he told her, as she looked from him to the scones. "I drusht couldn't holp it."

When her mum had finished with him, Mandy took Satish back upstairs. On the landing she reached out for his hand and pulled it towards her. She gave him little squeezes — at his wrists, on his thumb — then turned it, palm-up. From behind her back she produced the scone and lowered it onto his hand.

"You can have the rest," she said. "You've earned it."

He said they should stop the game now, but Mandy told him: "No, you have one more go. Truth or Dare me."

"No. Let's do something else."

220

"Just one more. Then we're evens."

He sighed. "Truth or Dare?" The scone was good, that slight fizziness coming through.

"I don't mind. A big truth or a big dare. You choose. I'll do anything: trip up Paul Chandler, say Fuck to my dad, run down the street in my nuddie . . ."

"Truth."

"Right. What truth? I'll tell you anything."

He thought of some of the things he could ask. "I don't know," he said. "Tell me . . . tell me something no one else knows."

She went quiet, so that the only sound was Satish chewing, the scone rolling stickily in his mouth.

"OK," she said. She pulled him into her room, shutting the door behind her. Then she opened her wardrobe door and hauled out a basket. It was brimful of cuddly toys: penguins and giraffes, teddies and pandas, which she unloaded by the handful. When she had excavated the last one, she took out something else and held it behind her back.

"I will tell you something no one else knows," she said. "But this is something properly, properly secret. You cannot. Tell. Anyone. OK?"

"OK."

She laid it in front of him: an old toffee tin, navy blue, with silver bits that were flaking off in places. There was a picture on it of a man in knickerbockers and stockings and big-buckled shoes, and there was a dent on the top left of the lid, right next to his hat.

"If you tell, Mum'll kill me. If you tell I'll . . . honestly, I'll . . ." Her face had taken on the same hard focus that he saw in Cai when his friend was hell-bent on something. It was like a trick of the light: she had caught his look completely. Disconcerted, Satish moved to reassure her.

"Hang on. I won't tell anyone. You won't have to do anything. I promise."

"OK." She levered up the lid with her thumbnail and pushed the open tin towards him. Inside were girls' things: a leather pendant on a thong, decorated with a rainbow design; a glass vial of Miners' lipgloss (peppermint flavour); a pack of hairgrips. Two-and-a-half white chocolate mice nested in the bottom on pale dust from their own eroded edges.

Satish had no idea what he was meant to say. He didn't know how to connect these very ordinary things — the sort of things you'd see in her room most of the time anyway — to Mandy's hissed injunctions. He examined each object at length, handling them all except the white mice, looking at them from different angles. He hoped she would say something soon, something he could pick up on so he wouldn't seem stupid.

"Do you know why they're secret?" she asked.

"Umm . . ."

"It's not because of what they are. It's because of *how I got them*." Mandy looked at the door and leaned in closer, beckoning him nearer in turn so that they were face to face. "I got them because I *stole* them."

"You —?" He drew back to look at her. She was biting her lip.

222

"All of them. I stole them." And when he frowned in disbelief, she said a bit louder: "I did! I took them from the shops up the road. Wavy Line, the chemist, Valerie's."

"Mrs Weston's?"

Mandy paused. "Yeah," she told him. "Yeah, I did."

Mandy going into a shop, saying *hi* to the shopkeeper because she knew each one by name, they all did. Mandy pretending to look for something while she slipped something else into her pocket, something small she hid all the way home. The shopkeepers of Bourne Heath puzzled by the absence of that small something the next time they checked. Mandy keeping it in the bottom of her wardrobe.

"You steal them? Then you put them in there?" He pointed at the tin, which lay between them. "Is that what you do?"

"Mostly." Mandy replaced the items and pushed the lid back on. "Sometimes I give people things. I've given Sarah a few things. She doesn't know I took them."

He watched Mandy covering her tracks, piling the soft toys back into the basket, moving the basket into the wardrobe. After she'd shut the door she turned to him.

"I've never given you anything I've taken. Never. And I won't, OK?"

"OK. Great." He sensed this was a compliment of some kind, but he was floundering badly. Did all girls do stuff like this? Was this normal?

"Do you . . . Why do you do it, Mandy?"

She considered. "Well, it's exciting. It is — you should do it, just once!" He started to decline, muttering, but she talked over him. "You go in, and they chat with you about school or something, and you dare yourself to do it, and you can do it in different ways, depending on how brave you feel. When they can't see you at all, or when they're just turning away. Or, one time, I did it when the Wavy Line woman was actually next to me, putting more Black Jacks in the box!"

"Why do you keep everything in the tin?" he asked.

"Don't know." There was a pause. "I look at them again and I think about when I took them. I remember what it felt like."

Satish nodded sagely although he was none the wiser.

"OK. So, why do you give them to people, then?"

Mandy looked straight at him. She was biting back a grin. "Honestly, Satish, it's funny. Sarah, especially. I give her stuff and she sort of likes me more! It's just stuff, but if she's being a bit funny, it works on her. It's so easy. You just give her things."

Satish thought of Sarah, and he knew that what Mandy was saying was nasty, really nasty. But she was right: it was funny, too. He thought of Mandy feeding Sarah stolen goods like she fed her cat, to keep him close by, and he sniggered, then Mandy did, too. They both put their hands over their mouths to hide the naughty laughter, but they laughed anyway, guilty and delighted.

224

CHAPTER
TWENTY

There's nothing else she wants to keep hold of from that day. It can all go to hell. She holds a memory of Satish, and one of her mum, and that's all she wants.

She'd fancied Satish for ages. Everything else — Cai, the mucking around with Sarah — it was just a bit of fun, practice. Satish she really liked. There was something held-back about him. None of the other boys held back. It was all action, talk, showing off. Satish watched, and he listened. She knew she could say anything to him: he'd never tell. Satish kept his cool: about her dad's bedroom, about the stuff she took. He never corrected her when she said the wrong thing. He never laughed at her.

She was pretty sure he didn't fancy her, though. Certain of it, until Jubilee Day, up in his room. That morning, things felt different. He stood close to her a lot, touched her. He was even quieter than usual. Then, very suddenly, he was looking at her in a different way and stepping towards her, holding her arm and coming close to kiss her. She'd imagined it often, but not like this. In her daydreams he would burst into her classroom, public and unashamed, and they'd run away together, or they'd meet by coincidence on holiday and sneak away from their parents and kiss on a beach. Instead here they were, in his room, and it was really happening.

She offered her face to him, tilting it upwards and closing her eyes. Later, accused by Sarah, she told the truth — he didn't smell horrible. He did smell different though, gloriously alien and boyish. His lips pressed her skin firmly, leaving a wet trace, a hair's-width of coldness that soon warmed and disappeared. When he moved away from her, she waited just a beat to see if he would come near again. He didn't, so she grabbed his hands and stroked the backs of them with her thumbs.

"Mandy," he said quietly, and she could tell: he didn't know where to put himself.

Before she could get nervous she stepped right up to him, enjoying the luxury of his height, the necessity of leaning up, and anchored his hands so he'd have to let her kiss him on the lips. His mouth was trembling and he didn't open it, but he let her stay there for a few seconds, and she wondered if he was breathing in her smell, as she was his. I love him! she thought. I really love him!

She was moony and dreamy for the rest of the morning; the kiss had changed everything. She'd kissed two boys and loved one of them and it was a secret. Things went slowly, because she stopped a lot, trying to re-live the moment. When she first knew he was going to kiss her! When he stepped towards her! The way he said her name! Sarah's visit nearly wrenched her out of that, almost transformed them so they were just two kids snogging, but then Mandy remembered how it had

226

felt, and she took a minute to let it all fall into place again. Sarah might be trouble, though. Mandy should warn Satish; it was a good reason to see him. She wrote the word on the back of a poster and held it up to her window: TROUBLE. She waited for him to come to his window and see it.

Later, when it was time to put out the food Mandy was commandeered by her mum: "Can you open the door, Mands? It's all a bit wibbly-wobbly!" There were four plates of fairy cakes, thick with icing, piled artfully in pyramids of red, white and blue. Her mum took a platter in each hand, fixed her eyes on her cargo and stepped gingerly out of the front door. She sent her feet out first, nosing for danger with the tips of her shoes before trusting each step.

It's a lasting memory of the day: her mum stepping stately away from her and out into the street, Mandy's shift of focus as she caught a movement in the background, on the other side of the road: two fleeting figures running out of Cai's side gate. Satish was just in front, pelting towards home, and behind him, Cai. It looked as if Cai was reaching out to grab Satish, as if Satish was fending him off, but it was over so fast. As they disappeared her mum turned towards Mandy and tipped her a wink. She smiled back, suddenly unsure whether she'd seen the boys properly after all.

CHAPTER
TWENTY-ONE

Satish is with Colette, and she's hungry. They sit at the back of her favourite café in the unseasonable April heat. It's sweltering, but he's been denied the luxury of air conditioning because she doesn't like the other places in town. She says they're faceless, corporate, bastions of globalisation and cultural imperialism that leach money out of the local economy and so they've come here, where the Lebanese owner flirts with Colette and slips extra baklava onto her plate. Satish can appreciate the upside, but he's still sweating into his T-shirt and thinking he'd probably be flexible about the cultural imperialism if it bought him a little air-con.

"Hell in a handcart," Colette's saying. "This feels like July, or August. Imagine what the real summer will be like! You've heard all the findings on climate change? They say it's moving quicker than expected. God, I'm starving." She shoves a piece of baklava in her mouth.

Satish watches Colette for the signs of addiction: Is she excessively talkative? A tough one to call. He'll bide his time, drawing her out.

"I know," he says. "Asha's been coming home from school full of it, too. I think they have global warming lessons, or something."

"Good," she says, chewing. "They should. Maybe they'll do better than we have."

"Are you really worried by this?"

"Are you not?"

"Well . . . I . . ." In truth, he's not. Or maybe he would be, but what's the point of trying to fix the future when there's enough to do just to make the here and now bearable? But he knows how inadequate this will sound, and he tails off.

"My friend Harry says we'll all be dead in twenty-five years," she tells him.

"Your friend Harry's unbalanced."

"Still, though." Her coffee has come with a thick head of foam, and she leans towards the mug, tilting it towards her, and slurps the foam off the top. He can see what she's doing, trying to harvest it without disturbing the coffee underneath.

The other people in this café are overheated, too. They're dressed in clothes pulled early from storage, or in winter gear stripped down to make do. Their legs are white and tender, their faces flushed. At a nearby table, a man holds a toddler on his lap. The child twists in discomfort, settling, then fidgeting, then settling once more, and her father supports her lightly, maintaining the minimum of contact between them.

Colette is barely clad on top — Satish notes his faintly paternalistic disapproval — wearing little more than underwear, really. He can see her bra strap (black), and there's a sort of vest thing on top of that. She puts her coffee mug down and he checks the inside of her arm for tracks. There are none.

"Are you enjoying your tea, Satish? Are you sure you won't have anything to eat?"

"No thanks, I'm fine. The tea's fine."

There's a pause. There's something about the way she organised this get-together, friendly but with a bit of grit to it. When she rang to set the date it felt less like socialising, and more like being called to a meeting. He wonders what's on her agenda. He knows what's on his.

"OK," she says. "So, here's the thing: Sarah's mum — you know she still lives in Cherry Gardens? — she's been doing research about the photograph. She's taken it up as a kind of project. Been trying to trace people from back then, so they can be in it."

He can imagine it — Mrs Miller, ever the Bourne Heath hostess. He thinks of her with her clipboard and her impeccable organisation. He wonders how frantic she's been about her sick grandson, whether this new project was something to take her mind off him.

"She's got in contact with people?"

"She's tried to. She's tracked down Miss Walsh — you remember her?"

"The teacher?"

"Yeah. The teacher. She had long hair." Colette trails a hand down her throat. "She wore these big pendants. God, I had such a crush on her. When the rain came on Jubilee Day she let me shelter in her house. Her boyfriend was there. I couldn't nail it at the time, but there was this sexual charge around them. I remember the sense that there was something going on I wasn't part of."

"You were six!"

230

"I know, I know. My hair was wet because of the rain, and Miss Walsh brought a towel down to dry it. Her boyfriend was sitting there, watching me, and he was smoking or something, because he was holding his hand away from his face and it made his T-shirt ride up, and I saw his, you know, his pubic hair, what do they call it? Crab ladder — I saw his crab ladder. Don't look at me like that, Satish. I'm sharing, here."

"I'm waiting for the point."

"It's just . . . There was something about him, the way he watched me, just waiting to see what would happen next. No judgements, no intervention. A sort of amorality. You know where else I've seen that? Dealers."

He waits for the confession.

"Dealers," she says again, quieter. "The ones I knew, anyway. Do you think Miss Walsh's boyfriend was a drug dealer?"

"I think he was an accountant. What do you want to tell me?"

"Well, Mrs Miller found Miss Walsh but she's living in Scotland so she's not going to come."

On Colette's plate is her last baklava, a little diamond with grey paste oozing from the middle. He considers reaching out for it, but just as he's decided to, she takes it herself and bites it in half. As the layers of pastry succumb to her teeth, the whole thing squashes down and the paste leaks out of the sides. Sometimes, they get very hungry. Is this appetite normal?

"You want?" she asks as she offers him the remains.

He shakes his head. "Who else did she find then?"

"Hang on." She chews slowly, pointing at her mouth occasionally as he waits for her to finish. "Sorry about that. The thing is, she's been trying to trace the Chandlers."

Lukewarm tea slops on the floor of his mouth. He swishes it from side to side with his tongue. If he didn't have to respond, if he could hold it in for a while longer, his mouth would cool slightly, and the tea would warm a bit more.

"Satish?"

He swallows finally. "The Chandlers?"

"Yeah. She managed to find someone who knew someone . . . you know. You remember how she was? She could find bloody Lord Lucan. Weapons of Mass Destruction."

"So, I suppose she found them, then?"

"Well, she found Paul."

Paul Chandler, his dense body packed into his school uniform, appears briefly before Satish. He can see Paul's cold eye, Paul's jaw adorned with bum fluff.

"I need some more tea, Colette. You?"

"I'm fine."

He goes over to the counter and deliberates over his choice of cake. When he sits down again she hasn't let it go.

"So, Mrs Miller found Paul. He moved to Australia a few years back. I don't know what he's doing out there."

"So?"

"So . . . he's not coming, obviously. But she's looking for Stephen now. He hasn't emigrated or died or anything. He's back down south, apparently. You know, Satish, she'll find him."

The Chandlers had left a few months after the Jubilee party. The Jubilee was like a centrifuge, he sometimes thinks, its events sending them all spinning away from the centre: Cai and Colette to South Africa, the Chandlers up north. It wasn't like that at all, of course, they'd have gone anyway. The real centre was Satish, and they spun away from him all right. In that last half term at primary school, he was alone. He'd have nothing to do with Sarah or Cai, and Colette was too young to be a real friend. Mandy he ignored completely.

Being alone was bearable, but being publicly alone was really hard. Satish found new ways to look busy. He chatted to a bemused Sima on the walk to school. Once there, he avoided the playground altogether; he read books, he helped teachers. At weekends, his mum started to notice that he wasn't playing out, and he told her he had lots of homework to do. Once the holidays started, he got out of Cherry Gardens altogether most days, taking refuge at Ranjeet's place. When his mum remarked on *that*, he told her he was talking to Dinesh about secondary school, and it seemed to satisfy her. Certainly, she never brought up the subject again.

But for all his meticulous planning, he still bumped into the Chandlers from time to time. They shared the same road, of course, and there were those few weeks after the summer holidays when they were all at Bassetsbury Boys' together. Satish had to steel himself when he saw them coming. He could cope, though. He had a trick. When he saw them, he'd imagine he was armed. He had guns, at least two or three of them, concealed all over his body, like a spy. When the Chandlers appeared, he could feel the guns: knocking against his hip; strapped to his ankle; snuggling under his sock. There was nothing those bigger boys could do that would be a match for the guns. The slightest sign of trouble and they'd find themselves staring down the barrel of a Smith and Wesson.

I'm armed, Satish would tell himself as he spotted Stephen or Paul coming towards him. He'd square his shoulders and his hand would hover near his waist. He'd stare at them, and they'd stare right back, and they'd pass each other like that. But after Jubilee Day, the Chandlers never touched him.

"You're right," he tells Colette. "Mrs Miller will find Stephen."

"And then she'll invite him to the photo. He might come." She paused. "Bugger, eh?"

And it's those words that break him. The cunning of it, the disingenuous sympathy. She isn't using. She's clean and nasty, and he doesn't know why. His anger comes out in a rush.

"Don't give me that!" Colette jumps. "This was always going to get out of control, wasn't it?"

"What do you mean?" she says, her voice perilous.

"I mean, that you were so keen for me to do this, weren't you? Well, that's why I didn't want to. This was utterly predictable. *You* should have known it."

"It's not my fault!" she says.

234

"It's interesting you should say that. Because it *is* your fault, really, isn't it?"

"What do you mean?"

"I mean . . ." and he takes a breath, but he needs to lift this rock, see what's underneath it. "I mean that you tell Andrew Ford you'll make this happen — and I'm still interested in exactly how that came about. Then you track people down. And you call Maya, just to chat about it, all innocence. And you — don't interrupt me. And yes, before you ask: I'm *cross* — you break into my house in the middle of the night and spin me a line about your poor, poor, fraudulent father."

"Don't!"

The man with the toddler glances across at them. Satish lowers his voice. "And when I still don't comply, you do this." He pulls the note out of his jacket pocket and slides it across the table towards her. Colette looks at it for a second or two, then opens it.

"Do the photograph," she reads. "Or I'll tell your secret?" She gives the last word an upward inflection: a question. She stares at Satish. "What is this?"

"Don't give me that."

"What the *fuck*? Did someone send you this?"

"Don't bother, Colette. Don't pretend."

"What the *fuck*?" she says again. "Are you serious?"

Around them, Satish can hear muttered discontent. The man raises his hand for the waiter, but Colette has gone quiet, and she's looking at the paper that lies between them. Suddenly her expression changes.

"I don't believe it!" she says. "You . . . horrible . . . bastard!" She snatches up the note. "You think *I* did this. You think I would do this to *you*. You nasty little bastard fucker!"

Her forehead and chin and lips are trembling. Pain, or a very good approximation of it, moves across her face like a cloudscape. But he can't be sure. He presses on.

"Well . . . yes, I do. And I'm not the one at fault here. You were very keen for me to do this. You pressured me."

"I was upfront with you!"

"You pushed and pushed."

"Not with a bloody blackmail note, I didn't!"

She shoves it in his direction and starts collecting her things, her scarf, her purse, her mobile, stuffing them into her bag.

"You stupid, stupid bastard. Don't you know? I would never do this to you. I'm your friend, you thick bastard. Your friend! And I don't *care* about your secret, whatever it is. You could tell me anything, you stupid fucker!" And she gets up and walks out, pushing back her chair, so that it topples to the floor with a clang.

In the wake of her departure, as heads turn towards him, Satish covers his face and curls forward onto the table. He doesn't know what to think. The things she said feel true. Real. And if they are, he's a *nasty little bastard*, wrong and ashamed — *and* he still hasn't found his blackmailer. If she's lying, then he hasn't done anything to derail her; he's just made her angry.

He can hear it scattering down towards him, the shower of stones disturbed from somewhere higher up:

236

this thing isn't controllable any more. There's nobody left to remonstrate with, nobody to appease, and there's only one thing he can do to stop his world from coming apart. He'll have to do the photograph. He closes his eyes against the thought, but then he remembers what you say to parents when they resist treatment for their child: the alternative's worse. Now, he follows his own advice. If he doesn't do this he'll be exposed. He'll lose his job, lose his parents' respect, maybe even Maya and the kids. So he'll do the photograph. He'll do it because the alternative's far worse.

And the Big Deal that Colette wanted to tell him about, the search for Stephen Chandler? That's no mystery at all. Stephen will be found. He wants to be found. He has, after all, already sought out Satish; and Stephen found Satish with no trouble whatsoever.

CHAPTER
TWENTY-TWO

It happened four months ago. He was at work and he'd left his office for just a moment. When he went back, Stephen was in there waiting for him. Satish didn't recognise him at first. He registered a man just inside the door, and the man was looking around him as if he wasn't sure whether he should be there.

"Hello?" said Satish. "Can I help you?"

He was sinewy, tan-varnished, and although he was dressed formally, it looked all wrong: a surfer in a suit.

"Can I help you?"

"Satish Patel?"

"Yes."

"I don't know whether you remember me. I'm Stephen Chandler." He held out his hand.

Satish was ashamed, later, of having recoiled. But it couldn't be helped, and he found himself out in the corridor.

"Bit of a surprise, isn't it? I was in the area."

"Were you? Well, I'm afraid . . . I'm afraid this isn't a good time. I have patients to see."

Stephen followed him out into the corridor, stood close. "I thought we might catch up," he said.

"I have patients waiting right now. I can't."

"It'll just take a minute. Can we talk?"

There was a sound from further along, double doors opening as Niamh pushed through them. "Tea?" she said, and he remembered that he'd asked for some.

She handed it over, regarding Stephen with interest — "Any for you?" — but before he could answer, Satish said: "No, he's fine, thanks," and pushed past Stephen into his office, leaving him behind.

When he made to shut the door, Stephen bounced it open again. "It's only for a minute," he said, shouldering inside and closing it. Satish moved behind his desk.

"I'm very busy here." Satish kept hold of his hot tea. He looked at the sharpened pencils next to the phone.

"I think I know what this is about — can I sit down?" Uninvited, Stephen sat in the chair reserved for patients. He was a composite thing, a middle-aged man, and a boy, and — somewhere — the young man Satish had never seen. Lines had been carved into his skin, and it was more than the normal ageing process. There had been sun and wind on him over the last thirty years. Stephen's hands came to rest on the arms of the chair, and a middle finger rubbed at the finial. Then he shifted in his seat, crossed one leg over the other and plucked at the knee of his trousers. There he was! Stephen, the boy, caught in one of his characteristic quick movements, like a sudden dumping of energy.

"Look, I think I know why you're reacting like this," he said. "I know why you didn't answer my letters."

"I really don't have the time . . ."

"I understand. It was Jubilee Day, wasn't it?" He looked cautiously at Satish. "All that palaver before the street party? Blimey, that was nearly thirty years ago! What were we like, eh?" He grinned invitingly, but Satish didn't respond. Stephen was trying to take more control of his body language now. He slowed his movements down, became carefully expansive. The silence grew, and Satish let it. Stephen's smile flattened.

"Just kids, really, weren't we?" he continued. "When I look back . . . Well, we all had stuff to be embarrassed about, didn't we? If it wasn't your attitude it was your haircut. No point in being young otherwise. What we used to get up to . . ." He shook his head and smiled. Still Satish said nothing. Stephen talked on, hauling up more memories, the convenient ones, as he did so. The white noise of the computer filled the pauses.

"That school. Your mate Cai, footie in the street — do you remember? Different times. Well, we're all grown up now. And look at you. You've done well."

When he finally stopped, Satish stood. "I'm afraid I have to go now," he said. "Probably best to leave."

Stephen stood, too, and Satish's fingertips felt for the edge of the desk.

"Come on, Satish."

"I said, it's best if you leave."

Stephen pursed his lips and looked at the floor. "You know, you were a lucky bastard, Satish," he said. "A lucky, *smug* bastard, some might say. I'm sure you felt hard done by and whatever, but the truth is, you lucked out on Jubilee Day."

240

Was Satish suffering from some sort of latency? Certainly, he was a beat behind everything Stephen was saying.

"Do you know what the halo effect is?" Stephen went on. "It's what you got that day. They've proved it: if people know one good thing about someone, they think they're good at everything." He took a step closer. "If they know you're rich, they'll think you're clever. If they know you're popular, they'll think you're successful. Get one thing right — you know, really *right* — and you get the best jobs and the best partners and money and whatever. You got that." He flicks a finger at Satish. "You got it from that photo: that's all people thought about, you at the centre, the Jubilee boy. It made you *interesting*. It made people notice you. How do you think you got all this?" His quick gesture took in Satish's office, the hospital and — presumably — Maya and the kids, miles away and oblivious.

Satish opened his mouth, but Stephen was on a roll. "Don't tell me it was hard work; lots of people work bloody hard, and then they have a bit of bad luck and they don't get even close to this. That photo started everything. What were you, before that happened? Nobody. So don't come the martyr with me."

"In point of fact —"

"Oh, come on! *In point of fact?* Stop being so precious. It was the seventies! Everyone did it, or had it done to them. That's what childhood's about. Do you think I escaped?"

Stephen being whacked with his plimsoll, Colette listening on the other side of the wall.

"Stephen, why have you come here?"

"You did fine by that photo. The rest of us got fuck-all."

"This again? You still want this? You can't *sue* Andrew Ford."

"I don't want to."

"Or picket him, or tell the papers about him —"

"Listen to me. I don't want to." He paused. "There's more than one way to skin a cat."

Satish saw the pelt in Stephen's hands, dripping; a lump on the floor, muscle and bone.

"Forget suing him. We can do something else. It's the thirtieth anniversary of the photograph this year. We could contact Andrew Ford. Suggest a reunion. Bet he'll do it if you ask."

There was a stapler on his desk, and glass in the picture frame, and a heavy clock which told him it was just before four. He walked straight past Stephen.

As soon as he was out of the office, he felt better. He pounded along to the end of his corridor, put a hand out to the fire door but heard a hammering of footsteps behind him. He turned quickly; Stephen was jogging towards him, hands held up in mock surrender.

"Wait!"

"I have a patient to meet."

There was a family due in for a preoperative check, a private case. A boy, three months old, large VSD requiring pulmonary artery banding. Satish pushed through the fire door and kept going.

At the end of his corridor was the outpatients' waiting room, peopled by nervous adults and their

242

charges. Oversized cuddly toys loomed over them, each one a gift from a grateful parent. Stephen stayed quiet as they passed, then he was off again.

"Hang on, don't do this. Christ! Just ask him. He'll pay us to be in it this time — he'll have to."

"I didn't reply to your letters. Any of them. What does that tell you? I'm not interested." Satish looked at Stephen, who was a little out of breath from trotting behind him. "I don't know why you are."

"Think about it: money to be in the picture. Money to be interviewed about it. Newspapers, magazines — don't you think they'll all want a piece of this?"

"I don't want his money. I don't want to have anything to do with this."

"Please."

They stopped at an intersection of corridors. To have Stephen pursuing him again, even after all these years, even in this public place . . . Satish took a step backwards.

"You need to leave now."

"We never got our share. And now . . . It's been thirty years. How much longer will people still be interested? It's all right for you, with your posh job and your nice house and that. What about the rest of us?"

"You're unbalanced. That's a *professional* opinion. Leave me alone. If you care about it that much, ask Ford yourself. See how far that gets you."

"I did."

Satish considered the lift, its confined space, and headed off right instead, up the stairs. Stephen's voice echoed in the stairwell.

"I asked him and he's not interested. Not unless you do it."

They passed Clare Munroe going down. She nodded a greeting. Stephen was silent until she'd reached the floor they'd just come from, then he started up again.

"The problem is, he's not interested in *me*. He thanked me politely. Do you know what it means, when someone thanks you politely?" Stephen moved quickly, placing himself in Satish's way, on the step above him. "I bet no one's ever thanked you politely, have they? It means they're not interested. If someone thanks you politely they're showing you the fucking door."

Satish was finding it hard to listen. He was back in 1977, pulled there by this sense memory, this view of Stephen from below. Not Stephen's voice, not his restlessness — not even his smell, which came to Satish now, the cumin smell of sweat — nothing brought back the past like this simple perspective: him being smaller, Stephen being bigger.

"He doesn't know who I am. But he'll listen to you. Even if you don't need this, the rest of us do. Talk to Andrew Ford."

Satish sidestepped him and kept climbing. He could see the doors leading to the ward. He opened them and realised that Stephen wasn't following.

"Just talk to him!"

The words were silenced as Satish closed the doors behind him. In the waiting area a couple sat close together, a baby lying across the man's lap. Satish ducked into the disabled toilet and rushed for the bowl, heaving and coughing, vomiting in long, pumping retches. He spat then puked again, grabbing toilet paper to wipe his mouth. For a long time, he couldn't get up.

Stephen, and the smell of him. Skinning a cat. He gagged again.

It took a while to settle down. Satish made himself breathe regularly, washed his mouth out and waited by the basin.

Then he left the toilet and went to see his patient. He had a job to do.

Later that day on his rounds, Satish had to administer diazepam. Afterwards, the part-empty bottle had seemed like an invitation. He had slipped it into his pocket, telling himself he could bin it later. He transferred it to his briefcase the next time he went to his office, and walked out with it when he left the hospital that night. He kept expecting the security man to come after him, braced himself for the sound of running, shoulders tensed until he turned the corner into the next road. But there was nothing.

When he got home, he'd taken his briefcase into the garage and put the bottle on his workbench. He'd backed away and stared at it for a long time. He could hear Maya in the kitchen, banging around making dinner, fiddling with the volume on the radio. Diazepam: it was what you gave patients to calm them down before a procedure. Kids are infinitely adaptable. When they're ill, they're a lot more accepting of things than adults are. It's what parents don't realise when their child is first diagnosed, and maybe what ends up being most painful to them: their child's stoicism. This can sometimes break down though, often in the last few minutes before a procedure, when the kids get scared, want their mums. Diazepam relaxes them and lulls them to sleep. It stops them fighting the inevitable.

When Stephen Chandler came, Satish had known what those kids felt like, that rising sense of panic in the face of uncontrollable events. He'd witnessed it hundreds of times, but when Stephen came he'd *felt* it, he was feeling it now. He knew if he took a light dose he'd calm down and sleep well that night. His muscles would relax, he'd feel less anxious.

He thought about the perils of self-medication, then he dismissed the thought: it just didn't apply in this case. If he went to his GP, she'd only end up prescribing it for him, he was sure. It was what you did for anxiety; he was just cutting out the middleman. He had the same training as any other doctor, the same instincts, and in his informed opinion this was fine, a one-off.

He'd calculated the dosage with precision, taken just two spoonfuls — a conservative amount — then tucked the bottle back into the briefcase. No one's being deprived, he'd told himself, waiting for it to kick in, no one will know.

It took a while for the calm spread of the medicine to reach him. He put Stephen out of his mind: him and his brother, the loose cannons of Cherry Gardens. He thought instead of the others, his memories moving in the clarity of black and white down the table towards himself: Mrs Miller, Miss Walsh, Mandy, Cai, Satish.

Mandy, Cai, Satish.

246

CHAPTER
TWENTY-THREE

Satish is knuckling down. Faced with a choice which is no choice at all (the rock, the hard place) he's contacted Andrew Ford and agreed to be in the photograph. His decision comes with certain consequences, and here's one: it's a Sunday morning and Satish is being borne, laboriously, towards Cai. Maya and the kids in the Volvo, easing forward on the M25. Cai had rung and offered lunch, and Satish had struggled briefly, stacking up excuses, then he told himself: as well now as later, it will give me a chance to make some things clear, and he'd said: All right, then.

On the way he fields Mehul's questions: Who are we going to see? Where do they live? Why are we seeing them? Why haven't we met them before?

"I used to play with Cai a lot when I was a child," Satish says. "He lived next door and we went to the same school. But he moved away to another country when I was twelve and we haven't seen each other since."

He didn't see any of them. Once he'd started at Bassetsbury Boys' he fell in with the Nareshes and the Amrits and the Sanjays, bussing over to the next town if he wanted company.

"You'll both be famous now," says Asha. "Will Cai be nice?"

"I don't know," he tells her, and he sees Maya frowning at him. "I'm sure he will."

But Cai was never *nice*. More exciting than that, most of the time. More scary sometimes. He had dreamed of a great future for them both — and here it is, on some level: a consultant driving to see a lion keeper for Sunday lunch. Lion keeper. Cai might have been happy with this, had he known. But that wasn't the plan. The plan was for them both to be spies.

They'd seen *The Man With The Golden Gun* on telly at Christmas, and after that they only wanted to be 007. Cai's mum said Roger Moore was rubbish, that Sean Connery was the best James Bond — "he can leave his gun under my bed any night" — but it was too late. They could look like Roger Moore, easy, said Cai, in the Kung Fu scene. He showed Satish how, wearing his pyjama bottoms and dressing gown and striking a Kung-Fu pose. The next day, Satish turned up in slacks and a shirt with the first three buttons undone. Cai looked at him for a long time before saying, "Brill! We can both do that, can't we? See — it's *easy!*"

Cai knew all about being a spy, he assured Satish. He'd read about it. When you grow up, there are spies whose job it is to find other spies. When you're about to leave school they find you. They take you to a secret place, and they show you the stuff they'll give you, the car and the guns and the gadgets that Q has made for you. There are also beautiful women. They will give you all of this, but you have to say you'll leave right now.

They'll change your identity and you'll never see your family again, but it will be worth it because you're doing it for your country. For the Queen. If you agree to it, they'll take you away in a helicopter.

"Which people do they pick?"

"Us," said Cai. "They'll pick us because we're already interested, and practising, and dressing right. They like people who are good at PE because of all the fights. You've got to be good at PE."

They practised. Satish wasn't sure about the PE idea, but he tried. At home, they chose their numbers (008 for Satish, 009 for Cai) and had a go at spying, setting each other tasks and reporting back. Satish had to find out what Cai was having for tea without his mum seeing, and Cai had to take one of Sima's books from her bedside table.

They'd say the lines they heard on TV, drawing a bead on each other with imaginary guns. Cai had a go at doing the title sequence, walking along and then suddenly turning sideways and firing. He tried it a few times, got it down pat.

His friend was right, thought Satish, Cai could be a spy — easy. He wasn't so sure about himself, though. Weren't spies meant to be inconspicuous sometimes? When they weren't facing down a villain or gambling in a casino, weren't they meant to blend into the background so they could find out secrets? He didn't fancy his chances much. But in that last winter with Cai he suspended his disbelief and they carried on preparing for the day when, coming home from school, they'd be intercepted by a man in a sharp suit with a glossy car, ready to helicopter them away to a life of gadgets, and guns, and girls.

Maya is bored. She's slipped off her shoes and put her feet on the dashboard, a bad habit of hers. He thinks about mentioning the airbag, but decides not to.

"You never talk about Cai," she says to him.

"I haven't seen him for thirty years."

"I know but there must be childhood things. You still see Colette." Not at the moment he doesn't. "I know more about him from Colette than I do from you."

"There's not much to say. He lived in my street when we were kids."

"I don't know what to expect."

"Nor do I."

"OK then."

They round a bend and the motorway is glittering with cars. Satish steps on the brake, reaching out to click on the hazard light. "Papa!" says Asha. "Careful! I lost my place!"

"If you look at the road you will see there's something of a traffic jam," he tells her. "If I hadn't stopped we'd have crashed."

"You could have done it more carefully."

"Eleven going on fourteen," mutters Maya.

"What?"

"It's *pardon*, Asha, and I said you were rude. Be polite, please. Papa's trying to get us there safely. You shouldn't be reading anyway. It'll make you feel sick."

"Fine." She snaps her book shut. "What will I do now?"

"Well, you could enjoy Papa's fascinating stories about his childhood. They're *filled* with incident."

"When will we get there?" asks Mehul.

"I have no idea," says Satish. "Could be twenty minutes, could be another hour at this rate." Both children wail in unison.

"Can we listen to some music?" Asha asks.

"Tell us about the incident," says Mehul.

"What do you mean?"

"He means the childhood incident," says Asha. "Mum said."

He tries to crawl forward but stalls. For a few seconds, there's just the ticking of the hazards, and he waits for what she's going to say next.

"No," Maya says slowly to the kids, but not taking her eyes off him. "I said they're *filled* with incident. But I was joking, teasing Papa. He doesn't have any stories. Do you?"

"No."

Behind them, there's hooting. Satish starts the car again; it's barely worth changing up from first. Satish has been careful, *scrupulous*, about what he has told Maya. She was his fresh start, his clean sheet. So maybe it's innocent, all this probing.

"You must have some stories," says Mehul.

"That child should be strapped in," says Satish. "Look at that! No seatbelt. On a motorway."

"Tell us about Cai. When you were naughty."

Satish can see what's causing the jam now: a van on its side on the hard shoulder, the driver in the back of an ambulance, blanket-draped. They crawl by, rubber-necking like everyone else. The kids go quiet.

"Throw him a bone," says Maya. "Throw me one. Throw us a scrumped apple or something."

"All right. I once made Sima eat a grasshopper when she was a baby, in Uganda. She was too small to do anything about it and I made her eat it anyway."

"Urghh! Yuk!"

"That's, like, gross," says Asha.

"Does she know? I'm going to tell her," says Mehul.

"That's naughty," Asha agrees. "But tell us an English one. Tell us about you and Cai."

The traffic's moving freely now. They're on their way.

"We listened to music together. We played football."

"No, Papa! What was, like, the *worst* thing you and Cai did? What was the worst thing Cai did?"

He's nearly past the junction when he decides. He cuts across one lane, then the next, a neat piece of geometry that sends him sailing up the slip-road. When he reaches the roundabout he barely looks right. They wrap round it, passing signs to places he doesn't want to go, heading back the way they've come.

"Hang on," says Maya. "This is . . . Are we . . . ?"

"Sorry," he says. "I'm feeling rough. We'll cry off."

He can't see Cai. Not yet. They're back on the motorway and going to the only place he wants to be right now: home.

CHAPTER
TWENTY-FOUR

Satish at home on Jubilee morning, waiting for the party to start. Up in his room and staring out of the window. He keeps remembering it, that one word: TROUBLE! scrawled on a big sheet of paper, a smiley face dotting the exclamation mark, and Mandy's own smiley face gurning beside it. Satish watched her, pressed up against her bedroom window as he was against his. He'd flipped a quick thumbs-up and turned, then clattered downstairs and out of his front door.

Halfway across the road he checked: no one down his end. At the other end of Cherry Gardens he could see Mr Miller up a ladder, fixing a length of bunting that had come down. Mandy's dad was talking to him from the street below.

Mandy's front door was open, like his own — most were at this late stage of the morning — and Satish slipped quickly inside. He would have gone straight up to her, had in fact just placed his foot on the bottom step, but then he stopped because he could smell the cakes.

The air in the hall was heavy with their scent, and he knew that behind the closed kitchen door there was

253

another wave of it, damp and glorious. Smelling it, he knew what those cakes would be like, fresh out of the oven, still warm, their tops darker than the sponge underneath, that thrilling contrast between the fissured, almost-crusty surface and the soft mouthfuls below. The golden circle at their base would still be shiny with melted butter. All that would go once the cakes had cooled down. Better to slip into the kitchen right now, see if he could talk Mandy's mum round. Maybe she'd let him take one up for Mandy, too. Satish reached out for the door handle, then —

"Take it."

It was a man's voice. Satish thought about who he'd just seen in the street: definitely Mr Hobbes. So who was this? He heard a little click, the sound of a tongue detaching itself from the roof of a mouth, the sound you hear when someone's getting ready to speak. Then the voice came again.

"Take it!"

The words came out solid and weighty. Satish imagined them shooting across the kitchen towards Mandy's mum. And then he knew he shouldn't be there. He looked up the stairs for a moment, deliberated: Mandy was waiting for him. Then he turned the other way, slipping in through the open sitting-room door. James Bond, he thought, and he wished he had his dressing gown on. There was a wall that divided the sitting room from the dining room, and an arch cut into it, just like in his house. He could peek through the arch into the dining room and maybe see through the serving hatch, if it was open.

"Pete." That was Mandy's mum's voice. She said it quietly. Who was Pete? and then, "I don't need it."

Satish crouched low against the wall and edged round to the arch. Wait till he told Cai. Cai would love this.

"Just take it." Inside the kitchen he heard the man sigh.

On hands and knees, Satish inched along until he could see the hatch, one door bolted closed, the other open. The opening was blocked by the man's back. He was wearing a red jumper.

"Red jumper," Satish imagined whispering into Q's communication device. "Please identify."

Then the man turned and picked up something from the counter; Satish ducked out of the way. He'd seen the man, though. It was Mr Brecon. It was Cai's dad. One side of his shirt collar stuck out of his jumper at a funny angle, and his signet ring caught the light when he moved his hand. What was he doing there?

"Put it away," Mr Brecon told Mandy's mum. "A nest egg. You might not need it now, maybe not for years. But if you put it away somewhere safe, then you've got the option. Leave yourself some options."

Satish could hear movement in the kitchen: a step, a rustle. He dared himself to look. Mandy's mum was leaning back against the sink, her arms folded. The cakes were next to her, lined up on a rack. She'd iced half of them in royal blue then she'd stopped. She tilted her head to one side and her dark hair swung down and touched her shoulder.

"I have options," she said. "Plenty. You don't have to provide me with any. And what about Don? How do I explain it to him?"

"You don't. You open an account and you don't put his name on it. I won't be around anymore."

"Of course."

"You understand? I won't be back. It's for good."

"I know." She smiled and reached out a hand, then withdrew it.

"It's three hundred quid. The only thing I've ever —" And there was a *bang!* which made Satish jump out of sight. He sat for a second with his hand on his chest and his eyes wide while in the kitchen the *bang* happened again, and he realised Mr Brecon was hitting the counter. "God, you're stubborn! Bloody hell!" Mr Brecon — *Pete* — was saying, "What if you hit a bad patch? What if you needed . . . Bloody hell!"

At this point, James Bond would step in, Satish thought. There was a woman in there, and a man who was hitting things and swearing. Should he go in? He took another peek. She didn't look worried. Her arms were still folded and she was watching Mr Brecon. He had moved closer to her, and his face looked hard, angry. He looked determined, the way Cai did sometimes, the way —

"Pete, calm down. He'll be back in a minute."

"I'm not taking it back. I'm leaving it here." He pointed to the counter. "You're going to keep it."

Mr Brecon turned away from her, facing the open hatch door, and Satish went to hide again but he realised he didn't need to, because Mr Brecon had

256

pressed his lips together tightly and shut his eyes. How angry was he, wondered Satish. What would he do? He looked as if he was trying to stop something bursting out. Then he turned round again and Satish could see only his back.

"Mandy should have it," said Mr Brecon. "If you don't want it, at least take it for her."

"Absolutely not. Now, you have to leave."

This was impenetrable. Satish wondered, momentarily, if they were playing Spies too, if they were using some kind of code. The things they were saying didn't make sense. Mr Brecon wanted to give Mandy three hundred pounds (why?). She'd love that, Satish knew, yet her mum didn't want her to have it (why again?).

"Take it for her," Mr Brecon repeated. "She's my girl."

"Shut up!" Her words came out before he had finished. Satish flinched. "You just shut up and don't say that again in here."

He thought of Mr Brecon's determined face, the way Cai looked sometimes. The way Mandy did, sometimes. He thought of Mrs Hobbes's bedroom and the Indian bedspread, and Mr Hobbes's with the closed curtains and no pictures on the walls. He thought of Mr Hobbes shouting into his own letterbox, asking to be let in. Then it was like a puzzle that you shook, and things rearranged themselves, and Satish felt stupid and clever all at once. Mandy. Mr Brecon. Mandy and Mr Brecon! Mrs Hobbes was really angry, so it must be true. His best bit of spy work ever — ever! — and he knew at once that he could never tell Cai.

"Pete, you have to leave now."

In the kitchen, there was a long silence. After a while, Mr Brecon spoke. "When I'm gone, will you send photos?" His voice was low and tight.

"You have no idea how this works, do you?"

"You could write sometimes, tell me how she's doing."

"How it works is, you're gone. That's fine, that's your choice, but I can't do letters. I won't do photographs."

"OK. OK."

"Pete, you're impossible . . ." On the other side of the red jumper, Mandy's mum moved. A second later her hand was on Mr Brecon's arm. She rubbed it. Satish could hear the sound of a kiss being quickly deposited. Upstairs, floorboards shifted. Mandy had called him over ages ago. Maybe she'd seen him coming over. Maybe she'd wonder what he was doing.

"She's a good girl," Mr Brecon said.

"I know. She's a very good girl. She's *my* girl."

"Keep an eye on her, eh?"

"I always do."

Up on the landing, a door opened. Satish jumped. He could hear footsteps coming to the top of the stairs, then pausing. If Mandy came down, she would see him spying. If her mum came out to see Mandy, she'd discover Satish too, and know what he'd heard. Only a few feet away from him was the kitchen door. It could swing open at any time. In the dining room, the yawning hatch waited to reveal him. Beyond the kitchen the front door was ajar, but it was too late now because (one, two, three) Mandy had started to come down.

258

"*Really* keep an eye, though," said Mr Brecon.

Mandy's mum answered slowly: "What do you mean?"

Four, five, six. He'd counted the stairs in his own house; they were just the same, so he knew where she was. She was rounding the curve of the banister.

"Pete? What do you mean?"

Two more steps and Mandy would see him.

Satish waited, grimacing, but the steps never came. Mandy had stopped for some reason. Then there was the sound of friction, of a foot turning on carpet, and he heard her mumble something, and — yes! yes! — retrace her steps. He slumped down, reprieved, as Mr Brecon carried on talking.

"She's growing up, and she's . . . Have you noticed how she . . .?" Mr Brecon stopped.

In the quiet that followed Satish thought: that's it, I'm off, and he rolled onto his knees, ready to ease upright and make his way upstairs. No cakes for him now, he realised, and even in the drama of the moment, hiding in someone else's sitting room, hearing secrets he was never supposed to know about, he found that he was disappointed.

"Do you know what I saw her doing this morning? Do you know where she was, Pam?"

Satish did. He let out a little "oh" of fright, bumping back onto his bottom, and then was frightened in case they'd heard. That morning, Mandy had been with him, in his bedroom. They'd been kissing. In a hot rush he saw it all; him and Mandy together, and Mr Brecon (her dad!) seeing them. He pulled himself out of sight of the serving hatch as if his embarrassment made him more visible, as if Mr Brecon could *keep an eye on him*, even with his back turned.

From inside the kitchen, he could hear Mr Brecon telling Mandy's mum what he'd seen, every word of it mortifying. Satish waited for her to be cross and she was, her voice sharp as she replied, but — the surprise, the relief — he found that she wasn't cross with *him*. She reserved her anger for Mr Brecon — "I take exception to that, actually. It's scarcely your business" — but Satish put his face in his hands anyway. He had thought himself and Mandy to be completely enclosed for those few moments, sealed off from anything external. The news that there had been a witness wrenched his vision of the thing, and he suddenly saw the open door of his bedroom, the treacherous window. He imagined the front of his home hinging open like a doll's house, exposing him and Mandy to view. Everything would be known; everything would be punished. And what else was public, if that was public? He thought of Cai's hidden record, of Mrs Brecon crying in her room.

"You want to be watching out for that. She'll only suffer in the long run. Cheeky Paki bugger!"

"Be careful, now. I take good care of her. She's turning out lovely. You'll be six thousand miles away in no time and you still think you've got the right —"

"She's my daughter. I think it's fair enough."

"I said shut up about that! You can't say that in here. Don could come in at any time. Get out now."

As she said this, the garden gate banged back on its hinges. From inside the kitchen, there was a drawing of breath.

Satish got to the bottom stair just as the handle started to turn. *Leg it!* He bounded upstairs, galvanised by contradictory impulses: Be quick! Be quiet! Have they seen you? Don't look back! Shit! Fuck! Bugger! Bum! All the forbidden words tumbling in him like dice. Behind him, he heard it: Mr Hobbes coming in the back ("All sorted now"), Mr Brecon diving out the front. Satish ducked down behind the low parapet on the landing and breathed, in, out, in, out.

Up here, behind her bedroom door, was Mandy. Cai's dad was her dad, too. She was Cai's sister — sort of. Satish tried to pull himself back to what was happening before he knew all this. TROUBLE! He remembered: she wanted to see him. Act normal. She must never know about any of this. Satish knocked and went in.

CHAPTER
TWENTY-FIVE

Mandy was standing on her mattress, Sellotaping the corner of a poster to the wall. She heard him come in, turned and dropped onto the bed with a little bounce.

"Blimey, Satish. What took you? You were ages."

Her bare legs kicked rhythmically against the divan drawers. Satish watched her for a moment and found his thoughts sliding away from her mum and Mr Brecon and the panic of discovery. There was just the bang-bang-bang of her kicking pulling him backwards through the day to the moment of their kiss. He thought about the wet mystery of it, the softness and the taste, and the embarrassment. How did you talk about it to the girl afterwards? Mandy seemed to be taking it in her stride. A year younger than him, but looking straight at him without shame: no need to do as he did now, removing his gaze to something else, no wobbly hot feeling in her limbs or on her face. Then he thought that she had asked him a question, and that he had been quiet for too long.

"Just my mum. Stuff to do — you know."

"Yeah."

"You said there was trouble."

"Real trouble," she told him. "Colette saw us earlier. And her dad. Now Sarah knows. She's furious."

Satish took this in. If Sarah knew then there really would be trouble. Sarah was *furious*, Mandy said.

"Why's she so angry?"

Mandy did look away now, down at her feet, which were still beating against the side of her bed: one-two, one-two.

"I don't know. She just is. She was surprised. She was cross I hadn't told her."

Did girls always go like this? he wondered. Angry. *Furious.* He saw, with clarity, the peril he was in. Colette, Sarah, Mr Brecon: the secret leaking out on all sides. Mummy and Papa would hear about it; *that* was furious, he thought bitterly. You want to see angry? Try my parents. It would leak down the street to the school, trickle into the playground. Oh no! It came to him suddenly: Mandy would be in for it too. The unspoken rationale for their secrecy hung over him: she was a girl, and younger. He was an Asian. They were both liabilities. There were lots of ways they could suffer for this; she could be shunned. He'd watched her enough with Sarah to know what that would mean, and he couldn't imagine — not for a moment — that she'd ever think it was worth it. As for him, he'd kissed a white girl, an English girl. He didn't want to think of all the things that could be messed up by this. He searched for something to say to Mandy.

"Don't worry about it," he offered, though it occurred to him that she scarcely seemed worried at all.

"I'll think of something. Go to the party. It might just — it might just be forgotten."

Mandy snorted. "You should have seen Sarah. I'm fed up with her, anyway. I don't care what she thinks. She's not in charge."

"Yeah, I know. Look, Mandy, I've got to go home, get ready. I'll see you in a bit."

At her front door he paused, peering out to check that no one would spot him leaving. Over the way, his own house was quiet. No movement from Cai's, either. Nobody, he thought, would see him slipping away from Mandy's place and across the road to home. The door shut behind him with a click, and he legged it.

CHAPTER
TWENTY-SIX

They're lying in the dark, each pretending they've drifted off, neither fooled by the other; it's hard to fake that shallow-sleep breathing. Just a little longer, surely, until his dose kicks in. Around them, the house has closed down for the night. They've heard his mother's bedside light clicking off, Mehul has shuffled to the toilet for the last time. There's the ground bass, felt more than heard, of his father's snoring.

Beside him, Maya whispers: "You can tell me anything."

He thinks if he waits for a while, he might still get away with it. Then she says: "Chocolate?" The family joke, the word you'll always respond to, even through strategic deafness, and he laughs, despite himself. The mattress dips as she squirms onto her side.

"You can tell me *anything*. I'm not going anywhere."

"Nothing to tell," he says. "Go to sleep. I'm tired."

"Liar."

"Go to sleep."

She moves closer. There's the warmth of her — and those cold, cold feet. She hooks one over his, her arch across the front of his foot. "OK," she says. "Stop me when I've got it right. You've gambled away all our money, you want to join a circus, you want to be a girl, you've lost your job —"

"Stop it, Maya."

"Is it the job?"

"Please. Sleep."

She switches on the lamp and he slams his eyes shut, hiding behind his hand: dark red. He lifts his hands and it's a screen of red-orange. Beautiful. He looks at it as long as he can.

"Satish, talk to me. Open your eyes!" When he does, she's sitting up against the headboard, knees scrunched to her chest. "Come on."

"*Come on* what? What do you want me to say?"

"Shush!" She glances towards the door. "Don't raise your voice. Why make this so hard?"

"Well, I don't know what you want from me."

She pinches her nose and frowns. "There's something wrong, I know there is."

"It's . . ." He looks over at the clock. ". . . one o' clock in the morning and I've got work tomorrow. This is silly. It's disproportionate."

The wrong word, maybe: too cold, too pompous. It moves her up a gear.

"I hate it when you do that," she says, slapping her hand down between them. "You treat me as if I'm stupid."

"I don't."

"Yes! As if I'm really stupid. And this is not *disproportionate*. This is . . . evidence-based!"

"Evidence-based? Am I some kind of patient, then?"

"God! I'm just saying . . . I'm trying to do this in a nonthreatening way."

Something shifts in him. "Oh, are you? And if you wanted to be *threatening*, what would you do then, Maya?"

He turns away from her, his legs hanging over the edge of the bed, and doesn't know what to do next. He can tell from her silence that she doesn't know either. They stay suspended like this until he thinks she's about to speak, and finds he's afraid of what she might say. Then he propels himself forward and out of the room.

The fridge light spills out into the kitchen. He likes the darkness of the rest of the room, the privacy it gives him. It calms him down. He pours himself a glass of juice to give himself something to do, a reason to be down here so he can tell himself he hasn't just walked out on his wife in the middle of an argument. He hasn't. He's thirsty. He puts the glass down and leans over, hands on the counter, head dipping down below his shoulder blades. He's like that when she comes in.

"Did you really just do that? Did you just flounce off in the middle of a discussion?"

"*Flounce?*" he says, addressing the glass, his hands. (*Discussion?*)

"Don't jump straight in and dismiss me. There's something wrong. Let me —"

"This is ridiculous."

"See, right there? Right there, dismissing me. Look: imagine you're living with someone, and they start behaving oddly. They start . . . doing things out-of-character."

"This is me now?"

"I think it is. Listen to me. Stuff like . . . not sleeping so well. You feel them beside you. They can't sleep. They don't talk to you so much. They're withdrawn. Look at me, Satish!"

"You are blowing this up out of all proportion."

There's no warning of his father's approach, locked into each other as they are. He comes through the kitchen door and into the gravitational pull of their argument, a new satellite.

"Oh." His dad stands at the door, not coming in, not leaving. "Sorry. I heard a noise. I wanted some water."

Maya turns away and fiddles with something by the sink.

"I woke up," his father adds.

"Yes. We were talking."

"Yes." His dad edges forward slightly. "I'll just . . . a glass." He moves round them both, leaving a wide berth, as if touching them would set something off. He gets his water then glances behind at them as he leaves.

"So, I'm *blowing this up out of all proportion?*" She enunciates with the kind of precision you use when you're trying not to shout. "I'm sure your dad will enjoy mulling that one over. And your mum, come to that."

"That's not my fault. I didn't hear him."

Maya steps closer to him. He tries not to step back.

"Listen to me," she says. "Because this is important."

"Please, let's just go to bed."

"You are withdrawn. You aren't sleeping." She counts it out on her fingers. "When you do it's this dead-to-the-world sleep, and when you wake up it's like I've pulled you from the bottom of a swamp." She stops mid-flow, as if recalling something. He thinks she's foundered, but she plunges on. "Something's wrong. I say things and suddenly it's the wrong thing, and I don't know why. I mean, all these years together, and I've got used to you and this even keel of yours, and now . . . what about that time when we were boxing? What was that about? What happened on the way to Cai's?"

"You are overreacting. In the morning this will all seem silly."

"If you loved someone and you knew something was wrong, you'd do something about it, wouldn't you? I love you, Satish."

"I love you, too," he says immediately. "Now let's go back to bed."

"So is that it? Is that your response? Is that all I get from you?"

He doesn't know what to say. He wants comfort, for himself as well as her, wants to do something reassuring but noncommittal. He reaches out to her, but she's already leaving, and he doesn't know who moved first, whether she knew he was reaching out and just didn't want him touching her.

"Fine." She goes over to the door. "Fine, but I'm not letting this go. If you won't believe me in the middle of the night, then sleep on it — if you can. This won't go away, Satish."

269

He hears her treading back along the hall and up the stairs. He can plot her course as she moves above him: into Asha's bedroom, into Mehul's. Long silences, absences of movement. Upset as she is, she'll stay a little longer than she needs to, getting a bit of comfort from her sleeping kids. Then finally back to their room, where she'll lie awake for a while. There should be a way to make peace without giving her what she wants, but he can't see how. It's too delicate a navigation and he feels ponderous, clumsy. He'll stay down here, keep himself busy.

Because Maya's right about one thing: he isn't sleeping, even with the diazepam. He makes himself acknowledge it: *I've built up a tolerance.* He hasn't tried kicking it again, not after that last blackmail note, so he takes it each night and it keeps the jitters at bay, but that's all it does now. What a bloody idiot, the worst kind: a doctor with a fool for a patient. As it turns out, his body is subject to chemistry, like anyone else's. Like anyone else, he will suffer now if he stops, an ironic assault comprising just those things he needed help with in the first place — anxiety, panic — only much worse than before. He could raise his dose for some relief, but he can't bear to — that's what addicts do, and he's not an addict. So he's in limbo, prowling the house at night anxious and sleepless. And the threatening notes . . . he's still waiting for the next one. With no idea who his blackmailer is, he can't tell them: *you win, I'm doing the photograph.* He doesn't know if they'll hold off until the reunion, whether they'll leave him alone after that.

270

Right now, he'll find something useful to do; he'll try to keep going until he's ready to drop. That's the key: distract himself for long enough to get tired, so that when he finally falls into bed he will sleep straightaway. No lying there in the dark, worrying over this present crisis, or slipping back into the past — and back, and back — to Jubilee Day.

CHAPTER
TWENTY-SEVEN

Cai couldn't wait for the barbecue. It was the burgers that got him. Even though they were all pinky-red with white bits of fat in them, and cold and a bit slimy, and you could squish them just a little with your fingers so that you left a dent in the greaseproof circle, even though they still had that dead-meat smell, you knew they'd be just lish really soon. The barbecue was burning, getting ready, and he'd asked his mum to get some of those cheese squares, the yellow-orangey ones that tasted creamy, and then he could squish tomato sauce onto it and squash the whole thing down in the bun. When the cheese and sauce dribbled over the edges he would take a bite and get all the flavours and textures at once.

He'd have the first burger. He always made his dad do that, and he didn't let his mum see, because he liked the insides a bit pink, still a bit bloody, and she'd have said, no, that's not safe, stick it back on, Peter. He liked to see the bite through the centre, to look at it side-on and see a thin black outside, a brown layer next and the pink right in the middle. That was a good burger. He couldn't wait. They wouldn't be on yet. His dad would still be poncing around. *What have you been doing with yourself, then*? Well, wouldn't you like to know? That's for me to know and you to find out. He imagined saying it, his hands in his pockets and his chin angled upwards. Dad didn't like hands in pockets. He didn't like you dragging your feet or saying *what* instead of pardon, or *bu* — er instead of butter. He didn't like Satish. Ha! That was for sure.

The thought of Satish made Cai feel sour. He drew his knees up to his chest and hugged them. This was a good place to sit. He could hunker down in front of the gatepost and no one would see him from inside the house, or from the back gate. He could look at other people's houses and watch people going by but no one at home could find him. Right now he can see the tables all set out. He can see underneath, where the legs and feet will be, and the top, all neat, laid out ready for the party. God Save the Queen? Johnny Rotten would *smash* this party! He'd push all the stuff off the table onto the ground and bash it with his guitar. He'd gob and vomit onto the table. No future! No future!

There was going to be a "Stuff the Jubilee" carnival in London today, Stephen Chandler had said. He'd talked big about it, said he was fourteen now and could easily go. Said he would catch a train and — stuff it! — just leave. But here he was in Cherry Gardens, and so was Cai, because he didn't know how to get there and his parents would kill him, just kill him, if he did go. If Johnny Rotten were here he would climb a ladder, grab that stupid bunting and pull it all down. He'd swing on it, and rip the flags to bits. Dad would look on, horrified, but not be able to do anything about it. His hands would go up to his mouth, he'd wave his fist at the Pistols. Or he'd be like a teacher, all straight and disapproving, like Bill Grundy on that programme, and they'd all take the piss.

When that programme went out, Cai hadn't even heard of the Pistols. In the months afterwards, he'd spent his time having Kung-Fu fights in his dressing gown and trying to look like James Bond. What a kid! What a fucking child! Thank God he'd woken up at last.

Over the road a door slammed, and he jumped: Mandy's place. Mandy. He stayed still, hoping she wouldn't see him. *Mandy and Satish!* He didn't want to talk to her, but it was no good. A voice called to him: "Cai? Cai!" and there were footsteps.

It was Sarah. Her face looked grim and her cheeks were pink. Her mouth was a hard line.

"Cai. I've just seen Mandy." Her arms were crossed over her chest and she stood tall above him. Really tall. He glanced down; she was wearing high red shoes. She looked grown-up.

He got to his feet. "I'm off," he said, turning away from her and setting off down the road. He passed the Chandlers' place and Sarah's semi on the other side but kept going. She followed him down the corridor created by the newly set table in the centre of the street. He could hear the clonk-clonk of her heels on the road. It was hard for her to keep up.

"I've seen Mandy," she tried again. "And I'm afraid I've got something not nice to tell you, only I feel I have to tell you, because it's not fair otherwise." She lengthened her stride to come level with him. "I know you fancy Mandy." She waved away his protests. "She told me everything, and I'm really sorry to tell you this, but she kissed Satish this morning. I thought you should know."

Fuck Mandy (she told me everything), and fuck Sarah (I thought you should know). He sped up, rounding the corner into the cul-de-sac, heading for the end of it, where they usually went to play footie.

"I know she kissed Satish. So what? My dad told me."

His dad had put a picture in his mind which he didn't want there. In this picture, Satish had kissed Mandy and she had closed her eyes for a long time. Satish had touched her and she liked it. Maybe the worst bit of this picture was that his sister and father had seen it all.

"Mandy said you'd kissed, and you fancied each other. It's all right. I haven't told anyone."

"You reckon? I don't fancy her. I did kiss her but I don't fancy her, and I don't care if she fancies Satish."

"But you —"

"I don't care!"

They'd arrived at the end of the close. Through the gap between the tree and the fence he could see the front wall of his school, and the teachers' car park. He sat down, wedging his bum against the base of the tree. Sarah hesitated — her clean jeans against that dusty earth, he guessed — and he looked away from her, willing her to leave. Instead she lowered herself, arranging the back of her top before she leaned against the trunk. Her feet stuck out in front of her.

A ripple of wind made its way down the street. Cai felt the cold on the back of his neck, the hairs rising.

"OK, so you don't care," Sarah said. "But I do."

"Yeah?"

"I do. Mandy doesn't know what she's doing." He stayed quiet and after a bit she carried on. "What does Satish do, at playtimes at school?"

"What do you mean?"

"Where does he go? Who does he hang around with?"

Cai thought. "Dunno. Hangs around in the playground. He sometimes talks to my sister."

"God!"

"Sometimes plays with Lee Davis."

"Satish is *lucky*."

Sarah leaned across and touched him. He looked down at her fingers on his skin. The nails were short arches, varnished a pearly pink, and he could see where the polish had slipped onto the sharp, sticky-up bits at the side of her nail. He considered pulling her hand up to his mouth and biting off those little shards. They'd feel prickly on his tongue. When he tugged at them, the soft parts would come off, too. It would hurt her. Cai's gaze skated down her fingers, along her hand and arm, and up to her face. She was looking back at him.

"He's lucky you even let him hang around with us. It is you that lets him, isn't it?"

"I —"

"Maybe because you're leaving, he thinks it's OK to do this sort of thing."

Behind them, in School Close, a woman suddenly raised her voice: "Pippa! It's after twelve! Get a move on!"

Not much time left now. He'd have to go home and dress up: the navy shirt, the blue trousers. No rips, no safety pins, no black. No future. He remembered the shadowy swastika on his thigh. He'd drawn it with a Biro, pretended it was a tattoo, but watched it fade night after night in the bath, nervous in case his mum came in. What a joke! Stuck here today, making no difference to anything at all. Next to him, Sarah's face creased in concern.

"It's outrageous," said Sarah. She pronounced the word — one of her mum's, he thought — with relish. She was right, though, it was *outrageous*, and suddenly he saw it with clarity: this wasn't about him and Mandy at all. He thought of Stephen Chandler trying to rub off Satish's colour, and himself, Cai, laughing along with the joke. And here he was now, imagining Mandy and Satish together, when any time he could just, he could just . . .

Sarah was getting up. "I'm off," she said. "I bet *Stephen* will do something about this." And she pulled herself upright, her shoes raising her higher than usual, so that when he said, *yeah, but you're*, he said it to her calves, and those calves strutted off as she walked up the road and turned the corner into Cherry Gardens. He didn't see the next bit, but he knew what it would be. Can you believe what Satish did? What a Paki did? And Cai's just let it happen.

He had two months to go in Cherry Gardens. It was hard to imagine South Africa at all, let alone what the kids there would be like, what kind of friends he might have. Two months to go as one of the gang. No, more than that: their leader. They listened to him, he decided things. But now there was Satish kissing Mandy as if it was OK to do that sort of thing, and Sarah going off to Stephen as if Cai didn't matter any more, as if he'd already left.

Cai went straight over to Satish's house. He was going to charge up to his room, he'd decided. If they made any noise Satish would have to tell his parents why and they'd kill him. As he got closer he glanced over at Mandy's, at her window and noticed a movement by her front door. Satish! Coming *out* of there, preparing to cross the road! Satish! It was true, then. Bastard! Cai felt his muscles bunch up and he started to run, clenching his teeth, but making himself hold back, hold back until you've got him. Satish had reached the middle of the road before he saw Cai, and he didn't look scared even then, not until Cai's outstretched arm had grabbed him by the shoulder of his T-shirt and pushed him backwards so that he had to scrabble to stay upright.

"Hey! What are you doing?"

"You wanker, Satish! You fucking wanker!"

He'd backed him up Mandy's driveway and against her garage door.

"What?"

278

Cai checked for witnesses; nothing. The blank walls of Miss Walsh's house, of Mandy's. Everyone was inside now. He felt Satish's heart banging against his hand. He held him against the door for a second, then let him go, then shoved him back into place again when Satish tried to move away.

"Stay there! I'm going to fucking have you! You kissed her! You kissed Mandy!"

He grasped Satish's shoulders, dug his fingers right in, and started to shake him. Satish's head was tossed backwards, making the metal door shiver. Then after one of the rebounds it shot forward, and Cai could see Satish's face coming towards him, and there was an impact, and pain, and Cai was kneeling in the centre of the driveway, his face in his hands.

"You fucking nutted me! I'm going to have you!"

"I'm going to have *you*, you — you bastard!"

Then Satish was on him, and they were pushing and pulling and trying to hit and trying not to get hit and trying to get a leg free to kick. Where was the punching, the clean strokes they saw on telly? Cai couldn't do it, so he went for any bits of Satish he could get to. His fist found Satish's side. He felt bone against his knuckles and heard a cry. Good. Then there was a hand slapping against Cai's face, twisting his head round. Cai heaved back and rolled on top of Satish and heard him shout out again.

As they struggled Cai could hear him muttering something, moving in and out of clarity as his mouth was muffled by the movements of their bodies. Cai pushed against him hard and scrambled to his feet.

279

"What?" Satish was panting. They both were. Cai stepped back, out of reach of hands and feet. "What are you saying?"

"I said, I kissed her. So what? Why are you doing this? Why do you care?"

Cai's mouth was filled with the things he couldn't say. He opened it and found it blocked, so he launched himself at Satish again, kicking and pulling and shaking and shouting.

"Stop being such a fucking girl! I don't *care*!" he yelled into his enemy's ear. "But she's not yours! She's not yours, Paki! You're a Paki!" He was sitting on Satish's hips, pinning his arms behind his head. The simplicity of it came as such a relief, he felt like crying. He got close to Satish's face — not too close — and told him, "That's just it! You're a Paki, so you can't kiss Mandy. You're Splatish."

Satish didn't say anything. He turned his face to the side and didn't look at Cai. Then he bucked and kicked, trying to throw Cai off him. There was no point to this any more. Cai waited until Satish stopped, then quickly hopped up and away.

"I've had enough of you," Cai told him. "I can't be bothered. Stay away from me, or I'll beat you up some more."

Cai crossed the road and went through his own back gate. The kitchen door was unlocked, the kitchen empty. He sat on the floor next to the oven and pulled his knees up to his chest. He waited there a long while, until he felt clearer and could decide what to do next.

CHAPTER
TWENTY-EIGHT

Satish had been beaten up by Cai. No: he and Cai had fought. He'd given as good as he'd got. After Cai left, he didn't know which direction to go in: back to his house, where his parents would see him? Unthinkable. He didn't want them to be involved; he couldn't have said if it was more for their protection or his. At the end of Mandy's drive the street was deserted. He didn't want to walk into it. He couldn't go into Mandy's garden, but he could stay here, tucked into the angle between Mandy's house and her dad's garage, and hope no one would see him.

He prodded himself to assess the damage. His ribs were painful on the left side and the back of his neck hurt, probably from Cai banging his head against the garage door. There was a graze on his right elbow, little wellsprings of blood rising through it. Come on, you didn't do badly, he told himself, and then it came back in a frightening rush: Cai calling him a Paki, calling him Splatish. They weren't friends any more. He tried to comfort himself — Cai was leaving anyway — but it didn't work. Cai! If he was a Paki to Cai, he was a Paki to all of them. All of them, even the ones he hadn't met yet: in his new school, wherever he went.

Satish made himself breathe a few times, taking deeper and deeper breaths that deliberately hurt his ribs, so he could practise. He couldn't go home yet. He thought of Cherry Gardens, its glaring windows. School would be safe, though; just round the corner, the buildings shut for the day, and Satish knowing all the best places to hide.

He set off, staring straight ahead as if he had somewhere to go. He'd nearly made it to the end of the road, skirting the trestle tables on his right, when he heard the shout: "Oi! Splatish!" The Chandlers. Not wanting to face their casual taunting, he jogged up to the end of the road and turned left. He could see the tree, the gap you went through to get to the school. He could see the school gates.

"Oi!" They must have sped up. They were rounding the corner now.

"Leave me alone!"

Satish flapped a hand behind him to bat them away, but they kept on coming, and someone else with them: Sarah, clip-clopping in her high heels, a few paces behind. He reached the tree and looked back again; they had nearly caught up, and there was something in their bearing, in Paul's head-forward impetus, Stephen's nearly-smile, that made him afraid. Stephen was holding something behind his back.

The gate was locked, so he had to vault over it. When he went to swing his leg over he was caught by a jab of pain in his side, and as he steadied himself they reached him. He expected them to pull him off but they didn't. Paul grabbed his foot and levered him over the gate so that he fell on the other side with a cry as his ribs and arm were hurt again. When he dabbed at the graze on his elbow blood came off on his fingers.

"Leave me alone!" he told them again, scrabbling to get up as first Paul and then Stephen straddled the gate. Sarah was pacing on the other side, searching for a different way in.

Satish ran towards the building, veering off to the right, past the climbing frame where the Chandlers had made the boy fall all those years ago, and into the adventure playground. He heard the crunch-patter of feet following him, heard panting and laughing. Ducking behind the climbing net, he saw Paul and Stephen face him through the squares of rope. They swayed on their feet like goalies, the bag Stephen carried with him bumping against his leg.

With a sudden, twitching burst of energy, Stephen made a feint towards him.

"Come on, Splatish," he said, beckoning. "Let's be having you."

"Cai's already done it! We . . . he hit me. Look!" He pointed his elbow at them.

Stephen laughed. "We're not going to hit you. Are we, Paulie?"

"Nope." Paul shook his head.

Then Satish saw Sarah arrive behind them and the boys moved to the ends of the net so they could rush him from each side, and he ran towards the slide, and climbed its steps because it was the only place to go. He looked down to see Paul at the bottom, arms wide like a father waiting to catch him, and Stephen behind, climbing up the steps, the handles of his Wavy Line bag balled up in his fist.

Satish thought of Mrs Hirsch, the playground supervisor they always tried to avoid because she was so strict. What would she say about this? What would she do to Paul and Stephen if she were here? But there was no one in the playground; the doors of the school were locked, the windows empty. Two against one. It would hurt more than before, but at least Satish could get some of his own blows in. No choice, anyway.

He slid down to Paul, feet out, hands out, and when Paul caught him at the bottom Satish kicked and thrashed, hitting out at any parts he could reach. Then he felt a wallop as Stephen slid down, his feet hammering into Satish's back. After that, it was easy for them.

They dragged him into the cramped space under the slide. Satish twisted round but Paul held him easily.

"Now, Splatish. We've got a little lesson to teach you." Paul raised his eyebrows and a cartoonish grin stretched across his face.

Satish pulled away in a sudden jerking movement. Paul, unfazed, reached out to grab him again. Big and stocky, and so much older, he could subdue him without really trying. His strong hand squeezed Satish's upper arm.

"Stay," he said softly.

Satish noticed the clean white T-shirt over his jeans, and wondered if he was dressed for the party already; he told himself that no one would dress like that if they really meant to get into a fight. And he was too young,

284

anyway, or they were too old, fourteen and fifteen and going to secondary school. He saw himself as they might see him, a kid, and thought perhaps that in itself might protect him. Then he remembered the stories about the National Front demo in Ranjeet's street, and Ranjeet's neighbour pulling his little daughter to safety as she shouted at the marchers.

"We need to teach you a lesson," Sarah was saying as she came over.

We? He wanted to laugh. She was eleven — eleven! — and dwarfed by the Chandlers, even though she was wobbling on her too-high heels.

"Go away, Sarah. Go home."

Beside Satish, Paul snorted.

"Go away! Go home! A good bit of advice, Splatish. Do you ever feel like taking it?"

Sarah was undeterred.

"You kissed Mandy. You kissed an English girl. Pakis shouldn't do that. We're going to teach you a lesson," she repeated.

Stephen joined her, the four of them crammed under the apex of the slide. He was pulling something out of his bag.

"Yeah, if you feel like a snog, go back to where you came from." He pulled a box out of the bag, and something out of the box; something red. He balanced the object on his palm. "If you have to do it, do it with some other brown bastard." Then he turned to Sarah.

"So, tell me again about the beef?"

Sarah passed her tongue over her upper lip.

"Satish can't eat beef. He thinks cows are *sacred*. I heard him tell Cai."

"Yeah, I've heard something like that," said Stephen. "But I would think, and tell me if I'm wrong here, I would think that's something he got from his own country? Isn't it, Satish? That's not an English thing, is it?"

The thing on his hand was a beefburger: raw, broken in half, the spots of fat showing white against the meat.

"We do eat beef here in England," Stephen went on. "Boiled beef and carrots! Roast beef. We love the stuff! Today we're having beef burgers to celebrate the Jubilee and I would suggest . . ." He shifted the burger in his hand, grimacing. ". . . that there's no better time for you to try it, Splatish. You want to live here, you like English girls, you'll love English food. Open up."

This couldn't happen. It could not happen. Satish clamped his mouth shut and turned his head away. It banged against the bottom of the slide. He kicked out towards Stephen, who sidestepped casually and berated his brother, "Legs, Paulie!"

Paul snaked his own leg round and brought his heel down onto Satish's left foot. The movement swung the two boys together and as they crushed up close Paul confided, "I will do that again," as if Satish needed the warning. His foot burned, the tender toes delineated by precise lines of pain.

Stephen was close now, the dreadful lump of meat closer still, right in front of Satish's face. He brought down his lines of defence — the teeth, the lips — and tried to make them solid and unbreachable as Stephen

286

pushed the burger up against his mouth. He heard Sarah shouting encouragement: "Go on, Stephen!"

The meat was cold and soft. It moulded itself round Satish's lips as he resisted. He clamped down on them, rolling them inwards so they touched as little of the meat as possible, then shuddered as he felt some of it rolling inwards. He closed his eyes, as if that might make a difference, then all of a sudden his nose was pinched by a strong hand. He tossed his head back and forth, but the grip remained constant, and he knew that in moments he would have to open his mouth.

I'm British! I'm British! he wanted to say — a stupid thing in any case, because he couldn't say anything, couldn't open his mouth. It came out as a lowing, a moan. He *was* British; he did a thousand British things. There was really only one thing left, and it was this: he did not eat beef. There was a pressure in his chest, a pain in his forehead and then his body betrayed him, betrayed him utterly, and his mouth snapped open to take a breath.

The beef came in with it, piling over the barricade of his teeth and flopping onto his tongue. Terrible, terrible, get it out! He shook and waggled and pushed out his tongue to get rid of it, but it fragmented into little bits. It was fatty and metallic, and he gagged. He felt Paul dropping away from him smartly, but he wasn't sick.

He spat two, three times, using his fingers to scrape it all out, then pulled up his T-shirt and scrubbed at his tongue with it. When he'd finished, the inside of his mouth was coated in a greasy film. He was filled up with the taste of the meat. He'd eaten beef. When he saw the bits on the ground he gagged again. He became aware of himself doing this and what he must look like. The other three had retreated. They'd done it now, anyway. They'd done the worst thing. There was nothing left. He rushed at Stephen, arms flailing, then brought his foot up sharply into his balls.

Stephen went down and Satish took his chance and ran, not bothering to look behind him, not bothering to listen for them coming, just pelting for the gate and over it, running for Cherry Gardens, and adults, and safety.

CHAPTER
TWENTY-NINE

Before Satish turned into Cherry Gardens, he heard the impact: a clattering noise, a crash, a man's voice rising, "Woah! Verity. *Verity!*"

A front door slammed. He bolted into the street, thinking only of finding an adult, someone he could tell, someone who could take charge. A paper plate somersaulted towards him, spinning like a flipped coin. He saw more on the ground, and cups, and a glass jug smashed next to an overturned trestle. Skewed across the street was Miss Bissett's little blue car. She was getting out of it. Mr Brecon was rushing to help her.

"Verity. Are you all right? What were you doing?"

Miss Bissett tugged her cardigan down over the top of her skirt and sidestepped his open hand. "I'm fine, thank you very much, Peter. A slight misjudgement. I think something must have blocked my view."

"Please!" Satish was with them now. He pulled on Miss Bissett's sleeve. "Help me!" In his peripheral vision, he saw three figures scurrying across the entrance to the street: Sarah and the Chandlers. They kept going. They would loop round Cherry Gardens and come in at the other end.

"Help me!" he said again. "They . . . they've . . ." The relief of it broke him and Satish felt his face crumple. He put a hand over his eyes and let himself cry. "It was just terrible . . ."

Mr Brecon shook his head. "OK. This can wait, Satish. Can't you see what's just happened here? Have a bit of sense."

"No! They made me —"

"Bloody Nora!" said Mr Brecon.

"I just wanted to nip into Graham's driveway," Miss Bissett went on. "I don't like to think of the car sitting on the main road all day. I was going to park it in there."

Other people had come out of their houses now. Looking up, Satish could see Mr and Mrs Hobbes hurrying from the other end of the street. The Millers' door had opened, and Mrs Miller was bustling towards them. Mr Chandler arrived from his side of the road. Satish wiped his mouth again. He opened it and took a few breaths to let the beef taste out, but it just made it stronger.

"What a carry-on!" It was Mrs Miller. "You all right, Verity?"

Miss Bissett started to reply: "Yes I am, thank you. I'm not sure it's worth —" But Mrs Miller cut across her.

"Right! Let's get this sorted, shall we?" She rolled her eyes at Mr Brecon, who grinned back. "Peter, can you move Verity's car for her? Pop him the keys, will you, Verity? Pam and I can tidy up. Don and Ed, could you sort out the table? Lovely."

"*Wait!*"

Satish could see them ranged in front of him: the cavalry. Mums and dads, the adults he'd grown up with. They were already starting to disperse, Mr Brecon reaching out for the keys, the other two men bending to the fallen table.

"Help me! Please. Stephen and Paul, they did something awful . . ." He looked at Mr Chandler. "Sarah was with them. It was *terrible*."

Saying the names seemed to stop everyone, and they all turned towards him. Mrs Hobbes pushed past Mrs Miller and went straight to Satish. She put an arm around his shoulders. "What's wrong?" she said. "What happened?"

Mrs Miller's eyes narrowed. "What did Sarah do?"

"Little fuckers," said Mr Chandler. "Excuse my French. What did they do now?"

Satish leaned into Mrs Hobbes and she pulled him close. "They chased me into the school. We were in the playground." He was still crying, he was snotty, all vowels.

Mrs Hobbes held him away from her and searched his face. When she spoke, her voice was hard. "Where did they hit you?"

"They didn't. It wasn't that."

"Oh." She smiled, and he could feel movement around him.

The adults relaxed. Someone laughed. He heard Mr Chandler say: "Small mercies."

"If you're sure you're happy to park it," said Miss Bissett.

291

"It was worse! Much worse!"

"Maybe this is something for you and I to chat about," suggested Mrs Hobbes at his side.

"No," he told her, and then: "No!", shouted, so that they all stopped again. "You need to hear this! You all need to know about this!" It was Satish's last chance. His face was still chilly with tears, but he wasn't crying any more. "They didn't hit me. It was much worse. What they did! They made me eat *beef* . . ."

He looked up and he saw Sarah, Stephen and Paul coming into Cherry Gardens. Colette caught sight of them from her front garden and tagged along, trotting behind. They came towards the car and the small crowd of adults, but stopped a few yards short; they'd seen Satish.

"They *forced* me. Stephen and Paul did, and Sarah was there . . ." He saw Sarah look, horrified, at Stephen.

Mrs Miller glanced at Mrs Hobbes and grimaced. Mr Brecon let the keys slip in his hand and they clinked against his palm. He sighed. "I'm sorry. I don't —"

"I *can't* eat beef! It's not allowed! It's a thing, a taboo thing. Hindus can't eat beef." Satish looked at each adult in turn, waiting for them to realise what had happened.

"So what did Sarah do?" asked Mrs Miller.

"She was part of it. Do you understand? I'm not allowed. Cows are sacred. She *wanted* them to do it."

Miss Bissett turned to Mrs Miller. "Are you going to let him talk to you like that, Jane?"

292

"I'm sure Satish isn't trying to be rude," said Mrs Miller, tilting her head to one side. "I think it's all got a bit much, with the party and everything. You ate beef, Satish. It's scarcely the crime of the century."

"Beef is forbidden! And it was *raw!*"

Miss Bissett winced, but Mr Brecon said: "Boys will be boys, Satish."

"I think you'll survive," said Mr Chandler. He smiled round at the other adults. "And you know what?" He leaned down to Satish's level, dropping his voice. "There's a reason boys like you get messed about by boys like them. Show them a bit of backbone. A bit less snivelling. Then they'll leave you alone."

Behind him, Stephen mimed vomiting. Colette was staring at Sarah. She was still staring as the three older children turned and made off down the street, away from the adults.

"Right," said Mrs Miller. "Peter: car. Don and Ed: table. Verity, why don't you go home and put your feet up? We'll sort this out. Pam, I'll get a bag for us to put that glass in." She gave Satish an admonishing nod and headed back to her own house.

"Come on, out of the way," said Mrs Hobbes. She led Satish onto the pavement opposite and Mr Brecon started up the car. Next to them, the men righted the table. Satish could hear Mr Hobbes telling Mr Chandler:

"You'll always have problems with an 850. Rustbucket."

"You OK, Satish?" asked Mrs Hobbes

"No, I'm not OK! It was horrible and wrong and no one cares! I don't know what to do."

"I'll tell you what we're going to do. Right now."

"Really?"

"Really."

In his relief Satish sagged against her, put both arms round her and tucked his head under her chin. He let her stroke his hair and he didn't care how childish he looked, or what people might think.

"You and I are going to go back to my house."

"OK."

"We're going to sit you down and get you a cup of something hot, maybe find you a flapjack."

"OK. Yes."

"And you're going to calm down and get settled so that you're ready to enjoy this lovely party."

"What?"

She tutted and ruffled his hair. "You daft h'a'porth."

"What do you mean?"

"You silly boy. I know the Chandlers are *awful*." She said it quietly, Mr Chandler just a few feet from them. "They're awful boys, but you're tougher than that. It's only a bit of beef."

"It is not!"

"Come on, Satish. It's time to calm down. You know what they're like. They'll have their fun and move on. Now, let's get a bite to eat?"

Satish knew now that he wouldn't go to her house or anyone else's. Only his own. He broke out of her enclosing arms and walked away. He heard her call his name but he kept on going, away from the site of the

294

accident, where Miss Bissett's little blue car was inching into the driveway.

He walked back down the length of the table towards home, between a line of closed front doors and the endless repetitions of the Union Jack. The flags fluttered above him; the table beside him was a streak of red, white and blue. People would sit here and laugh together. They'd drink Ribena and Coke and eat burgers and jelly and fruitcake. That's what the adults were preparing for. He glanced back at them: industrious and good-humoured, calling out to each other, making jokes. They had forgotten him already.

He walked and he could hear English sounds: a lawnmower in someone's back garden, a radio station jingle from a transistor. Drawing level with Cai's house, he was hit by the smell of smoke, of beef cooking. There was a small billow drifting over Mr Brecon's garage, over his own, and dissipating above his garden.

Satish couldn't go in just yet. He felt it expand around him, huge and oblivious: the street, the village, England itself. And in every street in England, the same food, the same flags, the same celebration, and none of it had anything to do with him. They couldn't move on again. This was it: there was only England, nowhere else to go, only this village, and this street, and Satish here alone in it.

The beef taste was fading a little. When he got inside he'd scrub out his mouth. Lots of toothpaste and hot water, swill with mouthwash and try to get that oiliness out of him. He would work at it for as long as it took. He would scour it out of him for good.

CHAPTER
THIRTY

Satish scrubs himself clean — his nails, his hands, his arms. He's the last to arrive. They're waiting for him in the cath lab. He can see them through the glass-panelled doors: the patient out cold and wired up, Charles attending to him. Jac Timms, the radiographer, chats to Clare Munroe. They wear, as he does, a surgical mask and bouffant cap: part robber, part dinner lady. Mediated by the mask, everything they say will be softened, muffled.

Softened and muffled. He's finally upped his dose, and he can't imagine why he held off for so long. The best night's sleep he's had in weeks, and this morning, everything seems mellow. Adrift on a diazepam sea, this ritual — the painstaking scrubbing, hands held up, water draining down his arms — anchors him.

When he enters, elbows first, Charles nods towards him. Clare is singing something in falsetto, making Jac laugh.

Dance, dance, dance . . .

She shimmies in her scrubs, hands held out in front of her.

"Morning, Clare."

She stops singing. "Morning," she says. Jac adjusts the plates of the X-ray machine.

"So," says Satish. "We have Moustafa Saad. Pulmonary stenosis, previous valvuloplasty. Here today for a catheter study. Charles?"

"He's fine," confirms Charles.

Moustafa is seven. Satish lifts his hospital gown to prepare him for the procedure; he paints pink antiseptic onto him, to the left of his groin, then drapes him in green, exposing a window of skin.

"It's Mike's wedding party on Saturday," Jac says. "His send-off."

"Yes," says Charles. "There was an email."

"A secret one. You know he's not to be told?"

"OK. I'll keep schtum."

"Can you *all* keep schtum, please?" asks Satish.

They fall silent. Satish knows they'll exchange glances once his head's down. He doesn't care. He's going to burrow through this child's vein towards his heart. He's going to learn what's going on in there, the things you can't see even on an echo: the pressures in the chambers, the balance it's held in.

"Clare?" he says. "Covered needle, please."

The ventilator marks time with its piston-breaths. Charles' stool squeaks as he turns on it. Satish watches his own hands push the needle into the femoral vein.

"You hear all that bollocks about how they started going out?" asks Jac, eyes on the monitor.

"The cycling thing?" says Clare. "No, it's true. I heard it from his fiancée at the Christmas do."

"Go on," says Charles. "I'm always out of the loop."

297

Satish is having trouble with the introducer. It should fit nicely into the vein, opening a path for the guide wire, the catheter and its little passenger, the transducer, which will make its way to the heart and send back dispatches. Something's wrong, though: it won't slip in. He can't work out whether it's a problem with the vein or the equipment. Nothing's moving the way it should.

"So," says Clare. "She meets him at a conference. She decides she fancies him. She finds out he's this keen cyclist, where his club is . . ."

"OK."

"And she joins. Only, she isn't a cyclist at all."

"Come on! This is classic Mike," says Jac.

"Seriously," Clare assures her. "She's barely even cycled to the *shops*. She buys all new gear: new bike, new clothes, that Lycra stuff. She *distresses* it in the washing machine so it looks used —"

"Clare, could we have quiet, please?" It comes out sharper than Satish would like, but they're distracting him. "And could you move, please? You're a little close."

He sees Clare glancing at Jac, but she moves anyway and that was the problem, obviously, because now the introducer goes in quite smoothly, and he's ready to start. "Four French," he says, and she comes near again, and passes him the catheter.

There's purposeful movement in the room now, and Satish is happier with that: Charles is attending to the patient; Jac is making sure the angle of the X-ray camera is right. The catheter's moving, too: unseen up the vein, towards the heart. He pushes it along the wet darkness, feeling the resistance and give of its progress against his fingers.

"All right," he tells Jac. "We'll need that X-ray on, please."

A few seconds later, the catheter reaches the right atrium. He can see it on screen, a filament of white in the dark of the chamber. On his other monitor the numbers are in rhythmic flux, rising and falling with the contractions of the heart. Right atrial pressure's at four.

Beside him, Clare is the only one not occupied, and that stupid song is still in her brain, he's sure, because out of the corner of his eye he can see her fingers tapping against each other. And now he's in the right ventricle: pressure twentyfive over four.

He needs to twist the catheter round its hairpin bend, up into the pulmonary artery: there's a knack to it, but it takes concentration and he can't focus, not with this constant disturbance in his field of vision.

"Clare, would you mind?" He nods his head towards her twitching fingers and she stills them.

He turns the catheter at his end and sends a twisting ripple up its length. He watches the screen, waiting for it to arrive in the heart. Nothing for a few seconds, the transducer unmoving against the ventricle wall. Then it curls round and noses upwards into the pulmonary artery.

"How are those pressures looking?" says Jac.

He looks at the numbers pumping away on the screen. Pressure: twenty-three over thirteen. And the previous ones were . . .

"How's he looking, Satish?" says Charles.

"Hang on." He lines them up in his head, but it takes a moment to make sense of them. He needs to get this right.

"His heart function's good," he says eventually. "The pressures are stable. He won't need another intervention." He begins to retract the catheter. Out of the heart and back down the femoral vein: its homeward run.

"Distressed Lycra," says Charles.

"Yes," says Clare. "She goes along but she hates it. Absolutely hates it. But she gets her man, and then she doesn't know how to break it to him, and they've only been going out a few months — wet weekends up hills, stuff like that. Hold on . . ."

Clare stops talking and moves to Satish's side again, ready to hand him what he needs. The catheter comes out, tracing worm-lines of blood on the drape. Nearly there. He can have a cup of tea soon, clear some paperwork.

"I hope he's worth it," says Charles.

Clare clears her throat. "Anyway. They book a cycling holiday in the Pyrenees, she agrees to it but is dreading it. At the last minute something big comes up here and he tells her they have to cancel. She really turns it on: *oh, I'm so upset! I couldn't wait for that holiday!*, that sort of thing . . ."

Satish only knows there's something wrong when he sees the blood. It's pouring out of the catheter site, and he's sitting there with the introducer in his hand. He's ripped it right out of the vein, just tugged it out. He didn't even realise it was about to exit.

He grabs a pad of gauze and presses it to the bleeding.

"Right, that's done then," he says. Clare's still talking (he catches *pouring with rain, halfway up . . . he proposes*. Charles laughs). How much has Clare seen? There's always some blood at the puncture site — five minutes of compression at least, the nurse handling it more often than not. But this is different; there's blood round the edges of the gauze, red soaking up through the top layers already.

"Might need a bit more gauze," he tells Clare, and when she goes to fetch it he takes a look underneath. There's a haematoma. It's huge, the size of his palm, and bulging under the skin. He must have nicked the femoral artery. The wound keeps bleeding. He changes pads.

"You want me to compress?" she asks.

"No. I'll do it."

The other three have stopped talking, and now that they have, Satish wishes the gossip had continued. Because now there's just him, and them looking his way.

"Clare," says Charles. "I think I might give him a bit of extra analgesia. Can you pull out some rectal diclofenac for me?"

Satish can't work out how this happened. He lost concentration for just a second, that was all it took. He was focused on it and then . . . Was it Clare, fidgeting and distracting him?

She goes to the drugs cupboard. "Just don't ask for morphine. You're on your own."

Satish changes pads again, keeps the pressure on the wound, willing the blood to coagulate. He'll send Moustafa back to the ward but that won't be the end of it; nurses don't miss haematomas. For now, he'd be grateful to leave this room with his mistake undetected. Ten more minutes of compressing and it'll be all right. It will. Then he can take something to steady himself.

"There a morphine problem?" says Charles.

"A controlled medicines problem." Clare passes the diclofenac to him. "Sheila's pure raging about it."

"It'll be cock-up, not conspiracy," says Jac. "It's always cock-up."

Satish makes himself hold still. It might not be that. It might not be him.

"What's the problem?" he asks, watching the gauze soak red.

"I don't know," says Clare. "Sheila thinks something's gone missing. There's a memo." ("There's always a bloody memo," mutters Jac.) "Anyway, we've got to follow strict protocol."

"It was rife at my last place," puts in Charles.

Satish's face, his body, his hands. They are all giving him away. He is a sign advertising his own guilt. They can all see it. He doesn't want to move, to attract attention. And then he tells himself: no, keep moving or they'll notice. Get the job done. He reaches for another pad.

"What does she think's gone missing?" he says.

"I don't know. She's going to do a stock-take later this week. Then there'll be another memo . . ."

Jac is moving the arms of the X-ray machine back from the patient, preparing to leave.

"Why does she think there's something missing?"

"Dunno," Clare tells him.

But Satish knows. He imagines an envelope on Sheila's desk, a note inside. A hint, a nudge in the right direction.

"I'm off," says Jac.

Did the note name him? Surely not. What good would that do? But if he backs out of the reunion, will there be another one, pointing the finger right at him?

"This one's taking a while," he tells Clare. "More gauze?" He sees Charles look at the blood, the catheter, him.

"Strict bloody protocol," mutters Clare.

"Yeah, and mind you obey it," says Jac, on her way out. "Or I'll tell on you."

Satish looks up. There's something . . .

"Yeah, yeah," says Clare. "If you think you're hard enough."

Satish's mouth opens, involuntarily. It's come to him like a gift, unlooked-for. He knows who his blackmailer is.

CHAPTER
THIRTY-ONE

The last time the Chandlers took him, he didn't even care. It was quick: Satish sitting on his back step, tongue roaming his mint-bleached mouth, checking the crevices for anything he'd missed. They came in the open back gate, not even checking for Satish's parents first.

Paul grabbed a handful of Satish's hair and pulled him across his driveway into Cai's garden. No Cai there. Satish felt the scorch of the barbecue across his side and face; the air around it was solid with heat.

"We're going to show you what we do to fucking snitches," said Stephen, and he pulled back his fist.

Satish looked at him. "Go on, then," he said.

Stephen faltered. He looked around him, and his gaze came to rest on the barbecue. "Right!" he said. "Is that what you want? Hold him, Paulie."

Satish searched Cai's window: blank. But next to it, in Colette's room, he saw a face. Colette was transfixed, hovering behind the glass, her mouth open. Go, thought Satish. Go and play. I don't want you to see what happens next.

Paul pushed him up against the fence and moved his hand round to change his hold on Satish. He used his thumb to push up Satish's T-shirt sleeve. Stephen came towards them with something that flashed silver . . .

And then the sound turns off in Satish's memory and he's twisting in Paul's grasp, and he knows he's shouting but the noise of it is blocked out by the wall of pain in his arm. His body folds up, he pukes on the grass and the Chandlers step away from him. He's on his knees because he can't stand up. The hot tongs fall. There's a smell: it's him, the smell of barbecue coming off him. His arm is huge; it's all pain. When sound fades in again he hears himself too, the formless crying out.

Satish looked up and Cai was there, coming towards him.

"Get out of my fucking garden!" he shouted, and then he stopped.

He looked at Satish down on the ground, at the puddle of sick next to him. He looked at the Chandlers. Satish pushed himself to his feet, cast round for something that might help and found himself looking at Mr Brecon.

He was looking out of the French windows at the back, just a few steps away from Satish. Reflected in the glass, Satish saw the Chandlers watching, saw Cai turn and notice his father. Mr Brecon stood as if braced for a fight: arms at his sides, fists clenched. He could see what was happening but he made no move to stop it.

Cai had become very still, and Satish wondered if this at least could benefit him. Surely he couldn't be attacked while Mr Brecon was actually watching? He caught a sudden flare of memory, a night in Kampala five years earlier. There was a voice in the dark, his mother's, and Sima's head nestled into their father's neck as they jogged across the tarmac towards the plane. They'd made it to safety then, guided by their own blunt-headed determination. Perhaps he could save himself now.

He took a step away from the fence, and then a second, feeling the swell of pain as he moved. Another brought him behind Cai, who still hadn't budged. When Satish looked at Mr Brecon again, he saw why.

Satish's line of sight was now the same as Cai's. From here you could see Mr Brecon behind the glass. But you could see Cai's reflection too, the boy superimposed on the man. Both were tensed for conflict, welcoming it even, arms stiff at their sides, hands bunched. Both were jutting their heads forward, their expressions combative. Mr Brecon could see only Cai, of course. But Cai could see them both, and the sight had stopped him short. His eyes were fixed on the glass, and Satish could not tell which one of them he was looking at: himself or his father.

Mr Brecon blinked once, slowly, then turned away from the window, his lazy movement the final confirmation; he would not stop his son doing whatever it was he was about to do. Then the window was empty and dark again, and Satish was alone.

Cai was still looking across at where his dad had been. Satish told himself: Do it! Do it now and you'll stand a chance! But even as he formulated his plan Cai turned quickly and grabbed Satish by the arms. There was a fresh heave of pain.

Satish yelled, anger and pain together, incoherent. Cai pulled at him and Satish, resisting, reached out and hit Cai's face with his good arm, and now Cai was shouting something, using Satish's name but shouting it away from him, shouting towards the house.

"Satish!" he yelled. "It's OK! It's over!" He threw it like a stone against the window where his dad had been. "We're mates! You're OK!"

"Let go!"

But Cai carried on bawling. "We're mates! It's over!" And he glared up at the indifferent house, his mouth set in that way that was him and Mandy and Mr Brecon all at once. Satish shoved him aside, staggered towards the gate and made a run for it.

CHAPTER
THIRTY-TWO

His scar is the shape of an incomplete circle: a pair of brackets, opening and shutting with nothing in between. It's the shape of the two curves of metal at the tip of the barbecue tongs. Those tongs were probably thrown out when the Brecons moved to South Africa. Maybe not, though, Satish thinks; they do a lot of barbecuing there, don't they? *Braai*, they call it. So maybe those little jaws survived the emigration after all, another household object shoved into a tea chest, in which case they might be under South African soil by now, part of some urban landfill, bedded down in the same strata as the other things disposed of twenty, ten, five years ago. Or perhaps they've held on in a shed somewhere in Durban, fallen out of sight behind an old lawnmower, some garden chairs, a can of oil. But before they went, wherever they went, they left a little of themselves in England. Their mark is here, on Satish's right arm, an inch or so south of the shoulder joint. It's the sort of place where people choose to put a tattoo.

Satish is sitting at his desk at work, a week before the reunion photograph. His finger finds the scar easily and moves round the broken circle, skipping the gaps each time: on and off and on and off. His hand is tucked into his shirt and he closes his eyes, the better to concentrate. The skin is hard, contracted down, the edges puckered. It has led a curious double life this thing, kept from his parents by sheer luck and ingenuity, revealed to Maya under a false identity. He is intimate with it, though; his hand brushes over it daily in the shower, he catches sight of it in the mirror when he dresses, and whenever he does so he never fails to appreciate its final irony. Like most deep scars, the colour leached out of it within months; it's a part of him that will always be white.

He is sitting with his hand tucked into his shirt, circling his scar, meditative. In front of him is an ECG printout. The patient, a fourteen-year-old boy, collapsed while playing football. He's been bounced to Satish from neurology; they can't find anything wrong. But Satish can. Stretching across the red grids of the graph paper, the boy's trace shows a long QT interval. There's the extended slump of the ST segment and the sharp peaks of abnormal T-waves. The boy's heart went into arrhythmia, beating fast but futile: a cartoon animal, legs a blur, suspended above a canyon. No blood to his brain, no warning of what was coming — he'd have lost consciousness instantly.

On and off, on and off. Satish's finger moves over his scar. He needs to double-check the history, make sure it isn't caused by any medication the boy's been taking. He's thinking about this next action: pull your hand out of your shirt, get a pen, write a note . . . and then Stephen Chandler walks in on him. No warning: he doesn't even knock. There's a rush of heat to Satish's face, as if he's been caught masturbating. He pulls his hand free, and then he registers who it is.

"I had to come back," says Stephen, advancing into the centre of the room. "I need you to hear me out." He's ditched the suit and looks more fluid, less restricted in his T-shirt and jeans. As if he could move quickly, if he wanted to. "Ford won't let me do the photograph," he says.

Satish once met an air stewardess who told him she checked for fire exits every time she walked into a new environment — a restaurant, a shop, a friend's home. He wonders how she'd assess his office: one window, one door. One man blocking access to both. He buttons up his shirt. "I'm sorry about that, Stephen," he says. "But it's not in my control."

"Not control, no. But *influence*. Listen —"

Satish keeps his seat. "I think you should leave."

"Please, listen. I know I came across . . . last time, I was . . . aggressive, maybe. Wound up. I'm sorry. I've thought about it . . ." Stephen huffs air out of his nose. He looks around the office as if seeking something that might help his cause. Before Satish can speak, he carries on. "The photograph's going ahead, but Ford's not interested in me. He doesn't remember me. He doesn't believe I was there."

"There's nothing —"

"Hear me out!" The moment he's shouted, he's patting the air down with his hands. Satish doesn't know which of them he's trying to pacify. "Sorry, sorry.

310

But all you have to do is tell him who I am. That's it. End of."

"I can't help."

"I don't understand. It would cost you nothing but it could turn things around for me. You know, they're saying Neil Listick might turn up. Riot Act! Think of the exposure we'd get. Everyone would want the story."

Part of what makes this hard is the disproportion of it all: Stephen's reliance on this one, tenuous thing. It's unbalanced enough to nearly be funny; Satish doesn't know what to expect next, a punch or the punchline. He tells Stephen: "None of it makes a big enough difference. Not Andrew Ford, not Riot Act. This won't turn anything around."

"Please. I need to try everything, every avenue. I should have said before. I've lost my job . . ."

"I want you to leave now."

". . . custody of my daughter. She's called Lily. She's eight. She . . ."

"Stephen! Stop!"

And then there's a knock on the door. The two men look at each other.

"Hello?" It's a woman's voice.

Satish gets up. "Stay there," he tells Stephen. He opens the door a crack.

At first, he struggles to recognise the woman waiting outside. Then he remembers: it's Alice Roberts. He last saw her harried and pale, standing next to her daughter's bed in borrowed scrubs. He'd had to tell her they were keeping Jess on the ward for longer, and watch as she tried to hold things together. But Jess has done well; she's come with her mother now and is leaning against the opposite wall of the corridor, staring at her feet. She still looks a bit wan, but she's on the mend. Her jeans have a chain hanging from the belt, and her T-shirt proclaims her a "Beastie Girl".

"Doctor Patel! I hope you don't mind. We so wanted to see you," her mother says. She's carrying a large bag, which she hefts onto her shoulder when she sees him. There's a scarf hanging out of it, made of some kind of slippery material and as she bumps the bag higher, it starts slithering out.

"Do we have an appointment? I wasn't aware . . ."

She bends down to rescue the scarf. "Oh! No. We just decided to take our chances. Jess has been home for a few weeks now. She's doing great, aren't you?" Jess nods sullenly. "Suraya's looking after us and it's all been fine. I just wanted to come and see you all, after our appointment today. We're doing the rounds! ICU, Mike, everyone. I wanted to say . . ." Here, her voice wobbles a bit.

Behind her, Jess tuts and sighs. "Not again, Mum. This is tragic."

Mrs Roberts laughs, but the action seems to jump-start her weeping, and by the time she speaks again she's crying in earnest. "Well, you can see she's better, can't you? I feel I have to say this — it's terrible, when something like this happens. You think your child — I mean, you just want to protect them. And I was very scared." She looks at her daughter. "I'm sorry, but I was. You gave me a terrible fright. It's an awful thing, but what I wanted to say . . ."

312

Satish is horrified. He needs to stem this somehow, but can't, for the moment, find a way to do so. He sends quick glances up and down the corridor: no one coming. Mrs Roberts gushes on.

"I wanted to say that you all made it bearable. You were kind and straight with me, and you got Jane Oshodi to look after me, and she was brilliant.

"And what I wanted to say, if you don't mind, I wanted to tell you what it's like, when someone's missing from a family like that, the whole family's messed up. We just — we couldn't go on together if something had happened to her. But we didn't have to do that. We got her back. So I wanted to say, thank you. And we've made cards."

She reaches this hiatus and opens her bag, sniffing; Satish can see a fat pile of envelopes inside. She flicks through them and retrieves one. But instead of holding it out to him she comes towards him with it. Behind her, Jess is looking at the floor again, and suddenly Mrs Roberts has her arms around Satish and she's pinned him in a hug. He looks out over her head and doesn't know what to do. He can feel his chest vibrating as she continues to talk.

"You're all brilliant, all of you. Bloody brilliant," she sniffs.

Unsure of the etiquette, Satish tentatively hugs her back. Spurred on, she squeezes him harder. This should be awful, worse than the talking; it's uncontrolled, disempowering. It's embarrassing. But under cover of having no choice — *she became very emotional, I couldn't get rid of her* — he discovers to his surprise that it isn't as unpleasant as it should be. He and Mike and the rest of them, they have changed this woman's life. Maybe she has a right to this verbal arrhythmia.

"You're worth your weight in gold," she's saying now. "I hope you know that. She's here now because of you." He tilts his head against Alice's, just a little, and hears Jess say, "Oh, God," and her mum draws back from him.

"OK, now that's three times I've made a fool of myself today," she says. "I'll let you go."

Satish makes an effort to steady himself. He knows he should say something. "It was lovely to see you both," he tells them. There's a damp patch on his shirt.

Mrs Roberts says her goodbyes, a lengthy, garrulous process, and Satish is left alone in front of the closed door. He re-adjusts his shirt, tightens his tie. Stephen is waiting for him.

He's sitting on the chair, but when Satish enters he stands up suddenly.

"Just contact Ford. Please. I just want this chance. You're wrong; it *will* make things better."

Satish looks at Stephen, at his T-shirt referencing a rock concert of some twenty years past, at the leather thong on his wrist. He sees things he didn't see the first time: the other man's hair is receding, there's a pale stripe across his bare ring finger. And there's the troubling vision of his daughter, Lily; Satish doesn't even know if she exists.

He thinks about the prosecution of ancient wickedness, about how often it has failed. Stephen

314

could be Pinochet, rising from his wheelchair on the tarmac. Let him.

"All right," says Satish.

"What?"

"I'll do it. I'll email Ford. I'll tell him you were there. After that, you can take your chances."

"Oh, God," says Stephen. "Thanks." Even as he's talking he's moving past Satish, getting out while the going's good. He almost makes it to the door, then looks back.

"No harm done, yeah?" he says.

"What?"

"Back then. We were just kids, all as bad as each other, yeah? We straight now?"

No: harm done, thinks Satish.

He does it before he's even aware of what he's doing. He makes a fist with his right hand, thumb outside, to protect it. Stephen opens his mouth. Satish studies his face briefly, locating his jaw, his eye, his nose, and he pulls his arm back and swings it, with all his adult strength, and he hammers it against Stephen, who stumbles against the door, and Satish likes the feel of it and the sound of it and it does seem the appropriate thing to do so he does it again: once, twice, and then finally he feels satisfied.

CHAPTER
THIRTY-THREE

Satish is waiting for her when she comes into the bedroom. He's sitting on the bed, the blackmail notes in his hand. She sees him and her face goes still.

"Oh, Papa." She starts to cry: instantly, no segue.

"Close the door, Asha."

She closes the door.

He waits and lets her cry some more. She's still got her rucksack on and as she bends forward to weep, it shifts sideways.

"Take off your bag. Sit down." He's set up a chair opposite him. He thinks, if she's sitting next to him on the bed, this will be harder. It's in his muscle memory: to reach out for her, to give her a cuddle and kiss the top of her head.

"Why did you do it, Asha?"

"How did you know?"

He waits.

"*Do the photograph, or I'll tell your secret,*" he reads. "*I mean it. I will tell about the medicine. Do the photograph.*"

She cries, wordless.

"Do you know what that's called? It's called *blackmail.* You know that, don't you? If you were an

316

adult, the police would *arrest* you for it. Did you know that?"

"No!" She wipes her nose with the back of her sleeve. He sees the cuff frayed where she's been chewing at it: they always tell her off for that.

"Asha, I don't know where to start. What was going through your head?"

"You wouldn't do the photograph."

"But —"

"You just wouldn't. I knew you had a secret."

"How? I mean, what made you think . . .?"

"You were really cross with Mum when she had your bag."

He wants to stay in control. He keeps it measured. "She had my bag — my briefcase?"

"Yeah. You stopped her. You *hurt* her."

It was that Saturday afternoon, weeks ago. He thinks about the way Asha would have seen it, what she'd have heard. He knows what he saw: Maya's face, bobbing behind those stupid pads he had to hold up. He remembers wanting to be elsewhere. Asha was on the stairs, chatting to them. She grew bored and went up to the landing, he recalls, but she'd have heard everything. Asha, deep in her beanbag, reading her book. Putting it down to listen when things got interesting. She'd have had a half-view of them downstairs, all legs and arms, glimpsed in between the bannisters. Asha seeing him lose it, her dad pounding away at all his ghosts. And later: Asha sneaking into the garage, looking through his briefcase, finding his bottle, his spoon.

"What did you think you'd found?"

317

She shrugs. "A secret. I thought maybe you were, like, drugging yourself, or you'd stolen it."

Maybe it's the shrug, the carelessness of it, but he feels a rise of anger.

"And did you not think," he asks her. "Did you not think that if this was a secret, if it was as serious as that, that it would be really dangerous to *blackmail* me about it?"

"Dangerous? Why?"

"Because, Asha, you could hurt me!"

"I get told on *all the time*. Every day! But I'm not the only naughty one, am I? Why does nobody search *your* bag?"

No, absolutely, he wants to say. We're all at it. He wants to feel righteous indignation, but he can't. He can't claim the moral high ground; she's asking all the right questions. And he remembers the limits of her world: she knows nothing of disgrace, of professional ruin. She never imagines they might lose each other. She knows what it is to have a cigarette found in your bag and be grounded for two weeks. Maybe she thought she'd be grounding him.

But there's something he still doesn't understand. He asks her: "Why did you care so much about the photograph?"

"It doesn't matter."

"Tell me."

"OK, then," she says. Her hands make fists in her lap and she looks straight at him. "I hate it that you're sad all the time."

"I'm sad . . .?"

318

"See? There's no point telling you. You'll just say I'm wrong."

"Go on."

"You're, like, sad and grumpy *all the time*."

"That's not true, Asha. It isn't."

He's found somewhere else to look, but she ducks across, moving her face in front of him. "It *is*, Papa."

"That's a different discussion. Why did you care about the photograph? What's the point of making me do it?"

"I know you think Mum's wrong, but I bet she isn't. She said you'd be famous if you did the photograph. You would! I found out about it. Look!" She gets up and rifles through the mess on her desk, displacing other mess as she does so.

"Look!" she says again, pushing a CD towards him. It is — of course — *The Only Language They Understand*. "That's you!" she tells him.

"I know it's me. They used it . . . they did it a long time ago."

"Yeah, but don't you see? They did, like, adverts and everything. Loads of stuff. You'd basically be a celebrity again."

He smiles. "Not much of a one," he says. "Not for long."

"Papa, honestly," she tells him. "It would happen. It really would. You've just got to do the photo. Because it would make you happy."

Behind Asha is the picture of the boy popstar, the one who found fame when his school was on TV. The boy grins over her shoulder, clean and unthreatening. Is he happy? He looks happy in the photograph, and that's enough for Asha. Imagine if being a celebrity was the best thing that could happen, a guaranteed path to joy. Imagine someone's miserable, and too sad or dumb or stubborn to do what's best for themselves. Imagine they needed a little push.

The door opens. It's Maya. Satish and Asha look round, Satish folds up the notes.

"What's this?" she says.

"Nothing," says Satish. "It's just a school thing. I'm dealing with it."

Maya looks closely at Asha. "Oh yes? Fill me in."

"I will. But right now I need to deal with this." Satish waits, but Maya shows no signs of leaving. "Really. I'm in the middle of it. I'll fill you in later."

"Right." She waits for something else to be said, and when it isn't she turns and leaves. They both watch the door close, watch the handle dip and rise again. Asha looks back at Satish.

"You really don't want her to know, do you?"

"No."

"Even now you've, like, caught me and everything?"

"Yes, even now."

Asha considers this. He waits for her to realise his weakness, her strength — to capitalise on it; he can see her processing. It's a strange moment, waiting for guile to surface in Asha's face. This is how she loses her innocence, he thinks. And suddenly he'd do anything to stop it happening. It seems like the worst thing in this whole catalogue of worst things, stretching right back to the summer of 1977.

320

Then her face folds in on itself and she bursts into tears.

"Oh, no, Papa," she says from behind her hands. "Papa, is it really that bad?" It takes him a moment to realise the way this has turned, that she's not angry or defiant or threatening; she's frightened for him. He pulls her off the chair and onto the bed next to him. She pushes her face into his chest and sobs. "It's really bad isn't it, Papa?"

She can't see his expression: he can let himself go, for a second or two. He hopes she can't feel his chest contracting.

"No," he tells her, keeping it short. "It's not that bad. Really."

"But Mum doesn't know."

"No."

"Then it must be really, really bad."

He draws breath to deny it again, and then he thinks: you idiot. You bloody idiot. She's the only one seeing this clearly. It is *really, really bad*. She's eleven, that's all, and look what you've dumped on her shoulders now. She's scared for you. Grow up, he tells himself.

"Listen to me," he says, cupping her cheek and tipping her head so she can look at him. "You are right. It was bad. *Was*. I was . . . very, very stupid. Mum doesn't know yet, but she will. I'll tell her, I promise. And then, when Mum knows, it won't be a secret, and things will start to be all right. Do you understand?"

She looks at him warily.

"I mean it," he says. "I'll tell her today. No more secrets."

And he can see what she meant, where it might come from: Asha wanting things to be better, a different sort of life — and, God knows, he understands how that feels. Cai would have, too.

"Will you tell her what I did?" she asks.

"No. You didn't understand what you were doing. I'll tell Mum everything except that. We'll keep just that one secret. All right?"

She nods into his chest. "I'm sorry, Papa. I just wanted . . ."

"Shush," he tells her.

"How did you guess it was me? How did you know?"

"Asha, you said you'd *tell* on me. Only kids do that."

"I'm not a kid."

He smiles. "You are."

"I'm not!"

"You are," he says, stroking her head. "You're just a kid."

It comes to him that he doesn't have to do the photograph now. He thinks of himself walking into the frame, Satish grown up, made new. Asha would love it. There's nothing to make him do it any more. But there's nothing to stop him.

CHAPTER
THIRTY-FOUR

Satish is late. He was meant to leave the hospital at six, which would have left him plenty of time, but work never goes that way, so now he's hurrying, walking with a long stride because he can't stand the indignity of running. There's a chance that he's not just late, but *too late*, in which case he can go home and quite reasonably claim that he did his best, that it wasn't his fault.

In his hand is a bit of paper with an address, and he keeps looking at it. Without this constant reiteration, he thinks, he might end up going somewhere else entirely. He wonders whether, if he looks at it enough, it might have mercy on him and change its instructions. *Go to the cinema!* it might say, or *I've booked a table for two!* Or, best of all: *Come home.*

He's a full fifteen minutes late now, and just as he decides that's his limit, he rounds a corner and it's right in front of him: the church, a breeze block with a steeple, a place where he doesn't belong.

On the pavement people swerve round Satish, tutting. They glance at his face and they know why he's here; they must do. He's not sure whether to brazen it out and stroll across as if he owned the place, or keep his head down. He crosses the street with his eyes on the tarmac, and halfway over there's a squeak of tyres. A car horn sounds, very near, and he jumps; the car's right next to him, the bumper inches away, and the driver behind the windscreen shouts soundlessly, her hands on her head. Satish scurries on, through the iron gates into the churchyard.

He's in no state to do this. Heart pounding, he's replaying his near-miss, catastrophising. Six inches closer, he thinks . . . He really, really needs to sit down, and the only bench in the churchyard has a pile of dog faeces next to it. A sign directs him up a grave-lined path to the church hall. There's an ice cream carton on the doorstep, half-full of water, fag ends floating in it leaking plumes of yellow. The curtains are closed; he can't see inside.

Behind him there's a crunch of gravel and it's this, in the end, that propels him forward and away from witnesses. He's in a lobby: coathooks and stacking chairs and a noticeboard for a mother and toddler group. Through a rectangle of wired glass he sees a room in semi-darkness, a group sitting round a low table: mostly men, one woman. She's bent forward on her seat, a cup tilting in her flaccid hands. The table's covered in leaflets and books. A candle gives out a soft light.

Too late, thinks Satish. And then one of the men sees his face through the glass and raises a thumb. There's a black tattoo climbing out of the man's T-shirt, curling up his neck and wrapping itself round the side of his shaved head. He smiles broadly and beckons again.

324

The handle squeaks when Satish enters. Heads turn. He makes for a chair near to the door, stumbles against it, goes to sit down then bobs up again: the tattooed man's made a noise, a sort of *whisht*, and he's grinning and pointing at the empty seat next to him. Satish clatters his way there, round the back of all the chairs.

He sits as he is: coat buttoned, briefcase on his lap. The tattooed man shakes him by the hand. Satish raises his head to meet the gaze of the group, but they're not looking at him.

They're looking at another man. He's clean-cut and suited. He could be a banker, or a lawyer, or a teacher. He could be a doctor.

"Hi. I'm Phillip," he says. "And I'm an addict."

CHAPTER
THIRTY-FIVE

The bunting looks fantastic; they must have been at it all morning, thinks Satish. Then he sees the white van, the crew of men in matching black T-shirts (*At Your Service: the events people*) and he remembers: it won't be two blokes and a ladder this time. He's standing near the quiet end of the road, in the cul-de-sac that leads to the primary school. Cherry Gardens is closed to cars, so he's parked here instead. He's a bit early.

There's still a tree at the end of the close, and next to it a gap through which the kids still — he assumes — pass on their way to school. They must do, because the gap seems wider and more formalised, the overhanging branches neatly trimmed to adult height, the fence on the other side in good repair. He wanders over to it, squeezes through and stands outside his old school gates. Since he left they've done some redevelopment at Bourne Heath County Combined. Most childhood things look smaller when you revisit them, but his school has grown. It's done well. The curved wall of a new classroom bellies out into the playground. In front of him, in the old music room (terrible, terrible noises hauled from reluctant instruments by enthusiastic Juniors), he can make out a bank of computers, a gift, he's sure, from the good burghers of Bourne Heath and their active PTA.

It's a Sunday afternoon and the school is deserted. Satish thinks of the playground, round the corner and out of sight on a different day, long ago, the climbing net, the slide and he finds he can think of these things now without flinching. It happened. But it's not happening now. He considers the intervening decades, the children who have inhabited this place. He thinks of cricket and footie and twenty-one and British Bulldog, and the songs of the girls: *Keep the kettle boiling, miss a loop you're out — you're in!* and *Vote, vote, vote for little Annie* and all the shoving and running and slapping and kicking that mark out children's tenancy of their playground. He wonders whether there is any part of this place that has not received the touch of a child's hand or foot or bum at some point during the last thirty years. It is there in front of him, printed invisibly on brick and tarmac, smudged onto glass and cleaned off and smudged on again.

When he passes back between the tree and the fence he wants to sit down. He perches on the kerb, the same place they always used to sit on those do-nothing afternoons, him and Cai, Mandy and Sarah, and sometimes the Chandlers. Sitting like this, he can see the street from much the same height as when he first came to Bourne Heath. The cars in the driveways have changed, and not just because time has moved on; you need a bit more money to live here now, he thinks. The Minis and Datsuns and Morris Minors have been ousted in favour of Chelsea tractors.

327

He's so caught in this shift between then and now that when a figure emerges from Cherry Gardens and heads towards him, looking familiar yet strange, he isn't surprised at all. She's grown curves — she's voluptuous, even — and that hair, which has entered his imaginings from time to time, is no longer the sleek bob he remembers. She would change, wouldn't she? A girl like her would never stay still. She's a woman now, and that hair is long, fixed up elegantly at the back. Some things never alter though. He can tell as she's walking towards him; she's still trouble.

"Mandy?"

She comes up to him and it is her: Mandy, groomed with Gallic style. She's aged, as they all have, but it's Mandy nevertheless. She looks at him keenly, making the same transition, then opens her arms wide. They embrace in the French way: one, two, three air kisses with their cheeks touching, and Satish feels a little jolt: that was easy. They pull back to look at each other. Mandy winks at him, then reaches up on tiptoes — it all comes back! — holds his hands in hers and plants a fourth kiss, deliberately, onto his lips.

"It's so good to see you. So good," she says, rubbing her lipstick from his mouth with her thumb.

They walk back to Cherry Gardens together. He says, "So, here we are then!" and she giggles.

"It is just lovely to see you, Satish. Best thing about the day."

"You're looking wonderful. You're looking . . . French."

"I live in Paris! Did you know that?"

"I did. I cheated — internet. But you do look . . . there's something, anyway."

Cherry Gardens has been decorated only as far as the photographer's end of the table. The space behind won't be in the photograph, so there's no point. The rest of the houses, including Satish's and Mandy's, stand bare, unadorned. It puts him in mind of an old film, a spacecraft landing in a field outside a quiet town, the ship all the more alien for the ordinary things around it. A little bit of the past has crashlanded in Cherry Gardens.

"Tell me about France."

"Well, I'll never be properly French, evidently." She stresses the final syllable. "But I've lived there long enough. I've had a French husband." She looks at him, raises an eyebrow. "In fact, I've had two."

No, she hasn't stayed still. Two of them! And French! He can see them in their beautiful suits, knowing what wine to order, and using that accent . . .

"Two, Mandy? You've been busy."

"I'm never idle. Do you want the run-down? Do we have time?"

"I don't think they can start without us."

The greenery is more lush than he remembers, the trees more mature — of course — and the houses they shade have grown, too. All those street-facing doors have gone, obliterated by new extensions.

"Well." Mandy nudges against him as they walk. "Potted history. I married Luc when I was 24 — too young, of course. He was a bastard. I know they all say that, but really. After we separated his mum rang me. She *apologised*. Then I met Jaffa."

"Jaffa?"

"Jean-Francois. He was fun, but it was brief. Quick marriage, quick divorce. These Catholic boys."

They've stopped halfway down the street and she's looking at him.

"You need a new hobby," he says, grinning.

"*Oh coquin!* Anyway, I got one. Do you really want to hear all this? We'll do you next, I promise. OK. So I left my job — *terrifying* — and I set up this business and language school. Business English, Anglo-American business practices, all that."

"You did well."

"Yes, I did. Well, that's it, really. That's me. I don't need to ask about you, do I? Well, not the job. Know all about that. Do you smoke?" She feels around in her bag.

"No."

"Can I? Do you mind? French habit." She lights up.

"Look," he says, pointing to the house opposite. "Sarah's place."

She squints at it. "Yes, of course! So that means . . ." She counts down with her cigarette. "Miss Walsh and me and Miss Bissett — God, what a bitch!"

He turns, and they're standing right outside it. "The Chandlers."

"Little bastards." They look at the house in silence. Plastic window frames and blotches of colour in the flowerbeds. A people carrier in the drive. Then the front door opens and Satish runs out, Satish small but not scared and not running from anything. He comes right up to the two of them.

"Hello," he says. "Are you in the picture?"

"Sandeep!" comes a voice from inside. The boy flicks round again and runs back.

Satish realises he's holding Mandy's arm.

"I'm sorry," he says, letting go.

Mandy laughs.

"Yeah, I know. Spooky. But think about it. Little Sandeep. He's living there."

They look back at the house, front door closed again, and Satish sees her point. He's living *right there*. His laugh rolls out generously. It's authentically funny, and now Mandy's laughing too, both of them curling over slightly, touching each other and setting each other off again.

"I think you'd call that the last laugh," she says.

After a bit they make their way down to Mandy's house on the opposite side, skirting the party table. Satish sees, in his peripheral vision, food, drink, the red-white-and-blue. A few seats from the end, there's a "Reserved" sign, and Satish thinks of Stephen.

"You now," Mandy commands him. "Tell me about you."

"You know about my job, then?"

"Yes. Very flash. It's perfect for you, being a doctor. A kids' doctor."

"I'm a paediatric cardiologist."

"OK. So, what about the bits I couldn't Google?" They pass the end of the table, a gathering of people and equipment.

"I haven't had any French husbands."

"Careless." She fish-mouths, blows a smoke ring, skimming under it as she walks.

"I'm married, though. Maya. We have two kids."

Mandy presses her lips together. "When did you get married?"

"In . . . umm . . . she'd kill me for this . . . 1993."

"Long-service, Satish. You'll have to tell me how. Are you happy with her?"

It escapes him uncontrolled, half-gasp, half-laugh. The cheek of it! All this time and she's still asking questions like that.

"Yes," he manages. "Of course."

"Of course," she says.

They're standing outside her old house and he looks up at her window, like he always used to, but there's nothing for him to see there now. Mandy takes a couple of steps up the driveway.

"What are you doing?"

"Come on." She cranes round to see in through the front window. "I don't think anyone's in." She strides down further, beckoning to him. "Come on! Don't you want to see?"

"Mandy, it's someone's house!"

"Yes, but it used to be mine. Come on!"

"What if they're in?" But he's already taken a few steps forward. "They're probably round the back."

"So what? We'll plead curiosity, or ignorance or something."

He takes the cigarette from her hand — "They'll smell it!" — and carries it back to the road, stubbing it out and leaving the butt on the pavement. He has a quick look to see if anyone's watching them and hopes she doesn't notice and think he's a coward. She's already at the gate, lifting the latch. As it clicks up she grins: "Just like old times."

The garden is immaculate and empty. There's a new conservatory blistering out from the back of the house. Through it, he can see Mandy's old dining room. Mandy goes right up to the back door, framing her face with her hands so she can see through it properly.

"Posh new kitchen," she reports. "Marble worktops. Not a spoon out of place. They even have a *wine cooler*, look."

But Satish is scanning the windows, top and bottom, making sure they're not being observed. "Come on, you've seen it now," he says.

"Do you remember the melamine, and that fake wood?" asks Mandy.

"Yes. Let's go."

"Just a minute. Don't you want to see what the rest of the downstairs is like?"

She grabs his hand and pulls him towards the conservatory, and he feels a rush of adrenaline. When she lets go they stand side by side, both cupping their faces now, peering through a foreground of bookcases and wicker chairs to the dining room beyond.

"It's very . . . tidy," he says.

These neat people have tidied away part of his childhood. They, or their predecessors, or *their* predecessors, have got rid of the arch between the lounge and dining room, and sealed up the serving hatch. They've stripped away the fingerprints he once left on her wallpaper, and chucked out the carpet on which he trod.

"It's smaller," says Mandy.

"I know," says Satish. "It always is."

Back in the safety of the street, he asks her, "When did your parents move?"

"Well, in '84, the day I got my A level results — I had the letter in my hand — Mum came in and told me they were getting divorced."

"Were you surprised?"

She does that eyebrow thing again. "What do you think?"

"So they both left Bourne Heath?"

"Yes, and it was a good thing, too. I never wanted to come back."

"So what's your mum doing now?"

"She died," says Mandy. "Cancer."

"I'm sorry."

She looks away from him. "It happens."

Satish watches a young woman rearranging a pyramid of cupcakes. She takes one off the top, stands back, and looks at the rest. After a few moments, she replaces the cake.

"You know," Mandy says, turning to him, "I've been trying to work out what made you come here today. I'm so glad to see you, but — let's be honest, Satish — this was an appalling place back then. Appalling attitudes. Why would you come back?"

He smiles. "It's a long story."

She waits. When it's clear there's nothing forthcoming, she says, "There's something we need to say to each other. I want to talk about what they did to you that day."

Suddenly she's too close to him.

"You know . . ." he tells her, shaking his head. "Long time ago, not worth . . ."

"I bet no one else says this. I bet everyone else here today pretends it never happened. But I don't want to do that. I want to talk about it and I want you to let me."

"It's been thirty years, you know . . . I don't have much to say about it. I'm fine."

"I'm very glad." She bites her lip, draws breath. "I'm not fine, though. This is something I've thought about a lot."

"What? Jubilee Day?"

"A lot. After I got older, especially. It occurred to me . . . I mean, I have always felt quite strongly that . . . Did you ever think about the irony, that it all happened because of me, and that in the end I was the one who wasn't there, so I couldn't stop it?"

This eccentricity pulls him up short. He pauses, considers it. "It would never have occurred to me. You couldn't have stopped it."

"I might have done."

"You couldn't. And it didn't happen because of you."

"It did!" Her stridency comes from nowhere. "It was the kiss they were so angry about, wasn't it? It was as if I set it all going, then sort of abandoned it. Abandoned you."

"No. That's not true."

"I had a responsibility that day. What they did to you . . ." She reaches up to him and, before he can stop her, her fingers are stroking his upper arm.

"Mandy, don't."

She pushes back the material of his shirt over his scar.

"Here it is. God, I want to bash them all in! God, Satish!"

He breaks away from her and smooths down his sleeve.

"It's not so bad," he says. "It's all in the past."

"Don't say that! It was a terrible thing."

"It was a terrible thing at the time," he says. "I don't think about it much now. It hasn't defined me or affected me. It's not who I am. I don't mean this cruelly, but your guilt is misplaced. Nobody could have rescued me. I rescued myself."

"I'm sure you did," she says. "You wouldn't let me do it, that's for sure." It's the nearest she's come to bitterness. "You barely ever spoke to me again, after Jubilee Day."

"You're reading too much into this," he says firmly. "It was bad, but it happened a long time ago and you were a kid. Those people were looking for an excuse, and I gave them one. You need to — what do they call it? — you need to absolve yourself."

"Hmm." She doesn't say anything for a while. Satish is going to speak again, but then she says, "Well, how selfish that would be. That would be self-centred, wouldn't it, to come here and think about my own

336

absolution? The thing is, you're probably right." She looks up at him, appealing. "But I don't think it's something you do for yourself, Satish. I think someone does it for you."

"Fine." He makes a swirl in the air with his finger. "Consider yourself absolved."

"You think?"

"Absolutely. Absolution."

They stand there for a while longer, but he can't think of anything new to say. They turn away from her house, towards his, and Mandy takes his arm.

"The absolution is good," she says. "But it's not why I came back."

"To this *appalling place*? So why did you?"

"You won't believe me. You'll think it's flim-flam."

"Go on."

"You're easy to Google. But I wanted to *touch* you."

CHAPTER
THIRTY-SIX

Mandy leaves; she's spotted Colette at the other end of the road. Satish watches her move away from him, and stays watching as the two women reunite, a piece of silent theatre: there's Colette's polite puzzlement, recognition, delight, her open mouth, her wide eyes. They move in for a kiss which Mandy performs air-style, as she did with him, but Colette does it the old-fashioned way, a smacker on each cheek. They hug, they pull back to look at each other, they hug again. It's been weeks since his last meeting with Colette — the row in the café, his shameful accusation. He needs a reunion with her, too, but he can't face it just yet. He leaves them to it.

Satish is alone outside his old house. After the photograph, he'll do a meeting. He's found one nearby. Ninety meetings in ninety days, that's what they say you need to do. We have a disease, they say, but we do recover. Each day we are given another chance.

There's a young couple outside, watching proceedings. They've left his — their — door open, and through it he glimpses neutral colours: linen and calico, they'd be called, pebble and bamboo. In the window of the front extension there's a taupe blind. Blue hydrangeas still squat in the front garden, but the driveway's changed, its cracked concrete replaced by a spread of black tarmac. Down the centre of this waddles a toddler, stiff-legged and rocking from side to side. Her father's gaze never shifts from her, tracking her progress towards the pavement.

Satish sneaks a look up at his bedroom window. Not much to see there: a silver light fitting, the creamy backs of curtains, the pale wood of a wardrobe. But, like the school playground, it is a palimpsest, full of what used to be there. He can see a boy behind the glass, his hand pressed against the window, his eyes watching another window over the road. He can see the mark this boy's hand makes. The lad is dwarfed by his own shirt collar. His hair curves in a shiny pudding-basin, a little long at the back perhaps; he's uneasily halfway between child and man. Satish can see a girl in the room with him, moving towards him. He sees them come together and beside him in the street there are faint traces of the other watchers who saw this, too. He sees the boy being marched out of his back gate, sees him running for home. Satish, grown-up now, bids them goodbye: the watching boy, the kissing boy, the victim, the runner. Each day we are given another chance.

The woman moves away from the wall towards the toddler, and towards Satish. As she looks at him her face opens in recognition, her mouth already framing a question. He nods at her and turns away.

The table is loaded with goodies. At the age of twelve, he'd have been hovering over them, assessing them, doing a recce in preparation for the party. Now he swipes a pretzel for old times' sake. That's what they've used, in place of his mum's chakli. There's also a beige pile of something damp to stand in for the coronation chicken. But Mrs Hobbes' cakes have been reconstructed in glorious Technicolor (he remembers them, half-iced, on her kitchen counter), and not much has changed about the jugs of squash. The remarkable thing is the proliferation of Union Jacks: on the tablecloth, the cups and plates. Plastic Union Jacks on wooden sticks — just the same kind as Colette was holding in the original photograph — have been put next to some of the place settings along the table. Where did he find those, wonders Satish — eBay? Twenty years ago this would have been unacceptably nationalistic. Ten years ago it would have been ironic. And now? Well, now it's probably retro, or something like that.

At the end of the table there's a tripod, a man crouching down to adjust its height. Andrew Ford, surely? The wildness has gone from his hair; it's salt-and-pepper now, curly still but cropped close to his head. With that assertive nose of his there's something oddly Roman about him. When he sees, Satish, he smiles.

"I don't need to ask. It's Satish, right?" He holds out his hand.

His assistant Georgia is stage-managing this, he explains, and he indicates the young woman who rearranged the cupcakes so fastidiously.

"Georgia knows pretty well how I work," he tells Satish. "She'll be sorting out the stuff that goes under my radar." He waves his hand vaguely in her direction. "Gives me time to focus on the important things. Like

340

you, and the other veterans of *Glorious*. Looking forward to it?"

"Umm . . . yes. Happy to do it."

"Great, great. Now, I'll be wanting you to recapture exactly what you were doing when that first photograph was taken — same seat, same body language, the lot. OK?"

"All right."

"Pretty familiar with the original? I bet you are. I can't go anywhere without hearing about it. Haunts me!" He laughs and shakes his head.

"Yes, I know the feeling."

"Well, another fifteen minutes of fame, eh?"

"Yes."

"Great. Be ready in a bit. See you then."

Colette is perching on the wall in front of Miss Walsh's old place. She's fiddling with one of the beads on her skirt, catching it under her fingernail, releasing it and catching it again, Satish watches her, unsure whether this is the right time to fix things. But just as he thinks: yes, it's time, someone else gets to her first, a man in a leather jacket, and she looks up at him with such open pleasure that Satish retreats. It's Oscar, of course; she grabs a fistful of his jacket and pulls him close, burying her face in the leather. She's good at getting what she wants. There's something she wants more, though. When she sees the old man appear at the end of the road, she's off.

He's shorter; not just because Satish has grown up, but because the other man has somehow grown down. He's become compressed, he stoops. Colette walks at his side, solicitous, leaning into him slightly, looking up at his face. As Peter approaches, Satish draws himself up higher. He's young and strong, and this time being younger has its advantages.

"Dad, you remember Satish," Colette declares, stagily. The two men clasp hands. Peter's is a fleshy paw; Satish cannot recall ever having touched him before.

"Of course," says Peter, his voice diminished too. "How are you getting on?"

"Excellently." He lets the word hang for a moment. "And you?"

"I'm . . ." He looks round him, across at his old house, then shakes his head suddenly. "I'm fine! Never better! I'm working in London, so I get to see Colette from time to time. And Cai, of course."

Like Satish, Peter has chosen a suit for the photograph. His is a little shiny, and there's a worn patch on his left shoulder, the sort you'd get from a bag strap. Satish wonders what Peter takes to work with him in that bag. The suit is dated, even Satish knows that, and his shoes have been deformed by bunions over the years. All this Satish sees, and he's aware that it should engage his sympathies.

"So," says Peter. "Colette tells me you're doing very well, Doctor!"

"Yes. And I'm working in London, too."

"And we meet right here, after all these years. Strange thing, eh?"

"I heard about your situation," Satish tells him, feeling the swell of a nasty joy. "I'm sure you'll be back on your feet soon."

Satish sees the T-shirt before he recognises its wearer. It's a vivid yellow — a punch of colour at the end of the road. There's rough black lettering across the top and a pink strip over the middle, pushed into a curve by the man's paunch.

Colette runs by him into the stranger's arms. The man is stout and bald and for the first moments Satish stares at him as if this new face were not a face at all, but a room in which he is searching for someone. Then he can make out a mouth, unchanged, and eyes which, isolated from the skin around them, are still the eyes which look at you from the photograph. Yes, he thinks, this is Cai. This is what Cai would look like if he had grown up.

Cai — the new Cai — breaks away from Colette and comes towards him. "Satish," he says. "Hello, stranger." He holds out his hand. Satish hesitates, then takes it. It's muscular, scratchy with hardened skin. Satish thought it might set off some kind of reaction in him, this touch, but they're just two middleaged men shaking hands. He doesn't know what to say.

"Let's get this out of the way," says Cai. "I was a horrible little tosser and I'm sorry." He waits, and when Satish says nothing, he adds, "A late apology, I grant you."

"Well . . ." Satish begins.

"I would have said sorry a couple of weeks back, but . . ."

"Yes," says Satish, remembering the last-minute funk which sent him home that day. "Sorry about that. Like I said in the email, I wasn't very well."

"Yeah?" says Cai. "Well, whatever. We're here now, right?"

"Yes," he agrees, "we're here now."

And then there's nothing more to say. All the other things — remonstrances, epiphanies, absolutions — they are surplus to requirement. The two men stand opposite each other, waiting for the next thing to happen. Satish searches his bank of small talk for some currency. He points at Cai's T-shirt.

"*Never Mind the Bollocks?*"

Cai nods, laughs. "Yeah — out and proud! Couldn't resist it. Souvenir T-shirt. Maybe not quite part of the Punk ethic, yeah?" Looking up, he seems to check himself, then suddenly moves away from Satish, back the way he's come, round the end of the table and down the other side.

"I'll just tell them I'm here," he says. "Andrew Ford . . ."

Behind him, Satish hears a click of annoyance: Colette has reappeared, and beside her is her dad. Peter stares at his retreating son, then spots someone else seated at the table a few places down, unlit cigarette in her hand, rifling through her handbag.

"Mandy? Is that you?" He moves towards her and she rises to greet him. He takes her hand and squeezes it between both of his.

She pulls back slightly. "Mr Brecon?"

"Peter."

"Yes, of course. Well . . ." There's a brief silence as Mandy looks from Peter to Colette. When nobody says anything she continues. "Funny circumstances to meet in, after all these years. How are you keeping?"

344

Peter pulls Mandy towards him. "Come here," he says, wrapping his arms around her. She angles the cigarette away as he closes the space between them. Colette starts forward.

"Dad?" she says.

Mandy stiffens, and after a moment Peter releases her.

"I'm sorry, I'm sorry." Peter tugs his jacket down. "Just . . . being back, you know."

Mandy folds her arms across her chest. "How are you keeping?" she repeats.

"I'm keeping well. Back in Britain for a while, like you."

"Yes," she says warily. "Mother country . . ."

Peter opens his mouth to say something, but there's a young woman moving purposefully towards them, a toolbox in her hand, a toolbelt round her waist. When she reaches them she points at each of them in turn.

"Satish, yes? Peter? Colette? Mandy? Great. Four for the price of one. Don't go anywhere." She grabs a nearby chair and then plonks her toolbox on it. When she opens it up, Colette lets out a little, "Oooh."

"Make up!" says Mandy, and Satish sees that the box is filled with tubes and pots and palettes. There's a pack of baby wipes and a clump of cotton wool.

"I'm Saffron," she says. "Andrew's asked me to pop on a little make-up, OK? We'll start with you, Mandy."

Wordlessly, Mandy pushes back her fringe and closes her eyes. Saffron snaps open the pack of wipes and passes one over Mandy's face.

"Nice job," she says. "I bet it took you ages to do this, and here's me taking it all off again." When she's finished she dips a sponge in a pot of something flesh-coloured and starts dabbing it on.

"Is this necessary?" asks Peter. "For all of us? For the men as well?"

"Don't worry, boys," Saffron tells them. "Everyone thinks they'll end up looking like something out of the *Rocky Horror Show*. I'm just improving on nature, that's all." She reaches down to her belt, which, Satish now sees, contains brushes rather than tools. "Hold still."

She strokes powder over Mandy's nose, her cheeks and chin and eyelids. Then there's something pink. The rest of them watch, silenced.

"Copy me," she instructs, and Mandy does, opening her mouth slightly, pulling it a fraction wider. There's a thing with a pencil, and then a brush, and Mandy's lips are done. She looks as if she's on television, and someone's turned the colour up.

"You look beautiful," says Peter. "More beautiful."

Mandy frowns and dives into her bag. "Anyone mind?" she asks, producing her lighter. She's lit up before anyone can answer.

"Watch the lipstick!" Saffron warns her. She turns to Peter.

"I don't want it to show," he says, and she tuts at him.

Mandy sighs and looks back up the street. Satish follows her gaze and sees Cai leaning back in a chair, feet on table.

"I'm off," she announces.

"Wait!" It's Peter. Saffron's hand is clamped on the top of his head, so he can't turn to her, but he says it loudly enough. "Hang on, Mandy. Before you go . . ."

"Stay still," Saffron tells him.

"Mandy, wait. It's been so long. I just want to know. Are you happy?"

She stops mid-stride. She looks at him, puzzled, and Satish can see her trying to fit it all together, to work out Peter's strangeness. She opens her mouth to speak, cuts her gaze away from him, then closes it again. The silence becomes painful and Satish is just starting to feel awkward when Mandy finally answers.

"You know, that's a very strange question. And I don't know why you'd care. But for what it's worth, I think I am happy. I'm living in a city I love, and I'm doing what I love. I've had my ups and downs, but who hasn't, by this age?"

"Thirty's rough," puts in Colette, and Mandy smiles.

"Yeah, thirty — evidently. But we're here, aren't we? We're still here. I know what they say, the pessimists, but to tell the truth, I'm not one of them. What's that expression? The triumph of hope over experience. Well, I actually believe in it. I would uphold that every time. So yes, I suppose I'm happy."

Peter ducks under Saffron's restraining hand, evades the brush she's reaching out to him, and grabs Mandy by the shoulders. He squashes her against his chest.

"Well said, my girl. Well said."

And Satish doesn't want to see it any more, the way this situation might unfold, the surfacing and suppression of family secrets, so he walks away.

Sarah's looking better than she did the last time they met. Satish encounters her as he loiters near her parents' house, and she comes too close for him to pretend he hasn't seen her. She's recovered her poise, dressed in sharp little boots and the kind of wrap top he sees on the wealthy matrons of his town. She must have been on holiday; her skin is a couple of shades browner than it was under the fluorescent hospital lighting. The two of them look at each other. She opens her mouth and he shakes his head — no — but she's already moving towards him.

"Satish, I . . ." And she stretches out to touch him. He desperately doesn't want her to but he can't pull away because he's English after all and that would be a Scene. Her hand comes to rest lightly on his arm.

"Louis's great," she says, removing it. "He's doing really well. It was a glitch. They say he'll be fine."

"Good. I'm glad to hear it."

"And I'm sure you understand, about what I said. I was under a great deal of pressure that night. Every parent . . . You just try to do what's right . . ."

"Yes."

"It's very tough. You have no idea. But you — you fixed him."

"Actually it's my job. The Hippocratic oath? I'd never have done anything else."

She looks at him for a second.

"I'm glad he's doing well," says Satish.

"I told my mum," she continues, gesturing to a woman sitting halfway down the table. The woman looks at Satish and her face resolves into Mrs Miller's. She raises her hand and smiles. "She's very grateful. I think she'd endow Central Children's with the rest of her pension if I let her."

"I have to go," he says, and gestures out towards the rest of the street, to nothing in particular.

"All right," says Sarah. "Thanks."

He tries to look busy as she leaves, setting off purposefully. A moment later he glances back and realises he needn't have bothered. Her attention's not with him, but with Mandy, who she's bumped into on her way down to Andrew Ford. *Bumped into* isn't right, though; quite the opposite. The two women pass back-to-back, ignoring each other with scrupulous care.

And now it really is time to fix things with Colette. She's back on Miss Walsh's wall and just for a short while there is no new lover claiming her attention, no needy father or recalcitrant brother. The currents and eddies of this strange reunion are calm for the moment. She's nicked a cake from the far end of the table and is nibbling it.

"I'm horrible," he says. He sits down beside her. She starts licking the top of the cake. "I'm a —" He checks to see who's near them. No one. "I'm a nasty little bastard . . . fucker."

She still doesn't look at him. He can see the path her tongue has driven through the blue icing.

"Go on," she says.

"I'm a thicko."

"Uh-uh." She shakes her head.

"All right. I'm a stupid little bastard."

"What are you?"

"I'm a horrible, horrible fucker."

"Louder."

"Do I have to?"

The cake is denuded of all icing now, just a wash of transparent blue over its top. She takes a big bite and speaks through the mouthful.

"Wow-er," she says.

He laughs. He shouldn't — this isn't in the bag yet. But he laughs, and he waits for her to swallow. She says: "Louder. If you want to redeem yourself."

"I'm a horrible, horrible fucker!"

It really isn't in the bag. When she faces him she's stopped joking.

"No, Satish. Say it really loud because it's really true. You were a horrible, horrible fucker, because you thought I'd blackmail you even though I've been your friend for years and years and that's not something friends do. You should have known — I never would."

It takes him two goes to get up on to Miss Walsh's wall. Once there, he places his feet carefully so he won't stumble, then clears his throat.

"I," he says (Andrew Ford and Mandy turn his way; Cai looks round), "AM A HORRIBLE, HORRIBLE FUCKER." He looks down at the toes of his shoes and hears someone clapping.

"OK," she says. "You're done."

He stays with her until the white van has gone, and people are starting to sit down. Peter is in his place, with Cai diagonally opposite. Cai studiously avoids eye contact with his father. Andrew Ford positions himself

350

at the head of the table, and now there are two other photographers as well, marking him like conscientious defenders, shadowing his movements and taking their own pictures of Andrew Ford checking his camera, Andrew Ford in discussion with Sarah, Andrew Ford surveying the table.

"That one's from the *Sunday Times*," Colette tells Satish. "The other one's from the *Gazette*."

The *Bucks Gazette*. Ford's *alma mater*: the paper which printed the original picture. Satish wonders if Ford sees anything of himself in the young lad they've sent today. Maybe not, but the *Gazette* boy will have seen it for sure, allowing himself to hitch a ride on the possibility of glory: glory on the turn of a lucky moment.

"Oh my God!"

At the end of the street, a black car has stopped and disgorged a man. Colette shades her eyes against the sun and watches as he makes his way over to Andrew Ford.

"Oh my God! I'd heard a rumour, but . . . Shit! Neil Listick!" She makes as if to stand, then thinks better of it. The man is wearing a trilby, and a long coat swirls behind him.

"Doesn't he call himself Neil Wilson now?" asks Satish.

"Yeah, I know. But seriously, Satish. Neil Listick! Fuck!"

Neil Wilson reaches Andrew Ford and the two men pump arms and pat each other's shoulders. People stop their conversations and watch. There's a patter of clicks from the press photographers.

"He did those margarine ads last year, didn't he?"

"Yeah. But . . ." She looks at Satish. "Shut up! I know: mighty, fallen. But come on, give him his due. The man was a god."

Georgia leads the new arrival to a spare place at the table, whisking away the "Reserved" sign. Everyone's looking at him, can't take their eyes off him, so at first it's only Satish who sees the figure coming in at the other end of Cherry Gardens. Stephen — shoulders back, chest out, a bloom of purple around his eye — makes for the unfilled places nearest Andrew Ford. But then Georgia spots him and waves him away, up to the unfocused end of the table, turning from him before he can remonstrate.

"Did you fix it?" Colette asks Satish.

"Fix it?"

"The blackmail stuff. Is it sorted?"

"Yes. Sorted. If you want to know . . ."

"I don't."

It's nearly time. Just one more thing to do.

"There's a question I've kept asking you," he says. "And you keep not answering it. How did you get involved in all this?"

There's a pause. "I told you," she says. "My dad. The money."

"No. I understand that part. But the rest of it. You said Andrew Ford got in touch."

"Yes . . ."

"But I don't think that happened, did it?"

"Um . . ." She's fiddling with her bracelet. It's suddenly become fascinating.

352

"I won't be asking you to stand up and shout or anything. I think I know why, anyway."

"Oh, fuckadoodle-doo. It wasn't Ford. I mean, it didn't start with him. It started with . . ." She looks across at the table and he follows her gaze; Stephen is talking with the woman next to him, pointing at Andrew Ford, gesturing to himself.

"It started with Stephen, didn't it?"

"Yes! How did you know?"

Stephen's script coming out of her mouth, that night in his lounge: the promise of money. She'd made it happen.

"Stephen came to you and told you you'd be paid for this. You wanted to help your dad."

"Yes! But it's not just that. He . . . Stephen's good at finding people. He kept sending me these letters, for years, trying to make some money from the photo. Don't look at me like that! I never did anything about them. I got rid of them, straightaway. But then this one came, and it was nasty. Do you already know about this?"

"Tell me."

"He'd found out about my addiction. About what I was like, before I got clean. I don't know how. He tracks people down."

"Yes, he does."

Satish looks over at Stephen, now holding forth to the small group around him. He knows how this story ends, and it makes him want to go over there and lay into him all over again.

353

"He knew what I'd done, and he guessed Dad didn't. He said he'd tell him."

"He asked you to get me involved. He knew I wouldn't do it otherwise."

"Yes! And I just had to . . . Honestly, Satish, I wouldn't have done it without that. It would kill Dad if he knew, finish him off. You don't know . . ."

But he does, of course. He knows the terror of revelation, and Stephen does, too. Nasty little bastard. So that's that: Stephen and Colette and Satish and Andrew Ford, all of those dominos falling to bring them right here.

Ford is standing at the head of the table. He signals for quiet.

"Right," he says. "We're going to set up the shot."

Satish puts his arm round Colette and kisses the top of her head.

"Forget it," he says. "It's over and done with."

It's time to go. They're waiting for him.

CHAPTER
THIRTY-SEVEN

Someone said a photographer would be coming. He was from the *Bucks Gazette*. He'd turned up a few minutes before they were all due to start. There were a lot of parties that afternoon, but he wanted to do theirs. Miss Walsh had said he was welcome.

After the branding, Satish had pushed Cai off him and run into his own house. His mum wasn't in the kitchen, but he didn't know how long that would last. There was a pan on the stove and a bottle of oil next to it. A red mound of powdered chilli sat on a plate. With the pain building, worse than ever, he had to get somewhere more private.

Satish had gone up to the bathroom. He'd curled up on the floor and hummed quietly, trying to think about the humming and not the hurt. He put off what he had to do for as long as possible, but time was getting on and he had to . . .

Satish counted aloud, trying to trick himself like his dad tricked him when he had to do something painful: count to three but do it on two. One, two . . .

He shouted when the T-shirt came unstuck from the burn. He couldn't help it, tried to keep it down but it was such a terrible thing. He sat on the toilet seat until the dizziness went. The idea of putting anything on the wound was unbearable, but then he thought about his parents seeing it so he opened the medicine chest with a click and pulled out some Savlon and a bandage. It took a long time, with lots of rests in between, but in the end he had a passable dressing, one that would get him through what he had to do next. He found a packet of aspirins and took two, crunching them dry because he didn't want to lean down to the tap for water, and then he left.

Miss Walsh was over by her house, talking to a man with curly dark hair. He had a camera round his neck, a serious-looking one. It had a long, chunky lens. From time to time his fingers would make gentle contact with it, as if he were checking it was still OK. Miss Walsh was touching her hair a lot, and laughing.

At Sarah's house, Mrs Miller was delighted to see him.

"Any port in a storm!" she told him. "All hands on deck!" She'd made two big bowlfuls of coronation chicken, and they needed to be taken out to the table. Would he be a dear? He would, one at a time.

Coronation chicken was a banned substance in the Patel family. Since the Food Meeting his mother had repeated her injunction that none of them should touch the stuff. On his way to the table he looked down at the creamy mess. It was sprinkled with slender white ovals: flaked almonds, Satish reckoned. The smell made him feel sick.

Paul and Stephen Chandler were already seated, facing each other over a plate of dhokla. When Satish came near, Paul stared at him. Satish couldn't hold that gaze, but he could do this: he edged the dhokla to one side and placed the bowl of chicken right in front of them. He did it slowly, keeping his right arm straight by his side.

The photographer was walking up and down the table, holding up his camera every now and then and looking through the viewfinder. His finger wasn't hovering over the button, but the others didn't notice that; they kept sitting up straight when he came near, and smiling. Satish headed for the end of the table, where there were still some empty places, and sat down.

Colette couldn't sit down, not yet. She was in her driveway, opposite Satish's seat, jumping about in excitement. When she saw him she stopped her jumping and came up to him, eyeing his right arm warily.

"Your poor arm, Satish," she said, reaching out to touch it.

He winced. "Better not, Colette. Hurts a bit. Listen, don't tell anyone about it, will you? It's a grown-up secret. Can you keep a grown-up secret?"

"Yes," she said.

No, he thought. But maybe till the party's over. Then her dad came up and pulled her to the other side of the table, to sit on his lap. Satish felt his own breathing coming quicker. He looked straight across at them. Finally Colette's dad noticed and Satish kept staring until Mr Brecon had to look away: *I know what you did*. Colette reached for a paper cup and started fiddling with it. Her dad popped it out of her hand and put it back on the table. Then she leaned over for a cake and he told her: "Not till later," and pulled a plastic Union Jack off the table, slotting it between her thumb and forefinger.

"Here," he said. "Play with this."

There was a buzz and a screech, and the music came on. Satish heard the rise of strings and brass, a few scattered cheers from along the table. A couple of people clapped.

Come fly with me, let's fly, fly away

If you can use some exotic booze there's a bar in far Bombay

Mr Brecon nodded his acknowledgement. Behind him, Satish saw his own front door open. His dad had changed into a clean shirt and tie. After him came Satish's mum, holding Sima by the hand. Mother and daughter were dressed in matching long dresses . . . no saris, he noticed, but a new thing: English party frocks. They passed him, his mum smiling at the ground as if already disowning compliments. Sima saw Satish and tried to run to him, but his mum tugged at her hand and pulled her close, steering her into a seat halfway down the table.

Two places to Satish's left Mandy sat down, an empty chair between them. He'd taken his punishment already, but she hadn't. Perhaps, if no one saw them talking to each other, she could get away with it. He studied his cup and reached for her under the table

358

with his good arm. His little finger touched a knee, and bounced off in fright. Mandy frowned. Satish's hand ventured across again, hovered over her lap, moved until he bumped against her arm. He found her hand and held it. She looked down at her plate. She was murmuring something.

"I'm sorry," she was saying. "They told me. I hate them. I'm so sorry."

His palm, against hers, was sweating but he held on anyway, their thumbs pressing on the backs of each other's hands, their fingers curled round each other.

In Llama land there's a one-man band and he'll toot his flute for you

Come fly with me, we'll float down in the blue

Satish thought about what would happen next. It wasn't enough just to keep clear of her this afternoon, he realised, not for a week or even a month. It would never be OK for her, to be seen with him. Mandy looked up and emitted a disgruntled "huh!", and there was Sarah, seated just across from them.

Mandy made to pull away, but he held on for a bit longer. He concentrated on her hand, on filing its details away in his memory: the soft swell at the base of her thumb, the crenellations of her knuckles, the sticky heat of her palm and the cool of her fingertips. Then he felt a movement behind him, and suddenly Cai was there. The edge of Mandy's nail slid across the backs of his fingers, and they parted.

"Mind if I sit here?"

Satish did, hugely, but he couldn't summon up the energy to say no, and in any case the request was a formality; Cai had already parked himself between Satish and Mandy. Satish went to scratch his head and touched a hat instead, and remembered he was wearing it — he alone of all the kids — but he couldn't be bothered to feel embarrassed.

The man with the camera had finished circling the table. He crouched down at their end, and held up a black gadget which he clicked repeatedly, moving it around in front of him.

"We're OK, Satish?" said Cai in his ear. He'd swivelled round so that he was side-on to his chair, and faced his friend.

"Go away."

"I know things went wrong, but that's over. We're OK."

"I don't care. Go away."

Andrew Ford raised the camera to his eye.

They're having some trouble placing Colette in the photograph. Satish watches from his post on the wall; he's the last to sit down. He'd like to stay here for a while, see how everyone else settles in before he goes over. At six, Colette perched happily on her dad's lap. At thirty-six, it looks a little odd. Andrew Ford thinks so too, he can tell. There's lots of good-natured oohing from her and her dad, some mock-solicitous enquiries about the strain on his legs, but Satish knows what Ford is thinking: it's awkward and ungainly at best.

Ford gestures Colette further towards the edge of Peter's lap, and the pose takes on an unwelcome burlesque quality. When she replaces herself more centrally, she overwhelms her father, blocking him from the camera. They start again. Peter runs a finger inside his suit collar. Next to him, Sarah is making determined conversation with the woman seated to her right. Occasionally she sneaks a glance at Mandy, chatting animatedly with Neil Wilson. Sarah's not the only one, thinks Satish. Peter's taken up with Mandy too, his gaze resting on her for the moments when his attention is not claimed by Colette or Andrew Ford.

Everyone's different now, Colette had told Satish, and he had disagreed. All they'd done is grown up, he'd replied. They hadn't changed at all. Maybe he'd been right about that; here was Cai, resolutely offering his father the cold shoulder. Here were Sarah and Mandy, the wall between them still in place. Here were the unspoken secrets Peter still kept close.

Something has changed, though: Satish has. He has treated with the past, has negotiated terms with it. He won't be hearing from Stephen again. And Cai? In June 1977 Cai was just a kid, and we're all better than the worst thing we've done. As for Satish, he can see himself more clearly now: Satish isn't a victim after all, but tenacious, a survivor. That's the joy of history: its clear, backward glance. Satish has endured. He's stuck it out and made a place for himself, a good place: a home.

"Hey! Satish!"

Cai has turned in his seat and is gesturing him over. Satish realises that everything else is ready: they are only waiting for him. Colette is standing behind her father, her arms around his shoulders, their logistical

361

struggles resolved. Mandy and Sarah are still finding other things to pay attention to, before Ford requires them to pay attention to each other for a short while. When Satish takes his seat at the end of the table, Cai, uninhibited, throws his arms around him.

"Fantastic!" says Andrew Ford, raising the camera to his eye. "That's just . . ."

He presses the shutter release. The aperture opens for one two-hundred-and-fiftieth of a second.

One two-hundred-and-fiftieth
of a second

It was less than the time it takes to form a conscious thought. But there were shadows of thoughts: precursors, or echoes of those just past. When the shutter opened, the back of the camera was flooded with light. For that fractional time, the silver bromide crystals underwent extraordinary changes, and tiny silver deposits formed an invisible image which would later resolve itself into a table set with party food, a father holding his daughter, two girls oblivious, and — right at the front of the photograph — two lads tussling, entwined. Less than the time it takes to form a conscious thought. But there were shadows of thoughts.

Mandy and Sarah were armoured; each was outraged, each convinced of the rightness of her own position. Now they had caught each other's gaze, neither would break it. Sarah was hell-bent on this and this alone, but Mandy had only half a mind on it. She could still feel the place where Satish had held her hand, and as the shutter-release opened she was engaged in mapping the area he had so recently touched and wondering when the opportunity would come for him to touch her again.

Colette, ensconced on her father's lap, could feel him surround her, and that made her secure and warm. Next to her was Sarah, and she didn't want to look at Sarah, just in case Sarah had already gone home and seen the mess Colette had made of her bedroom, just in case Sarah guessed and told on her. Sarah with her high shoes and her new necklace: she'd made them hurt Satish. The posters were all torn down, all the popstars and film stars, and it didn't matter to Colette because she knew she'd never, ever want to go into Sarah's room again. Now the man wanted to take a picture of her, and she knew how smart she looked in her new outfit. She wanted to give her best smile. She wanted not to wriggle, to stay still for the picture, so she pulled and pulled at the flag Dad had given her, transferring all her energy to that. She beamed: her brightest smile.

Peter was staggered by grief. It came on him unawares in the seconds before the picture was taken. There was Colette fiddling, fiddling, claiming his attention, and then, just as she stilled herself he looked across at Mandy and was hit by it: his girl! She was lovely and young and foolish and he would soon be gone, unable to help her with anything. Three hundred pounds was derisory: he saw that clearly. It was nothing next to the dreadful, untenable reality of his departure, of their separation. How could money possibly stack up against that? Was it too late to change his plans now? What had he been thinking?

364

Cai was aware of his father opposite him, of the thrilling fact of his own rebellion. It was the best rebellion he could imagine: *I am not you.* He was ready for the fall-out. He welcomed it. His dad was looking, so Cai held Satish close to him. As he leaned into his friend, he felt the cold bar of a safety pin pressing against his bare skin. With his navy shirt buttoned up no one would ever see the T-shirt, his secret protest, but his other protest was less secret: two fingers up to them all. The moment the aperture opened, Frank Sinatra was cut off, mid-line: *It's perfect for a flying honey —* and the first note of *God Save The Queen* broke in, discordant. It would be several seconds before everyone realised what was happening but Cai, with his burgeoning dissent and his access to his father's recording equipment, knew it was coming. He couldn't wait.

Satish had his own protest to make. Against the insistence of the pain and between the two clicks of the camera, two clicks so close they sounded like one unless you were listening very carefully, he subliminally registered the first howls from the centre of the table. They came from near his parents, from the place where the Chandlers were sitting, and they carried with them the sound of fury and disbelief. Those chillis of his mother's had been chosen in Bassetsbury from her favourite greengrocer: she was fussy. She'd brought them all the way back here on the bus and hung them in the airing cupboard. She'd pounded them tenderly that morning, wanting them to be as fresh as possible for the party dishes. Crushed to a powder, they'd

365

mingled with the flaked almonds on top of the Coronation Chicken. In one two-hundred-and-fiftieth of a second he'd heard the sound of revenge. Not his best revenge — not yet — but a temporary one, at least.

The shutter closed.

Acknowledgements

I am hugely grateful to the following people for the help and support they have given me in the writing of *Jubilee*:

My agent Jo Unwin: an absolute corker, both personally and professionally. Respect is due.

My editor at W&N, Kirsty Dunseath, for being exacting, insightful — and brilliant.

The team at Orion, for their enthusiasm and expertise, and for making me feel so welcome.

The Literary Consultancy for their unwavering belief in the novel, and Harry Bingham for making it all happen.

Dal Dhariwal and Sonia Holloway for telling their childhood stories with such candour.

Kishor Joshi for the astonishing generosity with which he shared his stories of family and food. And for the best cup of masala chai it will ever be my privilege to taste.

Chandrika Little Dragon, Mumta Sharma and Seema Mehta for wading through early drafts with patience and an eye for detail.

Thanks to J for helping me understand the world of Narcotics Anonymous, and for trusting me with the knowledge of her own addiction: "it will stay here".

My friend and ace paediatrician Dr Maeve O'Sullivan, who dealt womanfully with the constant stream of medical queries I sent her. Thanks also to Alder Hey cardiac nurse Gill McBurney, and to Dr Louise Dubras, for medical consultancy above and beyond the call of duty. Any mistakes which remain are mine alone.

Professor Martin Elliot and Dr Rob Yates at Great Ormond Street Hospital, for helping me find the best part of Satish; I will never stop thanking you.

To Rob Sheffield for teaching me *My House, Your House* and for telling me, with such vividness, what it felt like to listen to the Sex Pistols in Cwmbwrla.

Thanks to Jenny and Dick Harris for everything — from the first word you read me, to the last one in this book.

To Seth and Caleb: I love you so much I could pop.

And finally to Alex, who has given me a room of my own and so much more than I could ever say here: thank you.

Also available in ISIS Large Print:

Pigeon English

Stephen Kelman

Newly arrived from Ghana with his mother and older sister, eleven-year-old Harrison Opoku lives on the ninth floor of a block of flats on a London housing estate. With equal fascination for the local gang — the Dell Farm Crew — and the pigeon who visits his balcony, Harri absorbs the strange elements of life in England: watching, listening, and learning the tricks of inner-city survival. But when a boy is knifed to death on the high street and a police appeal draws only silence, Harri decides to start a murder investigation of his own, unwittingly endangering the fragile web his mother has spun around her family to keep them safe.

ISBN 978-0-7531-9050-0 (hb)
ISBN 978-0-7531-9051-7 (pb)

The Making of Us

Lisa Jewell

Lydia, Dean and Robyn don't know each other. Yet. And they are all facing difficult changes. Lydia is still wearing the scars from her traumatic childhood and, although she is wealthy and successful, her life is lonely and disjointed. Dean is a young man, burdened with unexpected responsibility, whose life is going nowhere. And Robyn wants to be a doctor, just like her father — a man she's never met. But is her whole life built on an illusion? Three people leading three very different lives. All lost. All looking for something. But when they slowly find their way into each other's lives, everything starts to change . . .

ISBN 978-0-7531-8914-6 (hb)
ISBN 978-0-7531-8915-3 (pb)

A Moment Like Forever

Martina Reilly

Andrea and Lexi thought they would be best friends for ever. Through thick and thin, growing pains and wild nights out, they were inseparable. But it was their biggest adventure that was to tear them apart: travelling through Australia. Andrea and Lexi were involved in a catastrophic accident. Andrea was left scarred but her best friend was nowhere to be found. What happened to Lexi?

Two years later, Andy's scar means she's too scared to leave her flat. Instead, she spends her time with her grumpy cat Baz and her hopeless boss Alistair. And Lexi still hasn't been in touch. When Andy's sister needs somewhere to stay, bringing her boyfriend and all their dramas with her, Andy realises she's been hiding for too long. Just because she's keeping secrets buried doesn't mean they'll stay that way . . .

ISBN 978-0-7531-8846-0 (hb)
ISBN 978-0-7531-8847-7 (pb)

Jubilee

Eliza Graham

During celebrations for the Queen's Golden Jubilee, Meriel watches her aunt Evie as she scrutinizes the crowds enjoying themselves on the village green. They both remember what happened on that day 25 years ago, when Evie's young daughter Jessamy vanished.

Meriel gets on with her life, but when news comes of Evie's death, Meriel must return to the village to sort out her aunt's estate. Neighbours tell her of Evie's increasingly eccentric behaviour in the weeks before her death and how Evie collected photographs of the Queen's Coronation and examined them with a magnifying glass.

Determined to work out what was gripping her aunt, Meriel immerses herself in family history, starting with Marion, Evie's mother, who made a "terrible mistake" around the time of the Coronation in 1953. Meriel is convinced that the key to Jessamy's disappearance lies in these events.

ISBN 978-0-7531-8674-9 (hb)
ISBN 978-0-7531-8675-6 (pb)

The Swimmer

Roma Tearne

This tender story of love and loss is deftly infused with the sights and sounds of a hot Suffolk summer
Daily Mail

43-year-old Ria is used to being alone. All her life, she has struggled to form a meaningful relationship with any man. Her existence, ultimately, is a solitary one — until she discovers the swimmer.

It is midnight when she first sees him, across the river at the bottom of her garden. His name is Ben and he is a Sri Lankan doctor, awaiting a decision from the Home Office on his asylum application. He is also 18 years Ria's junior but despite this, their friendship steadily grows. At first, she resists anything more than his companionship, but in the long, blistering summer days that follow, under wide Suffolk skies, they are powerfully and irresistibly drawn to each other. Until, that is, tragedy occurs, and in one single act of violence the lives of everyone in this small rural community are changed forever.

ISBN 978-0-7531-8762-3 (hb)
ISBN 978-0-7531-8763-0 (pb)

ISIS publish a wide range of books in large print, from fiction to biography. Any suggestions for books you would like to see in large print or audio are always welcome. Please send to the Editorial Department at:

ISIS Publishing Limited
7 Centremead
Osney Mead
Oxford OX2 0ES

A full list of titles is available free of charge from:

Ulverscroft Large Print Books Limited

(UK)
The Green
Bradgate Road, Anstey
Leicester LE7 7FU
Tel: (0116) 236 4325

(Australia)
P.O. Box 314
St Leonards
NSW 1590
Tel: (02) 9436 2622

(USA)
P.O. Box 1230
West Seneca
N.Y. 14224-1230
Tel: (716) 674 4270

(Canada)
P.O. Box 80038
Burlington
Ontario L7L 6B1
Tel: (905) 637 8734

(New Zealand)
P.O. Box 456
Feilding
Tel: (06) 323 6828

Details of ISIS complete and unabridged audio books are also available from these offices. Alternatively, contact your local library for details of their collection of ISIS large print and unabridged audio books.